A GIFT FROM
TIFFANY'S

melissa hill

 st. martin's griffin ❧ new york

A GIFT FROM TIFFANY'S. Copyright © 2011 by Melissa Hill. All rights
reserved. Printed in the United States of America. For information, address
St. Martin's Press, 175 Fifth Avenue, New York, N.Y. 10010.

ISBN 978-0-62090-719-1

First published as *Something from Tiffany's* in Great Britain
by Hodder & Stoughton, an Hachette UK company

Acknowledgements

There were lots of wonderful things going on while writing this book, not least the arrival of baby Carrie right in the middle of it. Huge thanks to her for taking it so easy on her clueless parents in the early days, thus allowing me to complete the story with minimum disruption.

Thanks and much love to Kevin who effortlessly kept things on an even keel throughout possibly our busiest year ever.

Huge thanks to Dr Dockeray and the wonderful staff at Mount Carmel hospital who got family life off to a great start, and made our first days with Carrie so special.

To my fantastic parents, sisters and in-laws who are always there to offer a helping hand, it means so much, thank you.

Heartfelt thanks to super-agent and great friend Sheila Crowley – a true miracle-worker. I just couldn't ask for better and I owe you so much.

To my amazing editor Isobel Akenhead, working with you is such a joy, and my stories are so much richer for your input, thank you.

To Breda, Jim, Ruth and all at Hachette Ireland who work so hard on my behalf, I'm very grateful.

To everyone who buys and reads my books, and who has sent me so many lovely messages through my website www.melissahill.info. I love hearing from you and treasure every message.

My thanks once again to the booksellers all over the world who give my books terrific support; it's very much appreciated.

Finally, massive, massive thanks to my brilliant publishers Hodder, who are amazing to work with – and who inspired this book by introducing me to the wonders of a certain little blue box . . .

Dedicated with much love to my
beautiful baby daughter, Carrie

Chapter 1

The significance of what he was about to do wasn't lost on Ethan Greene. It was a big moment in his life; it would be in any man's, he guessed.

But as he battled through the Manhattan crowds on possibly the busiest shopping day of the year, he wished that he'd chosen a better time.

Christmas Eve on Fifth Avenue? He must be mad.

Taking a deep breath of the cold air, which was refreshing and not as damp as it usually was in London, he couldn't help but think how little had changed since the last time he was in this city and, at the same time, how much had.

Arriving in New York only two days earlier, he'd surprised himself by how well he remembered the landmarks and how easily he found his way around. The jostle of the subway ride from midtown to downtown and back again, the scent of well-worn vinyl taxi seats and the endless hum of a billion sounds – human or inanimate – buoyed him. The unmistakable buzz of the place put a new spring in his step, something he hadn't felt in years.

But now Ethan was in a hurry and acutely aware that the minutes were ticking by and the crowds seemed to be growing thicker. There wasn't much time left.

Alongside him Daisy squeezed his hand briefly as if sensing what he was thinking, yet she couldn't possibly know

what he'd planned. All he'd said was that he needed to make one more stop before they returned to the warmth of their hotel. Conscious of how much he hated crowds (and shopping for that matter) she was probably just trying to put him at ease.

How would she react? OK, so the idea had been on the cards for a while and had been mentioned more than once recently, so by rights today shouldn't really be too much of a surprise. While she seemed keen, Ethan now realised that he really should have spoken to her about today – it was unlike him not to discuss such matters with her in more detail – but the truth was that he was nervous. What if her reaction wasn't as positive as he'd anticipated? As he wondered, an anxious lump appeared in his throat. Well, he'd find out her reaction soon enough, especially when they reached their destination.

She looked especially pretty today, he thought, wrapped up in a multitude of layers to keep out the teeth-chattering cold, her blonde curls creeping out under a dark woollen hat, and her red nose appearing above a black embroidered scarf. Despite the cold, she was loving New York just as he'd known she would, and everyone knew there was no better time than Christmas to visit the city that never sleeps. Yes, this was a good idea, Ethan reassured himself. Everything would work out fine.

Finally, having negotiated their way through the mass of last-minute shoppers, they reached the corner of Fifth Avenue and Fifty-Seventh Street. He looked at Daisy, and her eyes widened in surprise as he took her hand and steered them both towards the entrance.

'What's going on?' she squealed, glancing at the familiar nameplate beside the doorway, its typically clean-line wording on polished granite today surrounded by verdant pine branches especially for the Christmas season. 'What do we need *here*?'

'I told you – I need to pick something up,' Ethan replied, leading the way and giving her a brief wink as the revolving glass doors deposited them in the hallowed halls of Tiffany & Co.

Daisy was immediately captivated by the vast, high-ceilinged sales floor and its column-free design, and she gazed in amazement at the long rows of glass-fronted cases, their precious wares twinkling alluringly under the spotlights.

'Oh wow, it's all so beautiful,' she whispered in awe, standing in the middle of the aisle as crowds of equally spellbound shoppers and tourists milled around her, each one fascinated by the breathtaking jewellery displays. The store was one of the few in Manhattan that didn't utilise lavish festive decoration; its sparkling wares required little embellishment, and combined with the unmistakably romantic Tiffany's allure this was more than enough to create that magical Christmas feeling.

'It is, isn't it?' Ethan agreed, his nervousness dissipating somewhat now they were here. He took her arm and guided her between the various display cases and down towards the elevators at the back, his tired feet temporarily soothed by the soft-carpeted floor.

'Where are we going?' she asked, moving forward reluctantly. 'Slow down a bit! Can't we take a look around? I've never been here before and . . . Where are we going?' she repeated, bemused, as the elevator doors opened.

'The second floor, please,' Ethan requested.

'Certainly, sir.' The besuited lift attendant complied, graciously bowing his top-hatted head. He smiled at Daisy. 'Madam.'

'But . . . why would we be going there?' she asked, her

voice hushed, and he deduced she'd read from the directory display overhead what was on this particular floor. She was certainly taken with the place, but however enthralled she'd been downstairs, he knew she would really be impressed by the second floor.

Ethan's heart began to hammer in his chest as the elevator doors closed. Would she be OK with this? Again, he probably should have just come right out and asked, but he figured that she'd enjoy the surprise, and he also thought it was important that she felt very much a part of it.

His voice was light. 'Like I said, I need to pick something up.'

Now Daisy gazed open-mouthed at him. 'You're not . . .' she gasped, immediately understanding, but from her expression Ethan still couldn't quite gauge her reaction, and he guessed the presence of the attendant was intimidating her into asking no further questions.

Within seconds, the elevator doors reopened and he and Daisy stepped out into the wood-panelled room on Tiffany's famed Diamond Floor, where he had come to collect his purchase.

'I can't believe this!' she was saying as they approached one of the hexagon-shaped wood-and-glass display cases, her head swivelling from left to right as she watched various happy couples around the room being served champagne while they made what would arguably be the most important purchase of their lives. 'I really can't believe it! *This* is what you're picking up?'

Ethan smiled nervously. 'I know I should have said something but—'

'Ah, Mr Greene.' An elderly and distinguished sales assistant addressed Ethan before either had a chance to say anything more. 'Pleasure seeing you again. Everything is in

4

order and ready to go. We weren't sure, and I forgot to ask on the phone, if you preferred your purchase already gift-wrapped, or wanted to show the lady first . . .' He smiled at Daisy, who beamed back at him, wide-eyed.

'Oh yes, let me see, please!' she exclaimed and then put a guilty hand to her mouth, conscious that she really should be showing a little more decorum – especially in a place like this.

Ethan hid a smile.

'Well, here we are,' the older man said, his voice low and gentle as he presented them with the world-renowned little blue box. Placing it ceremoniously on the glass display in front of Daisy, he pulled back the lid to reveal the platinum marquise solitaire Ethan had chosen a couple of days before.

The ring had needed to be sized correctly, which was why he was picking it up today, and now considering it afresh he was pretty sure he'd made a good choice. It was the classic Tiffany setting: the diamond lifted slightly above the band and held in place by six platinum prongs in order to maximise the stone's brilliance.

'So what do you think?' he asked Daisy, but it was pretty obvious that she was captivated by the beautiful ring, although that wasn't really the question Ethan was asking.

But when she turned to look at him, her delighted expression told him everything he needed to know.

'It's the perfect choice, Daddy,' Ethan's eight-year-old daughter assured him, 'and Vanessa is going to absolutely *love* it!'

Thank goodness her reaction had been positive.

All day – no, strike that, all *month* – Ethan had worried about how Daisy would feel about this. Especially when

this New York trip held a special significance for both of them.

Earlier that day, over a couple of hot chocolates in a midtown café, he had watched his daughter pick at an iced lemon cupcake, and known that something was on her mind. Just as her mother had always done, Daisy got that squinty look in her eyes and offset her jaw ever so slightly when deep in thought.

'Did you like Times Square?' he asked, fishing. 'With all the lights and everything?'

'Everything's just so beautiful,' she replied and then paused, looking out of the window at the bustling street. 'Mum said Manhattan was like one big Christmas tree at this time of year. She was right.'

'You really remember how much your mother talked about it, don't you?' he asked.

She gave a little smile. 'I know I was only small, but I loved hearing about it.'

Ethan nodded. 'Of course, she was right about it being like a big Christmas tree. Your mum was right about lots of things.'

Suddenly, the significance of sitting here with his daughter in the city that her mother had adored so much washed over Ethan and almost took his breath away. Swallowing hard, he tried to gather his thoughts.

'You know what else she was right about?' Ethan added, and Daisy looked intently at him as she always did whenever he had something about her mother to relate. It wasn't lost on him that his daughter was seldom more attentive than when he offered some piece of the puzzle, whose parts probably seemed quite scattered to her; to him it was as if she were an archivist of some sort, gathering and assembling the pieces of a great legacy and putting them in order.

Ethan continued with a smile, 'She was right that you would grow into a bright and beautiful girl.'

Daisy grinned and turned back to the window to watch the goings-on of a very busy Fifth Avenue on Christmas Eve.

It had been nine years since his last and only other trip here. Jane, Daisy's mum, had convinced Ethan to see the city and, making the trip from their home in London, see it they did.

Jane was a born and bred New Yorker and just couldn't bear to spend another springtime 'without a stroll through Central Park as the leaves begin to change'. She said dramatic things out of the blue like that every now and then, to which Ethan usually responded by asking if it were actually she and not he who was the English language lecturer. 'No, Professor,' she would say with a wink. 'You're the brainy, creative one around here, whereas I'm just a born romantic.'

Jane's parents had retired to Florida in the meantime, so she didn't get to visit the city of her birth as often as she'd have liked.

Daisy had been conceived in the Big Apple during that visit. The running joke between Jane and Ethan – one that Jane had no problem sharing with their friends and family – was that Daisy existed because they'd taken the expression 'the city that never sleeps' quite literally.

As a personal trainer and nutritionist, Jane did her best to keep Ethan in tip-top shape, a fact that was all the more ironic when she developed ovarian cancer and discovered that, unless the chemotherapy worked a miracle, she had only mere months to live.

Daisy was five at the time. Jane and Ethan were head over heels in love but had never got round to getting married, and he'd wanted to change that, especially once they heard the news.

'Don't be ridiculous, sweetheart. We've been happy so far; why change now?' Jane insisted. 'Besides,' she added jokingly, 'soon I won't have enough hair left to wear a veil!'

By then Ethan would have gone along with anything she wished and Jane had several last wishes.

One of them was that he took their daughter to visit New York at Christmas when she was old enough to appreciate and enjoy it. She had spent hours weaving for Daisy tales of the magic of Manhattan and of her own childhood Christmases there.

When, a few months back, Daisy herself started talking about making the trip, Ethan knew it was time.

One evening over dinner he mentioned the idea to his girl-friend, Vanessa, who he hoped might be keen to join them. Although he knew the trip to the city would hold particular significance for him and Daisy because of its association with Jane, he also felt it was important that Vanessa be included. Their relationship had taken a serious turn over the last six months, and maybe, just maybe, it was meant to be that the three of them should spend time in New York together.

Perhaps this trip would be a kind of rite of passage into the next stage of his and Daisy's life? It was three years since Jane's death and Ethan was pretty certain they had her blessing to move on; another of her last wishes was that he shouldn't remain alone.

'Go and find a woman who'll bake you bread,' she'd laughed, in what Ethan knew was a reference to a long-standing joke about their dietary habits. Jane's strict healthy-eating obsession meant that they rarely ate heavy refined starchy foods like bread or potatoes, something a carb fan like Ethan had always struggled with. And in the end, it hadn't mattered what any of them ate; the cancer had taken her from them anyway.

But he knew there was a metaphorical element to the remark too, and although at the time he couldn't bear the thought of moving on with someone else, as the years went by that feeling lessened. A woman who'd bake him bread? Ethan wasn't sure if this described Vanessa exactly, but he did know he loved her and felt she would be the perfect female role model for his rapidly maturing daughter.

And when Ethan had suggested the three of them spend Christmas in New York together, Vanessa was all for it. She knew the city well, often travelling to Manhattan on business or to visit friends.

'Do you think Mum would be proud of me?' Daisy asked then, bringing Ethan back to the present. He looked at her and cocked his head inquisitively. 'She always said she was proud of me every time I trusted myself and tried something new,' his daughter continued. 'And here I am in her favourite place, trying something new.'

'I can guarantee it, buttercup,' Ethan told her softly, his blue eyes watering slightly.

Then, checking his watch, he realised how late in the afternoon it actually was. He thought of Vanessa, remembering she would be back from visiting her friends soon and he, true to form, still had some very important shopping to do.

Madness really, he thought. It was all so last minute. Daisy was tired, and focused on her mum, but they were expecting him at the store.

So the debate had continued in Ethan's head about whether to finish what he'd set out to do, or to retreat to the comfort of their room at the Plaza hotel. That buoyant feeling he'd had about it all over the last few days was now starting to ebb a bit and he was feeling nervous. Get it together, he told himself.

'Do you know who else is proud of you?' he asked Daisy.

'Yes,' she replied without hesitation, before finishing the last of her hot chocolate. 'You are. And Vanessa is too. She told me on the plane.'

Ethan smiled. That was all he needed to hear.

Now, as he and Daisy waited together for the Tiffany's assistant to gift-wrap his purchase, he was relieved that everything seemed to be working out. Of course, there was still the small matter of Vanessa's reaction to all this, but he was pretty certain he knew what that would be.

To the ring, if nothing else.

He'd learned from Jane, who used to wax lyrical about Tiffany's, that the famous little blue box was almost a by-word for true New York-style fairy-tale romance. According to her, there wasn't a woman in the world who could resist it;, the store and its wares enchanting the dreams of millions.

Something from Tiffany's had certainly always made Jane go weak at the knees, and Ethan's one big regret was that he'd never had the chance to present her with one of their famed diamond rings.

He hoped Vanessa would appreciate it just as much, and he was pretty confident she would, given her appreciation for the finer things in life. Her dedicated work ethic ensured she was able to afford the best and, as far as Ethan was concerned, the best was exactly what she deserved.

Thinking about the cost of the ring, he gulped, once again thankful for those stock options that had come good a few months ago. The shareholding had been a gift from his father, and it was only because of that lump-sum windfall that Ethan had been able to spend so much on the diamond, or indeed a suite at the Plaza hotel.

'Would you prefer our classic white ribbon for the box

or perhaps something a little more festive for the holiday?' the assistant asked him. 'A red bow, perhaps?'

'Daisy?' Ethan urged, letting her decide.

She seemed to think for a moment. 'Definitely the white.'

'Ah, classic Tiffany's style,' the assistant agreed with a smile. 'Good instincts, young lady.'

Daisy grinned again and looked from the assistant to her father. 'My mum used to tell me about here,' she said shyly. 'She told me that Tiffany's is a very special place filled with magic and romance.'

The assistant looked at Ethan and he smiled, silently acknowledging that Daisy was at the age where this kind of fanciful stuff was important.

'Daisy's mum is no longer with us, but she was very much a Tiffany's devotee,' he told him. Ethan knew that Jane would no doubt have waxed lyrical to Daisy about the store in the course of her many tales about New York. The love of his life had been a romantic old soul, the type who believed in whimsical things like fate and the mysteries of the universe.

For all the good it did her, he thought, but lately some of that seemed to be coming through in Daisy. Then again she was an eight-year-old girl who had posters of princesses and unicorns all over her bedroom walls, so he supposed this was normal enough.

In any case, Ethan was relieved to discover this more imaginative side of his daughter; since her mother's untimely loss, she could sometimes be a solemn, fretful little girl, prone to worrying about the slightest thing.

'Ah.' The man nodded, as if understanding. He hunkered down to Daisy's height. 'Well yes, this *is* a special place, and as you can see, there's lots of romance happening right here at this very moment.' He indicated the other customers, all

enclosed in their own starry-eyed bubble. 'And I must admit I myself have experienced a few magical moments through-out my time here. Like meeting you today, for instance, young lady,' he added with a wink and Daisy blushed happily.

Ethan looked on, his heart soaring at the sight of his little girl's smile.

Then, when the all-important package was nestled safely in the small robin's-egg-blue bag, and the assistant handed Ethan his purchase, Daisy beat him to the punch and grabbed the soft handles herself. 'Can I carry it?' she asked, staring at the bag as if it contained something rare and precious.

Which indeed it did.

'Of course you can.' Ethan was beaming as he put the accompanying documentation into his jacket pocket. He couldn't have hoped for a better reaction, and felt more certain than ever that he, Vanessa and Daisy being together in New York was merely the first step on the wonderful jour-ney they all had ahead of them.

Then, taking his daughter's hand, he wished the friendly Tiffany's assistant a merry Christmas and he and Daisy headed back outside to rejoin the crowds on Fifth Avenue.

Chapter 2

'Hey there, gorgeous, what's up?' Gary Knowles said, answering his mobile from inside the changing room at the Bergdorf Goodman men's store. He placed the handset between his cheek and shoulder so he could have both hands free to carry on with what he was doing.

Turning sideways he threw back his shoulders to size himself up in the Ralph Lauren shirt he was trying on, and smiled at his reflection in the dressing-room mirror. 'Yep . . . glad you're enjoying it,' he continued absently, turning his head to get a better look at his back, at the way the tapering shirt fitted his torso. 'Hmm? Yeah, just finishing up now.'

Nodding approvingly at himself in the mirror, Gary brushed aside some strands of sandy blond hair (tinged with just enough peroxide to give him an up-to-the-minute edge) and figured that this shirt was another definite. 'Shouldn't be too much longer. Why don't you go ahead and get yourself ready for tonight,' he suggested, 'and I'll meet you back at the hotel later? Can't say for sure . . . round about seven, maybe? I still have a couple of things to do here.' He raised an eyebrow. 'What, you've got all yours done already? Not bad – and for a girl too!' Laughing at his joke, he slipped out of the shirt and now studied his bare chest. His six-pack looked especially impressive in this light, he reflected. Shame nobody else

could see it. 'Grand. I'll see you there then? Yup . . . me too.'

With that Gary ended the call and put the phone back in his pocket. Then he put his own clothes back on, grabbed the pile of bags at his feet and headed back out in the direction of the cashier's desk.

He was soaking up every minute in the Big Apple. It was a trip he had wanted to take for years, but for some reason he had never got round to it. And now that business was so slack these days he couldn't really justify laying out the cash for it.

Back in the glory days of the Irish house-building boom, Gary's one-man construction company was charging telephone-number prices for sticking up extensions the size of a telephone *box*, but unfortunately those days were long gone.

He had a few quid salted away, of course, and wasn't destitute quite yet, but trips to New York were a good bit down the pecking order when you had four buy-to-regrets (two of which were currently without reliable tenants) and an expensive motorbike hobby to maintain.

Luckily for him, along came Rachel, who, nine months into their relationship, gave him the trip to New York as a present for his thirty-fifth birthday. They'd decided to hold out for a while longer before taking the trip, as his girlfriend had been to New York a few times before and assured him that Christmas in the city was really something special and definitely the best time to go.

His head held high, Gary navigated his way through the crowds of other shoppers towards the nearest check-out queue. However, a display of TAG Heuer watches nearby caught his eye, and before he knew it the small 'Christmas Eve Price Reduction' sign forced him into a bit of a dilemma. Eventually deciding he had a watch, and perhaps one was enough, he made his way along the jewellery case to see what other bargains he might encounter.

Now, they weren't on sale, but the Paul Smith cufflinks certainly would look well – especially for meeting the bank manager. Stuff like that was always an asset, he told himself. In his line of business, and especially in these tough times, a fella had to look the part at all times. The cufflinks were a bit pricey, but wouldn't they be an investment in his future?

At Gary's request the assistant took the box out of the display case so he could take a better look. 'And perhaps something for the lady in your life too?' he suggested, and not for the first time Gary was impressed by how switched on these guys were when it came to selling. They could be a bit pushy at times too, mind you, but he reckoned if sales-people were like that back home in Ireland the country would still be booming. 'We have some wonderful specials at the perfume counter . . .'

But that was all Gary heard, as the salesman's sugges-tion reminded him of something.

Rachel.

He had looked at some nice underwear for her earlier but it had just dawned on Gary that he hadn't actually *bought* his girlfriend anything.

'Uh, no . . . no. Just the cufflinks, thanks,' he said, his mind racing.

He couldn't get her perfume again as he'd bought her that for her birthday, but what other options were there at this hour on Christmas Eve? It was almost six and he had told Rachel to be ready around seven. They both knew he was always late so in reality that actually gave him an hour and a half or so of leeway, but at the same time he was

getting hungry and the shops would be closing soon.

Paying for his shirt and cufflinks, he decided to head back out onto Fifth Avenue and try the next place that caught his eye. After all, he told himself, Rachel was having a great time anyway, and was clearly happy just to be there in New York with him. Any gift at all as a token of their time here would do, wouldn't it?

When he spied Tiffany & Co. just ahead Gary breathed a sigh of relief.

Some famous jewellery shop or something, wasn't it? Perfect. Somebody somewhere was obviously looking out for him, and this might be less hassle than he'd thought. He pushed open yet another of those blasted twirly doors – they seemed to be everywhere in Manhattan and they made Gary dizzy – and went inside.

A glass display counter on his right immediately caught his eye, not so much for what was inside, but rather for what was behind it. The beautiful and nicely buxom blonde smiled in his direction and drew him in.

'Happy holidays,' she greeted as he approached.

'Hello, there. Same to you.' Gary ran a quick gaze over the display of swanky-looking necklaces, and suddenly his skin broke out in a cold sweat. Christ alive, look at those prices!

'Welcome to Tiffany's. What can I help you with? Are you looking for anything specific?'

'Well, no, not really,' Gary muttered. 'Just something nice for . . . I need something for my sister.' If he told her it was for his girlfriend your woman would think he was a right tightwad if he didn't spend big. 'Nice but not too . . . well, you know yourself.' He felt like a right eejit for thinking he could just randomly pick something out in a place like this.

'Ah, I think I've got just the thing. Follow me,' she said

walking ahead of him to another counter. 'Now these charm bracelets are always a popular choice, especially for the season,' she said, pointing out a row of silver bracelets. 'People just love them. The perfect gift for a sister, I would think: thoughtful but not too intimate.'

'Er . . . can I have a look?' he asked nervously.

'Of course.'

Studying the bracelet, Gary quickly sought out the price tag and breathed an inward sigh of relief. Yep, this would do nicely. Thoughtful, not too intimate and, more importantly, not too pricey. 'Right then. That'll be perfect. Amanda,' he added, reading her name tag.

'You'll take it?' She chuckled, her blue eyes wide with surprise. 'That was fast, I must say.'

'Yep,' Gary said with a little wink. 'I don't hang around.'

'You know, I just love your accent,' she said, looking closely at him. 'Are you English?'

'Christ, don't insult me!' he quipped, feigning horror, then seeing her dismayed expression he shook his head. 'Ah, don't worry about it. It's a bit of an old joke. I'm Irish. From Dublin. Ever been?'

'I'm afraid not. Maybe one of these days . . .' Amanda said, laying the bracelet inside a soft felt pouch before putting it into a square blue box. Then she tied the entire package together with a white satin bow. 'Here you go. I know your sister is just going to *love* this little blue box – every woman does!'

'Yeah, yeah, I'm sure she will. I'll be the favourite brother this year,' Gary muttered, whipping out his Visa card. After ringing up his purchase, Amanda handed him back his card along with a small Tiffany's carrier bag and Gary had to admit that he felt a bit of pride picking it up.

Tiffany's, no less! Rachel would be thrilled.

'Thank you, sir,' the assistant said with a smile. 'Enjoy your visit to New York and I do hope you have a fabulous time here.'

'That I will. And you, gorgeous, have a lovely Christmas,' he said, winking.

'Why, thank you. I'm sure I will!' Amanda giggled and Gary gave her one last appreciative glance before picking up the rest of his bags and heading back out onto the street.

Mission accomplished, he thought, a grin on his face. With his arms weighed down with bags he almost felt like a victorious hunter, home afresh from the field.

Just then, his mobile phone rang again and shunting the bags from one arm to the other, Gary reached into his pocket and checked the display. His stomach dropped. He'd thought it might have been Rachel calling him back but no, it was actually the last person he wanted to talk to.

Especially today, and perhaps even more so because of where he was. Talk about bad timing! If she could see him, she'd surely kill him. Well, he'd worry about that some other time, Gary thought, determinedly ignoring the call, though it was much harder to ignore the by now familiar flutter of unease in his chest. Christ, he was no good at this kind of thing!

The ringing stopped and Gary exhaled, relieved that he'd potentially dodged a bullet.

Now, he needed to find a quick way back to the hotel in SoHo.

Where was his motorbike now that he really needed it? He groaned, flustered and frustrated in equal measure. Even with all these bags hanging off him, having his Ducati just then would be a hell of a lot easier than trying to hail a cab amid all the people already attempting the same feat around him.

Oh well, Gary decided, lifting an arm and stepping out

into the road like they were always doing in movies, when in Rome . . .

Completely shopped out, Ethan and Daisy had also just exited Tiffany's.

'So how about it, buttercup? Do you want to head for the Disney Store now?' Ethan suggested, although truthfully he hoped Daisy was as tired as he was. It had been a long day and he wasn't sure he could handle much more of these crowds.

She wrinkled her nose. 'Nah, I think we should head back now.'

'I think you're right.' Ethan took her hand, and was just about to say something else when a loud shout interrupted him.

'Thanks for nothing, ya gobshite!' came a yell to his left that, remarkably, rang out above the cacophony. Ethan thought this could well be because the unmistakable accent was familiar to him, since Vanessa was Irish by birth.

They both turned to look at the man nearby. 'Don't worry about that, darling. It's just some guy trying to hail a cab, and good luck to him in this crowd. So what do you—'

Again, a sound interrupted them, but this time it was the loud blare of a horn followed by the piercing screech of braking tyres. Ethan turned back to see the same man now lying in the middle of the street, shopping bags scattered all around him.

'Freakin' idiot!' a cab driver yelled out of his window.

Oh dear . . . Holding his daughter's hand tightly, Ethan pushed through the quickly gathering crowd. As a university lecturer, he was certified in CPR and as such felt obligated to step in when an emergency like this presented itself.

'Someone call an ambulance – quickly,' he ordered, as he made his way out into the road.

Kneeling at the injured man's side, Ethan could immediately see that he was still breathing, and with some relief he took to clearing a space around him.

'Is he OK?' the driver of the taxi was saying, a shell-shocked expression on his face. 'Man, he just came out of nowhere. I couldn't have avoided him, seriously.'

'I can't honestly say.' Ethan gently wiped the blood from the injured man's brow, and ensured nobody else tried to move him while they waited for help.

'I swear to God, he just came out of nowhere. My fare will back me up on that and – oh man . . . !' Ethan followed the driver's gaze back to the cab, which was now empty of passengers. Typical New Yorkers, he thought wryly, in so much of a hurry they couldn't wait around long enough even to see if the guy their own cab struck was dead or alive.

'Try not to worry. I'm sure he'll be fine,' Ethan reassured the driver, who seemed even more distraught now that he'd lost his witness. Worried about a lawsuit, perhaps, Ethan wondered, but then he realised that maybe he was being unfairly cynical.

There was a large crowd gathered, and while the man's health was foremost on Ethan's mind, he was also rather mindful of his belongings. The last thing this guy needed was for some quick-thinking thief to steal his packages, especially on Christmas Eve.

'Can you gather up all his things?' he directed Daisy, who was standing there looking very worried indeed. 'It's OK, poppet, he'll be OK,' he added quickly, almost sorry now that they'd got involved in something that could potentially be quite traumatic for her. 'We just need to make sure no one steals his shopping.' That seemed to make sense to Daisy, and she quickly leapt into action, much to Ethan's relief.

Eventually a blast of sirens could be heard in the background, although it seemed to take forever for the ambulance to navigate its way through the sea of Fifth Avenue traffic in order to reach them.

Once the medics were on the scene and had taken charge, Ethan's next priority was simply getting his little girl back to the warmth and safety of their hotel.

Telling the medical staff what little he knew about the incident, he was free to go as soon as they began loading the still-unconscious man – and his plethora of packages – into the ambulance.

'Hey, mister,' a gruff voice called to Ethan. It was another yellow-cab driver, who must have been watching the scene from nearby. 'That was mighty nice of ya. Howz 'bout I give you and your little girl a lift to wherever you're headed? It's on me.'

'Thanks, that's really very kind of you,' Ethan answered, thinking that perhaps New Yorkers weren't nearly as brash as people made them out to be. 'But we're only up the block, and I think we need to walk this off anyway. Thank you all the same. And merry Christmas . . . I mean, happy holidays.'

'No problem. Same to you.' The driver tipped his baseball cap, and Ethan and Daisy continued on towards the Plaza, which, luckily for them, was only a short walk away.

Back in their hotel room, Ethan helped Daisy unbutton her winter jacket and warm up her hands. Vanessa was still out, and in truth he was glad to have some more time alone with his daughter after what had happened. Since losing her mother she was prone to worrying about every little thing, especially (and perhaps understandably) about losing Ethan too.

Melissa Hill

In fact sometimes she was like a mini version of Jane, scolding him about his diet and telling him he shouldn't eat too much junk food. Ethan also blamed TV advertisements, the ones that continually peddled cures for heart disease and diabetes, for scaremongering his eight-year-old into worrying about health problems, when at her age she should be concerned with little more than the outcome of the fairy tales she read.

Following the accident, it seemed the old worrisome Daisy was back and he needed to try and restore her confidence.

'You OK?' he asked, and she nodded uncertainly. 'You were such a big help back there. Sad to say, but there really are people who would have stolen that man's shopping. You helped him just as much as I did, you know. We're a good team, you and me.' At this, Daisy smiled proudly and his heart lifted a little. 'So why don't we order some room service while we wait for Vanessa, and then we can tell her all about it? Fancy another hot chocolate?'

'I don't know,' she said hesitantly. 'We had one really big mug already today . . .'

'Well, as your mum used to say, you can never have too much hot chocolate in New York at Christmas.'

Daisy grinned. 'Really? Well, OK then.'

'Great. I'll phone room service now, and while we're waiting why don't you go and wash, change into your pyjamas and meet me back here when you're ready?'

'OK.'

Fifteen minutes later, Daisy was relaxing in the chaise longue with a cup of hot chocolate topped with marshmallows, just the way she liked it, Ethan seated in a cosy armchair across from her. It was a strange day, he thought; he sensed that she was feeling it too.

Well, a lot of things had happened today.

'You're very quiet,' he said, moving across to sit on the end of the chaise longue. 'I hope you know that the doctors will do all they can to help that man.'

'I know. I've seen stuff like that on TV, Dad.'

'Good, then you know he's in good hands.'

So it wasn't just the accident she was thinking about. Ethan wasn't entirely sure if this was a good or a bad thing.

'How are you feeling about the engagement ring? About me asking Vanessa to . . . to be your stepmother, I mean?' he said, reaching for her hand. 'Vanessa has been in our lives for a while now, and you know she really loves you, loves reading with you and taking you to dance class and everything. It would be nice to be a family again, don't you think?'

Daisy took a long sip of her chocolate and stirred the marshmallows with her finger. 'Yeah. Being a family would be nice.'

'Of course, you and I have always been a family too,' Ethan said, and, suddenly overcome with emotion, he had to pause before he could go on. 'I remember,' he continued, turning over her hand in his and opening her palm, 'I used to hold your tiny hand in mine and marvel at how much the same and yet how different the lines in our palms were.' He traced his index finger over the lines, while Daisy listened attentively. He knew she adored hearing stories about what she was like as a baby. All children did, he supposed, but perhaps Daisy even more so because all those stories tended to feature both of her parents together. 'You and I share so much, inside and out. You'll always be my baby, but I can see you growing and changing every day – becoming more and more of the person you are. It's been so wonderful and yet . . . Well, it's been

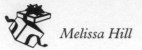

hard sometimes without your mum,' he said, his voice faltering a little. 'But I love being here for you, buttercup, and I want you to know that. I just . . . Look, I'm probably not making any sense.' He ran a hand through his dark hair, wondering why all of this felt so surreal now, when back at Tiffany's it had seemed so right. Covering her little hand with his big one, he continued: 'Just know how much I love you. You will always be my number-one girl. But maybe now, as your mum used to say, we *both* need to trust ourselves and try something new?'

For the first time since they'd left the accident, Daisy smiled. 'Mum *would* be proud of us,' she said, setting down her mug and giving her father the biggest hug he'd got from her in a long time.

Chapter 3

Rachel Conti loved New York at Christmas. Although a visit to the city was always a treat, at this time of year Manhattan was truly at its finest: all decked out in sparkle and full of holiday cheer.

As she sat drinking mulled wine and looking out of the window at the lights of the skyscraper opposite her SoHo hotel, she was mildly sorry she hadn't gone the whole hog and booked somewhere uptown like the Plaza, or at least stayed in a place with views over Central Park. It would have been so much more romantic, especially as it was forecast to snow tomorrow, but midtown was all Rachel could afford at the time she'd been making the reservation. She and Gary were only two of the vast hordes visiting New York at Christmas, and most of the better hotels were either fully booked or way too expensive.

She wished her boyfriend would finish his shopping and come back soon. He'd spent quite some time at the shops today, Rachel thought, even longer than she had; but since they were only here for a few days, she supposed she could hardly blame him for wanting to prolong the New York experience for as long as possible.

Rachel couldn't help but wonder about what he might have chosen for her as a gift this time round. Since they had been together only a couple of months at the time, she had given him the benefit of the doubt on Valentine's Day

when she'd received one of those gift-shop single chocolate roses wrapped in coloured foil. Then on her birthday, a few months later, she'd been disappointed again when he'd presented her with a bottle of perfume and a gift certificate for a well-known discount clothing store. Useful certainly, but hardly thoughtful, and she'd figured Gary just wasn't the type who went for grand gestures or over-the-top sentiment.

Still maybe, just maybe, this time he would really step it up. After all, she had given him this magnificent trip as a birthday gift; so surely he would rise to the occasion now in return? Not that she'd had ulterior motives in doing so – far from it, despite what Justin seemed to think. He was the head chef at Stromboli, the bistro Rachel co-owned with a friend back in Dublin.

'Oooh, that's quite an investment,' he'd teased. 'So are you hoping he makes a big one in return?'

As well as an employee, Justin was a friend, and while Rachel was by now used to his direct, sardonic manner, even she was taken aback by this.

'Don't mind him,' Terri, her best friend and business partner, had soothed. 'Just because *he* needs an ulterior motive to do something nice doesn't mean everyone does.'

However, she sensed that her friend too had been somewhat taken aback by her generosity, particularly when she and Gary hadn't been seeing one another that long. But despite Gary's best attempts at hiding it, Rachel knew that his business was going through a rough time at the moment, and seeing as hers was booming she'd wanted to do something to help cheer him up. There was nothing more to it.

They'd had a wonderful trip so far. Last night they'd gone to see *The Lion King* on Broadway (which, much to her surprise, Gary actually enjoyed) and tonight they planned to go out to a steakhouse nearby for a nice relaxing Christmas Eve dinner and a couple of drinks before coming back to the hotel and . . . Rachel smiled. She supposed she'd better start getting ready. Gary had said he'd be back around seven, although – knowing his time-keeping – she definitely had a half-hour or so to spare.

Stepping out of a quick shower and into a suitably festive red dress, Rachel looked herself up and down in the full-length mirror.

As always she was glad she kept her dark hair relatively short. It was easy to manage and, of course, much more hygienic for cooking at the bistro, and she liked the new choppier style her hairdresser had given her recently; it looked fun and rather flirty. She shook her head, remembering how as a teenager she had hated her petite frame and not being supermodel tall, but now she loved the way her just-curvy-enough hips offset her distinct waist and more-than-a-handful breasts, as Gary called them. A direct result of her Sicilian heritage, as was the relatively uncommon combination of blue eyes and sallow skin.

She smiled. Yes, surely her boyfriend had something wonderful up his sleeve; Rachel could feel it. She didn't want something grand or expensive, just something thoughtful, something he'd carefully chosen just for her.

Fastening her strappy, four-inch silver heels and intentionally bending over to make sure her breasts were securely situated inside the plunging neckline of the dress, she decided to lay out Gary's gifts on his pillow for him to find when they returned from dinner.

An hour later, Rachel had placed and rearranged the packages several times, ordered more mulled wine from room service, eaten three cookies from the hotel minibar,

and touched and retouched her lipgloss over and over.

But of course that was Gary: chronically late and always pushing the limits. And while it was mostly endearing, this time it was kind of irritating, given the night that it was. Reaching for just one last cookie, Rachel was both startled and relieved when the hotel-room phone rang. Odd that he wasn't calling her mobile, though.

'Good evening, this is Nancy Moore, and I'm calling from Mount Sinai Hospital,' a strange voice said, and instantly Rachel blanched. *A hospital?* 'Do you happen to know a Gary Knowles?'

'Yes . . . of course,' she replied, her heart hammering. 'Why?'

'I apologise for the nature of the call but I'm afraid there's been an accident,' the woman continued, her tone steady. 'Mr Knowles is in a stable condition, but hasn't regained consciousness yet. We found his hotel key and called this hotel hoping to find next-of-kin.'

Next-of-kin? Oh no, that could only mean. . . 'Oh my God,' Rachel could barely speak. 'Is he OK? I'm his girl-friend . . .'

'He was hit by a cab, ma'am, but his injuries aren't severe at this time,' the woman confirmed, and Rachel quickly exhaled the breath she'd been holding. 'We expect him to regain consciousness soon, but feel free to come down and see him whenever you like. Your name, please?'

'Rachel, Rachel Conti. Yes, yes, of course, I'll be right there . . .'

Changing only her shoes (into a pair of flats so she could get around faster), and wrapping up in a warm coat, Rachel managed to make it to the hospital in under forty-five minutes, which wasn't bad for a cab ride on Christmas Eve. It didn't take her long to find directions to Gary's room and she soon collared a nearby nurse to get all of the details.

'He suffered a few bruised ribs in the blow, and then a laceration to the head and subsequent concussion from the fall,' said the woman, reading from the chart. 'Twisted ankle too. Apparently some Good Samaritan stepped in and kept the crowd back, cleaned him up a bit and kept the wolves from carrying off his packages. Stuff's right there,' she said, pointing to a pile of colourful bags on the chair beside Gary's bed.

'Will he be OK?' Rachel asked nervously.

'He'll be fine, but don't expect him to come round properly till morning. He woke about half an hour before you got here, but we sedated him to keep him still and resting. Feel free to stay for a while, but you may as well take the bags and head back to get some rest yourself. He's not going anywhere for at least a couple of days, maybe three. Oh, and happy holidays,' she finished.

Rachel barely raised a hand to acknowledge her as she leaned over Gary to gently kiss his forehead and stroke his arm.

'Bloody gobshite . . .' he mumbled almost imperceptibly.

The nurse looked enquiringly at Rachel. 'He's been mumbling stuff like that all evening. Any idea what he means?'

Rachel actually felt the hint of an unexpected smile. 'It's just an Irish expression.'

'Ah, I see,' the woman said, nodding quickly as if this explained everything. 'I guess I don't blame the poor guy. Have a great evening.'

'Thanks, you too.' Then Rachel turned back to Gary. She lifted his hand and held it in her own. 'Poor baby, look at you . . . always pushing it,' she whispered, holding back tears

as she moved to caress his forehead. 'I hope this didn't happen because you were rushing back for me.'

Rachel sat there with him for an hour or so, trying to discern the extent of his injuries and wondering if there was anything the nurse hadn't told her.

Apart from the bruises and head wound, he seemed OK, although she would have much preferred him to be awake and able to speak to her.

Eventually, when there were no further signs of him stirring, Rachel decided to take the woman's advice and head back to the hotel. It was late, visiting hours were long over, and there wasn't a whole lot she could do here, not when he was so heavily sedated. She gathered up his bags, deciding it was probably safer to take them back to the hotel rather than leave them out in the open.

Just as she was leaving, an orderly met her with yet another bag, this one containing Gary's clothes and other personal effects.

Heavily laden, Rachel turned to look at her injured boyfriend one more time. 'I love you, Gary. Merry Christmas,' she whispered, pausing for a moment before leaving the hospital mere minutes before Christmas Eve gave way to Christmas Day.

'A little late to be finishing up Christmas shopping, ain't it, lady?' the cab driver joked as Rachel piled in with all of Gary's bags and boxes.

'I wish,' she replied, her tone short, before calling out her hotel's address. 'Please,' she added then, somewhat more gently. After all, it wasn't *this* cab driver's fault that poor Gary's Christmas had been ruined.

Back at the hotel, she plopped herself down on the couch, letting the packages fall around her feet. She felt tired and defeated, and while she was sure Gary was in good hands, she couldn't help but worry.

In addition, the twinkling Christmas lights from the streets, glowing faintly through the window, seemed to be mocking her now, and all Rachel could think about was the poor thing lying there in the hospital.

Should she contact his mother? She didn't know Mrs Knowles at all, they'd never met, but her number would surely be programmed into Gary's mobile. She bit her lip. Perhaps better to wait until morning when she'd spoken to the doctors and knew more. If she phoned Mrs Knowles out of the blue now, the woman's Christmas would be ruined with worry too, and she didn't want that.

Getting up to pour a glass of wine seemed like a much better idea, so that's exactly what she did. Then, tossing her red dress on the bed and slipping into the hotel's fluffy robe (instead of the sexy little negligee placed neatly on Gary's pillow) she remembered Gary's bag of clothes and decided she should make sure everything was in order.

It might be weird, but she just didn't like the way everything was bundled away like that in a bag on the floor; it almost made it seem like he was dead or something. No, much better to tidy everything up and have all his clothes washed and ready for him when he got back.

Rachel picked up the plastic hospital bag and settled back on the bed. Taking everything out, she set Gary's wallet on a nearby bureau. His jacket was dirty and bloodstained from the head wound, as were his jeans, so they needed to go to the laundry. Rachel checked the pockets of each for receipts, or anything else that might be destroyed in the wash. From his jeans pocket, she pulled out a list, which, judging by what was scribbled on it, must be her boyfriend's Christmas shopping list.

In true Gary fashion, Rachel thought, smiling as she read through it, there was one column for names and one

column for corresponding stores, presumably where he'd either bought or intended to buy the gifts. Hmm . . . where was he planning to buy her Christmas present, she couldn't help but wonder. Gary was somewhat evasive when it came to his family, and she was interested to try and figure out his relationship with various family members by the kind of gifts he was buying for them. Then, immediately conscious that she was prying, she set the list down on the nightstand beside her. Switching on the TV, she turned off the bedside lamp and took another taste of her wine, this time with something more akin to a swig than a sip.

She glanced towards the list again, her interest also piqued about what Gary had in mind for her. Oh what the hell, she reasoned, reaching for it, it was a list of stores, not actual gifts. So what could it hurt?

Before Rachel knew it, the list was back in her hands and she had clicked the lamp on to have a better look. At first glance, she didn't see her name written down anywhere. At a second more careful look, she still didn't see it. Frowning, she put down the list.

Then it hit her. What was wrong with her? Of *course* her name wasn't on the list. Gary would no doubt have known exactly what he wanted to get her for Christmas, so why would he have written it down?

With that, Rachel poured herself a second glass, and it was a bit more of a generous helping than before. It was essential really; she was, after all, alone and worried in a New York hotel room on Christmas Eve.

Going back to the bed, she climbed under the covers this time, then gently, one by one, plopped the gifts she'd bought for Gary onto the floor next to the bed. First went the negligee, next went the heavy box with the leather motorbike trousers in it, and third went the handcrafted wallet mono-grammed with his initials. And then went her mind, inevitably back to wondering what Gary had got for her.

Her gaze moved to the pile of bags not more than five feet away from her. Inside one of those was her gift, unwrapped.

Rachel knew Gary must have bought it today because she'd already searched the room and his empty suitcase in the hope of finding some clue of what she should expect to get from him. It was silly and she hated herself for it, but she just couldn't help it.

'No, I'm not going to look,' she said out loud, grabbing the television remote and starting to click through the chan-nels. Cinemax, MoreMAX, Pay-Per-View . . . some of the show titles looked rather intriguing. 'Yikes, who watches skin-flicks on Christmas Eve?' she asked herself rhetorically and kept clicking until she came upon *It's a Wonderful Life* right around mid-point.

Just perfect.

By the time George was hearing bells ringing and start-ing to believe, Rachel had the empty wine bottle in one hand and Gary's list in the other. With tears streaming down her face (as they did every time she watched that film), she headed without a second thought to the couch, where she promptly started matching gift bags with the names and stores on the list.

With each matching set she found, she moved the corre-sponding bag to a pile. By the time she'd come to the end of the list there was one bag from Bergdorf Goodman, with men's clothes and some expensive-looking cufflinks in it (for Gary's brother perhaps?), and, conspicuously, one small but gloriously familiar blue gift bag.

'Oh my goodness . . . Tiffany's!' she cried aloud. Her

heart pounding in her chest, she checked the list again, turning the paper over and over in her hand. Nothing.

Could this be hers? Had Gary *really* bought her something from Tiffany's?

He must have!

Rachel's eyes sparkled even brighter than the festive lights outside. Checking her watch, she swallowed hard.

Well, it *was* officially Christmas now, wasn't it? Holding her breath, she peeked inside the bag.

Only to find the world-famous little blue box.

Chapter 4

Unable to sleep any longer, Ethan got up at dawn, and was standing at the window watching the sun come up over Central Park and the surrounding buildings. In fact he was up before Daisy on Christmas morning for the first time since she'd been old enough to be excited about it. Snow was gently falling, and, thanks to the Plaza's in-room facilities, he was sipping freshly made coffee. It was a picture-perfect New York Christmas morning, even if he was yawning after tossing and turning all night.

Ethan thought again about Daisy's mother and smiled a little as the coffee aroma took him back in time. Jane wasn't enamoured of his habit and had always insisted that if he *had* to drink coffee, it should be organic or nothing. In turn all Daisy's baby food had been home-made and, yes, organic too. Jane had been an amazing mum, he thought, and he had a healthy, happy daughter because of her.

Happy? His train of thought halted at the word. Sure, Daisy was generally a happy child, but it still seemed to him that there was so much missing, so much he wasn't giving her. Ethan ran a hand through his thick brown hair and felt his eyes fall gently shut as he thought about the three years he had spent alone, and how many nights he had sat with Daisy and cuddled her until she could fall asleep, her last words always about missing her mummy. Those instances had become less frequent as the months passed, but still

there was nothing Ethan wanted more than to be a family again.

It was best for Daisy. Not to mention that he really did love Vanessa. Yes, he had been hesitant in the early days, but over the course of the last year they had grown especially close, and now he was certain she was the perfect person to turn their little unit into a real family.

He'd met her at a book fair, of all places. His good friend Brian, a former work colleague at the university at which Ethan lectured, was now a highly successful and well-respected novelist. Just over a year ago, after much coaxing and cajoling, Brian had convinced Ethan that leaving Daisy with her grandparents for three days while they made the trip to Frankfurt did not make him a neglectful parent.

'After all, mate, it's basically a business trip,' Brian reassured him. 'We're going to talk about my book this time, but we'll be going for yours next year. Maybe this'll inspire you to get your arse in gear and start writing that Great British Novel,' he teased, referring to Ethan's latent ambitions. 'Not as great as my own, mind, but I'm sure there's room for us both on the Booker shortlist.'

Ethan couldn't really argue with this (the reason for the trip, that is; he had no illusions about getting anywhere near any list, Booker or otherwise), so in the end he decided to go along.

And then on day two of the fair he saw her: the not classically beautiful, but poised and immaculately groomed blonde who was heading their way.

Ethan had caught her eye a couple of times as he and Brian browsed through the stands, and found himself intrigued by her calm self-possession. When she first approached them, Ethan suspected she might be one of Brian's many literary 'groupies', but gathered from the polite yet familiar conversation that ensued that she and Brian had crossed paths before at publishing events. It turned out that she too worked in publishing and was senior editor of a literary imprint at a major London publishing house. The next thing Ethan knew, the three of them were having lunch, and he discovered that Vanessa lived in the vicinity of Teddington, not far from his home in Richmond. And not long after that, just the two of them were having dinner, at first there in Frankfurt and then back in London. He enjoyed her company and lively conversation; they had a shared appreciation of great literature and the arts, and he also admired the single-minded determination with which she ran her professional life, having worked her way up in a highly competitive field. And still her ambition didn't end there. Vanessa wanted the most respected and accomplished literary authors for her list, and laughingly informed Ethan that her original intention in approaching them at the fair was to see about poaching Brian from his existing publishing house.

She was so different from Jane – she was focused and driven as opposed to having Jane's relaxed approach to life – that Ethan surprised himself by first becoming intrigued by her and then eventually falling for her completely. Sometimes she made his head spin with her broad and intricate knowledge of travel, food and wine, as well as the seemingly effortless confidence with which she approached everything. This self-assurance was one of the first things that had captivated him, but there was also a somewhat enigmatic side to her that had made him want to get closer.

Still, he had waited almost six months before introducing her to Daisy. Just because he was moving on, there was no reason to force his daughter to do the same, he reasoned.

When the big meeting did finally occur, Ethan arranged

for Vanessa to meet the two of them after Daisy's weekly Saturday dance class. He had done his best to ensure it was light and informal, and to keep the focus on Daisy, but he wasn't fooling his wise and perceptive daughter. As the three of them walked along by the Thames eating ice cream, Daisy kept giving her father the same look her mother had always had. Ethan called it the sideways-squinty-eyed look, one that often appeared on his daughter's face during poorly disguised homework bribing and early-to-bed coaxing.

Over time, though, Daisy came around. She loved it when Vanessa read to her; storytelling was one of her favourite things. She especially loved Vanessa's accent, a rich combination of a decade and a half spent in cultured London coupled with the lilt of her Irish roots. It was something that at the beginning had greatly appealed to Ethan too, although Vanessa liked to insist that fifteen years of living in England had eradicated most of her native brogue.

He always wished that Vanessa would read more than just one bedtime story at a time, but reminded himself that it was different for people who'd never had children of their own, and no doubt she would gradually get a feel for that kind of thing.

He should know; he had never considered himself the doting-father type but had fallen completely in love with his baby daughter when she wrapped her tiny newborn hand around his index finger in the delivery suite. And when afterwards he'd cuddled her fragile little body close to his bare chest, skin to skin, Ethan had given her his heart there and then.

Given time it would be the same for Vanessa, he thought; Vanessa and Daisy would share a moment that would cement their relationship. It couldn't be forced. It would probably happen once they all lived together, when they spent time together like a real family. Sadly, due to Vanessa's inability to conceive (something she'd disclosed frankly to Ethan early on in the relationship) there would be no additions to that family, but he was fine with that too.

As daylight gradually crept across the park, Ethan lifted his head, wondering how long he had actually been standing there daydreaming. The sun was peeking through the clouds, and despite the brief flurry of snow a clear sky was visible in the distance. Ethan thought that this was a good omen seeing as it had been overcast and grey in the city since they arrived. Today was different for a reason, he realised; the powers-that-be must be smiling on him and his intentions . . .

'Merry Christmas, darling.'

At the sound of the voice nearby, Ethan jumped, and coffee splashed on his bare chest through the opening of his bathrobe.

'Oops!' Vanessa laughed, coming up alongside him. 'Sorry, I didn't mean to startle you . . .' Her voice trailed off as she rushed to the bathroom, and in a flash she was back with a cool washcloth and a fresh robe.

'It's my own fault. I was miles away,' he replied, smiling at her. 'Anyway, it's cold by now.'

'Why so jumpy? Still thinking about that accident yesterday? I'm sure the guy is fine.'

Holding the cloth to his chest, he stood there in his boxers, assuring her she had just caught him in a daydream. 'No, no, it's fine, honestly. I just didn't expect anyone else to be up so early.' Ethan handed her back the cloth, and put on the dry robe. 'Join me for a fresh cup?'

She smiled. 'I'd love one.'

Ethan moved to the cafetière and poured a steaming cup

of coffee for the woman he was about to propose to. Coffee pot in hand, he noticed he wasn't nervous as such, but not quite his usual calm, cool self, either.

Evidently so did Vanessa. Taking the cup from him, she put her other hand on his before he had the chance to let go. Ethan looked up to see some sort of knowing look in her eyes, as if she could guess exactly what he was thinking. It shot right through him. Resisting taking a step backwards, he knew he must be looking startled again, because she seemed to quell the slightest smile as she turned away.

Goodness, she knows! He wondered how that could be. Maybe she'd noticed that one of her rings had gone missing? A little while back, he had secretly purloined one of Vanessa's costume rings from her jewellery box so that he could establish the correct ring size.

'So, as I was saying, merry Christmas,' Vanessa repeated, reaching forward to kiss him. 'It's so wonderful being here in New York on Christmas morning with you and Daisy. It means a lot – especially when I know how important it is to you two, because of Jane, I mean.'

She was so perceptive, and always so generous and understanding about Jane's memory that Ethan felt himself fall in love with her all over again. Living in another woman's shadow would undoubtedly be a challenge for some, but thankfully this didn't seem to be the case with Vanessa. Well, Ethan decided, even if she did have any qualms – hidden or otherwise – those would surely be erased once he produced that little blue box.

'Thank you for asking me to come with you,' she went on, her voice slightly hoarse. 'You were right: New York at Christmas time really is something special.'

Ah, that was it, Ethan realised with some relief. Vanessa

had no idea what was coming. It was just the Christmas thing and she was emotional about that.

'Me too, and I'm so glad you're here. This is a really special time for us, for all of us.' He paused. The light coming through the window caught the hazel in her eyes, and the weight of what he was about to do took his breath away for a moment. 'I love you too, Vanessa. I do. I mean, I . . .' he stammered, recognising the Freudian slip in those two words. 'I mean, I do love you.'

She smiled and gently rested her hand on the side of his face.

'Merry Christmas!' Daisy squealed from the doorway connecting to her bedroom, as if poised for a grand entrance. She raced towards them, leaping and landing on the big double bed with a flourish. 'Let's open our presents!'

'How about good-morning greetings and some breakfast first?' Ethan replied, his tone half-scolding.

'Yes, you'll need to get your strength up for all the presents you'll be opening,' Vanessa chimed in.

'So do you,' the little girl replied with a demure smile, and Ethan gave her a warning look, which made her giggle.

'OK, let's get some room service organised,' he said, practically diving for the menu in order to change the subject.

'Hot chocolate. I suppose that's our first priority?' Vanessa teased, sitting down beside Daisy.

'That's not very healthy, you know, Vanessa,' she replied solemnly and Ethan and Vanessa shared a smile. His girlfriend was fully aware of Daisy's frequent bouts of anxiety and Ethan hoped that once they were all together as a family she'd feel more secure and such tendencies would wear off.

'But it's Christmas morning!' Vanessa insisted with a grin.

'I'm sure one day of indulgence won't kill us.' Ethan couldn't help but wince at her unfortunate choice of phrase, but luckily Daisy didn't seem to notice.

'You're right. Can I have an iced cinnamon roll too, Dad? I love iced cinnamon rolls.'

'You can have whatever you want, poppet. Any requests, Vanessa?'

She shook her head. 'What Daisy's having sounds good to me.'

'OK then, hot chocolate and cinnamon rolls all round,' Ethan said, picking up the phone to order.

Half an hour later, the three of them were sipping hot drinks and sitting around the little tree they'd bought and decorated especially for the occasion. Daisy tucked her legs up beneath her on the floor and licked the remains of the icing off her fingers.

'All right then, let's see what have we here,' Ethan began, handing a brightly wrapped package to Daisy.

'No, Vanessa first,' she insisted, grinning coyly.

'You're in an excitable mood today, even for Christmas morning,' Ethan said, giving his daughter his own, more subtle version of the sideways-squinty-eyed look. 'Go ahead and open yours first, OK?'

She gave a big, exaggerated sigh. 'OK, Dad.'

'Yes, please do,' Vanessa laughed. 'I think you're going to like that one, or at least I hope you will. It's from me.'

'Great.' Daisy sat cross-legged as she tore open the wrapping. A collection of soft-cover books landed in her lap. 'Animal stories?' she said, looking at the covers of a Thornton Burgess story collection.

'Yes. I had those when I was a little girl. They're just at your reading level, so you can read them to yourself at bedtime.'

'Oh . . .' Daisy said flatly, twirling one of her curls with her index finger. 'Thanks.'

'But one of us can still read them to you too, honey,' Ethan put in quickly, picking up on her obvious disappointment.

'Vanessa's turn now,' Daisy said easily, as if the last comment had gone in one ear and out the other. Typical.

Ethan looked at his daughter and smiled. At least she was still excited about the proposal, more so than he could have hoped. Giving her a surreptitious wink, he said, 'I do believe you're right,' and Daisy giggled with delight and clapped her hands.

Vanessa raised an eyebrow. 'Daisy, you've got me intrigued now. This must be a pretty good gift,' she said.

'Well, I certainly hope so.' Ethan handed her the Tiffany's gift bag. The distinctive blue box and ribbon combination was so unmistakably elegant it seemed a travesty to wrap them any further. 'This is from me, but Daisy helped me pick it out. She has great taste,' he added, giving his daughter a smile, which she giddily returned.

Vanessa seemed taken aback. 'Oh my . . . something from Tiffany's?' she gasped, her face lighting up as Ethan had hoped it would.

Jane was right: there really was something about the packaging alone that turned even the most sophisticated of women to mush.

Letting the little blue box rest in her hand for a moment, Vanessa went to untie the white bow, but then paused and looked up. 'Daisy, I've already told your father this, but I just wanted to let you know too how happy I am to be here, to be sharing Christmas with both of you. It means a lot, darling.' She reached over and patted Daisy's hand, receiving a huge Cheshire Cat grin in return.

'Go on, open it!' the little girl urged and Ethan smiled, enjoying the moment.

He moved closer to Vanessa, and reached out to take Daisy's hand.

Smiling at Ethan, Vanessa pulled slowly on the soft satin ribbon as if savouring every second. When it gave way and fell in her lap, she took a deep breath before finally lifting off the lid of the box. As she did, her eyes grew wide.

'Well, what have we got here?' she murmured happily, opening the little felt pouch and reaching inside. 'A charm bracelet . . . How lovely!'

What the hell . . . ?

Ethan stared at the box, unable to believe what he was hearing.

He glanced sideways at Daisy, who was just as wide-eyed. If he didn't know better he could have sworn that Vanessa was joking, but it wasn't really the kind of thing to joke about. Moving closer to get a better look, he checked to see what she was holding in her hand. Yes, there was no mistake – it was indeed a charm bracelet.

Cute, but no diamond solitaire.

Christ, what the hell was going on?

'Yes . . . we, er . . . picked it out together, didn't we?' he said, catching Daisy's eye. She sat there looking just as shocked as he was. 'It seemed like a lovely keepsake of our trip, of our special time here in New York, just the three of us.' Ethan's mind was racing. Lecturing had its advantages in that it helped him think quickly on his feet.

'Yes, we got it at Tiffany's,' Daisy said, rather unnecessarily. She looked at Ethan as if trying to gauge what they should do or say next.

'It's beautiful. Thank you,' Vanessa said, but Ethan barely heard her.

For a moment, he wasn't sure how to react, but knew deep down that he had to try to rescue the situation before Vanessa noticed something was amiss. Eventually he reached for her arm. 'Here, let me. I want to see how it looks on,' he said, lifting the bracelet from Vanessa's palm and fastening it around her wrist. 'Gorgeous . . . much like the woman wearing it, of course.' He gave her a broad smile but was sure that she would be able to see through its falseness. He'd always been dreadful at deception.

'Thank you – both of you.' Vanessa twirled the bracelet around on her wrist. 'It's just . . . amazing, and the perfect memento of this trip.' Sitting up straighter, she took a deep breath and smiled conspiratorially at Daisy. 'Well, Daisy, I think it's your dad's turn now.'

'Oh no, no . . . we should really let Daisy open the rest of her things first,' Ethan interjected quickly, running a hand through his hair and making a great show of looking around for his coffee cup. Any excuse to extricate himself from this uncomfortable and really very mystifying situation.

'No, I insist. Really. We should take turns.'

Daisy gave him a look. 'Yeah, Dad. Your turn now. It's only fair that way.'

'OK, I defer to the ladies,' he replied, effecting a ridiculous bow in an attempt to break the discomfort and retain some of the Christmas cheer. But given what had just happened, Daisy was edgy and, while he could very well be imagining it, he was almost certain from the look on Vanessa's face that she knew something was off. He sat back on the floor and leaned against the end of the chaise longue.

'Here it is,' his girlfriend said, reaching under the tree, and Ethan sensed some slight affectation in her voice as he took the long rectangular box from her hand. Perhaps it wasn't intentional, but sure enough it was there, beneath the

surface of her tone and the facade of her smile. She picked her cup of now-cold chocolate off a side table and looked away while taking a long sip.

Ethan felt the urge to say something meaningful again about how special this Christmas was, but as he opened his mouth to speak he realised that this seemed pointless now.

'Were you going to say something?' Vanessa asked.

'Ah, no . . .' he replied, peeling back the pieces of sticky tape with uncharacteristic deliberation.

'Hurry up, Daddy,' Daisy urged, moving closer.

'OK, OK.' Opening the box, a relieved smile (this one genuine) came over his face. 'Well, would you look at this! How perfect! See – great minds really do think alike.' With some relief, he held aloft a silver bracelet. It looked antique and very masculine, a series of rectangular pieces joined together. What were the chances?

'There's an inscription,' Vanessa pointed out enthusiastically.

'Oh.' Ethan's immediate thought was to wonder whether or not the bracelet she'd got by mistake was inscribed with anything. If so, maybe it would provide a clue as to where the hell it had come from? Then he read the inscription on Vanessa's gift for him, the words delicately etched into the individual pieces, and felt his heart fall heavily into his stomach.

> She loved him with too clear a vision to
> fear his cloudiness.

'Vanessa . . .' He could hardly meet her gaze. 'I don't know what to say. Thank you.' He reached across to kiss her gently at the corner of her mouth and lingered there for a second.

The quote came from *Howard's End*, a story she knew

he loved. During one of their arguments early in the relationship, she had told him that this particular line always reminded her of him, in that he always seemed to hover in a haze within her reach. It had become a sort of running joke since – one of those poignant references between two people that reminds them of how far they've come, and unwittingly breathes life into the demons of their past. They had both quoted it off and on, over dinner and wine, and conversations about the future. Regardless, the reference had always been intended as a loving and intimate exchange, but this morning it felt more like an unintentional kick in the teeth. Poor Vanessa, if only she knew that today was the day that that 'cloudiness' should have been lifted.

'What does it say, Daddy?' Daisy asked.

'Um, it says that I'm just about ready to open the gift from my beautiful daughter now!' he teased, tickling the sole of her bare foot. She laughed out loud and pulled it back.

'OK then, here it is,' she said, extending her arm proudly. 'I wrapped it up all by myself at school.'

'At school?' Vanessa queried.

'Yeah, I bought it at the Christmas Gift Sale. People donate things so we can buy gifts for our parents without them knowing.'

Vanessa stroked Daisy's arm. 'I would have taken you shopping, darling.'

The little girl shook her head. 'That's OK. I wanted to do it this way.'

'But thank you, Vanessa,' Ethan said, reminding his daughter of her manners.

'Yes, thank you, Vanessa,' Daisy echoed cheekily.

Ethan unwrapped his daughter's gift with considerably more speed and anticipation than he had the previous package.

'It's a book with nothing in it!' she announced, when all the wrapping had been removed.

'Yes, I can see that,' he said, faintly puzzled.

'It's so you can fill it in yourself, silly – so you can write your own book. You know, like you talk about,' she clarified.

'What a very clever daughter you have, Ethan,' Vanessa said, cocking her head and smiling, but Ethan caught the meaning in her words.

According to Vanessa, another element of his 'cloudiness' was his all-talk-and-no-action approach to writing a book of his own. She was always encouraging him to put pen to paper.

'You're just so talented,' was her argument, 'and I want the rest of the world to know it too.'

He'd made a start and cobbled together some sort of outline, but finding the time to write and be a fully employed single father was like trying to count the number of raindrops that fell in London any given year.

'Thank you, honey. I promise I will carry this with me everywhere and write longhand whenever the Muse strikes me.'

'Yay!'

'I'll drink to that,' Vanessa said, tipping up her cup and slurping the very last drop of hot chocolate.

The rest of the morning passed quickly as Daisy opened her other gifts, which were modest for the sake of not travelling back to London with excessive amounts of extra luggage, and of course she already knew that the bulk of her presents came in the form of the trip itself.

Finally, when Vanessa left the room to shower and get dressed, Ethan snatched some much-anticipated time alone with his daughter.

'Can you believe it?' he gasped, running a hand through his hair. 'What on earth happened to our lovely ring?' Not to mention pretty damn *expensive* ring, but Ethan guessed Daisy wouldn't really understand his concerns about that aspect.

She put her bare feet up next to his on the coffee table and frowned deeply.

'I know . . . it's so weird, isn't it? I just don't understand it. I remember that happened to me at school once, though. I went to eat my lunch and got someone else's lunchbox, which only had ham and horrible plastic cheese on white bread with NO yoghurt. I was so annoyed!'

Despite himself, Ethan had to chuckle at the comparison. 'Erm . . . yes, I suppose it is a bit like that.'

'Well, of course I know this is different, but you know what I mean.' She paused and looked down, scraping something from beneath one of her fingernails. 'But what do you think happened, Dad, and what are you going to do now?'

'Well, there's nothing we can do now, is there? Today, I mean. I think Vanessa was disappointed, though. I think she might have known somehow or maybe expected . . . Oh I just don't know.' He sat forward. 'OK, buttercup, you and I are going straight back to Tiffany's in the morning to try to get this straightened out. There must have been some kind of a mistake while they were wrapping it up or something. Remember that nice man sent it away while we waited?'

Daisy nodded. 'Yeah, that has to be it. Um, Dad . . . ?'

'Yes?' he replied, expecting some helpful insight into his predicament.

'Am I going to have hair on my toes like you do?'

Ethan burst out laughing. 'Yes, definitely.' He moved his feet closer so that the outside of his right foot was touching

the outside of her left one. 'In another five years or so your feet will look exactly like mine. And I hear that touching our feet together will actually speed up the process.'

Daisy squealed and ran back towards her bedroom. 'Stay away then!' she cried, and while Ethan would normally have taken the cue and followed to tickle her, instead he just called out, 'Have it your way,' and walked over to the window again.

He checked his watch. It wasn't even close to noon yet. This would be the longest Christmas day he had ever spent. Where on earth was the ring?

He seriously hoped Tiffany's might be able to shed some light on it tomorrow, but what if they couldn't? What then? Should he tell Vanessa? No, that would be too anticlimactic. But what next?

More importantly, Ethan thought, as he looked out at a now misty sky above the park, what if Vanessa was right? What if his mind truly was marked by cloudiness? And what if – despite his best efforts – he just couldn't escape the haze?

Chapter 5

Rachel rolled over in bed, automatically running her hand through her hair.

One thing she loved about hotel stays were the thick curtains – so thick that if you had them closed tightly enough, and if it weren't for the seam of light at the bottom, you could scarcely tell it was daytime.

First as a chef and now a restaurant owner, leisurely mornings had always been a luxury for her. Being able to sleep late was something she savoured, given the chance; however her version of this possibly differed from most people's. For someone who was usually at work in the kitchen by six a.m., staying in bed until eight was quite a treat.

Although she'd woken at six that morning, full of thoughts about Gary and rushing to the hospital to see him, she'd then figured that it was far too early for visiting hours, even on Christmas Day. So instead, for the next couple of hours, she had cosied up with Gary's pillow and dozed and half-dreamed about the two of them and their soon-to-be engagement.

Then, relishing one last vision of herself in white, Rachel opened her eyes. Stretching her arms out in front of her, she gazed at her left hand and envisioned that stunning solitaire on her ring finger. She'd really wanted to go to sleep wearing it last night, but had felt so guilty about finding it in the first place that in the end she'd returned it to its little blue box.

Now, leaping out of bed, Rachel realised her excitement was, indeed, tainted by considerable post-alcohol guilt. She really shouldn't have rummaged through the bags, and she certainly shouldn't have opened the Tiffany's one. Still, to think that if she hadn't . . .

No, she realised, biting her lip and looking at herself in the mirror with a playful smile, she shouldn't feel guilty, and really she wouldn't change a thing. It was a wonderful surprise, particularly after the shock and worry of Gary's accident. It was also quite romantic, considering: finding herself all alone on Christmas Eve and discovering just by chance that Gary was about to propose! It was fairy-tale stuff and more than Rachel could ever have dreamed of.

But perhaps the biggest surprise of all was the discovery that Gary loved her even more than she had known. Yes, they had fun together and she loved him too, but because she hadn't yet met his family, she wasn't sure how serious he considered their relationship to be. Family was important to Rachel; she was an only child and had already lost her own parents, and as much as she wanted to meet Gary's, she figured he was just biding his time until the moment felt right. A proposal was the last thing she'd expected from him and she certainly hadn't expected anything like that ring! The beautifully cut diamond was big enough to take your eye out and being from Tiffany's it had clearly cost him a packet. Who would have thought it?

Everything happened for a reason, Rachel told herself, so perhaps finding the box was exactly what she'd needed to allay any misgivings she might have had about their relationship.

She eyed the shopping bags in the corner of the room, thinking that she just had to have another look at that ring.

God, to think that this was going to be on her hand for the rest of her life!

Rachel was giddy. Opening the box once again, she was startled afresh by what she saw. The shape and setting were utterly stunning and the diamond itself looked so much bigger in daylight, and, indeed, without the cosy filter of the wine buzz.

Yet again she was faintly shocked that Gary had spent thousands on a blingtastic ring when he had never even alluded to marriage. Strange too when, on the flight over, he'd been complaining about how much he was going to have to spend on fixing something that had gone wrong with his bike. While Gary could never have been described as generous, she'd noticed he'd been particularly careful with money over the last couple of months, and now she thought she knew the reason.

Rachel smiled. Clearly the bike thing had been just a ruse and merely went to prove how much he really loved her. Her ring was more important than the Ducati! She shook her head fondly. One thing you could say about Gary was that he was *always* full of surprises. But this had got to be the biggest, *bestest* surprise of all . . .

It then occurred to Rachel that she really should rewrap the box at some stage so that Gary wouldn't notice anything untoward when he got back, but then she decided it could wait.

Her first priority was getting to the hospital to spend at least part of Christmas morning with her future husband, so stashing the box back in the bag, she showered, then put on some make-up, jeans and a sweater, before bundling up and heading out to hail a cab. She could pick up something for breakfast at the hospital.

During the cab ride to the hospital she was this time only too happy to natter away to the driver, a chatty Greek whose

passenger seat was littered with gyro pitta wrappers, and she marvelled yet again at the melting pot that was New York. For many of its inhabitants Christmas Day was no different to any other.

A little while later she reached the hospital, and going up to Gary's floor she approached the nurses' station near his room.

'Hi there! Merry Christmas to you,' she greeted happily. 'I'm here to see Gary Knowles in room 303. How is he?'

'Merry Christmas to you too! Go ahead on in. He's fine and resting well,' the nurse on duty said in what Rachel recognised as a thick New Jersey accent. 'He's a fidgety one, though. I'm guessing it's the meds, but he's been talking in his sleep off and on all morning. Something about a Ducati?'

Rachel smiled apologetically. 'Yes, he's a bit of a motorbike enthusiast. Sorry about that. I'm sure there are things you'd rather be doing on Christmas morning than listening to such ramblings.'

'Don't worry about it,' the nurse chuckled, waving an arm. 'It's kind of funny – my husband has a Ducati too, and if I didn't know better I'd ask if his injuries were from riding. Al, my husband, slipped on black ice two weeks ago and had rib problems really similar to your husband's.'

'Oh, he's not my—' Rachel caught herself before she uttered *husband*. But the very thought of the word sent fresh flutters through her stomach. 'I mean, we're engaged, but no, he got hurt in an accident, actually. His first time in New York and he gets hit by a yellow cab,' she added, with an ironic half-smile. 'I'm sorry to hear about your husband, though.'

'Oh no, he's fine. Couldn't keep him off that bike if I

tried. Honestly, I think if he had to choose between me and that thing . . . I'd probably be a single woman by now!' The nurse laughed good-naturedly. 'Well, I won't hold you up. You have a nice visit.'

'Thank you . . . Kim,' Rachel said, reading her name tag. 'I'm Rachel, and I'm sure I'll see you on my way out.'

'Sure.'

But, peeking around the corner of Gary's room, the joy Rachel had felt all morning suddenly gave way to a potent dose of reality. Her boyfriend looked even worse than he had the night before. One side of his face was swollen, scraped and black and blue, and he was hooked up to an IV. He looked so still and pitiful that she felt her stomach lurch, and swallowed hard as she sat down in the chair next to his bed.

Wracked with guilt, she berated herself for being so carefree and happy when her poor fiancé was lying here in agony. Then, telling herself that he probably looked worse than he felt, and remembering that his injuries weren't extensive, she leaned over and kissed Gary tenderly on the forehead.

As he batted his eyes open slowly, her vision blurred a bit through her tears. This was all so strange, she thought. Did this man who spent most weekends riding with his bike club, and who was getting ready for a three-week European tour next spring really want to marry her? And what if his injuries *had* been from riding – how would she feel then? Or what if—

She stopped thinking and rebuked herself for being negative, especially when she was usually so good at focusing on the positive. Maybe she just was so caught off guard by Gary's intentions that it had really thrown her for a loop. The man had bought her a shockingly expensive diamond,

for goodness' sake, and was now ready to show her his sensitive side. Yes, that was it, Rachel told herself.

'Good morning, my love,' she said, when Gary moaned again. 'Merry Christmas.'

It took a good ninety seconds for him to turn his head slightly and begin to respond. 'Hey . . . was in a bloody accident . . .' he slurred. 'Some fool hit me.'

'I know, I know, a taxi. But you're OK. I mean, it's nothing serious and . . . God, Gary, I'm so sorry.' Rachel couldn't help but feel responsible. 'This was supposed to be the trip of a lifetime. I can't believe this happened. Should I call your family? I wasn't sure if—'

'Yeah, stupid gobshite . . .' he said, barely perceptibly, before his eyes fell shut once again. Hoping he was referring to the taxi driver and not her, it made Rachel smile. He was obviously high on the medication.

'Hey, I'm sorry for being nosy,' Kim whispered suddenly from the doorway, 'but what does *that* mean? He's been saying it off and on all morning too.'

Rachel was grinning. 'It's sort of an Irish swear word.'

'Ah, I see. Well, pardon me for saying so, but I think that accent is kinda sexy,' Kim chuckled, going to the top of the bed and doing something with the saline drip bag. 'Even with that bruised face, I can see why you fell for this guy.'

Rachel smiled proudly. 'Yes, I really did fall for him . . . hard and fast,' she replied. 'I just wish I could let him know that I . . .' Her voice trailed off, and when Kim looked at her questioningly, she shook her head. 'Me and my big mouth,' she continued, somewhat guiltily.

She didn't know if it was a combination of being basically alone in a strange city at Christmas, or just the excitement of bearing a big secret, but for some reason she felt very much at ease with this nurse. Or maybe it was the fact that Kim had experience of life with another motorbike enthusiast?

'Christmas,' Gary mumbled suddenly. 'You're gonna love what I got you . . . wait till you see it.' He seemed to be talking to himself and Rachel wondered if he was aware that she was even there. 'And you should see my new cufflinks . . .' That was the last thing he managed before the drugs got the better of him yet again.

'Well, now I'm intrigued!' Kim said, smiling at Rachel. 'Wonder what he got you that's s'posed to be so great?'

'Actually I kind of already know,' she confessed, unable to hold it in any longer. She winced, hoping that telling someone else might help absolve her of some of the guilt. 'I already opened the package.'

Kim was wide-eyed. 'You're kiddin' me! And what did you get?'

When Rachel didn't answer, but instead looked guiltily at a sleeping Gary, Kim raised an eyebrow. 'Somethin' tells me you could use a cup of coffee and a chat right now, sweetheart,' she said, grinning. 'I'm due to take a little break soon. Wanna join me? Trust me, he'll never know you left.'

Rachel looked from Kim to Gary. He certainly wasn't going anywhere. 'Thanks, I'd love to,' she said, meaning it.

'I can't go far, but let me grab us something from the machine and you can join me in the lounge,' the nurse said, already moving in that direction.

'Thank you. This is so nice of you.' Rachel was delighted to have someone to unload to. As it was she could never keep anything to herself.

'So I take it you had big plans for this Christmas?' Kim asked, as they picked up two cups of coffee, with creamers,

sugar packets and stir sticks. 'A flight from Ireland is no short jaunt.'

'Well, someone obviously had big plans –' Rachel paused as she stirred in her sugar '– but I knew nothing about them.'

Kim nodded in the direction of Gary's room. 'You mean that good-lookin' Irishman back there.'

'Exactly. The problem is that it was supposed to be a surprise. A big surprise. You see . . .' Rachel started to explain, but Kim cut her off, a question in her eyes.

'Wait a minute. You said before that you guys were engaged, but I've just noticed there's no ring on your finger.' Suddenly her eyes grew wide. 'Oh boy, I get it! He had his accident yesterday, on Christmas Eve. He was gonna propose today, and you found the ring in his pocket or something, right?'

'Not quite . . . at least, not in his pocket.' Rachel looked away but gave a big toothy grin that spoke volumes.

'But you did find it? And now you're excited, but frustrated that you can't tell anyone, yet at the same time guilty?'

'In a nutshell, yes.' Rachel laughed, relieved she didn't have to spell it out. She told Kim all about the Tiffany's bag that had been with Gary's shopping. 'I'll bet you're a good nurse, but I think you'd be an even better detective!'

'Well, don't be so sure about that. And don't feel so guilty either. See, he's a typical man. He didn't have his shopping done or gifts wrapped by Christmas Eve, then when he's rushing back to try to make up for lost time he goes and gets himself hit by a cab.' She shook her head in mock exasperation. 'If you ask me, it's his own damn fault you found that ring . . . and probably his own fault he got mowed down in New York traffic too!'

Rachel laughed out loud. 'Oh I really shouldn't be laughing, but thank you. Telling someone is such a load off my mind.'

Fifteen minutes after the start of Kim's 'ten-minute break', the two of them were still chatting away. 'It's funny,' Rachel was saying, 'I suppose you just never know who you'll end up with. I don't know . . . there's just something about Gary. This is so like him: hitting me out of the blue like this, catching me completely off guard. It's exciting. *He's* exciting.'

'Exciting is good. Hell, so are big rocks on your finger. Not that I would know, mind you,' Kim said with some sarcasm, looking at her own hands. 'But you be sure you've got the lasting friendship stuff going on too. That's one thing Al and I have. I was only kiddin' before about him choosing the Ducati over me – at least I think I was,' she said, smiling at her own joke. 'We're really pretty crazy about each other, you know. Got married young, and have been together a long time.'

'I want to be like that,' Rachel said dreamily. 'Gary believes in me and that means a lot. He's a builder, you know, and last year he helped my best friend and me turn our dreams of opening a restaurant into reality. He gave us the cheapest quote by far, and later admitted it was only because he wanted to ask me out,' she said, fondly. 'He worked day and night to get the refurbishments finished on time, and then the day before we opened he pulled up to the bistro.' She smiled at the memory. 'We were just having the equipment hauled in, and I was covered in dust and paint. I was exhausted and looked a complete mess, and suddenly I heard someone revving a bike. It was Gary. He insisted on helping us out, as a favour.' She shook her head. 'Looks like he's surprising me for the second time, and again it worked.'

'It *almost* worked,' Kim clarified. 'You make sure he gives you a proper proposal too. Don't you let on for a minute that you know about that ring.'

'No, of course I won't. I'm just dying to have it on my

finger, though. Oh you should see the size of it, Kim,' she cried excitedly. 'It's absolutely breathtaking. It must be worth a fortune.'

Kim smiled and Rachel noticed her twisting the wedding ring on her own finger. It was a simple gold band. 'I would say one thing – and don't get me wrong now, this is just the standard advice I give to all of my friends who have got engaged, mostly 'cos marriage is such a huge leap.'

'What?' Rachel sat forward, only too happy to get the benefit of this lovely woman's experience.

'OK, here it is: you just make sure that he thinks *you're* worth more than you think that ring is worth. There. And I don't just mean the way you look with that body and that hair and those huge blue eyes . . . uh, you can stop me any time . . .' She paused, laughing. 'But seriously. You know what I mean. Make sure he really, you know, knows you, loves you, cares about what makes you happy.'

Rachel didn't answer for several seconds. She took a long sip of her coffee.

Kim reminded her of Terri, in a way. Her friend was a real rock of sense, naturally cautious, and, unlike Rachel, wasn't prone to mad bouts of reckless enthusiasm. Just as well she was the business brain in the partnership, although of course Terri was an amazing cook too.

As Rachel thought of Terri, she remembered how her friend also tried to give her advice. 'Being impetuous can only get you into trouble,' her friend routinely teased. But Rachel guessed that her impulsive nature had come from her roots, as her dad was second-generation Sicilian. He'd been dead for over ten years now and Rachel had almost got used to being alone, having also lost her mother when she was much younger. Suddenly, a bubble of happiness developed inside her when she realised that after years of being alone, Gary would now be her family. She smiled.

'I know exactly what you mean, and I couldn't agree with you more,' she said, standing up. 'I suppose I'd better go and see if Gary's awake.'

'And I –' Kim said, checking her watch '– had better head back to the desk, half an hour too late. Ah, it's Christmas, so shoot me.'

'Thanks for this, I really enjoyed it. Will I catch you later? Or if not, will you be on duty over the next couple of days? Maybe we can do this again.'

'Of course. I'm not going anywhere and I'd love to. Believe me, I can't wait to hear how this love story turns out!'

'Me neither,' Rachel grinned, waving after her new friend.

Chapter 6

It was the following day, and Fifth Avenue was once again swarming with shoppers. While Ethan knew there would of course be crowds, this morning the surrounding buzz of activity merely exacerbated his worries and confusion.

All he could think about was Vanessa. Fortunately she had wanted to take advantage of the post-Christmas sales and had set off on her own for the better part of the day. That gave Ethan the chance to try to do something about the missing ring besides simply ruminating over it.

Yet he knew that Vanessa wasn't much of a shopper by nature, didn't usually care about sales, and hadn't made any mention of shopping throughout the trip. Not until a particularly awkward moment the night before.

From start to finish Christmas Day had been a disaster, and it seemed to Ethan that her new-found desire to shop was an opportunity for a break from the unbroken tension that had existed between them for the last twenty-four hours or so.

Just then a woman twice his size stepped on his foot with no regard, and stifling an expletive he tugged at Daisy's hand, pulling her out of the crowd and into a nearby café. 'Time for hot chocolate, I think,' he muttered darkly.

'Really, Dad,' she replied, giving him a disapproving look. 'We've been having way too much of that lately. I think you need to lay off.'

'Well, I'm sorry, but just now it's absolutely necessary,'

Ethan said as they each took a stool at the counter. 'Hot chocolate and a coffee, please,' he said to the barista. He winked at Daisy. 'The coffee's for me; is that better?'

She nodded, mollified. 'Much better.'

Stirring milk into the mug, he tried to take a moment to gather his wits.

Last night, after Daisy had gone to bed he'd hoped for a romantic night with Vanessa and had ordered a nice bottle of wine, a Bordeaux, from room service and had it delivered with a red rose on the cart.

When he wheeled it into the bedroom where Vanessa was already cosy in bed, she looked up and gave him a wan smile that made him feel kind of foolish, as if she knew somehow that he was trying too hard.

He'd poured them each a glass and then sat facing her on the bed.

'To us,' he toasted, looking into her eyes. She nodded and looked back at him somewhat quizzically, then raised hers to toast him too. He thought she looked particularly beautiful that night, and always loved it when she wore no make-up and was just fresh and natural. Still, despite the cushion of red wine and the relaxation it brought, the conversation between them remained stilted at best. It was then that she mentioned something about spending the following day shopping.

'Well, of course, whatever you like,' he said, surprised but wanting to be nothing but supportive. 'It is New York after all and you deserve to treat yourself.' This seemed like as good an opener as any to set aside the wine glass and then turn back to slowly kiss her neck. When she responded, he paused to turn on his iPod, which was docked in the Bose system on the nightstand. Roberta Flack's 'The First Time', a favourite of Vanessa's, filled the room.

Naturally, he expected the mood between them that night to be transformed, and had hoped his efforts would make up for the events (or non-events) of the day. Even with the wine and the music, though, the whole thing felt tense and mechanical, as if they were both just going through the motions.

Today, the scene played out over and over again in his head, leaving him feeling a little guilty for being so preoccupied while he was with Daisy. 'OK,' he said, trying to shake off these peripheral thoughts and once again turn his attention to tracking down the ring, 'let's get going on our treasure hunt.'

'What? But, Dad, you haven't taken even a sip of your coffee, and I've already finished my hot chocolate.' Daisy was perceptive, as always.

'Yes, but I'm thinking we really shouldn't delay too long – just in case.' Ethan plopped a couple of coins on the counter by way of a tip, and the two of them headed back out onto the street in the direction of 727 Fifth Avenue.

'Ah, Mr Greene, hello.' The same elderly Tiffany's assistant who'd sold them the ring greeted Ethan and Daisy effusively upon arrival. He smiled benevolently. 'So how did the lucky lady like her Christmas surprise?'

'Well, perhaps there is a lucky lady somewhere who is enjoying it very much,' Ethan replied, his tone sounding much edgier than he'd intended, and the man raised an eyebrow. Then he sighed. 'Look, I'm sorry, but it seems there's been some kind of mistake.'

'A mistake? Please – have a seat,' the assistant urged, looking genuinely concerned as he led them aside.

Ethan and Daisy both sat down in front of one of the octagonal display areas. He tried his best to explain. 'I just don't know how it could have happened. I absolutely remember seeing the ring I picked out in the box before you had it wrapped on my behalf. But when my fiancée – or should I say my intended fiancée – opened the package yesterday morning there was just a . . . a charm bracelet inside.' His palms became sweaty just thinking about it; he rubbed them on his jeans. 'No ring, no diamond solitaire – just a silver charm bracelet.'

'A *charm* bracelet?' the assistant repeated in bewilderment.

'Yes. I was thinking that maybe there was some kind of mix-up with the wrapping, or that I'd been given the wrong bag.' This was the most likely scenario, yet the one Ethan half-hoped wasn't the case, because it meant that his purchase was in the possession of one very happy stranger.

'But I can't think what . . . This is unheard of,' the man blustered. 'As it is, we sell only diamonds on this floor. Gift items are available on the ground floor or up on the third, the Silver Floor.' He looked thoughtful. 'Just a moment. Let me call my supervisor.'

Ethan's jaw began to work. Damn, this didn't look good. 'Of course. Thank you.'

While the assistant made the call, Daisy rested a hand on her father's knee. 'Dad, it's OK. I'm sure everything will be fine,' she said, sounding anxious. Ethan looked at her, and immediately felt bad for having to drag her through all of this rigmarole.

'I know, and I'm sorry for getting so flustered. Just . . . thanks for helping me out with this.'

The next thing Ethan knew, he and Daisy were being greeted very graciously by the Tiffany's General Manager and whisked away by him and a couple of other suits to take a look at the Christmas Eve security-tape footage.

It seemed to Ethan, sitting there in the dim room, that

there must be nearly as many security cameras as diamonds on the premises. Luckily this meant that they could watch his and Daisy's visit to the store and their activity on the Diamond Floor from multiple angles, but, disappointingly, nothing seemed untoward. There was certainly no switch of bags, and from what he could tell absolutely no mix-up either.

He figured that these guys were probably just as suspicious – if not more so – of him as he was of them, since no doubt it wouldn't have been the first time that someone had tried to claim a missing item. Yet the bottom line was that nothing at all was revealed in the store tapes. He and Daisy appeared to have definitely left Tiffany's with the diamond.

End of story.

Ethan thanked the manager and the security team for their assistance, and they in turn promised to offer all support possible, and asked that he keep them apprised of any progress. 'Thanks, and likewise,' he said, shaking hands all around.

Back outside on the street, Ethan couldn't have been more frustrated.

'What now, Dad?' Daisy asked.

'I really don't know, poppet,' he replied, wracking his brains to try to come up with his next move. If there was no mix-up, no oversight in Tiffany's, then what on earth could have happened? They'd gone straight back to the hotel after being there, hadn't they? Or had they stopped off somewhere else . . . ?

'Do you think we could maybe get something to eat now? Sorry, but I'm really hungry.'

Ethan looked at his watch; it was almost lunchtime and they'd been in the store much longer than he'd anticipated. 'OK, I suppose we could—' A sudden screeching of tyres in the background cut off the rest of his sentence. 'Of course,' he exclaimed, looking in the direction of the noise. The accident! That was it! That *had* to be it. He turned to Daisy, his eyes wide. 'Remember that man, the one who got hit by the cab, the one we helped on Christmas Eve? He had all those packages, remember?'

'Yes . . .' Daisy nodded, unsure what he was getting at.

'Don't you remember? When I asked you to gather his things up for him and keep an eye on them . . . is there a chance that there was some confusion, that the man's things and our things might have got mixed up?'

All of a sudden, she looked scared. 'No, no, Dad. I really don't think so . . .' She bit her lip; the notion that she could have been the cause of all this was obviously troubling her greatly.

'Honey, it's OK, it's really OK if it did, and it isn't your fault,' was quick to reassure her. 'But it makes perfect sense, doesn't it? Yes, that has to be it. Right,' Ethan announced, the weight on his shoulders suddenly feeling a hell of a lot lighter, 'let's go and find a restaurant somewhere. Might as well make the most of that New York pizza while we're here, yes? You can eat as much as you like. Me, I've got some phone calls to make.'

Chapter 7

'Look, sir, it's like I said. I'm sorry, but we just can't give out that kind of information. It's against hospital policy. I wish I could help you, though, I really do.'

'You don't understand,' Ethan said, stepping closer to the nurses' station and growing more impatient by the second. He wasn't usually one to play on his charm (not since his college days at Cambridge, anyway), but it was apparent that this young nurse, Molly, might just be a tiny bit smitten with him and his adorable daughter. And the accent probably didn't hurt either, Ethan figured.

After hours of dead-end phone calls and one fruitless hospital mission after another, he finally had a solid lead on the man who had been hit by the cab on Christmas Eve, and he was less and less willing to take no for an answer. Dodging Vanessa on the issue, and trying not to act suspiciously in the meantime hadn't been easy, but Ethan had come this far and wasn't giving up now.

He was a man on a mission, and readily willing to use any tools at his disposal. He moved closer to the desk, cocked his head and gave Molly his most winning smile.

'Sir –' another nurse, obviously more senior, stepped in and positioned her large frame between him and the desk '– I sympathise with you and your "situation", but you and those big blue eyes can just take it elsewhere. And you, nurse,' she said, turning to the younger woman, 'can get back to work.'

'But—'

She stopped Ethan in his tracks with a disapproving look. 'Yes, I overheard most of it, and let me tell you that you have no cause for disturbing this patient and no claim to his identity. You don't even know his name, for goodness' sake. Now I don't care where you're from, what your schedule is or when you have to fly home. And I don't know what you want from this poor man but I suspect that whoever he is, he's already been through enough. You simply may not see him. Period.'

At this, Ethan felt a prickling sensation at the back of his neck. He knew people generally considered him passive, something that actually irked him no end, as he was far from it; he was just very choosy about where he expended his energy. However, when he did commit himself to an idea, a cause or a person, he could not be swayed; and in this case there was a (very expensive) diamond, not to mention an entire relationship, at stake. Ethan was not backing down.

Taking a deep breath, he rounded on the nurse. 'Well, seeing as you're defending this man's privacy, and seem to know precisely who I'm talking about, then I can only conclude that he must be here at this hospital.'

'I said no such thing,' she protested darkly. 'Besides, if he's not a family member, as you say, why does finding this guy mean so much to you?'

Following a phone call to the first hospital, during which he'd spilled all of the details, Ethan had quickly realised that his story sounded implausible and he came off as a madman, so in all subsequent searches he'd decided to leave out the part about the missing ring.

'Look,' he told the nurse now, hoping to appeal to her better nature, 'I lost something in all of the mayhem, something important. And the thing everybody seems to be overlooking here is that if it weren't for me and my daughter, the guy might not have made it. We most likely saved his life.'

'Saved his life?'

'Yes, I gave him first aid while we waited for the ambulance to arrive, and my daughter here made sure to protect his belongings.' He ran a frustrated hand through his hair.

'*You're* the one who helped him?' the younger nurse piped up again. 'The paramedics were talking about you.'

'Yes.' Ethan crossed his arms and spread his feet in a solid stance as he continued to stare down the older nurse, who still didn't look convinced.

'Nice going, Employee of the Month,' she said, rolling her eyes at her colleague. She turned back to Ethan. 'OK, perhaps this changes things a little. I mean, no one does that sort of thing in Manhattan,' she said, shaking her head in bewilderment, and Ethan's shoulders relaxed a little as she paused, seemingly deep in thought. 'Well, since you extended yourself to help this man, there's possibly a grey area here, and I suppose we *could* allow you to see him – as long as you are supervised, of course.'

Ethan was thrilled, but contained himself. 'I'd really appreciate that.'

'And, no, Nurse Starks, I'm not looking for volunteer chaperones,' she said sharply to her younger colleague, who had risen hopefully from her station. 'In fact, why don't you keep an eye on the little lady here, while I get someone to take Mr Greene to the room?'

'Sure,' the younger nurse replied. 'Is it OK if I get her a soda and a snack?' she asked Ethan.

'Yes, whatever she likes,' he said. 'Is that all right with you, buttercup?'

Daisy nodded, and soon afterwards Ethan was led by a male aide to the room of what he hoped was their guy.

Poking his head around the door, he was instantly relieved to see that the patient in the bed was indeed the man he had helped in the street two days before. Ethan released a breath he didn't even know he'd been holding.

Finally!

'Can I speak to him?' he asked the aide.

'Afraid not. He's been in and out of consciousness since he came in. It's mostly the meds, but he's pretty banged up too.'

Damn. Ethan hadn't anticipated that. Still, at least it was the right guy – which meant that his own Tiffany's bag must still be among his packages, and given that the guy had been so out of it, chances were he still didn't have the foggiest idea about the mix-up.

So, really, all Ethan could do now was wait for him to wake up (which he seriously hoped he would do soon). They would talk, sort it all out and, quick as you like, Ethan and the girls would be on their way back to London. But first he'd ensure they'd once again gather around the Christmas tree in their hotel room, and Ethan would drop to one knee and propose to Vanessa just as he'd originally intended. It would be wonderful.

Then, over one last dinner in New York, the three of them would laugh about the last few days' turn of events, and chat about the new life they would build back home together. Ethan had it all worked out in his head and almost had to restrain himself from nudging the injured man awake.

But ten minutes later he still wasn't conscious and Vanessa was calling Ethan's mobile. She was finished with her shopping and wondering where he and Daisy were.

Waiting in the hallway outside the man's room – he'd since learned he was called Gary Knowles – Ethan had seen her number come up but had let it go to voicemail while he tried to concoct a reasonable story. 'Hi, darling,' he said, trying to sound offhand.

'Hi, where are you two?'

'Oh, down by Battery Park,' he lied. 'I took Daisy on the Staten Island ferry for a waterside look at the skyline.' He winced, disgusted with himself for blatantly deceiving her. But did he have a choice? 'But we're almost finished now and should be back in an hour or so depending on traffic.'

'OK, great. See you back at the hotel then?' She sounded tense and he couldn't blame her. He'd been so distracted and secretive over the last day or so that it would have been impossible for her not to pick up on it. He supposed he'd better head back to the hotel soon. If Knowles remained unconscious there was little point in hanging around here much longer and Daisy would be growing restless.

He decided to push his luck a little further and enquire at the desk for some more details about the mysterious Mr Knowles. He headed back towards the nurses' station, and immediately saw Daisy jump up to greet him. 'Is it him, Daddy?' she asked eagerly.

'Yes, it is him,' he grinned.

'Yay! Does he have the—' Seeing Ethan's sharp look, she caught herself just in time. 'Does he have our shopping bag?'

Ethan glanced towards the young nurse, Molly, who was watching the scene with renewed interest. He took a deep, frustrated breath. 'I'm sure he does, but unfortunately I can't ask because he's unconscious.'

'Oh no.' Daisy's face fell.

'Excuse me?' Molly, who (as Ethan had intended) had heard the exchange, piped up. 'Did you say something about a shopping bag?'

'Yes, why?'

'Well –' she looked around edgily as if terrified her overbearing supervisor would hear '– it's just that I was here when he was brought in, and he did have a lot of shopping bags with him. Some really nice stuff too,' she added.

'Yes, Daisy here looked after them while we waited for the paramedics. You know how people can be,' he continued, pressing home the point that they'd been looking out for Knowles's best interests at all times. 'I wonder . . . it's just that the bag we lost was very important and—'

'So, *you're* the guy who helped the schmuck in room 303?' Ethan looked around to see yet another nurse approach from behind.

Damn. Ethan cursed the interruption, sure he was on the verge of getting Molly to let him know where Knowles's stuff was currently being stored. 'That's right,' he said, forcing a smile.

'Very kind thing you did, helping out some guy in the middle of the street like that,' she continued.

'I suppose.' Ethan was getting tired of everyone telling him how wonderful he was; yet he still didn't seem to be getting anywhere. 'But I'm sure anyone else would have done the same.'

'In this town? I don't think so, honey. Chances are the injuries from the cab would have been small beans compared to the stampede to grab his loot.' She smiled at Daisy and winked.

'Yes, well, I'm certified in CPR and everything so it's really second nature to respond to things like that. By the way, I'm Ethan Greene and this is my daughter, Daisy.' He

thought he might as well be nice and try to get as many people on side as possible.

'Nice to meet you both,' she said, shaking Daisy's hand too. 'I'm Kim and Mr Knowles is one of my patients. Must say, it's good to see that kind of spirit alive and well, especially on Christmas Eve.' She laughed. 'You know, Mr Knowles's girlfriend Rachel will be here soon. She'll want to thank you in person, I'm sure. So, if you want to hang out a little longer . . .'

A girlfriend? This was something Ethan hadn't anticipated. So chances were *she* was the one in possession of the man's packages now. He wasn't sure if this was a good or a bad thing. On the one hand it could be good, as he wouldn't have to wait around for Knowles to wake up, but on the other, what if the girlfriend didn't believe his sorry story?

But, surely, if he explained everything as it happened on Christmas Eve, she would understand? It was a desperate situation, that was for sure, but Ethan was very rapidly becoming a desperate man.

Still, now that he was fairly confident the bags were no longer being kept at the hospital, he figured there was little point in sweet-talking the nurses. Instead he needed to see this girlfriend.

'She's coming here? Today?'

'Of course. She was here earlier but just popped out on an errand. I'm sure she'll be back soon.'

'I see.' Ethan thought quickly. 'Well, why don't we grab a quick coffee at the cafeteria ourselves while we wait?' he said to Daisy, who nodded easily. Poor thing, she was really quite distraught about her part in all of this, which was another good reason, Ethan realised, for getting it sorted out as soon as possible.

On the way, and feeling like a heel for lying to her yet

again, he called Vanessa to tell her that they were stuck in downtown traffic and might be a little later getting back to the hotel. But time was limited and this needed to be resolved – soon.

Now, seated over two bowls of chicken noodle soup, Daisy was quiet and Ethan was restless.

'Do you really think we're going to get the ring back, Dad?'

'Of course,' he replied. 'Now that we've finally found our man. And when his girlfriend gets here and we explain everything, I'm sure there won't be a problem.' The only thing was, he no longer had Knowles's purchase, as he couldn't very well take the bracelet back from Vanessa, could he? Still, he could explain this to the girlfriend and let her know that he would arrange a replacement as soon as possible. Which meant, of course, that he'd have to shell out yet more moncy at Tiffany's, but if it ensured he got his ring back, Ethan didn't care.

He realised Daisy was idly picking up noodles and plopping them back in the bowl. 'Not hungry?'

'Not really.'

'Why? You didn't eat much at breakfast either. Is everything OK?'

She hesitated for a minute, as if about to say something, but then shook her head. 'I'm just worried about the ring, that's all.'

'Try not to,' he said, feeling doubly guilty for involving her in all of this now and giving her a reason to fret. 'And remember, it wasn't your fault,' he assured her again. 'It was just a mix-up, that's all. I'm sure we'll get it back. Let's finish up here and see if we can get to the bottom of it once and for all, OK?'

'OK, Dad,' she said, but he could tell that this was really troubling her.

They returned to the nurses' station to find the nurses they'd spoken to earlier sitting behind the desk.

'Is Mr Knowles's girlfriend here?' Ethan asked the older one, Kim.

'I'm sorry, no. She hasn't arrived yet and he's still sleeping.'

His face fell. 'That's a shame; we really were hoping to speak to her today. As you can imagine we're heading home to London soon.'

'I wish I could help you,' Kim said, looking at the chart she held in her hand. 'Like I said, she should be back by now.'

'She's probably already out shopping for wedding dresses, or something,' Molly giggled conspiratorially.

Ethan felt like he had just been hit by a sucker punch. 'I'm sorry? What did you say?'

'Don't mind her,' Kim said, glaring at Molly.

Ethan's mind raced. No, this couldn't be happening. The girlfriend . . . she couldn't possibly have found the . . .

No, but of course not, he reasoned, mentally kicking himself for letting his imagination run wild. The couple were probably engaged long before now. In any case, the guy was unconscious so how on earth could he have proposed? Especially when he didn't even know he had a ring.

As he tried to figure out the various possibilities, Ethan's brain was moving too fast for him to keep up, and he tried to reassure himself that, really, everything would be OK.

'Mr Greene? Are you all right?' Kim asked then. The look on his face must have given his concern away.

'Daddy, maybe we should tell them,' Daisy said, tugging at his sleeve, and the nurses exchanged a glance.

'Tell us what?'

'It's nothing,' Ethan said quickly. The last thing he needed was these two busybodies involved. Yet they seemed to know quite a bit about Knowles's personal life.

'Wedding dresses . . . Well, isn't that nice?' he said, trying to gather his wits about him. He looked at Daisy, then turned again to the nurses, at a loss as to what to do next. Vanessa was waiting for them so he couldn't very well hang around here all day. 'Tell you what, when Mr Knowles's girlfriend gets here, can you please give her my number and ask her to call me? I'd really like to speak with her. And, of course, I'll want to follow up with Mr Knowles, see how his recovery goes.'

'No problem.'

Ethan duly wrote his name and number on the piece of paper Kim handed to him. 'Well, thanks again for your help – both of you,' he continued awkwardly.

'Pleasure,' Kim replied and Molly grinned. 'I'll be sure to pass on the message to Rachel, and it was nice to meet you. You too, Daisy.'

'Yeah, thanks for helping us,' his daughter replied with a smile.

With that, they went off to catch a cab back to the Plaza.

On the journey back, Ethan continued to mull over the situation.

He hoped this Rachel woman would phone him soon and give him answers, namely as to whether he had anything to worry about with the ring. All this talk of the other couple's engagement worried him. There was no way his ring could have had any hand or part in that, was there? Not when the guy hadn't been able to open his eyes, let alone muster up the strength for a proposal. And the girlfriend couldn't possibly have known what was in his shopping, unless they'd planned to get engaged on

Christmas Eve. In which case his ring really couldn't be involved in any of it, Ethan reassured himself.

'Daddy, are you OK?' Daisy asked him and he made a conscious effort to try to forget about the ring, so as not to worry her further. Still, given the importance and expense of it all, that was downright impossible!

'I'm fine, buttercup, just thinking about our flight home. I wonder if we should maybe stay on a little longer, just in case this takes more time than we thought to sort out.'

Her expression brightened. 'We could do that?'

'Sure.' He couldn't realistically leave the city without resolving this, and while an extended stay would cost a few quid extra, it would hardly be the end of the world, everything considered. 'Would that be OK with you? A day or two more wouldn't kill us, and as long as we're back in time for New Year . . .'

'Yay! Can we go Toys R Us on Times Square again? We didn't really get to see much of it last time.'

'Of course, darling, we can do whatever you like,' Ethan replied absently.

He wondered what Vanessa would think about staying on, though, or how he would explain this sudden decision to take more time in the Big Apple. He'd have to think of something, perhaps last-minute availability for a popular Broadway show he'd always wanted to see? 'I'll see what I can do. For the moment let's just go back to the hotel and have a nice afternoon with Vanessa. I'll wait for this Rachel's phone call; but when she does call I might have to come up with some other . . . erm, reason to slip away again. Do you follow me?'

Daisy nodded. 'Of course. We still can't let Vanessa know anything's going on, or tell her what happened with the ring.'

'Good girl,' he said, putting up his hand for a high-five, while at the same time feeling desperately guilty for having his eight-year-old daughter collude in such trickery. She raised her hand and smacked his palm.

'But put some gloves on, Dad; your hands are freezing!'

'Well, well, well . . . don't you have gorgeous hunks just crawling out of the woodwork?' Kim announced when, not two minutes after Ethan had left, Rachel returned to the hospital.

'What?'

'Well, you've got a good-looking blond in the room down the hall and a dreamy Michael Bublé lookalike just left you his number. And I'd call him too if I were you.'

'What are you talking about?' Rachel said, bewildered.

Kim laughed out loud. 'Sorry, I couldn't resist. Seriously, you won't believe this, but the guy who helped Gary after the accident came here today with his little girl. He's the one who waited with him until the ambulance got there.'

'Really?' Rachel had heard about this Good Samaritan and was doubly impressed that he'd followed up and enquired after Gary's health. 'I wonder how he found us?'

'No idea. All I know is that he's drop-dead gorgeous, and she's cute as a button.'

Rachel frowned. 'And he left his number? Why? I'm sure you told him Gary was going to be fine.'

'Sure I did, but apparently he lost something at the time and he wanted to see if you knew anything about it. As well as checking on Gary, of course. Honestly, you should call him.'

Rachel was confused. 'OK, I suppose I'd better call and thank him anyway. But if there's something he's lost I don't see how *I* can help him find it.'

'Oh well,' Kim said with a shrug. 'Only in New York, I guess.'

Chapter 8

Later that evening Ethan, Vanessa and Daisy were taking in the sights around Times Square, when the call came. Taking his vibrating mobile phone out of his pocket, Ethan didn't recognise the number that showed up on the screen, and figured it had to be Rachel. Wonderful.

He stepped outside the M&M store, only too happy to escape the place and leave the girls to the frantic, multi-coloured world of grinning candy.

'Hello,' he answered, trying not to sound too urgent, but his hands were shaking.

'Hi there, is this Ethan Greene?' asked a female voice in an Irish accent. 'I'm Rachel; the nurses at Mount Sinai gave me your number.'

'Hello, yes, thank you so much for calling,' he replied, exhaling with some relief. He looked up to see Vanessa watching him through the window, and waved nervously as she and Daisy waited in line at the cashier's desk to pay for something. Soon they'd join him outside and he deduced he had about thirty seconds of privacy before they reached him. 'Yes, I wanted to enquire after your . . . erm, Mr Knowles, but—'

'Gary's fine. Thank you for helping him,' she continued warmly.

'That's good to know. Has he regained consciousness?'

'Not yet, I'm afraid. But seeing as you were there at the time, it would be great to find out more about what actually happened. As you can imagine, it was all a bit of a shock for me, as I wasn't with him.'

Ethan exhaled in relief, pleased that she had given him an opening.

'Of course, I'd be more than happy to talk to you about that. Are you free to meet for coffee? Tomorrow morning, perhaps, as I'm flying home to London in the afternoon? I'd also hoped to speak to you about something else, as it happens.'

'Well, yes, the nurse did mention something.'

'It seems there was a mix-up at the scene and . . . well, it's a long story and is actually rather . . . delicate.' Ethan tried to choose his words carefully as Vanessa and Daisy had now rounded the corner and come up alongside him. 'But I've got some free time tomorrow morning, and it would be nice to speak to you in person in any case, so would that suit?' He smiled at Vanessa, who was watching him closely.

Rachel seemed hesitant. 'Well, I'm at the hospital mostly, but—'

'Why don't I meet you there? Say, eleven?' he said, hoping he wouldn't scare her off by sounding too pushy, yet at the same time he had little choice but to press the issue. And if he could get this done and dusted without having to change their flight home in the meantime, even better.

'Yes, I suppose that would be OK.'

'Fantastic. See you then.'

'What was all that about?' Vanessa asked when he hung up. 'You're meeting someone in the morning?' She looked puzzled. 'But tomorrow's our last day.'

Ethan had thought about coming straight out and telling Vanessa all about the ring in the hope of clearing up the tension that had formed between the two of them, but he just couldn't do it. That would be a million miles from what he'd intended, or how he'd always pictured it. He wanted

the proposal to be something special, something romantic she would remember forever, rather than a long and confusing story about some stupid mix-up.

Fortunately for him, he had a cover story already worked out in his head. 'Believe it or not, that was an agent I submitted my proposal to a while ago,' he said, with forced enthusiasm. 'I emailed her before Christmas to let her know I'd be here in New York around now and, lo and behold, she wants to meet with me!'

He knew Vanessa would be only too happy to go along with this; after all, she was constantly encouraging him to dedicate more time and energy to his writing. He smiled, as if unable to believe his luck. 'I can't really pass up the opportunity, can I?'

'That's amazing news!' she gushed, obviously not pausing to dwell on the unlikelihood of such a thing happening. Clearly she thought his ideas were considerably better than he did. 'Of course you must go. What agency is she from? Perhaps I know her.' Before Ethan had a chance to reply she smiled at Daisy. 'Wow, looks like we've got a girls-only day ahead of us tomorrow!'

'But I want to come with you, Daddy,' his daughter protested, looking hurt. 'Please?'

Ethan ran a hand through his hair, not at all sure how to handle this. While he could understand Daisy's concerns about wanting to be there when he got the ring back, surely she understood that he needed to be careful about this? But of course subtlety wasn't exactly a strong point among eight-year-olds, was it?

'Well, I suppose that would be OK. That way, you can have some time to yourself, darling,' he said, turning again to Vanessa.

'What? But I've had lots of time to myself. In any case,

Ethan, do you really want to bring your child to a business meeting?' she questioned dubiously.

'Ah no, it'll only be an informal chat. Anyway, I . . . I mentioned in my submission how much of an inspiration my daughter is, so I'm sure she'd love to meet her too,' Ethan insisted, but it sounded incredibly feeble and he knew it.

'Really?' Vanessa looked from him to Daisy and something changed in her expression, as if she'd figured out that this so-called meeting was some kind of cover story – but for what she couldn't tell. 'Well, all right then. I suppose I could find some way to pass the time, perhaps visit the Guggenheim again or something, and meet you two later.'

'Great idea,' Ethan enthused, trying to get through the unbelievable awkwardness of the situation by focusing solely on the reward at the end of it all.

Vanessa might suspect something was up now, but once all of this was sorted out she would understand completely, and the two of them would laugh about it in the very near future. It was because of that very future that he was being forced into this situation at all, so surely the little white lies couldn't really hurt?

Yes, by this time tomorrow all would be fine, Ethan was sure of it.

Reaching the hospital the following day, Ethan realised he had no idea what this Rachel looked like, but supposed he could ask the nurses when he got there. Assuming they would tell him, of course. As he'd already discovered, the Swiss Guard had nothing on the medical staff in this place.

As they went up in the elevator, Daisy held his hand tightly. He looked down at her and smiled. 'Come on then, poppet. Let's go get our ring back once and for all.'

Reaching the nurses' station just a little before eleven, he

immediately spied a curvy well-dressed woman with short croppy dark hair standing in front of it. This couldn't be her, surely; he hadn't expected someone so poised and . . . elegant to be with a guy like Knowles. While Ethan had been happy to help anyone in trouble, his overall impression of the man, judging by the yelling and cursing at the traffic they'd heard before the accident, was that he was rather obnoxious.

He walked up alongside the woman, hesitant now about approaching her. She immediately turned to look at him. 'Hello,' she ventured, with an uncertain smile. 'Are you Ethan?'

He nodded. 'Rachel?'

'Yes. I figured it had to be you,' she continued, smiling at Daisy. 'The nurses mentioned you had a very cute little girl. Hello there, sweetheart.'

'That's right,' he said, surreptitiously checking her left hand, but there was no ring. 'Thanks so much for taking the time to meet with us. I'm Ethan and this is Daisy.'

'Very nice to meet you,' she said, shaking hands first with him, and then bending down to greet Daisy. 'Thanks for coming in, but I should warn you I really can't talk long. The doctor will be coming round to check on Gary soon and I need to be there.'

'Of course, we won't keep you.' Damn, Ethan thought; this wasn't exactly the kind of thing that could be rushed. 'But you have time for a quick coffee, I hope?'

'Well . . .' She seemed torn. 'I suppose that would be OK.'

They walked to the hospital cafeteria, Rachel having asked the nurse on duty to call her when the doctor was on the ward.

Taking the seat across from her, Ethan distributed a plate of cookies and fresh coffee he'd bought at the counter.

'So, listen, I can't thank you enough for helping Gary

that night. Both of you,' she said, turning to Daisy, who smiled bashfully. 'I hear you were quite the little heroine, too. Gary's never been to New York before, you see, and I can't imagine why he thought he could just barge his way through the rush-hour traffic like that.' She smiled fondly. 'I'm assuming that's what he was trying to do?'

'Well, I didn't see it happen, but I understand he was trying to hail a cab at the time.'

She nodded as if this explained everything. 'Exactly what I figured. It was really good of you to intervene, though. Thank you. He can be such a handful at times.' She shook her head indulgently.

'No problem.' Ethan was anxious to get to the point. 'But actually—'

'How did you find him?' Rachel continued. 'Here at Mount Sinai, I mean.'

'Ah, just a few phone calls. It didn't take too much,' he said quickly.

'Well, regardless, I am eternally grateful. We're just here for a few days over Christmas – we're not locals, as you can probably guess.' She laughed lightly. 'And while the trip didn't turn out quite as I planned, it seems there's a silver lining to everything,' she said, with the hint of a smile on her face.

'Silver lining?' Ethan asked suspiciously, and he felt Daisy tap him lightly on the leg.

'Well, it made me realise that there are genuinely thoughtful people in the world, like you and your lovely daughter. What a gorgeous dress you have on,' she said to Daisy.

'Thanks, I like yours too,' she replied, clearly delighted, and Ethan sat forward, keen to move past the mutual appreciation and get to the real reason they were here.

'Yes, we're just in the city for a few days ourselves,' he said. 'Our flight back to London is later this evening actually.'

85

'Ours would have been too, if this hadn't happened. But the airline was great about changing, especially given the circumstances.'

'Of course. So—'

'You live in London? That's one of my favourite cities, and I love spending time there. Granted, I haven't been over for a while, what with the restaurant and everything,' she went on. 'My friend and I run a bistro and artisan bakery back home in Dublin. We cater too, on occasion.'

'Oooh, do you make cookies?' Daisy asked, intrigued.

Ethan smiled fondly at his daughter. 'Daisy's become quite the cookie connoisseur on this trip.'

'Yes, although I don't like to eat too many, of course. Too much saturated fat,' his daughter pronounced solemnly and Rachel smiled, briefly meeting Ethan's amused gaze.

'Well, I do make cookies, as it happens – *much* better than these, if I do say so myself,' she joked conspiratorially. 'We only use fresh ingredients too,' she added, and Daisy grinned. 'Yep, cookies and pastries and bread and all kinds of yummy stuff – you'd love it! In fact, tell you what, why don't you give me your address in London, and when I get home I'll send you a box of goodies for being so helpful to Gary? You don't have to eat them all at once. How's that?' she suggested, and Daisy looked thrilled.

'Yes, well, thank you very much, but on another note,' Ethan said, trying again to get to the point, 'I'm not sure if that nurse mentioned this to you, but actually it seems there was a bit of a mix-up that day and in all the melee—'

'Oops, that's my phone. Sorry about this,' Rachel interjected, taking a ringing mobile out of her handbag. 'It must be the nurse. Hello? Is the doctor there now? I'll just be . . . What?' Ethan watched her previously animated expression go dark. 'Oh my God! Is he OK? But what about . . . OK yes, yes, I'm on my way.' Her brow furrowed, Rachel disconnected the call. 'I'm so sorry but I have to go,' she said, jumping to her feet. 'They changed Gary's pain medication because they were afraid he was sleeping too much, but now it seems he's had some kind of reaction. I'm not sure exactly what's going on. I'm so sorry, but I really have to go.'

'Yes, of course. Shall we go back there with you?' Ethan asked, completely appreciating her panic, but also not wanting to let the possibility of retrieving the ring slip through his fingers.

'No, but thank you. You're so kind. Um . . . you have my number, don't you?' she added, flustered. 'Text me your address, and I'll send those cookies over as soon as I get home, I promise.'

Standing up too, Ethan ran a hand through his hair. 'Yes, OK. Well, good luck with everything. Hope he's all right,' he mumbled, feeling foolish, and also completely clueless as to what to do. He couldn't very well say anything now, could he? Not with the poor girl in such a state. Stupidly, he held out his hand to shake hers.

'I hope so too,' she replied, suddenly throwing her arms around him in a hug that caught him completely off guard. 'Thank you so much again for all you've done – it was wonderful. Bye, Daisy!' she added, waving, and in a flash she was gone.

For a long moment, Ethan stared after her, not sure what to think.

'I really like her, Dad,' Daisy said, completely unperturbed by the fact that, after all that, they'd got absolutely *no*where. 'She makes cookies. *And* she smells nice.'

Ethan smiled distractedly. 'Yes, yes, she's lovely.' What on earth was he going to do now?

Suddenly he felt completely exhausted by the events of

the last few days. He was all out of ideas. It was too late to change this evening's flight, and even if the airline was amenable they'd no doubt charge him a fortune to do so at such a late stage. In any case, even if they did stay on longer it wasn't as if he could camp out here at the hospital until Knowles got better. Vanessa was suspicious enough as it was.

He picked up his cup of coffee and drank from it, although he might as well have been drinking dishwater. In fact, he realised he hadn't tasted anything or indeed eaten properly since Christmas morning, when all of this started.

'What are we going to do now, Dad?' Daisy asked. 'Should we just go to Tiffany's and get Vanessa another ring?'

Oh the innocence of eight-year-olds! As if Ethan had tens of thousands tucked away somewhere . . .

He picked up the cookie she'd been eating, hoping that the sugar rush might help sort out his nausea. 'Give me a bite of that.'

'But, Dad, you're not supposed to eat too many!'

'Who says?' he teased. 'There's no such thing as too many cookies.' He shoved a handful of them into his mouth in a weak imitation of the Cookie Monster from *Sesame Street*.

She giggled; it was a sound that always made his heart lift. 'Dad, you're silly.'

'No, you are.'

'No, *you* are.'

And as Ethan continued to banter with his beloved daughter, he remembered that no matter what, there was always at least one woman in his life who made everything seem better.

Chapter 9

'I know, it's wonderful, isn't it?' Rachel said into the phone later that day. Though she and Terri had left phone messages for each other over the last day or so, this was the first time they had actually connected.

Despite the scary turn he'd taken at the hospital earlier, Gary was once again in a stable condition, but barely lucid, which meant that Rachel was still waiting for her grand proposal. As there was little point in her hanging around the ward, Kim had advised her to head back to the hotel and get some rest, and had promised to call if his condition changed.

In the meantime, Rachel had taken the opportunity to call her best friend and tell her the 'big' news.

'All I can say is that when he does ask you, he'd better get down on one knee, or the next time he comes in here, the only beer he'll get served will be right over his head. And don't think for a second that I'm joking!'

Rachel laughed. She and Terri always shared this kind of good-natured banter about Gary, but beneath it all was an undercurrent of mutual love and support.

They had met in catering school many years before, and right from the time they were partnered up during the bakery section of the course their connection had been fast and furious.

That first day, as they were braiding dough, Rachel broke off a piece, cupped it beneath her nose and breathed in the

aroma and warmth of it. 'God, what is it about the smell of fresh dough?' she'd asked, moaning softly and closing her eyes.

'I don't know, but before you have an orgasm here in front of me, save it for my famous sourdough,' Terri quipped. 'It'll make your mouth water and your legs quiver. In fact, it came between me and my last boyfriend. He was jealous; couldn't handle it.'

Rachel laughed out loud. 'Nah, just wait till a warm piece of my Sicilian olive bread passes your lips and melts on your tongue, then you'll know all about it.'

'Bring it on,' Terri had challenged.

And so it went. At that time, Rachel was a country girl new to Dublin and without many friends whereas Terri was Dublin born and bred. After lectures the next day the two of them got together at a nearby greasy-spoon café for dinner, and from then on they were inseparable.

Weekends were spent in St Stephen's Green, chatting over baskets of their own freshly baked bread, as well as cheeses, fruit and lots of wine. Over the course of the next few months they bonded over shared recipes – a blend of tastes, textures and fragrances – and respective life stories and dreams.

Their mutual love of food and cooking, especially baking, made the friendship seem fated. Out of it came plans for a low-budget world-food tour, with special focus on the food of the Mediterranean, and after graduation they spent a whirlwind summer travelling throughout Europe.

Afterwards they both spent several years in various different catering jobs, but remained firm friends, with a strong involvement in each other's lives.

Then, a year ago, Terri's father, who ran a small café/bar in Dublin city centre, became ill, and the two women decided to look into buying him out and refurbishing the café, turning it into a more high-end Mediterranean-style bistro, which they called Stromboli.

When it came to their shared enterprise, Terri's business sense and Rachel's creativity worked well together. Although their arguments were vehement at times, the laughs generally trumped the quarrels. Rachel loved Terri's pragmatism and wit; Terri in turn adored Rachel's passion and impulsiveness.

'I'm the looker, you're the leaper,' Terri would tease whenever their roles blurred at work.

Ordinarily it would have been Terri organising the renovations, but when her dad took a turn for the worse on one particular day Rachel had agreed to take her place at the meeting with Gary Knowles.

Now, sitting with her feet up on the sill of her hotel window, Rachel couldn't believe the strange twist in fate that day that had led to her meeting the man she was going to marry. It could just as easily have been Terri here in New York now bringing *her* up to speed on what had happened, but at the same time she couldn't see it. The two people Rachel loved most in the world didn't always see eye to eye (if ever) and as such she couldn't see Terri and Gary engaged and planning to spend the rest of their lives together.

Not that she and Gary had managed to do that yet either . . .

'Never mind getting down on one knee to do it,' she said to Terri now. 'I couldn't care less if he stands on his head, just as long as I get to reopen that little blue box.'

'Tiffany's! Who would have thought it?' her friend mused. 'Not that you don't deserve it of course, but I must admit I didn't think Gary had that kind of taste.'

'Really, and what kind of taste did you think he had?' Rachel tried to sound petulant but there was a smile in her voice. In fact she knew exactly what her friend meant; she'd even thought the very same thing.

'Oh don't give me that wounded-kitten act; you know what I mean.'

Rachel popped a piece of cheese into her mouth. 'I suppose it was a bit unexpected,' she replied, her mouth full. 'Oh wait till you see the ring – it's just incredible, and—'

'What are you eating?'

'Just some feta I picked up earlier.'

'Ah, feeling a bit homesick, are we?'

'If you're implying that I'm missing you, guess again. Any occasion for cheese, that's what I say. I passed a lovely little Greek deli on the way back from the hospital and picked up this cheese plate. Not as good as *our* cheese plate, mind you, but it'll do.' Besides that, Rachel hadn't been eating properly for the last few days. As it was, the last thing she'd managed until now was a cookie with that guy Ethan and his daughter earlier that morning.

Just then, Rachel heard another call coming through on her mobile. 'Cripes, it's the hospital,' she said to Terri. 'I'd better go.'

'No problem. Let me know when lover boy is back on his feet, and don't worry about this place; Justin and I can hold the fort till you get back.'

'Thanks. I promise I'll make it up to you. Say hi to Justin for me. Talk soon.' She hung up and clicked through to the other line. 'Hello?'

It was Kim. 'Did you manage to get some rest?' the nurse asked. 'Because chances are you won't be getting much of it from now on.'

'What do you mean?'

'Well, I'm very happy to report that your man is on the mend.'

Rachel's heart soared. 'He's awake?'

'Yep,' Kim confirmed, a smile in her voice. 'Looks like you'll finally get a chance to put that great big rock on your finger for keeps.'

Rachel felt a thrill bubble up in her throat as she entered the hospital and took the elevator to the relevant floor. She could hardly contain herself and did a little skip as she rounded the corner to the hallway that led to Gary's room.

She was about to burst straight through the door, but instead opened it softly and peeked around the edge of it. Gary was sitting up in bed with the TV remote in his hand, flipping through the channels.

Seeing him look so normal and well, a burst of emotion shot right through her.

'I can't believe you're really awake!' she cried, swooping in to give him a big hug.

'Whoa, whoa! I'm still sore, babe,' he replied, holding up a hand to warn her.

'Oops, sorry.' Rachel stroked his forehead and the side of his face, which was stubbly with almost three days of beard growth. 'So, tell me, how are you feeling? Do you remember what happened?'

Gary grimaced. 'I suppose I'll survive. Bloody taxi driver, mowing me down in the middle of the road like that.' He shook his head in disgust. 'I hope the cops got him afterwards, stupid gobshite.'

'You poor thing. It must have been awful.'

'Hey, was my stuff OK?' he asked. 'The hospital said you'd taken my bags. I hope nothing got lost, or stolen even

– some people would take the eye out of your head,' he added, gasping a bit as he tried to sit up straighter.

Rachel smiled inwardly. How funny; Gary was barely conscious and his mind was already on the engagement ring. 'No, nothing missing as far as I know, thanks to a very nice man and his daughter. They came to your rescue, waited with you and looked after your stuff till the ambulance came. Anyway, I'll tell you more about that later. I'm just so glad you're OK. I wasn't sure whether or not I should call your mum,' she said, hesitating a little.

'You didn't, did you?' Gary looked up sharply, and was she imagining it or did a shadow cross his face when he said it?

'No, I thought I'd better wait and ask you first – seeing as I don't really know her . . . '

'Good. I wouldn't want anyone worrying unnecessarily.'

'Yes, that's what I decided in the end. Of course I would have reassured her that you were fine and that she didn't need to worry.'

He bristled. 'I'm not that fine. These ribs are still bloody sore, you know.'

'Oh I know,' Rachel soothed. 'Anyway it's probably better she doesn't know, what with us being so far away and it being Christmas and everything.' She decided to change the subject. 'It's a pity you missed Christmas Day, but we can celebrate properly as soon as you're out of here.' She grinned. 'And exchange gifts then too.'

'Yeah, I suppose,' Gary replied nonchalantly. 'I can't believe I was out of it for so long, though. We'll need to get back home soon; I've got a job starting first thing on Wednesday. What date is it today? The twenty-seventh, is it? I think that's what the doc told me.'

Rachel's face dropped. 'But I got our flights changed because I didn't know how long you'd be here. Gary, you can't start a building job so soon after leaving the hospital. You said yourself you're still not a hundred per cent, so you need to take it easy, at least for a while.'

He seemed to be thinking it over. 'I suppose I could always ring yer man and tell him I'll be there first thing after the New Year . . .'

'That's more like it. Anyway, I thought that once you got out, maybe we could stay on in the city until New Year's?' Rachel figured he might be up for it in the circumstances, especially with his grand plans for a proposal going astray. New Year's Eve in New York would no doubt be amazing. They could go to Times Square and take in the atmosphere while waiting for the ball drop; it would help make up for missing Christmas.

Gary looked at her as if she was mad. 'Not a hope! You'll have to change them back, babe. To the earliest ones you can get. To be honest, after all I've gone through I can't wait to see the back of this place.'

'Oh.'

'And I'll need to get out there and start trying to get a few more jobs in. Money doesn't make itself, you know.'

'Oh. I see.' Rachel hadn't expected him to be quite so negative.

'Don't get me wrong. I appreciate this trip and every-thing. And I had a great time the first few days. It's just, you know, work and then the big New Year's motorbike ride, which I'm still doing despite these bloody ribs, I swear.'

'No, no . . . I understand that,' she said, raising a smile. After all, he was right. Money *didn't* make itself, and she reminded herself that he had already laid down a good chunk of that for the ring. Chances were he was planning ahead and budgeting for their wedding and honeymoon too, so thinking about it, a few extra days here would indeed be

 *Melissa Hill*

too much of an extravagance. Not to mention that Rachel also had her own responsibilities with the bistro.

No, it was probably better in the end, she realised. Gary would no doubt have already thought about this in detail, and decided that it was best to wait until they got home to propose.

Oh well, Rachel thought, it seemed she'd just have to wait that little bit longer to get that ring on her finger.

'That's my girl. Come here,' he said, motioning to embrace her. She duly leaned in and kissed him tenderly. 'Now let's get the doc to write me a prescription so I can get the hell out of here.'

He seemed unusually anxious to leave the hospital. Maybe he wasn't waiting until they got home to propose and wanted to do it as soon as possible, preferably before they took their return flight?

That would be much better; to Rachel, an engagement in New York – be it on Christmas Day or otherwise – seemed much more romantic.

'Hello there,' came a voice from the doorway and Rachel and Gary turned to look.

'Kim, hi!' Rachel greeted her warmly. 'Oh I'm glad you're here. I – *we* wanted to say thank you and goodbye. You've been so kind and I loved talking with you.'

'I wouldn't have missed it. I think he's being discharged tomorrow, but just in case I'm not here when you leave, I wanted to pop in and say hi. Hey there, Irishman,' she said, turning her attention to Gary. 'How does it feel to be back in the land of the living?'

'It'd be a lot bloody better if I had some painkillers,' he replied rudely, and Rachel looked at him, mortified. 'And why can't I get out today?'

'Gary, have some manners,' Rachel chided. 'Kim has

96

been looking after you very well while you've been here, and she's been brilliant to me too.'

'Well, someone had to keep your lovely lady company,' Kim replied, evidently unperturbed. 'I'm glad you'll be back on your feet soon. Quite a knock you had. She's been like an angel watching over you,' she told him, putting her hand on Rachel's shoulder. 'Anyway, I'll leave you two to your catching up. Just wanted to wish you well in case I don't see you. I'll find out from the doc when he's happy for you to leave, and come back and let you guys know.'

'Thanks, Kim, we really appreciate it.'

'No problem.' The nurse turned to go but then paused and looked back over her shoulder. 'And you, sweetheart, just you remember what I told you before, OK?'

Rachel flushed, and her eyes darted towards Gary for his reaction. Of course he had no idea what she was referring to, but still she felt a little caught off guard. She hadn't noticed the clock on the wall before, but all of a sudden the ticking from it could be heard clear as anything. 'Of course, of course I will,' she replied quickly. 'And thanks again.'

'What was all that about?' Gary asked after Kim had closed the door.

'Oh nothing . . . just some insider secrets on helping you get better,' she said, stroking his arm and trying to sound carefree. 'Anyway, I can't wait to have you out of here either. We've got a belated Christmas to celebrate.'

'Yeah, I hope you got me something nice; after all this, I think I deserve it,' he said, and Rachel had to smile at his ironic sense of humour.

Clever diversion, honey, she thought happily.

Chapter 10

As she prepared to close up Stromboli bistro for the night, Terri Blake was still reeling from Rachel's phone call from New York and the news of her best friend's engagement. Although she was thrilled for her friend, it was the last thing she'd expected, especially from Gary.

Terri had been surprised last year when, shortly after the bistro opened, Rachel had taken up with the builder who'd carried out the renovations. She remembered the way he'd gone the extra mile in helping them get the refurbishments finished on time, but it was obvious (to her at least) that this was purely in the hope of impressing Rachel. And it had worked.

Still, she'd never truly considered Gary Knowles a real match for her friend, not a long-term one anyway.

He was attractive certainly, in that coarse, dishevelled kind of way, but in her opinion he seemed rather immature and self-centred. For this reason Terri had never really taken to the guy, never really understood exactly what it was that Rachel saw in him.

She also didn't like the fact that Rachel hadn't been introduced to Gary's family, and knew little or nothing about them, despite being with him for almost a year. To Terri that was something of a red flag, regardless of Rachel's protests that he just preferred to take things slowly.

It also irked her that Gary routinely took advantage of Rachel's generosity; expecting to eat and drink at the bistro for free, and more often than not staying over at Rachel's flat. Granted his own place was further out of town so it made sense for convenience, but from Terri's point of view, give and take in Rachel and Gary's relationship had up to now been a one-way street, with Gary doing all the taking.

Rachel was aware of her misgivings and Terri knew that her friend took the odd barb and banter between her and Gary in good stride, often comparing them to quarrelling siblings. Luckily she didn't seem to notice that Terri was genuinely baffled by her interest in him.

But now Gary had gone and bought Rachel a diamond ring, and one from Tiffany's, no less.

Terri had heard that a ring from the world-famous jewellery store was supposed to be the epitome of romance. She wouldn't know about that. But she did know that the nadir of romance was the love of your life running off with your supposed best friend, as had happened in Terri's last relationship.

That had been almost eight years ago, she reflected with some dismay, but she didn't think she would have got through the devastation that followed if it hadn't been for Rachel, whom she'd met at catering college shortly afterwards.

It was strange but upon digesting Rachel's unexpected news from New York, a panorama of memories Terri and her friend had shared throughout the years suddenly seemed to fill her head from every side.

Student days spent lounging around in Rachel's flat with their feet up, drinking wine and talking about past or present loves; days out shopping and sharing wardrobe advice; staying up late discussing dreams for the future . . .

Then, of course, the huge excitement of deciding to go into business together, the subsequent haggling over the mechanics of the bistro and its bakery offshoot until, finally,

the opening day of Stromboli itself, which Terri was sure was the proudest moment of both of their careers, and a defining moment in their friendship.

She smiled, recalling the commotion surrounding not only opening the restaurant, but giving it a name.

While the two easily agreed on the type of cuisine to offer, she and Rachel simply couldn't come up with a name that encapsulated their intentions, yet was creative but not too pretentious.

Eventually they chose something that reflected both Rachel's Sicilian heritage and their explosive cuisine: Stromboli. It was the name of a volcanic island off the coast of Sicily. One thing could be said for certain: there was nothing like it in all of Dublin.

An eclectic blend of art, furniture, fragrances and Mediterranean foods, Stromboli drew people from miles around. The artisan bakery section was practically becoming a tourist destination in itself thanks to write-ups first in local newspapers and then in the *Irish Times*, followed by a special mention in the *Dublin Food Guide*. Within a few months of opening the bistro they'd had to post a 'Reservations Recommended' sign in the window.

Their focus on creating an authentic palate of individual dishes and blending flavours and textures from various countries had paid off in greater ways than either Terri or Rachel had imagined. Although they originally intended to keep the off-site catering aspect to small and intimate gatherings, their services were increasingly in demand.

The Mediterranean dishes, full of vegetables and rich in egg, meats and cheeses, were some of the most popular choices on both the bistro and the catering menus.

The more traditional Irish preparations of tarts, roasts and starchy vegetables enticed the tourists, and Stromboli's location a stone's throw from the Ha'penny Bridge helped considerably with bringing in custom. Their seafood paella, with which they served fresh sourdough (from Terri's leg-quivering recipe), had undoubtedly become the bistro's signature dish, and the reason their regular customers kept returning time and time again.

Also, the drinks menu, full of personal touches, reflected an impressive consideration of detail. Terri had chosen the majority of the list herself and was immensely proud of it. They carried a nice array of popular European wines along-side a line of various Spanish and Portuguese beers, as well as the most popular Irish ones. For additional colour they even had a few American microbrewery selections to choose from. Terri's own favourite was Arrogant Bastard Ale, which, Rachel joked, Terri only ordered shortly after first being introduced to Gary. It had been a staple on the bistro menu ever since and oddly, despite the in-joke, was one of Gary's preferred choices; he'd even bought a round of it for every-one on his birthday.

Everything about the bistro inspired Terri: the day-to-day running of it, the administration and ordering of supplies, the budgeting and book-keeping, even the madness that was the catering arm.

And even though Stromboli was her and Rachel's shared enterprise, it still felt a little like she was carrying on a piece of her dad's legacy.

Tom Blake had run a traditional old Dublin café from the selfsame location since Terri was very young, and although he'd raised an eyebrow at the refurbishments, and Stromboli's striking purple and orange signage above the doorway, she knew he was overjoyed that catering (albeit of a very different kind) was staying in the family.

For as far back as Terri could recall, cooking and food

had simply been an extension of her very self and the life she experienced all around her.

It was really only in the kitchen – her hands covered in sticky dough, her senses filled with the rich sweetness of the egg-and-sugar-laden mass and her arms tired from kneading – that she felt secure and confident in her life. Baking represented a link not just to her past, but to her passion in the present and her identity in the future.

On the wall of the kitchen in the bistro hung a plaque:

> When we no longer have good cooking in
> the world, we will have no literature, nor
> high and sharp intelligence, nor friendly
> gatherings, nor social harmony.

Her dad had given her this plaque on Stromboli's opening night and she'd since learned that it was attributed to a person called Marie-Antoine Carême. It confirmed for Terri that she was doing something of value, something that brought a sense of continuity to her own life and the lives of others.

She couldn't remember which book it was in particular, but there was a Toni Morrison story she had read in which the main character made bread time and again, sustaining her family and entertaining friends. The section of the story Terri loved most was the description of the woman kneading bread with her warm hands while, behind her, her lover held her closely, gently and firmly kneading her body too.

Thus came her passion for baking bread. Bread – like real love – took time, cultivation, strong loving hands and patience. It lived, rising and growing to fruition only under the most perfect circumstances. If the water was too warm, it killed the yeast; too cool and the yeast was not inspired to grow the bread. Without enough sugar, the yeast would starve, leaving the bread flat and lifeless; if the air was not humid enough, the yeast could not spur the bread to reach its full potential.

Many were the late nights or early mornings that Terri had spent in the kitchen concocting new bread recipes and kneading dough of various textures – herbs, spices, sausages and cheeses – until it gleamed and grew smooth under her persuasive hands.

Unfortunately, Terri thought wryly, as her mother kept telling her, the time and effort she dedicated to baking might have been better diverted to her love life. While she'd had a few flings over the years, she hadn't been involved in a proper relationship since Rob, and in all honesty she didn't particularly care.

It wasn't for the lack of offers, and although Terri knew she was a million miles from Rachel's drop-dead beauty, she figured she was OK-looking in her own right.

Her hair was probably her best feature, and customers often commented on her curly red tresses, which were so thick she could barely contain them beneath her chef's cap, and while she was probably a teeny bit overweight, there was no way she was forsaking her and Rachel's delicious food for the sake of 'finding a man'.

In addition, Terri had yet to find any man worthy of the time and effort required for a relationship. Most of the men she encountered these days were serial Romeos who had no interest in settling down, or newly single guys emerging from long-term relationships or marriages with all the extra baggage this entailed.

Rachel and their chef, Justin, were always teasing her about being too cynical and having unrealistic expectations, but what was so unrealistic about wanting to share her life with someone easy-going and straightforward? Terri had no

interest in the immature game-playing that seemed to go on between people who were supposed to have grown out of their teenage years a long time ago. She simply wanted someone to share her day-to-day life with, someone to come home to in the evenings and to chat and laugh with, someone who understood her hopes and dreams and who would be there for her whenever she needed him. Was that really too much to ask?

'I don't have high standards, just standards full stop,' she argued with Justin on a routine basis, but the truth was that at thirty-two years old, and after almost eight years of being single, Terri had just about given up on happy ever after.

And while it might have been a surprise (to her at least), she was glad that Rachel had found it.

Chapter 11

As it turned out, and much to Gary's annoyance, the doctors refused to discharge him from the hospital until the following afternoon.

In the meantime, Rachel once again contacted the airline and arranged, at considerable expense, to rebook their flights back to Ireland on the twenty-ninth, which meant that once Gary got out they would be spending one last night in New York.

Back at the hotel, she'd gone out of her way to ensure that their final night in the city would be extra special. All being equal, she was sure that Gary would have had his own elaborate proposal plans in place but, with the accident, everything had gone awry. Well, the least she could do now was try to make it easy for him.

So when at six p.m. sharp the knock on the hotel door came, Rachel leapt up from where they sat on the couch to answer it.

Tipping the room-service waiter, she wheeled in a cart with two prime-rib dinners, two lit candles and a freshly chilled bottle of champagne.

'Wow, pulling out all the stops, aren't you, babe?' Gary grinned, as she put an arm around him and helped him to the table

He was getting around pretty well on his twisted ankle but still seemed a bit crotchety, despite the Vicodin haze.

'Well, we did miss Christmas,' she said, giving him a wink and biting the inside of her cheek as she tried to hold back a giddy smile. Earlier he'd again brought up the subject of exchanging Christmas gifts, so it looked as though she didn't have too much longer to wait.

She managed to make it most of the way through dinner without her hands shaking too much. By contrast Gary was incredibly relaxed, and for this, Rachel was grateful. Part of her was afraid that, if he hadn't been seeing her through the rose-coloured glasses of pain medication, he might have been suspicious that she was on to his proposal plans.

'Ugh, I can barely move after that,' she said, scraping the plate with her knife and fork. 'I've been waiting for so long to have this nice dinner with you, I think I've overdone it. More champagne?'

'Perfect,' Gary said. 'I'd pour it myself if I could, but I don't think my ribs could handle the strain.'

'Don't worry; I've got it,' Rachel said. She glanced at the bottle, which, worryingly, was almost empty. They'd have to order another one to celebrate their engagement, if Gary ever got round to it, that was! Sometimes he could be so laid-back it was funny, but not this time. 'So,' she went on, trying to sound light-hearted, 'I suppose now might be a good time to break out the presents. I'll just get yours and we'll open them together, OK?'

'Great. I could do with some cheering up. While you're at it, would you grab the one I got you from my stuff?'

Rachel's heart raced. This was it! 'Sure, but how will I know which one is mine?' she asked, grateful that her strengths lay in cooking and she hadn't instead tried to pursue an acting career.

'Well,' Gary replied, raising his eyebrows playfully. 'That would be the one in the little blue gift bag.' He sounded uncommonly pleased with himself and she grinned.

'Sounds nice,' she said, feigning ignorance about the significance of the bag's colour.

A couple of minutes later, she returned to the table with the Tiffany's bag and several gift-wrapped packages meant for him.

'Tell you what, why don't we move onto the sofa for this? It'll be more comfortable for you,' she said. That way, there was less risk of Gary injuring himself when he got down on one knee.

'OK. Give us a hand, though, would you?' He stood up and Rachel gently guided him the few steps across the room. 'Grand, and don't forget my top-up,' he added, indicating the champagne.

'Hold on, I'll bring my glass too.'

Once they were seated side by side on the sofa, Rachel handed Gary her carefully wrapped gifts.

'You first,' he said.

'No, you go ahead,' she insisted. She appreciated his manners, but figured the engagement ring deserved to be the grand finale. He didn't seem nervous at all, but then again she supposed he was lucky; most men didn't have the cushion of Vicodin to help them through a marriage proposal.

Gary complied, and several minutes later had his motor-bike-riding trousers, leather wallet and a nice Hugo Boss shirt next to him on the couch. Rachel had picked up the shirt in the meantime, realising that the gifts she had given him seemed miserly compared to the huge amount he must have spent on her. 'Thanks, babe. I can't believe how much you've spoilt me! I'm so lucky to have you. Now your turn.'

Rachel looked at him nervously, waiting for some sign of

ceremony; then, realising that with him in his current state she should just be happy that she'd soon be wearing his ring, she reached for the bag.

'Oh wow, Tiffany's!' she exclaimed, playing her part to perfection.

Gary grinned. 'Yep, nothing too shabby for my girl.'

Taking out the box, she smiled up at him, hoping she had done a good enough job of retying the ribbon so that he wouldn't notice it had already been opened.

But it seemed he hadn't spotted anything amiss. 'Can't wait to see it on you,' he said, and Rachel swallowed hard.

Here we go . . .

She pulled at the delicate white ribbon and as it fell away she gently lifted the lid off the box. 'Oh my goodness,' she gasped wide-eyed, slowly opening the velvet ring box inside. By now, though, Rachel was no longer acting; the sheer beauty of the ring was more than enough to send her swooning all over again. 'Gary . . .'

'I knew you'd like it. I saw it and straight away I thought, yep, perfect for Rachel. She'll be able to wear that with just about anything.'

His sense of humour certainly kept her on her toes, that was for sure. This really wasn't the right time for joking around, although Gary was such a devil that she wouldn't put it past him to keep her on tenterhooks just for the fun of it.

Despite his best attempts at levity, Rachel still couldn't help but be overcome by the emotion of the moment. She smiled, tears pricking at the corner of her eyes. 'Well, yes, of course I will. I'll never take it off.'

She looked up at him, still waiting for him to make some sort of romantic gesture, even if he wasn't able to get down on one knee just yet.

'Let's have a look, then,' he said. 'Put it on.'

'Well –' she turned the box towards him '– I was hoping you'd help me with that.'

Suddenly Gary's eyes grew even bigger than hers, and for a long moment he couldn't seem to meet her gaze. The silence was just beginning to make her uncomfortable, when finally he spoke. 'So you . . . erm, like it, then?'

Rachel's eyes shone, and all of a sudden she understood. He was nervous; in spite of all his jokey bluster, the poor darling was terrified. 'Gary, I *love* it! And I love you. I will be so proud to wear it.'

'I . . . yeah . . . me too . . . I mean, proud to have you wear it,' he fumbled, trying to sit up a little straighter. She nodded at him encouragingly, still holding out the box.

'Oh . . . right,' he said, reaching to take the ring out.

She set the box down and held out her left hand.

'So, er, do you want to . . . will you marry me?' Gary asked, his jaw quivering a little.

'Yes, yes, I will, Gary. Of course I will!' Rachel replied, a tear streaming down her cheek. She could never have imagined this would be so emotional. Leaning over to hug him, she then sat back to see that he was still wide-eyed. 'You poor thing! I can't believe you pulled this off in your condition. We could have waited till you were feeling better.' Then she paused. 'Oh who am I kidding?' she continued, laughing and wiping another tear from her face. 'I'm so glad you didn't. It's so gorgeous. I love it. And I love you!' she beamed, holding the ring up so the diamond sparkled magnificently in the light.

'Yeah, me too. Ah, how about some more of that champagne?' he said, sounding weak – from the emotional strain of it all, no doubt.

'Yes, of course. A toast!' Her heart singing, Rachel topped up their glasses with what little champagne was left and

picked them up. She handed him his glass, waiting for him to say something meaningful, but before she knew it he'd knocked it all back in one go.

'To us,' she said, faintly disappointed that he hadn't waited, but what did it matter?

Taking a sip of champagne, she relished anew the lovely sensation of bubbles on her tongue. Here she was, in New York, engaged! And not only that but she now owned the most stupendous, amazing, *magnificent* Tiffany's ring.

It was every girl's dream come true.

Gulping down the last drops, she then turned and gave Gary a devilish smile. 'Now, I know you're not exactly in the best condition for any . . . energetic activity, but that doesn't mean you can't receive.'

She put her glass down and moved towards him.

'Well, OK,' was all Gary could say, and she felt him finally relax as she began placing feathery kisses on his lips, his neck, before gradually working her way down along his torso.

Looking back up at his face, she grinned mischievously. 'Just a little taste of what you'll be getting for the rest of our lives . . .'

'Sounds good to me.' Gary smiled, closing his eyes and resting his head on the back of the couch.

Later that night, well after Rachel had fallen asleep, Gary lay wide awake in bed beside her.

What the hell?

It was a question he kept asking himself for a very long time, the light from the digital clock on the nightstand reflecting off the side of his face in the darkness. Even after popping an extra Vicodin an hour ago, he just couldn't quieten his mind long enough to nod off.

Over and over again he replayed the scenarios in his head: shopping for the bracelet . . . seeing the shop assistant wrap up and place the *bracelet* in the bag . . . going outside to hail a taxi . . . waking up in the hospital . . . then tonight, Rachel beaming at him as he placed this colossal diamond ring on her finger.

Eventually, he drifted off but in his dreams he was back in Tiffany's, arguing with the blonde over how much his credit card had been dinged for. Was there some kind of girly conspiracy thing going on, or something?

Then, minutes later, he was once again wide awake, the images from his dream still clear in his head. Tiptoeing out of the room he slunk off into the sitting area and fired up his laptop to check his credit-card statement.

Gary took a deep breath. There it was in digital black and white; he had indeed only been charged a hundred and fifty dollars or so for the charm bracelet.

Well, OK then.

Granted, he hadn't planned on getting married, but there was no denying that he'd done well out of this particular deal.

And now, through no fault or effort of his own, he was an engaged man. Gary's stomach tightened. The timing wasn't the best, that was for sure; not when there were a few . . . loose ends in play. He'd be under pressure now to tie them up – and quickly.

He supposed he'd have to introduce her to his mother soon too. That could be tricky. Hopefully his ma would keep her mouth shut. Well, he'd have a word in her ear beforehand to make sure she let nothing untoward slip about the . . . other situation.

He sat back on the sofa, thinking about Rachel.

Did he want to marry her? He could do worse for a wife,

he reasoned, thinking of some of the girls he'd been involved with over the years. She was great fun, easy-going for the most part, and while she could be a bit overemotional at times, all women were a bit like that, weren't they?

No, if he thought about it properly, Rachel was a great catch: she had her own business, was scorching between the sheets and, most importantly, wasn't constantly in his ear about the time he spent off with the boys on the bikes.

Anyway, it was only engaged. A ring didn't necessarily mean they had to get married in the morning, did it? Rachel certainly seemed happy enough with just a ring on her finger, and if she was happy maybe he should be too. One thing was for sure: he might as well make the most of being in the good books for as long as possible. Because if she ever found out about the other thing . . .

Gary scratched his jaw. All considered, maybe he shouldn't look a gift horse in the mouth.

Powering off the laptop, Gary shrugged.

Like the man said, sometimes you just had to roll with the punches and take the hand life dealt you.

Chapter 12

Ethan felt Vanessa's gloved hand in his and decided that it was good to be back in London. Daisy was today catching up with her grandparents, and he was looking forward to spending some time alone with Vanessa.

His parents had been so supportive and helpful since Jane's death, Ethan mused. Having been married themselves for almost fifty years, they had become more than just a stable bedrock for him. They were a touchstone, a sort of third-eye perspective for his own life. He was well aware of that, and it was something that had comforted and cushioned him over the last few years.

But since he and Vanessa had dropped Daisy off at their house yesterday, something had been different.

He couldn't put his finger on it. He knew that the feeling didn't really have anything to do with his parents per se, but he couldn't shake the annoyance he felt at his mother's doting, lingering tendencies. His parents' black Lab, Bailey, had barrelled in from outside as they were saying goodbye to Daisy, and as the dog shook off the dampness – a long, controlled, full-body, rhythmic motion – Ethan felt almost envious.

He wished he could just shake things off like that too, get a grip on what was bothering him, and then play happily or lounge by the fireplace without a care in the world.

Whatever it was, it was reminiscent of a feeling he had

had while shopping on Christmas Eve, only this time he wasn't invigorated and feeling one step ahead of things. The opposite.

Now, unaware of his own pace until he heard the snow crunching beneath his feet in shorter intervals, he tugged on Vanessa's hand and told her that the quicker they walked the sooner they would be stopping for lunch.

'But, Ethan, I'm not that cold. I'm actually enjoying the walk. It's such a lovely day; let's make the most of it.'

He forced a sigh and watched his breath turn to vapour before his eyes. She was right, he thought. Since coming home, he had been too wrapped up in his own head, too fixated on nothing but losing that ring. He needed to relax.

'I'm sorry, darling. Just getting back into things after the break has made me a bit stressed, I think.' He squeezed her hand and shot her a smile. 'Yes, let's enjoy it. In fact, let's give that place over there a shot for lunch today. What do you think?'

'The Snug?' Vanessa said, stopping in her tracks. 'Why on earth would you want to go to an Irish pub?'

Despite her heritage, he didn't think he and Vanessa had ever been in an Irish pub in London together. She tended to avoid them in favour of more traditional English establishments; he guessed that to her they weren't remotely like home and actually rather kitsch and fake. Still, he'd always liked this particular one.

'I don't know. I suppose I just feel like trying somewhere different for a change.'

'Really? On the plane you were saying how much you were looking forward to getting back into our routine. You even mentioned our café.'

By 'our' café Ethan knew she meant the one they often

went to for lunch at weekends. 'Right, and I am – we are. But why not bring some new flavour into the routine? I haven't been to the Snug in ages. Besides, the gastro-pub food got four out of five stars in *The Times* recently, and we might even see a politician or two,' he added, offering a little background colour that he figured might appeal to her.

She laughed, looking incredulous. 'You researched this place?'

'Well, I wouldn't say I did any full-blown research, but I just came across a review – only yesterday actually,' he said, muddling his way through an explanation. 'Don't be fooled by the outside; I know it seems a bit shabby but the menu really does look impressive.' The look on Vanessa's face wasn't communicating much, and Ethan wasn't sure if she was impressed with his enterprising thinking, or suspicious of it.

'You've just never struck me as the Irish-pub type,' she finally said.

The observation set him off kilter. Just what type *did* she consider him? In fact, what type did he consider himself? As they stood there on the path across from the pub, the cold breeze suddenly became a wind.

'OK then, I must admit I'm slightly intrigued,' she conceded. 'As long as you don't ask me to guzzle back Guinness and start singing rebel songs, I suppose we could try it.' She smiled and brushed the snow out of her fair hair.

Ethan threw his head back, catching snowflakes on his tongue. 'Great. You'll love it.'

'You seem pretty sure of yourself.'

Did he? He realised that this was something she had never said to him before. In truth, he quite liked the sound of it as, since Jane's death, he hadn't thought it was possible to be

sure of anything. He grabbed her hand and led her across the street and into the Snug.

Seated inside the dining section at a table topped with white linen, Vanessa voiced her approval. 'Well, I have to admit it's not exactly what I expected. No neon shamrocks in sight. Actually, it's rather nice.'

'Good.' Ethan smiled, feeling almost as if he'd won a battle of wills of sorts. 'Seems I was right, then.'

Lunch passed pleasantly. Vanessa enjoyed brown bread and home-made potato and leek soup while Ethan devoured a platter of fresh oysters. Halfway through, he decided that a Guinness would complement the meal perfectly and since the glass was only halfway empty by the time his plate was clean, he then decided he needed something else to finish things off. Apple crumble with custard did the job nicely.

'Good God, Ethan. Did you bring this appetite back with you from New York?' Vanessa laughed. 'Because if you did, I suggest you return it quickly. I don't think I've ever seen you eat like this before.'

He chuckled. 'I know. Pretty good, eh?' But the mention of what he might have brought back from New York merely reminded him of what he *hadn't*, namely the ring.

He grew quiet for a while and Vanessa said nothing. It was as if the mention of New York had brought into focus the bubble of unspoken questions hanging between them. They hadn't talked all that much about the trip since their return, and although Vanessa had insisted she'd enjoyed it, he knew that she sensed, however vaguely, that something had shifted in their relationship while there. He could only imagine how his seemingly out-of-the-blue distraction and evasiveness since Christmas Day had come across to her.

She'd asked how the meeting with the 'literary agent' had

gone, and Ethan had been deliberately ambiguous, telling her that it wasn't really a meeting at all, more of a brief chat over coffee until the agent was called away on an emergency.

'So what did she say about the proposal you sent? Will she be offering representation?'

'I'm not sure. She needs to read a writing sample before she decides.'

'Well, you'd better get cracking on that then, hadn't you?' she'd teased, and Ethan had tried to divert her from the topic by presenting her with yet another gift: a little silver apple charm for her bracelet.

He'd picked it up in Tiffany's on the way back from meeting Rachel Conti at the hospital, and had hoped it would act as a peace offering of sorts, and a memento of their time in the city together.

Or more likely, Ethan had admitted to himself, a weak attempt to salve his own conscience for lying to her.

Now, two days back in London, he was still no further down the line to retrieving his engagement ring, and wasn't sure what his next move should be. Since his return, he'd called Rachel's number again under the guise of enquiring about Gary Knowles, but only got voicemail, upon which he'd left his own contact details.

There was a side of him that hoped the situation would automatically be resolved once the man recovered from his injuries and subsequently examined his bags, becoming aware himself of the mix-up. Then, with luck, he and Rachel would put two and two together and Ethan'd have the ring back in no time. At least, that's how he hoped things would play out, because for the moment he didn't have any better ideas. He knew something would have to be done, certainly; there was no way he could leave the situation up in the air.

But until he made contact with Gary Knowles, there was little else he could do.

'Shall we?' he asked, reaching for the bill.

'Absolutely. It's nearly time for you to pick up Daisy, and I need to go home tonight as I haven't quite unpacked yet. But I can still take her to her ballet class tomorrow afternoon, if you like. And then dinner?'

'Sounds good,' he said, leaning to one side to take his wallet out of his back pocket.

Later that evening, Ethan came in from the balcony of the two-storey town house he shared with Daisy in Richmond.

He sat in the leather chair adjacent to the dancing flames in the fireplace and, with his elbows on his knees, leaned forward and bit softly on the thumbnail of his left hand.

He stopped and smiled at the unbidden memory that arose on doing so.

Jane had always loved secretly watching him bite on that nail while he was lost in thought. She said the way his hair fell part of the way across his right eye made him look sexy. She loved his blue eyes anyway, but found them most irresistible 'when they're reflecting mysterious thoughts'. What she loved even more, though, were his hands. She used to say they were strong and masculine, yet sensitive and artistic. She loved the way they held a coffee cup and the way they held her, and especially the way they looked on her bare skin.

Hearing Daisy stir in the other room, Ethan shook off the memory and sighed as he sat back, the leather chair exhaling beneath his weight. He loved the earthy scent of that leather. It made that particular chair his favourite place to sit in the entire house. Rubbing a hand over his torso, he smiled as he thought about the lunch he had devoured earlier, and before he knew it his mind began replaying eating chocolate-chip cookies that day he and Daisy had met Rachel.

He wondered where she was now, the woman with his ring. Was she still in New York, tending to her injured boyfriend, or back in Ireland? The day after tomorrow was New Year's Eve, and she'd mentioned she ran some kind of restaurant so surely she would have to return to that at some stage during the festivities?

Ethan checked his watch. It was late, but not that late if she was still in New York. Should he try her number again, and this time just come out and explain everything once and for all? Then again, he couldn't imagine upsetting her in such a way, particularly with all the strain she was under. She'd seemed like an especially lovely person: kind, warm, with such an infectious laugh.

Immediately he shook the feeling off. It was almost Daisy's bedtime so really there wasn't enough time for telephone calls and explanations. He stood up and went to look in on his daughter.

'Almost ready for bed?' he asked Daisy, standing outside her bedroom doorway. If there was one thing he had learned about raising an eight-year-old girl, it was to never enter without announcing himself or asking permission.

'Come in, Dad. Just drawing,' she said, sitting on the bed in her nightgown.

'What are you drawing?' he asked.

'Just my favourite memories from our trip,' she answered without looking up.

There, scattered around her, was page after page of scenes from their time in New York. 'I want to show them to my friends when I go back to school next week.'

Ethan sat carefully on the edge of the bed so as not to

disturb his little artist at work. He surveyed the pictures of the moments that were apparently special to her. There was one of her sitting on the plane next to him, another of the Statue of Liberty, one of the two of them walking down what he suspected was Fifth Avenue, their view of Central Park from the hotel, and the Christmas lights on Park Avenue. Then, oddly, one of him tending to Knowles after the accident.

'You picked this as a good memory?' he asked, holding up the picture.

She nodded. 'Yes, Dad, because everyone says you and I were heroes that day.'

Ethan smiled weakly. 'I suppose we were.' Then he spotted another picture, this one of three people at a table eating chocolate-chip cookies and smiling. At first he thought it was a representation of the two of them and Vanessa, but it quickly struck him that the hair colour was wrong.

He raised an eyebrow.

'What?' Daisy asked, looking up. 'Don't you like them?'

'They're beautiful. So is Vanessa in any?'

'Yes, here,' she said, pointing to a picture of three people sitting around a Christmas tree. Sure enough, there was Vanessa, but sort of tucked halfway behind Ethan.

'Ah, yes. I see her now,' he said. It wasn't lost on him that Rachel's depiction was beaming and smiling, drawn from the front and centred in the picture, whereas Vanessa's sort of blended into the background. 'Did you have a good time, poppet?'

'Yes, very much.' She sighed and shook her head. 'You already asked me that so many times, Dad.'

'I know. I suppose it just didn't turn out exactly as we expected, did it? I still have to get the ring back and ask Vanessa to marry me. Are you still OK with that? You know, do you still think that's a good idea?'

She nodded. 'Of course. I don't think she had a very good time in New York, though, but I suppose that could change.'

Ethan grimaced. He'd half-hoped that Vanessa's distant behaviour had been nothing more than a figment of his imagination, but it seemed not. 'It was a bit topsy-turvy, our trip, wasn't it?'

'Yes.' Daisy paused and looked at him. 'Dad, did *you* have a good time? I mean, if you drew a picture of your favourite memory, what would it be?'

'Well . . .' Ethan was stumped. For a moment he honestly couldn't think. Then he chuckled. 'I suppose it would have to be the one of me force-feeding you M&Ms on our last night. Here, give me a piece of paper and one of those crayons!'

Daisy giggled with delight. Then, when Ethan was done with his own rendition of their chocolate feast, she raced into the kitchen to place it prominently on the fridge door along with the rest of her drawings, where Ethan had every intention of letting them stay until the edges were yellowed and cracked.

Chapter 13

'I'm telling you, I don't know how it happened,' Gary said, crouching down as he tightened the last bolt on a new fuel line he was installing on his motorbike.

He was glad to be back home, a wrench in his hand and a beer on the concrete garage floor. It had been a long flight across the Atlantic with his sore ribs, but at least not as long as the bloody hospital stay. He shrugged and looked at his best mate, Sean. 'Sometimes, when you realise the cards you're dealt, you've just got to bluff and keep your poker face on.'

'Well, you could have knocked me under a bus when you told me you were getting hitched, but with the way things panned out I suppose you couldn't do much about it,' Sean guffawed. 'Anyway, you could do worse than Rachel, you know. You'll never go hungry *and* you get to have those curves in your bed every night.' He grinned and raised his beer can to his mouth. 'Guess one of us had to take the plunge soon enough. Hate to admit it, you bastard, but you're looking at a win-win.'

Gary and Sean had been close buddies for over thirty years. They'd grown up together in the same area of Dublin and had always shared a fascination for things that went fast, from home-made go-carts to BMX bicycles, then eventually street bikes. Somewhere along the line between those came fast girls and then fast women.

While Rachel didn't exactly fit the 'fast' category, she'd certainly been lusty and spontaneous enough to catch Gary's eye and, more importantly, meet the approval of his mates.

He stood up, wiped his hands on a greasy rag and tossed it onto the workbench. 'Throw me another one of those,' he said to Sean, who reached into a half-empty twelve pack of Heineken and obliged. 'Well,' he said, as it opened with a loud hiss, 'in fairness, marriage is never a win-win, but if I have to take the plunge I suppose the odds are in my favour this time.'

'Yeah, well, just as long as it doesn't change you,' Sean said dismissively, waving the can in his hand. 'Although at least Rachel never tries to come between you and your mates. Hell, she even keeps the brew flowing every weekend after the rides. How many birds would give us the thumbs-up on that?'

'Cheers,' Gary said, not entirely comfortable with this line of conversation – about marriage and being changed and all that. He'd just wanted to hear Sean's take on what he should do about the ring if it all went south with Rachel. 'One more thing: you can't breathe a word of this. As far as the rest of the lads are concerned, I bought the ring and I proposed. I got it under control. OK?'

'Say no more. You have my word,' Sean said solemnly.

Gary laughed. 'I'd better! All right, throw us over your bike now. Mine's good to go.' It was almost an unspoken pact between them to meet at Sean's house on Sundays after their Saturday rides, to keep their bikes in tip-top shape. Because of his injuries, Gary wasn't up to riding just yet, but today was a good excuse to catch up with his friend.

'And speaking of coming up trumps, I suppose you'll

have a big payout coming soon – from the cab crowd, I mean,' Sean said.

Gary frowned. He hadn't thought of that. Sean saw the hesitation in his face and laughed. 'You do know you can take that crowd to the cleaners, don't you? I tell you, Gary, you'd be stupid not to. They'll expect that kind of thing. Sure, aren't the Yanks themselves always suing one another left, right and centre?'

Gary thought about it. Sean was right. The cab company were probably waiting for a summons to come through the post, and here he was sitting around like an eejit and doing nothing about it.

'You know, you could be on to something there.'

Sean shrugged. 'You'd be mad to let it go. From what you told me, it's all cut and dried.'

That was true, Gary agreed. There he was in the middle of Manhattan, minding his own business, when this gobshite comes out of nowhere and mows him down. Of course he should get recompense for that. And for all the money he'd had to pay out for the hospital bills too, although to be fair, his health insurance had covered a lot of that. But thinking about it now, wouldn't the cab companies have insurance for that kind of thing? So, really, Gary would be very stupid not to at least enquire about it.

'You're right.' He'd phone a solicitor first thing in the new year. In these troubled economic times nobody could afford to let opportunities like that go astray. And wasn't he entitled to it, after all? As it was he was still suffering, and if it wasn't for the fact that the boys were willing to wait for him, he'd be missing the New Year's bike ride. In fairness, he'd been forced to postpone one building job because of the hospital stay, and who knew how many others his injuries would put a stop to?

Not to mention that a few quid would come in handy

right now. Actually, it might very well be the answer to one or two of his more pressing problems. Sean didn't know the half of it.

'Listen, thanks a mill again for holding off on the big ride until I'm up for it,' he said to Sean. 'These bloody ribs will take a while.'

'No problem. Sure, we'll do it as a team, same as always,' Sean assured him. 'The rest of the lads are fine about it. They're all on for the party too.'

'The party . . . yeah,' Gary replied, grabbing a fresh cloth while Sean applied the engine cleaner. On the way back from New York, Rachel had come up with the bright idea of throwing a big do to celebrate their engagement.

'We could do it at the bistro on New Year's Eve – when everything's already set up for a party,' she'd gushed, her mind already racing with the possibilities, and Gary could do nothing else but agree.

'One thing I am learning about all this engagement stuff,' he grinned, 'is that there's lots of booze and partying leading up to the main event. Can't baulk at that, I suppose.'

'Too right,' Sean agreed, taking one last swig and tossing his empty can across the garage and into the recycle bin. 'I'll make sure you have the stag night to end all stag nights too. Rachel didn't waste any time pulling this one together, did she? A New Year's Eve engagement party.' He pulled his towel back and gave it a stinging flick that landed on Gary's arm. 'Very fancy.'

'Dickhead – you'll regret that when I'm back in fighting form,' Gary said, grabbing another beer from the box and tossing it to Sean.

'Sure, are you ever any other way?' his mate replied with a wink.

★ ★ ★

'Wait a second,' Brian said, pausing to take a sip from his wine glass and then setting it on the bar. He looked at Ethan in disbelief. 'You bought a two-carat rock for Vanessa?'

Ethan looked at his friend, wondering why he sounded so surprised. 'Yes, it's been on the cards for a while. I thought you knew that.'

'Well, yes, I knew you two were close but I didn't think it was that serious, actually . . . But, more to the point, then you went and *lost* the bloody thing?'

'In a word, yes,' Ethan replied. 'And thank you for summing it up in a way that makes me sound like an absolute pillock. I know I can always count on you for that,' he added, raising his own glass for a toast, which Brian gladly accommodated.

The two men had met years before at the university in which they both taught, and well before Brian had become the successful novelist that Ethan hoped to one day be too.

'Glad I can bring some consistency to your life,' Brian replied, finishing off the last of his Montrachet with one swig. He motioned to the barman. 'Another, please.'

Ethan shook his head. 'I thought we agreed to meet for *a* glass, not three.'

'No such thing as one glass – what's the point?' Brian retorted. 'Besides, you haven't me told me how Vanessa reacted when you told her what happened.'

'I didn't tell her what happened. How could I?' Ethan looked away and finished his own glass. Without thinking he raised his hand to his mouth to chew on his nail.

'So you haven't proposed yet?' asked Brian.

'No. As I said, how could I? What woman wants a proposal that ends in the man telling her he's lost the ring?'

Brian was silent for a moment before he spoke again. 'I just can't believe it.' He shook his head.

'I know I wouldn't have let that bag out of my sight for a second, let alone drop it on the street to help some stranger. You're way too nice for your own good sometimes, my man.'

'Well, that's the thing,' Ethan replied, explaining that the bag had actually been in Daisy's care. 'She's blaming herself, of course. But I've tried to reassure her that it wasn't her fault. It's not as though the bags got mixed up intentionally.'

Brian looked sideways at him. 'I take it she knew about the planned big Christmas proposal, then. How'd she handle it?'

'Brilliantly, really. She didn't know when it was happening until I picked up the ring in New York, but she was fine, really enthusiastic.'

'That's great, Ethan. I'm glad Daisy's OK with it. That kind of thing could have been a big stumbling block, especially when she's so attached to you.'

And why wouldn't she be? It had been just the two of them for so long, Ethan thought.

'Is she still just as gung-ho on the health stuff?'

He smiled sadly. 'Afraid so. The other day she brought home this leaflet she'd picked up from somewhere about superfoods.' It broke Ethan's heart to see that most of the items listed were being lauded for their cancer-fighting abilities. 'And she's doing her utmost to try to make me take up jogging as a new year's resolution,' he told Brian. 'Says it'll help keep my stress levels down.'

Which was another reason Ethan was still at pains to reassure his daughter that the mix-up with the bags wasn't her fault and that he'd be able to get the ring back with minimum hassle.

The problem was that he didn't know if that were true.

'She's a great kid. And you're a great father, Ethan, better

than I could ever hope to be. Not that *that's* on the cards,' he added sardonically. 'Or if it is, I know nothing about it, nor do I want to.'

'Thank you.' Ethan smiled, thinking that with Brian's reputation it was very likely that he might indeed have offspring somewhere that he didn't know about. Although Ethan didn't know if what his friend had said about him being a good father was true. He'd muddled his way along so far, but there was so much he didn't know about bringing up a little girl in today's world. Which was why he was so happy to have found Vanessa. There was no replacing Daisy's real mum, of course, but it was plain to see that his beloved daughter needed a strong female influence in her life.

'So what's your plan for getting this ring back, then?' Brian asked. 'I take it you're still going ahead with the big proposal.'

Ethan looked at him. 'Well, of course. Why wouldn't I be? Anyway, seems like I might need to take a trip to Dublin soon.' He explained how the numerous messages he'd left for the other party were so far unreturned.

Brian looked incredulous. 'And how exactly do you plan to get this mysterious trip past your lovely bride-to-be without telling her what's going on? Hell, Ethan –' he paused, shaking his head '– call me old-fashioned, but if you're going to marry the woman shouldn't you be able to actually *talk* to her?'

Ethan pushed aside his empty glass, and set his elbows on the bar. 'That's funny coming from someone who hasn't stayed with one woman longer than six months.'

'Point taken.' Brian grinned, unable to deny he was a renowned Lothario, his esteemed profession helping a lot in this regard.

'Anyway, as it turns out, things aren't that simple. The woman who has the ring . . . I met her in New York . . . Gary Knowles's girlfriend,' he continued, stumbling over the words a little. 'We had coffee, and exchanged phone numbers. So I suppose I'll just have to try to—'

'Hold on! *Woman?* What woman? You didn't mention a woman. I thought some bloke had the ring.'

'He did. At least I think he did, but he didn't . . . *doesn't* realise it.' Ethan glanced across and felt the weight of his friend's perplexed look, something he'd last seen when Brian's car had a flat and he'd admitted he didn't know how to change a tyre.

A couple of very long minutes passed during which Ethan noticed the music coming from the jukebox and the growing hum of people in the bar. It was Happy Hour and people were filing in. He felt diminished, as if all the great plans he'd had in mind had suddenly been bundled in the palm of his hand and inadvertently dropped and stepped upon.

'Look, I'm not trying to say that the way you're handling this is wrong,' Brian began, his tone suddenly serious. 'I just think you need to figure out what on earth you're doing and why. Anyway, what's happening here? You're usually the advice man and now you've got me being the touchy-feely-thinky one. I don't do this; I save it for the writing. So just get all this sorted so we can get back to our normal roles here, yes?'

Ethan raised a smile. 'You're right. I should just go and get the ring back, and give it to Vanessa as planned.'

Brian said nothing, but raised his glass and gave Ethan a look that said he wasn't quite convinced. They sat in silence for another couple of minutes before his friend spoke again. 'Actually, I'm not even saying that's the right thing to do. Get the ring back, yes – hell, if I'd spent that much

on a piece of jewellery I'd be *swimming* to Dublin to get it back, let me tell you. But in terms of proposing to Vanessa . . . just make sure it's really what you want. I know you're anxious about Daisy but don't sell yourself short as a parent either. Don't fool yourself into thinking you're on some sort of timeline – there should be no race to the finish when it comes to something like this.' He paused for a moment. 'Don't be afraid to take your time; make sure it's what you *both* want, and for the right reasons.'

'Thanks for the advice, but speaking of time –' Ethan gulped down about half of the newly poured wine, and set the glass purposefully on the bar '– I'd better go. Vanessa's coming over this evening. She's picking Daisy up from ballet class and then we're having dinner.' He checked the time on his watch; it was after six-thirty. 'They're probably there by now.'

Brian in turn set his glass on the varnished wooden bar and gave the barman a nod for the bill.

'Hoofing it or cabbing it?' his friend asked when they got outside.

'I'll walk, actually.' The two men stood there on the path for a moment, in the glow of red and green neon. 'Thanks,' Ethan said. 'Happy new year.'

'Same to you. Have a good one. And if you need any help sorting out that other thing,' he said – referring, Ethan suspected, to the ring – 'give me a bell.'

'Will do.'

As Ethan turned to go, he felt something at the edge of his brain. It was that feeling again, but now it was accentuated by Brian's comment about taking his time. Time was exactly what he *didn't* have. If he could just make a decision, some sort of decision, and act on it . . .

Yes, that's what he needed. And Daisy needed it too.

Action. Pulling on his gloves, Ethan noticed on his wrist the bracelet Vanessa had given him. He remembered the quote and mumbled it to himself: 'She loved him with too clear a vision to fear his cloudiness.'

'No, nothing to fear here,' he said, trudging towards home in the melting snow, with a warm cushion of alcohol to buoy him. He was going home to make dinner for his two girls. They would have a nice meal, maybe cosy up by the fireplace and watch some television.

Vanessa would stay the night and Ethan would make sure she knew exactly how he felt about her. Maybe he would even bring up the subject of the future. He still wanted the ring to be a surprise, but if they broached the subject as to where the relationship was headed, surely the tension that had existed between them since Christmas would dissipate?

A few minutes later he arrived back at the town house and, opening the door, immediately smelled garlic. The place was strangely quiet considering that Daisy and Vanessa were both there; at least Ethan assumed they were because Vanessa's Volvo was parked outside. 'Where are my lovely ladies?' he called out.

'Hi, Dad,' Daisy cried, coming straight from her room. She was still dressed in her leotard and pink tutu and looked adorable.

'Hi, buttercup. How was dance class?'

'It was fine. Vanessa was a bit late to pick me up, so I just practised for a few more minutes. Come on. She's in the kitchen. We've been looking at my drawings – and yours too,' she continued chirpily, leading to where Vanessa sat on one of the three bar stools in front of the small kitchen island.

'Hi, darling,' he said, kissing her cheek. Then he noticed she was just finishing some Milanese chicken. 'Oh! You've already eaten?'

'Yes, we couldn't wait. Dinner was ready for six, like we agreed.'

'Oh.' Instantly Ethan felt wrong-footed.

'I called your mobile to check how much longer you'd be but there was no reply.'

Sure enough, there was a missed-call notice on the screen of Ethan's phone. 'I mustn't have felt it vibrating while I was walking back. I just met Brian for a glass and a catch-up.'

'*A* glass? Smells like quite a bit more to me,' she replied, with a smile that Ethan knew belied her annoyance.

'I'm really sorry. I was sure we'd said seven . . .'

'It's OK, Dad. We saved some for you.' But Ethan didn't really hear Daisy. Instead, he was surveying the pictures she had drawn of the trip, which were sprawled across the island unit. Just as she'd said, she and Vanessa had been looking through them. 'I showed Vanessa where she is in this one,' his daughter continued.

'Yes, nice to see I am in one.' Vanessa laughed but he could hear the edge in her tone. She rinsed her plate and put it in the dishwasher. 'All your favourite memories of our trip – you should put those in a scrapbook, Daisy. Yours, too, Ethan.' Her voice had enough sincerity in it to appease Daisy, but Ethan knew well that she wasn't happy. 'That one of you and Daisy eating cookies is lovely,' she said, idly picking up the picture of their meeting with Rachel. 'And this must be the agent you met?'

'Yes.' Ethan nodded, non-committally.

'It was the best trip ever, wasn't it?' Daisy said, smiling, and he grasped at the opportunity to change the subject.

'Definitely. Especially because it was your first real trip, honey; but there will be more. The three of us will take many more trips together,' he said pointedly. 'Maybe next

time Vanessa can choose the destination.' He paused, waiting for her to agree.

'Maybe,' she replied. 'Are you finished with this already,
Daisy? You didn't eat much.'

'No, I'll have some more now. I just wanted to wait for
Dad.'

Ethan helped her up onto the stool and shrugged
awkwardly at Vanessa. He grabbed the plate and put it in
the microwave to warm it up. Then he warmed his own and
took a seat, while Vanessa kept moving about, cleaning the
counter and adding more dishes to the washer.

'Leave those; I'll get them later,' he told her. 'Come and
sit with us.' He reached out and gently rubbed her arm.
'There's some chocolate ice cream in the freezer for all of
us when we're finished. I'm so sorry I was late.'

She finally turned around. 'No, you two carry on. I think
I'm going to call it a night, actually. I'm planning an early
start tomorrow. Lots to catch up on.'

'No, no, please stay. I was really looking forward to us
having a nice evening, just the three of us,' Ethan said, dropping his fork and taking both of her hands in his.

'Ethan . . .' Vanessa looked straight into his eyes, the bar
stool putting them at the same eye level. 'Not this time.
Sorry.' She pulled away and grabbed her bag off the counter.
'Goodnight, Daisy,' she said, rubbing the top of the little
girl's head and planting a kiss on her wavy locks.

'Night,' Daisy replied, her focus squarely on the food in
front of her.

Ethan jumped up to see Vanessa out and she stayed ahead
of him the whole time, taking her coat off the back of the
couch and continuing into the hall without missing a beat.
He managed to slip in front of her by the door. Holding
her face in his hands, he looked at her intently. 'I'm sorry.

I know you're annoyed with me and I also know I've been a little . . . off, lately. It's not you, honestly. You're wonderful. I love you and Daisy loves you too. We're a team, the three of us, aren't we?'

'Dad, *Finding Nemo* is on soon! Can we watch it?' came Daisy's shout from the kitchen.

Vanessa closed her eyes for a couple of seconds and pressed her lips together.

'Just a second, hon,' Ethan called back, exasperated. He turned to Vanessa. 'Look, I'll phone you in the morning. Daisy's going to Tanya's house so let's have lunch tomorrow, just the two of us. That's if you're not too busy.'

Vanessa hesitated, then nodded. 'OK, that would be nice.' She turned to go, and Ethan listened to her footsteps move away from him down the path, just as Daisy's came towards him from the kitchen.

Chapter 14

At seven p.m. on New Year's Eve, Terri was running around the bistro making last-minute preparations before everyone started arriving for Rachel and Gary's engagement party. They'd closed the place after lunch today, as originally intended, Rachel suggesting they should use the night off as an opportunity to celebrate the big event.

For some reason, Terri felt that tonight seemed to mark a huge shift in her and Rachel's shared history; it was a separation of paths, as such. It was inevitable, of course, and deep down Terri always knew that Rachel would be the first one to settle down, but the engagement had happened so suddenly that she felt rather . . . bereft.

With a guilty pang, she tried to shake these negative (or were they envious?) thoughts out of her mind. Rachel adored Gary and, given this engagement, the feeling had to be mutual, so really she should be happy for them.

And she had to hand it to him for surprising Rachel in New York like that, and paying out so much for that whopper of a ring. Her eyes had nearly popped out of her head when she'd seen the size of it, and she felt bad for having clearly misjudged Gary Knowles, whom up to now she'd taken for a tightwad. She could hardly be blamed for it, given that the guy took advantage by routinely eating (and drinking) in Stromboli and yet never putting a hand in his pocket.

In preparation for tonight, Terri had spent the morning in a corner of the kitchen (much to Justin's chagrin), baking various breads and pastries to accompany the savoury canapés for Rachel's New Year's Eve-cum-engagement party.

Just then the chef walked through the swinging kitchen door, closely followed by an excited-looking Rachel.

'You still here?' he teased. 'Everything's organised and ready to go, so you girls should just go off and get ready and, more importantly, get out from under my feet.'

Justin had been with Terri and Rachel since the beginning and was practically a part of the furniture at Stromboli now. Besides his talent in the kitchen, they also appreciated Justin for his rapid-fire wit and good humour and for keeping the waiting staff smiling when the place was filled to capacity at weekends.

'Terri!' Rachel gasped and she could tell that her friend was already flustered. 'Why are you still doing things in the kitchen?'

'I know, I know – I'm going now.' She wiped her hands and put some fresh blinis in the fridge. 'Just wanted to make sure we have enough of everything.'

Rachel paused then, and by the look on her face Terri suspected she was about to go all emotional on them, as she was prone to do.

'Look, just in case I don't get to say it tonight,' Rachel began, tears shining in her eyes, and Terri smiled, 'thanks for helping me pull this party together so quickly. I know it was a lot to ask you to do, to give up your night off, and I want you to know how much I appreciate not just your efforts tonight, but the two of you as friends, and . . .' She paused, waving her hand in the air as if this would somehow stop her from blubbing. 'This is such a huge and truly unexpected step in my life, and thanks for helping me celebrate it.'

The sincerity in her voice merely made Terri feel worse for thinking badly of Gary before.

'Have you been on the vino again?' she joked, by now well used to Rachel's emotional outpourings. Her friend was an unbelievable softie and had this unyielding ability to remain positive and see the good in everything; it was something that Terri envied. 'You silly goose, of course we're going to help you celebrate! It's not as though we need much of an excuse, and anyway we're thrilled for you – aren't we, Justin?'

'You deserve every happiness, Rachel, and this is going to be a great party.'

Rachel beamed. 'Thanks, guys. And you're right, I'd better make a move, otherwise I'll be wearing my kitchen whites in all the photos. Back in ten?'

When she exited the kitchen Terri met Justin's eye. 'Nice dodge,' she said sardonically.

He shrugged. 'Unlike some people, I'm not going to lie and say I'm *happy* about it.'

'What do you mean? She's my friend; of course I'm happy for her.' Although Justin largely shared her opinion of Gary, Terri was horrified to think that the chef might have picked up on any misgivings she felt about the engagement. Or worse, that Rachel might have done.

'You're happy that she's marrying a Neanderthal? Some best friend you are.'

Despite herself, Terri had to smile. There had never been any love lost between Justin and Gary, who typically avoided each other like the plague. It was patently obvious that Gary was hugely uncomfortable about their chef's sexuality and, devil that he was, Justin camped it up to the hilt whenever Gary was around.

She shrugged and leaned against the kitchen worktop. 'What do you want me to say? If she's happy that's all that matters, isn't it?'

'Hmm, we'll see,' the chef replied. 'But from where I'm standing, this supposed fairy-tale engagement has horror show written all over it.'

In the small back office of the bistro, where she'd left a change of clothes, Rachel picked up her handbag and rummaged inside it for the gorgeous, sparkling diamond that she still couldn't believe was hers.

Since Gary had put it on her finger in New York she couldn't stop looking at the ring, and hated not being able to wear it all the time. Although – not that she was complaining, or would ever say anything to Gary – it was actually a bit big and awkward for someone who worked with her hands so much. This was something she hadn't thought about until she was back in the kitchen again and it had got caught up in some fresh cookie dough.

Still, this was a tiny inconvenience that Rachel could happily overlook for the privilege of owning such a perfect expression of love and devotion. Suddenly she put a hand to her forehead. Cookie dough! Thinking of cookies, she'd completely forgotten about that man Ethan Greene and her promise to send some to London for his little girl.

She had missed a call from him the day she and Gary got home from New York, and what with jet lag and organising the party, she had completely forgotten to call him back. She made a mental note to remind Gary to phone him soon; her fiancé would no doubt want to thank him, and they could make arrangements to have the cookies sent over.

Rachel slipped out of her chef's whites, jeans and T-shirt and into her red dress, the same one she had worn on

Christmas Eve. After all, Gary hadn't got to see it that night, so it seemed fitting that she should wear it now.

She pulled on her thigh-high stay-up stockings and fished her favourite dangly, faux antique earrings out of a pouch on the side of her handbag. Then, having applied just enough make-up to accent her almond-shaped eyes and redden her full lips, she finally smiled at herself in the mirror of the small adjoining bathroom. The lighting wasn't great, but she knew she looked the part. How could she not? She had never been so happy.

'Knock, knock . . .' she heard Terri say from outside the office door.

'Come in! I'm almost ready.'

'I don't know why you wouldn't just go upstairs to my place to get changed and . . .' Catching sight of her fully dressed, Terri's words trailed off. She raised both hands to the sides of her face. 'Wow, you look stunning! I love the dress.' Then she paused and shook her head. 'Look at the two of us and how far we've come since traipsing around as students barely able to make ends meet. We could hardly afford bus tickets back then, whereas now . . .' She shook her head. 'With this business and your wedding – suddenly I feel all grown-up.'

Rachel was taken aback. Unlike herself, who got emotional at the drop of a hat, it was very rare for her ultra-cynical friend to show her softer side. She hugged Terri, her eyes welling up again. 'Oh stop with the fuzzy stuff; you'll ruin my make-up!'

'Nonsense. A trail of mascara from your eyes to your cleavage is considered sexy these days,' Terri laughed, pulling back.

'Are you OK?' Rachel asked her softly.

'I'm fine. Actually, I don't know where that came from,'

she replied, sounding much more like herself again. 'We both know you're the sappy one in this friendship. And not only that but you're also the one who should be teary, what with being the bride-to-be and all . . .'

Rachel smiled.

'Ah, I don't know,' Terri continued. 'I think maybe the engagement just caught me so completely unawares that I'm still trying to get my head around it.'

'I know exactly what you mean.' As it was, Rachel felt as though her brain was still trying to catch up with her heart, or vice versa. 'Are you sure you're happy to be my brides-maid?'

Terri's eyes widened. 'Are you joking? Wild horses couldn't stop me, although I don't envy you having to find a dress to match this rug,' she added wryly, indicating her riot of red hair. With Terri's pale Irish skin, which contrasted widely with Rachel's sallow complexion, the two women couldn't have looked more different. 'So what did Gary's mum say? Was she thrilled?'

Rachel shrugged. 'Well I wasn't there when he told her, but I think she had pretty much the same reaction as every-one else, to be honest; she was a bit taken aback. Although Gary says she's delighted too, of course, and the great thing is, she's coming along tonight!' She was especially thrilled about that, and so looking forward to meeting her future mother-in-law. Her mother-in-law, imagine!

'Fantastic,' Terri said. 'Well, I suppose I'd better go home and get changed myself.' She didn't have far to go, 'home' being the little flat above the bistro. 'We're pretty much good to go outside, so you take your time getting ready and—' She turned for the door, but then paused.

Rachel looked up. 'What?'

Terri shook her head. 'It's nothing. I was just thinking

what a brilliant way to end our year. And next year will be even better, what with the big day itself, won't it?'

Rachel hesitated a little. She and Gary hadn't actually set a date yet; in all honesty, they hadn't really had a chance to discuss it since their return from New York. But yes, like Terri, she automatically presumed the wedding would be in the coming year. Personally, she hated long-drawn-out engagements – what was the point? And seeing as the proposal had more or less come out of the blue, she was certain Gary felt the same.

'Should be, but lots to sort out yet.'

'And plenty of celebrating to be done too!' her friend said with a wink, before going back out to the restaurant.

'You can say that again.' Rachel grinned, straightening the fitted dress along her thighs.

Chapter 15

Ethan was sitting in the kitchen of the town house drinking a glass of wine, waiting for Vanessa to arrive. It was New Year's Eve, and he had arranged for Daisy to spend the night at her friend Tanya's house as he really felt he needed some alone time with Vanessa.

He was determined to make tonight special. He had champagne on ice and had spent the day preparing a lavish meal in the hope of showing her a good time, and making her realise just how committed he was to her.

He couldn't help wishing that things could be different, and that instead of him secretly fretting about how he was supposed to get the ring back, they could tonight be discussing their impending nuptials. But he'd thought a lot about how he could at least show her he was committed; prove to her that their relationship meant a lot more than a simple silver charm bracelet – that *she* meant much more than that.

Then a thought popped into his mind and his pulse quickened. Of course!

But Ethan didn't have time to ponder his revelation further, as just then the doorbell rang and he got up to answer it.

Vanessa stood at the door looking exquisite. She always looked amazing but tonight she was dressed in a well-cut, black cocktail dress that fitted her slim frame to perfection.

Her blonde hair was piled elegantly on top of her head and a simple pear-shaped diamond pendant adorned her throat. His future bride, he thought. If only she knew it.

'Hello, darling. You look beautiful.' Ethan wondered why he sounded so wooden, so stilted all of a sudden. Why the uneasy formality?

She smiled and stepped into the hallway. 'Thank you.' Placing a light kiss on his cheek as she passed, she moved into the living room, taking off her coat.

'Why did you ring the doorbell? Did you forget your key?' he asked, trying to make light of the situation.

She blushed a little. 'I don't know really.' Again the formality. She looked around the room. 'Where's Daisy?'

'She's staying over with one of her friends. I thought it might be good to make tonight just about you and me.'

'Oh, that's nice.' Vanessa smiled again, but it didn't reach her eyes and Ethan felt his heart deflate. This is so awkward, he thought. It was as if all of their shared history had suddenly been erased and they were starting over from scratch.

'Would you like a glass of wine?' Ethan enquired.

'Yes, if you're having some.'

He moved to the kitchen and picked up the bottle of red that he had already opened. When he turned around, he noticed the tense expression on her face. It took him aback. He needed to change the mood here – and quickly.

'Here you go.' He handed her a glass and held out his own for a toast. But she didn't wait, instead bringing the glass to her mouth and drinking deeply. 'Er, cheers,' he said lamely.

'Oops! Sorry.' Laughing a little, she belatedly clinked his.

Ethan perched on one of the high stools at the edge of the kitchen island. 'Do you know, I heard that you should always try to end a year the way you started it.'

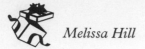

'Is that so?'

'Yes. And this time last year, you and I were very happy, remember?'

'Ethan—' Vanessa began, and there was a note of pleading in her voice.

'No, just let me finish, please. I know there has been some tension between us lately, especially since New York, and, well . . . frankly, it wasn't there before. I love you, Vanessa. Daisy loves you. I need you in my life and I want you to be happy.'

Vanessa lowered her gaze. Whether it was because of the emotion of the moment or the strain in the room, he didn't know.

'Ethan, I am happy. I just . . . You're right, there is some tension, and I thought . . .' she trailed off, shaking her head.

He got up off the stool and putting her wine glass aside, took both of her hands in his. 'Regardless, none of that matters now. Well, it does, but . . .' He shook his head, aware that he was babbling a little. 'I wanted to talk to you about something, a serious subject.'

She brought her gaze up to meet his. 'Serious?'

'Yes,' he said, swallowing hard. He hoped this idea would go over well; it was a temporary diversion of sorts, at least until he had the ring back.

'What is it, Ethan?' A strained smile played at the corners of her mouth and he wondered what she was thinking, what she was expecting him to say.

He cleared his throat. 'Well, I was thinking that maybe we should take our relationship to the next level. Start acting more like a family.' She smiled hopefully at him and he felt his heart begin to lighten. 'Vanessa, I was thinking that maybe

we should think about moving in together. I mean, you . . .
move in with us . . .'

There was silence for a moment and his hands started
to sweat. He couldn't believe he was this nervous; after all,
if everything had gone according to plan, they should already
be engaged. In truth, he felt almost silly for worrying about
her answer to this question. But what if she said no?

Finally, Vanessa spoke. 'Move in here, with you and Daisy?'
she asked, her face brightening.

Ethan smiled and nodded. 'Yes,' he replied and immediately saw her eyes becoming teary. 'We both love you, you
must know that.'

A tear crept down her cheek and she threw her arms around
his neck. 'Oh Ethan, I feel so silly. You have no idea what I've
been thinking this past week! I thought that my being in New
York with you might have been a mistake, that it brought back
too many painful memories of—' She shook her head. 'Of
course, of *course* I will move in with you. I'd love to!'

Ethan exhaled with relief. He felt fantastic. He wasn't
sure where the idea had come from, but clearly it had been
a brainwave.

Now, all was back on track, and even though she didn't
admit it fully Ethan knew *exactly* what Vanessa had been
thinking since New York. She had obviously been worrying
that his sudden withdrawal was down to the fact that he
was still pining for Jane. All because of that stupid mix-up.
This was the perfect solution, the perfect way to let her
know he was committed, and he didn't know why he hadn't
thought of it before.

He recalled Brian's comment about taking his time and
not rushing into anything. Well, if nothing else, this at least
gave him the opportunity to buy some time, didn't it?

Time to get that ring back from Knowles so he could move on with his life and make everything absolutely perfect.

Rachel was talking on her mobile phone and smiling. It was clear from her dancing eyes that she was talking to Gary. Her eyes always looked like that, Terri thought, when she spoke to him.

Just then, Rachel ended the call and practically danced towards her. She held out her arms and impulsively embraced Terri. 'Ah, life is good when you're in love,' she gushed happily.

'And so it should be.' Despite herself, Terri's voice cracked a bit, and Rachel pulled away to look at her.

'What's wrong? You sound . . . weird.'

'Ah, you know me. All this happiness and joy just pulls at my heart,' Terri said lightly, trying to inject her usual sardonic tone into her voice, but she couldn't help thinking about what Justin had said earlier. *Was* Gary the right man for Rachel? Yes, the engagement seemed a bit out of the blue, but it was an engagement nonetheless. And any fool could see that Rachel was blissfully happy, so surely that counted for something?

'Oh give over,' Rachel chuckled. 'We both know that deep down you're a real softie.'

'Yep, that's me.' Terri looked at her watch. 'Bloody hell, it's almost eight. People will be arriving en masse soon. Tell us, where's your knight in shining armour?'

'That was him I was just talking to there. He was on his bike so I could barely hear him, but he said something about making sure we have enough beer in.' She rolled her eyes. 'You know the way those boys won't be caught dead drinking wine.'

Terri did. Gary's mates were infantile and as far as she

146

was concerned should be grateful enough about being fed and watered for free at this party without starting to make demands about the supplies. But Rachel didn't seem to mind so perhaps she shouldn't let it bother her so much either.

Then, as if on cue, five bikes zoomed down the street outside the bistro. Rachel gave a little jump and clapped her hands together. 'Here we go – party time! I'd better freshen up,' she said, scampering towards the ladies' room.

Terri headed further down the restaurant to where Justin was already handing out canapés to the first of their guests.

'Mr Wonderful and his posse have just arrived,' the head chef muttered wryly.

'Yes, I witnessed the caravan,' she said.

Shortly afterwards, Gary and his leathered-up biker friends came through the door just as Rachel came out of the ladies'. He tossed his helmet onto a nearby chair and grabbed Rachel by the waist, spinning her around. The handful of onlookers already present applauded and Gary grinned while Rachel smiled demurely at him. Then she handed out beers to him and each of his friends, before pouring a glass of champagne for herself.

Terri saw Justin suspiciously eyeing the spectacle. 'How come his Highness is only rolling in now? Wouldn't you think he'd have been here earlier to lend a hand?'

'Give him a break, Justin; this is our speciality, not his. Unless you wanted the kitchen extended or something.' Now that he was engaged to Rachel, Terri felt somewhat duty-bound to defend Gary.

'Oh my God!' The chef was standing open-mouthed, motioning in the direction of the happy couple. 'Did I just hear her ask him if he liked the dress? She had to *ask* if he liked that dress? I think I need a drink,' he gasped dramatically and Terri had to smile.

An hour later, thirty or so people were grazing their way through tray after tray of quiches, cheese plates, blinis, and a plethora of other special-occasion goodies. The DJ had finally arrived; he was a friend of Justin's, who promised to play the perfect party-mix on his iPod through the bistro's sound system.

Some people were dancing, but Terri was nursing her second glass of champagne when she looked over to see a woman standing in the doorway. There was something vaguely familiar about her, and when someone else came in behind her and a gust of wind caught her strawberry blonde hair, revealing more of her face, Terri knew in an instant who she was.

'Hello,' she said, greeting the woman warmly. 'You must be Gary's mother.'

'Yes,' the petite woman replied, looking pleased to be noticed. 'Mary Knowles. I feel terrible for being so late, but I'm a nurse and . . . well, I got a bit delayed.'

'Not at all. Everything's just getting started really. Come inside and get something to eat. Can I get you something to drink? A glass of champagne, maybe?'

The woman appeared hesitant. Her small stature initially made her seem too young to be Gary's mother but, with a closer look, Terri noted the lines in her face.

'Oh, I'm sorry, I haven't even introduced myself. I'm Terri, Rachel's friend and co-owner of this place. Isn't it great news about the engagement? You must be so proud of your son.'

Mary took a deep breath, and cocked her head to one side, as if trying to buy time while constructing an answer. 'Very proud, yes. And a bit surprised too, I have to say,' she replied, taking a sip of champagne. 'That son of mine has been in love with those bikes for so long that I never thought a woman would be able to hold his attention.'

'Mam,' Gary called out, approaching them with a smiling Rachel by his side. 'I didn't think you were going to come.'

'Why wouldn't I?' She looked at Rachel and held out a hand in greeting. 'You must be the lucky lady.'

'I'm Rachel, yes. Oh, it's so lovely to finally meet you!' Terri had to smile as typically enthusiastic, Rachel reached forward and gave the woman a warm hug.

Evidently flustered by this unexpected show of emotion, Mary reddened a little and stepped back. She looked from Rachel to her son. 'Erm . . . yes, well congratulations, both of you.'

'Thanks so much. And this is the ring – isn't it just gorgeous?' Rachel beamed, extending her hand, and Terri watched with interest as Gary's mum did an actual double-take on catching sight of the ring.

'Stunning, isn't it?' Terri said, and Mary just nodded, apparently dumbstruck.

She looked curiously at her son, as if trying to work out when Gary had become Mr Generous all of sudden. 'I'd say you spent a fair few quid on that.'

Gary didn't meet his mum's gaze and Terri sensed that something unspoken was hanging between them. 'Ah, well, you know yourself . . .'

Mary smiled at Rachel. 'It's beautiful.'

'Thanks. I must admit it was a big surprise, but a lovely one. Your son really is an old romantic at heart,' she added, looking lovingly at Gary. Then she clapped her hands together. 'So, now that everyone's here . . .'

Terri watched her dash up to the DJ and seconds later the music dropped to background volume.

Rachel stood by the buffet tables and asked for everyone's attention.

'Thanks,' she smiled, as people hushed their conversations. 'First of all, Gary and I both want to thank you for spending your New Year's Eve with us and helping us celebrate our engagement.' She looked at Gary who just shrugged and looked back at her.

Out of sight of Mrs Knowles, Justin rolled his eyes at Gary's offhand response while Terri bit her lip and stifled a smile.

'Secondly,' Rachel went on, and her voice caught a little, 'as you know, my family is part Sicilian, and I'd like to continue a tradition we Sicilians have, in honour of my parents, who I know would be so proud to see this. It's also in honour of all of you, who have practically become family to me too.' Her eyes shining, she leaned down and took out a basket of bread from beneath the linen-covered table. 'Many of you will have tried my Sicilian olive bread or some variation of it already. Well, this,' she said with a sway of her hips and dramatic wave of her hand, 'is the authentic recipe. For those of you who don't know, it comes from my great-great-grandmother. In Sicilian tradition, this particular recipe is made only for special occasions, and is symbolic of sharing wholeheartedly in the occasion and its fruition. So, if I could ask my husband-to-be to come up and join me in taking a piece . . .' she said, entreating Gary with a smile. 'And then we'll pass around some for you all.'

Everyone clapped as Gary sauntered up to Rachel. She took one piece of bread in her own hand and gave another to Gary, entwining their arms in the traditional wedding pose used for a toast. She took a huge bite and then continued to eat the entire slice, smiling as she did so.

Gary ate a little of his before setting it back down on the table. 'One of the downsides of marrying a chef is that it's bad for the old waistline,' he joked, laughing and patting his stomach. His mates joined in the joke, raising their glasses and shouting.

'Oh . . . dear . . . God,' Justin said, coming up beside Terri. 'And I thought gay men were vain.'

'But there is something I would like to do,' Gary continued then and Rachel's face brightened.

'As you probably heard, I was in a very bad accident recently, and, believe me, if there's any justice in life the gobshite that did it will get what's coming to him,' he said, jaw tightening. 'Anyway, I was pretty battered and beaten by the time I got out of the hospital, but that didn't stop me from continuing with my plans.' He winked at his fiancée. 'If anything, it made the surprise even better. Poor Rachel probably felt a bit like I did when that cab hit me, although of course she didn't have to suffer these ribs.' Everyone laughed as he paused and made a great show of rubbing his midsection. 'So,' he said, turning to her, 'seeing as I didn't get the chance to do this properly the first time . . .' He cocked his head towards Rachel and, after a beat, she figured out his train of thought and took off her ring, handing it to him. With that, and after first making sure everyone had managed to get a good look at the ring, Gary dropped to one knee.

'Rachel Conti, will you marry me?' he asked and all the guests cheered.

'Of course I will.' There were tears in Rachel's eyes as Gary slipped the ring back into place.

Justin tut-tutted and shook his head. 'Drama queen,' he muttered darkly.

Terri was thoughtful. 'I don't know. Look, we've always thought that Gary was a prat of the highest order, but maybe we should give him a break? Looks like he's really into this.'

The chef sighed. 'Well, think what you like, but if you

ask me there's something very wrong with this picture. The guy has the emotional development of a sea urchin and I for one can't believe he was planning this before they left, let alone that he'd shell out for a rock that size.'

Terri's gaze returned to Rachel and Gary. They still had their arms around each other and looked very much like a normal, happy, engaged couple. She looked sideways at Justin. 'You're not jealous, are you?' she teased, nudging him. 'That Rachel is going to have this big white wedding?'

He snorted. 'Oh come on!' Then he shook his head. 'No, I just can't believe that our Rachel is actually going to marry this amoeba. Why? What the hell does she see in him? I know she says he makes her laugh, but is it intentional?'

Terri shrugged. 'Each to their own, I suppose. Just because you and I are hopeless in the relationship department doesn't mean we should be cynical about everyone else.'

'Speak for yourself, sweetheart. I know Bernard and I fight like cats but we're going through a really good patch at the moment.'

'Knowing you two, that will last for all of a week.'

'Actually I'll have you know that he's planning something really special for our day off tomorrow and . . . oh, speaking of which –' Justin reached into his pocket '– these two phone messages came in while you and Rachel were getting ready earlier. One from the accountant; he was rambling something about an end-of-year VAT return?' He shook his head. 'Don't ask; you know all that stuff is gobbledegook to me. And there's another from a guy called Ethan Greene, which I forgot to give to Rachel.' He handed her two slips of paper. 'He was calling from London – *very* sexy accent – and seemed a bit frantic to be honest . . . something about a big mix-up in New York with Gary.' He made a face and rolled his eyes. 'God only knows. Anyway, he said he called Rachel's mobile and got this number from her voicemail message. Can you pass it on to her tomorrow?'

'Of course.' Terri read the piece of paper, frowning. A mix-up – with Gary? What was all that about?

She looked across at Rachel's betrothed, who, having played the part of the dutiful fiancé, was now right back in the middle of his mates, handing out beer as if it was going out of style, while Rachel did the polite thing and circulated among the guests.

'What?' Justin asked, shrewd as always. 'I think I know that look.'

She shook her head. 'Nothing.'

But, for some reason, Terri had an underlying sense that this call was significant. What kind of 'mix-up' could have happened in New York? Something to do with the accident, maybe? Why else would some English guy be phoning here frantically looking for Gary?

She bit her lip. Maybe Justin was right; maybe there *was* something wrong with this picture.

What else had Gary been up to in New York?

Chapter 16

'Dad, you should phone the restaurant again,' Daisy urged Ethan, sounding much older than she was. He smiled at her advice. It was now the second of January and despite his previous attempts to get in touch with Rachel over the holiday period, she hadn't returned his calls.

He was loath to be too much of a pest, especially when she'd been so nice before; but nice or not, he needed to get his ring back.

'I know, Daisy, I know.' He picked up the phone. 'So you really are OK with Vanessa moving in?'

She sighed heavily. 'Dad, if you'd asked her to marry you she would have moved in eventually, wouldn't she? So, since I was OK with that . . .'

'All right, all right.' It wasn't exactly what he wanted to hear but Daisy was correct, and there was little point in pestering her with unnecessary questions. 'OK. Let's get this sorted out once and for all.'

This time there would be no pussyfooting around. He would explain the situation to Rachel and outline in full what had happened. Anyway, chances were she and Gary Knowles would have worked it all out by now and he wouldn't have to explain anything.

'Then why haven't they contacted you?' his subconscious mind asked, but Ethan chose to ignore it.

Having dialled Rachel's mobile number, he waited as the

line connected in Ireland. He really hoped she would answer this time, rather than leaving him to explain himself again to some worker at her restaurant, who obviously hadn't bothered to pass on his last message. Finally, on the fourth ring, the line was picked up.

'Hello?'

'Rachel? This is Ethan Greene.' When there was no immediate reply he added, 'We met in New York recently?'

'Ethan, of course!' she exclaimed. 'Oh my God, I'm so sorry. Don't mind me; my mind is all over the place these days. Yes, I got your message from before, and passed your number on to Gary. He hasn't called you back?'

'Ah, no – he hasn't.'

There was a brief silence. 'Really? I was sure he would have done by now . . . Look, let me apologise on his behalf. I know he's been up to his eyes since we got back, and with so much going on too . . . But I do know he really wants to talk to you, and to thank you, of course, for that lovely thing you did for him.'

'About that—'

'And we've just got engaged, so I think that's possibly the reason why he simply hasn't had time to contact you yet,' she went on blithely and Ethan went white. 'We've been so busy since we came back. We had a big engagement party and everything.'

Ethan wasn't sure what to think. There wasn't a chance that . . . no, surely not?

Gary Knowles wouldn't have been stupid enough to swipe the ring and use it to propose to his girlfriend, would he? What right-minded person would do such a thing? Then a thought struck him: what if the guy *wasn't* actually in his right mind? Perhaps his brain had been damaged in the accident, and he had a touch of amnesia or something similar, which

meant that he didn't know anything about a mistake and may very well believe the ring was his.

Trying to work it out, Ethan's mind raced and he saw Daisy look at him curiously.

'You just got engaged?' he mumbled. 'When?'

Rachel laughed. 'Gary proposed right after he got out of the hospital. I couldn't believe it. Apparently he had the proposal all planned for Christmas Eve, had even just bought the ring at Tiffany's and everything, but then of course the accident put the kybosh on that.'

Ethan's insides dropped and his fists automatically clenched. 'And how is he – after the accident, I mean?' he asked through gritted teeth. 'Did he suffer any lasting injuries?'

'Nothing major, thank goodness,' she confirmed. 'Really, you're so good to be concerned, but luckily it all worked out OK.'

'No head damage?' Ethan persisted. 'Memory problems? Anything like that?'

'No, nothing at all like that.' Now Rachel sounded a bit taken aback. 'According to the doctors he's fine. Why do you ask?'

'I just wasn't sure. I thought he might have had a bit of a bump on his head when I found him, but maybe I was mistaken,' Ethan said, thinking fast.

Damn, what the hell was going on here? Was the guy that much of an immoral crook that he would seriously try to pass off Ethan's ring as his own? It was obvious that he had no such proposal in mind before the accident, seeing as his Tiffany's purchase had consisted only of a simple charm bracelet.

Ethan's heart hammered. What on earth should he do now?

Or, more pertinently, what should he say?

Yet how could he burst this poor girl's bubble now by telling her the truth? Rachel seemed way too nice to be marrying someone so obviously thoughtless and devious. To think that the guy would be so barefaced . . .

Then a sudden anger flared up within him. Damn it, the time for talking was well and truly over. This was definitely something that needed to be sorted out in person, Ethan decided determinedly. He would go straight to Dublin and pay this Gary Knowles a visit. He'd sort out this entire situation face to face, man to man.

Realising that the line had gone quiet, he snapped back to reality. 'Well, congratulations.' Given what Rachel had just told him, it was the obvious response, although the word tasted like bile as he forced himself to say it.

'Thank you very much. Everything has happened just so fast, and of course there's so much to do and plan and . . . oh listen to me! I'm Bridezilla already! You don't want to hear about this.'

You can say that again, Ethan thought wryly.

'Actually, now that I have you,' she continued cheerfully, 'can you let me know your address so I can send your lovely daughter those cookies I promised her? I would have done it before now but, as I said, things have been so crazy since Christmas. I'll bake a fresh batch and send them over to you by courier today.'

At this, Ethan had an instant flash of inspiration. 'No, don't do that. I'll come and collect them actually.'

'Collect them?'

'Yes. You're in Dublin, aren't you? Well, as it happens, I actually have some business there next weekend, and you mentioned something about having a café? So if you let me know where you are based, I could pop in and pick them up. Perhaps catch up with your fiancé while I'm there.'

He knew it was a weak story but in all honesty he didn't care. What business would he – an English language lecturer – have in Dublin? He held his breath, almost waiting for Rachel to call his bluff or at least question his motives. However, if anything seemed amiss to her, she pretended not to notice.

'Oh. Well, it's a bistro, not a café, and it's called Stromboli. We're just on the quays, not far from the Ha'penny Bridge. Do you know the bridge? The building is painted deep purple and our sign is bright orange so you really shouldn't have any trouble finding us. We're hard to miss,' she laughed. 'Yes, it would be lovely to see you and I'll let Gary know you'll be in town.'

'Actually, probably best not to arrange anything too concrete for the moment, just in case I'm caught for time.' Ethan didn't want to give the fiancé too much of a heads-up about his arrival, in case the guy decided to do a runner. With a man like that, who knew? 'If I do have some free time, I'll pop in for lunch or something. Would that be all right?' He sincerely hoped he could get a weekend reservation at the Westbury, the only hotel he knew in Dublin that was centrally located.

'Yes, absolutely. But are you sure you don't want me to send over those cookies, just in case? I really wanted to do something, however small, to thank you. And it goes without saying that if you do have the time to see us while you're in Dublin, then lunch is on us!'

'Thank you, but really no thanks are necessary. With luck, perhaps I'll see you at the weekend.'

'Looking forward to it. Oh and tell Daisy I said hi, won't you?'

'I certainly will. Goodbye, Rachel.'

His brain hammering in his head, Ethan hung up the phone and exhaled deeply.

Daisy was using the famous squinty-eyed look on him. 'Why didn't you tell her about the mix-up with the bags, Dad?' she asked.

Ethan felt his mouth go dry. Yes, why didn't he? After all, he didn't know this woman, and it wasn't up to him to protect her feelings; he should really have just said something there and then. He looked at his daughter. 'Her boyfriend seems to have used our ring to propose,' he told her and Daisy's eyes widened.

'What? Oh no!'

'So I thought it might be better to say nothing just now, so as not to hurt Rachel's feelings.'

'That is really nice of you, Dad,' his daughter said, patting his hand. 'So that's why you're going to Dublin?' she asked. 'To sort everything out with that man?'

Ethan nodded tiredly. 'Yes.'

Yes, that was him, he thought irritably: too bloody 'nice' for his own good. Brian would have an absolute field day with this. Ethan knew his friend would have no compunction about telling it straight on the phone, especially considering the circumstances. But Rachel seemed like such a sweet person, and sounded so deliriously happy about her supposed fairy-tale engagement that he just couldn't bring himself to break the poor girl's heart by coming clean.

Well, come the following weekend, Ethan decided grimly, it remained to be seen how nice he would remain when Gary Knowles's thieving mug was in front of him.

Chapter 17

'Who was that?' Terri enquired when Rachel hung up the phone.

They were in the kitchen prepping for the bistro's evening sitting and she was up to her elbows in chopped peppers and red onions. 'Did I hear you say something about making cookies? I checked earlier and we've still got loads.'

Rachel was rolling out fresh pasta. 'No, it's fine. I was going to send some to Ethan, but there's no need.'

'Who?' Terri asked. The name sounded familiar but she just didn't know why.

'Ethan Greene. The nice English man who helped Gary after he had his accident in New York. Remember I told you about him before?'

'Of course.' She had forgotten about this so-called Good Samaritan until Rachel explained about him again when Terri had passed on the guy's New Year's Eve phone message. 'Didn't Gary phone him back afterwards?'

Her friend coloured a little. 'It seems not. It was a bit embarrassing, actually. I thought Gary would have got in touch with him in the meantime, considering . . . Still, I suppose he's been busy with work and everything.'

Some stranger saves Gary's life and he doesn't have the courtesy to pick up the phone and thank him? And even worse, the man who helped him was clearly anxious to hear about his condition and make sure he was OK. Not only that but poor Rachel was being saddled as go-between. Well, romantic proposal aside, this sounded very much like the Gary of old, Terri thought uncharitably.

'You shouldn't feel bad. It's not your fault that Gary hasn't bothered to call him back.'

'Oh no, it's not that; I'm sure it just slipped his mind. Anyway, it turns out he might be here on business at the weekend, so hopefully the two of them will get a chance to have a good catch-up chat then.'

'Who might be here at the weekend?'

'Didn't you hear me on the phone just now? Ethan Greene, of course.'

Terri frowned. Didn't Rachel say that this guy was some kind of professor or something? 'What kind of business would a professor be doing in Dublin?' she queried dubiously.

Rachel shrugged, her body language indicating that, unlike Terri, she was completely uncurious about it. 'A university lecturer, and I have no idea. Maybe he's organising some kind of field trip or something.'

'I don't remember any field trips to other countries when we were in college, especially at weekends, do you?'

'Well, who knows? And besides, what does it matter? If it weren't for him, Gary could have died or been robbed or something even more horrible than what happened. I'll be only too happy to get the opportunity to thank Ethan again in person.'

'And he said he's coming here to the bistro – to see Gary?'

It seemed very strange to Terri, or not entirely coincidental, that this Ethan Greene person, whom Gary had met in New York but lived in London and was a university professor, was suddenly about to appear in Dublin at the weekend.

'Yes, if he has the time.' Rachel paused and looked at her. 'Why all the questions?'

Terri stopped what she was doing and put one hand on her hip. 'Well, it just seems a bit strange, doesn't it? For someone who doesn't even know him, this guy seems very interested in Gary's condition. You said yourself he called the hospital in New York and he's been phoning here too.'

Rachel laughed lightly. 'Such a suspicious mind, as usual! I don't see how someone being interested in Gary's well-being is such a big deal. You weren't there, Terri; you didn't see how banged-up he was.'

'I know, but if this Greene guy is a stranger, why would he care?'

'Of course he's a stranger. What else would he be? He's a really lovely guy; you should have seen all the nurses mooning over him,' Rachel said.

Terri cocked an interested eyebrow. 'So he's good-looking too?'

'Yes.' Rachel looked sideways at her. 'Actually, if he does appear this weekend, maybe I should introduce you two,' she said with a knowing grin. 'Granted, he has a daughter, but for some reason I get the impression that he's single.'

Terri stiffened. 'Cripes, just because you're Miss Loved-up Bride-to-be, stop trying to foist me onto every male specimen in sight. I'm grand as I am, thank you very much.'

Still, if this Greene guy had the New York nurses mooning over him like Rachel said, maybe he might be a worth a look?

'OK, OK, you're right. I'm sorry.' Rachel laughed, Terri's love life (or lack of it) being a well-worn argument between the two of them. 'But, honestly, he's lovely: very English, all manners. He even offered his congratulations on my engagement earlier, which I thought was nice of him.'

Terri looked again at her friend, who'd continued calmly rolling out pasta, and couldn't believe why Rachel wasn't wondering more about this impending visit. But that was Rachel, wasn't it? Happy to take everything at face value, irrespective of the circumstances. Terri shook her head. Maybe her friend was right; perhaps she was too suspicious and sceptical about things for her own good.

But with Justin's suggestion on New Year's Eve that there was something 'off' about the engagement – as well as their long-held mutual misgivings towards Gary – she just couldn't help it.

The two settled back into their work, and were making idle small talk about this and that, when the door leading from the dining area burst open, and in strode the man himself.

Gary was dressed in his biking clothes, and Terri wrinkled her nose at the smell of leather and exhaust fumes drifting off him. She hoped Rachel would shoo him out quickly, as she didn't like having him around the food-preparation area dressed like that.

But that didn't happen, because as soon as Gary walked in Rachel's face lit up with a smile. 'Hey there! What are you doing here? Shouldn't you be at work?'

He shrugged indolently. 'Nothing much doing, to be honest, only a few jobs to price and I've done that, so I took the rest of the day off.' He stepped back a little as Rachel reached forward to embrace him. 'Hey, babe, watch that flour on my jacket,' he chided.

'Oh, of course,' Rachel said, pulling back. 'Sorry. I wasn't thinking.' She grabbed a dishtowel and began to wipe off the flour spots she had left on Gary's precious leather jacket.

Terri sighed inwardly. Yep, the dashing Romeo from New Year's Eve had now well and truly disappeared, only to be

replaced by the Gary they all knew and . . . didn't love. What on earth did Rachel see in him?

She watched Gary just stand there and let Rachel fuss over him. Then a thought suddenly popped into her head, and she bit her lip, deciding to see if this particular cat might upset any pigeons.

'Gary, you'll be interested in this. Rachel just got another phone call from Ethan Greene,' she said, watching him closely.

'Who's Ethan Greene?' Gary enquired blankly and Terri could almost picture the wheels grinding slowly in his mind.

'The man who helped you, silly – after the accident?' Rachel reminded him. 'He and his little daughter made sure you got to the hospital safely.'

A strange look flitted across Gary's face, and instinctively Terri felt the hairs on the back of her neck stand to attention. Something else was going on here, she was sure of it. The problem was that she couldn't figure out what.

'He called here?' he asked, his voice catching just a tad on the word 'here'.

Terri nodded. 'Yes, just a couple of minutes ago.' She kept her eyes glued to Gary's face; he was like an open book in situations like this. Probably because he wasn't smart enough to hide anything that might betray him.

'What did he want?' he asked, looking at Rachel.

She shrugged easily. 'He just wanted to check up on you, see if you were OK. It was a bit embarrassing actually, love. I thought you would have phoned him by now.'

'Yeah, I was going to but I – I lost the number.'

Yeah and I'm Nigella Lawson, Terri thought sardonically. Hmm, there was definitely something up here. But what?

'Yes, I thought it must have been something like that,' Rachel replied. 'Naturally, I told him you were fine. He's so nice really, but, to be honest, I think he was more worried than was strictly necessary.' She laughed lightly. 'Then again, I suppose I wasn't the one who picked you up off the street, was I? But thinking about it again, it truly was a wonderful thing he did for you, Gary, and you a complete stranger too. We should be very grateful to him.'

'Right,' Gary grunted, not having the look of a grateful man, Terri thought.

'Yeah, it was very nice of him,' she said, nodding in agreement. 'Of course, it doesn't matter that you lost his number because you might be able to thank the guy in person soon anyway.'

'What?' His head snapped up.

'Oh yes, I almost forgot,' Rachel told him. 'Ethan said he might be in the city this weekend and was thinking of popping in for a visit.'

'Here? In Dublin, you mean?'

Was it Terri's imagination or had Gary's face turned grey?

'Yes. Strange how it goes, isn't it? I'm glad, though; it means we might get the chance to repay him a little with lunch, or maybe even dinner, depending on how much time he has.'

'You mean, he's calling here – to the bistro?' Gary blustered and Terri noted his eyes were shifting from side to side at a very quick rate.

Now Rachel looked up, finally noticing the edge in his voice. 'If he has the time, yes. Why? Don't you want to thank him in person?'

'Well, of course I do but . . . Did he actually say he was coming here?'

'Not exactly. He just said he might be in town, and that if he had any free time he'd give us a call to see if we were available to meet up for a chat. It sounded like a very loose arrangement really, so I wouldn't worry about it; it's not as

though he expects us to get the welcome wagons out or anything. Anyway, why so touchy?'

'I'm not touchy,' Gary said, sounding decidedly so. 'Just . . . surprised, that's all.'

'Well, don't be. As I said, we might see him, we might not. But either way, it would be good for you to give him a call. It's been me he's been getting all the time, and I hate having to keep making excuses.'

'OK, OK, stop nagging me, Rachel.'

Terri harrumphed. *Nagging* him? The cheek of it!

But Rachel didn't seem the slightest bit bothered. 'So tell us, what brings you all the way over here? Missing your fiancée already?' she teased.

'Yeah. I was going to ask if you wanted to get a bite to eat? I haven't had lunch yet, so . . .'

'Sounds lovely. Where would you like to go?'

'Oh. Well, I thought we could just stay here,' he replied lamely.

Again, Terri felt like choking him. Of course, stay here so you can get it for nothing, she thought, gritting her teeth.

'I suppose that makes sense,' Rachel said. She turned to Terri. 'OK, if I take off now?'

'No problem,' she replied. 'Justin will be in at two, so I'll take lunch myself then.'

'Great! Let me just wash my hands and I'll be right with you,' she said to Gary.

'Hey, where's the rock?' he asked, frowning at her hand.

'Oh I usually have to take it off when I'm working,' Rachel explained, sounding a little guilty. 'It's so big it tends to get caught up in everything, and I wouldn't want to damage it, you know?'

He nodded, seemingly satisfied with this explanation.

Gary and Rachel went through to the dining area, and

Terri watched them go, wondering yet again why her friend stood for such egotistical behaviour. And the way he was going on about the ring – like some kind of overprotective father or something! Granted, it was obvious he'd spent a fortune on it so perhaps he was entitled to be concerned, but at the end of the day it was Rachel's now, wasn't it?

Something was tugging at the back of Terri's brain, pulling at the edges, and telling her to pay attention to some important detail, but she just couldn't put her finger on it.

Moving the tray of vegetables aside, she set about making puff pastry and thought a little more about Gary's reaction to the mention of Ethan Greene. He looked a bit thrown by his upcoming visit to Dublin, that was for sure, but seemed content when Rachel admitted that a meeting wasn't set in stone.

For Terri's part, she was certainly interested in finding out if this so-called hero would be putting in an appearance at the weekend, because from where she was standing it looked as though all this couldn't just be about simple consideration.

Of course, Greene's only knowledge of Gary was when he was knocked out, so clearly the guy had no idea who he was really dealing with. If he did, Terri was sure that Ethan Greene wouldn't be so concerned about Gary Knowles.

If anything, it would be the complete opposite.

Chapter 18

'So exactly how long are you going to be in Dublin, again?'
Vanessa asked Ethan from where she sat on the bed, watching him pack.

He smiled easily at her. 'Just overnight, maybe longer depending on how I get on.'

It was early Saturday morning and his girlfriend had not let up on the questioning ever since Ethan had mentioned earlier in the week that he planned to travel to Dublin. He had also asked if she would mind looking after Daisy while he did so.

Following their New Year's Eve conversation about moving in together, Vanessa seemed much happier, and had since stayed over a couple of nights at the town house, but it would take some arranging before she packed up her own flat and came to live with him and Daisy permanently.

'And remind me again why you're going? All of this seems to have just come out of the blue.'

'Well, not particularly,' he replied, trying to sound casual. 'You know how excited I was to meet that agent in New York. Well, I've simply decided that I'm going to get cracking on this book once and for all.'

'I see.' Vanessa's eyes widened slightly, as if the opposite were the case and she didn't see at all. 'And going to Ireland will help . . . how, exactly?'

Good grief, she was persistent! 'Well, for research, of course.'

'Oh. So there's an Irish aspect to the novel now?'

He smiled tightly, distinctly uncomfortable with this incessant questioning. 'There always was, to be honest. I just didn't do anything about the research side of it because, as you know, I was procrastinating about it all. But now, with it being the start of a brand-new year, and Daisy's not-so-subtle hinting,' he added, holding up his daughter's Christmas present to him, 'I've decided the time is right to jump straight in. New year's resolution and all that.'

'Well, I'm pleased to hear that, certainly,' Vanessa said, smiling, and Ethan exhaled, realising that this cover story was actually proving to be a bit of a life-safer. 'And, goodness knows, the critics do love an Irish element – all that good old reliable Catholic repression,' she joked lightly. 'So that New York agent must have been very positive about what you've come up with so far. What was her name, again?'

'Erm, Rachel Knowles. She was at one of the bigger agencies, but has just set up on her own,' he said, thinking quickly. Damn, he hated this barefaced lying, but wasn't it entirely necessary, given the circumstances? 'You probably wouldn't have heard of her,' he continued, smiling nervously, and at that moment Daisy walked into the room. Ethan wanted to hug her. Saved . . .

'Hello, darling,' Vanessa cooed as Daisy sat down on the bed next to her. 'I'm just trying to get your father to explain why he has to run off to Dublin this weekend and leave us.'

Daisy gave him a conspiratorial smile.

'For his book, silly.'

'I know, but . . .' Vanessa looked from Ethan to Daisy. 'Now here's a thought,' she suggested suddenly. 'Why don't we all go – all three of us?'

Ethan's head snapped up. 'To Dublin?' He gulped. The last thing he needed was a repeat of the scenario in New York, where he had to keep making excuses to sneak away.

'Yes, why not?' she said, smiling. 'We could easily get tickets for Daisy and me at the airport. It would be a good excuse, actually. I haven't been home to see Mum and Dad for a while and of course I didn't get to see them at Christmas, what with being in New York.' Vanessa's parents lived in one of the Dublin suburbs, but her visits home were infrequent, and Ethan had been there on only one occasion to meet them.

'But what about my piano class?' Daisy whined dramatically, and Ethan looked at her gratefully. His little girl knew exactly what was going on and had been fully briefed on his cover story over the last few days. 'I can't miss another one; I'm already behind after being in New York.' She gave Ethan her best petulant look. 'I don't want to go away again, Dad.'

He met Vanessa's eye and shrugged helplessly. 'It's a good idea, but Daisy's right. We've only just come back from a trip, so perhaps it's too soon to take another. Not to mention that I'll be mostly working, of course.' He turned back to his packing. 'Probably best to wait for a better opportunity – half-term, maybe? We could tie it in with a proper visit to your mum and dad then, and spend some time with them rather than just a quick flying visit now.'

'Perhaps you're right.' Vanessa seemed to be thinking it over, and Ethan knew that she wasn't altogether convinced about this so-called research trip.

He sighed inwardly. Well, there was really nothing he could do about that just now. This entire charade was ultimately for her benefit, so really he should stop feeling so guilty. He took a deep breath. Christ, all this fibbing, and ducking and diving questions was really taking its toll on him. Clearly he would never have been cut out for MI5.

'We'll be so proud of you when the book is published, Daddy,' Daisy said, smiling at him.

'Well, I'll try my best, but of course there are no guarantees,' he muttered, not wanting to add even more pressure to all of this by having to produce a publishable manuscript at the end of it.

Vanessa stood up from the bed. 'Yes, that is true, and no doubt the trip will all be in a good cause. Go and do your research, darling, and enjoy every minute of it. Daisy and I will be sure to have lots of fun while you're gone. I think I'll make some tea. Would anyone like some?'

Ethan nodded, eager for her to leave the room so he could have a moment alone with his daughter. 'That would be lovely, thanks.'

'Daisy, some orange juice, perhaps?'

'Yes, please.'

Vanessa went to do the honours, and as soon as she was gone, Ethan turned to Daisy. 'Good thinking, buttercup. For a moment there I really thought we'd all have to go.'

'That's OK, Dad. I knew you wouldn't want us tagging along.'

'Well, it's not so much that – more that I'll probably need all my time there to get the ring back from Rachel.'

Daisy shook her head. 'I just can't believe she's wearing your ring.' She looked up, her expression thoughtful. 'Does it fit, I wonder?'

'Sorry? What did you say?'

'The ring – does it fit Rachel, or did she have to get it made smaller or bigger or anything?'

'I have no idea, darling. I was so taken aback to hear that

she was wearing it at all, that it really wasn't something I thought to ask.'

Daisy nodded, as if thinking something over. 'Well, you should really check.'

'Yes, yes, I will,' Ethan replied absently, although in truth he couldn't care less about whether or not the ring fitted Rachel or if she liked it or any of that type of nonsense. What mattered was that the ring was *his* – and by rights it should now be Vanessa's – and for the sake of his relationship (and indeed his sanity) he just needed to get it back.

Up in the Wicklow mountains, Gary was in his element. He and Sean zoomed along the rough terrain on their bikes, bouncing the tyres along the granite trails and landing heavily on the surrounding bog. Hard on the old ribs, but Gary didn't mind. He'd had enough of sitting around on his backside for the last two weeks, and was itching to get back in the saddle.

It was bad enough having to delay the gang's usual New Year's ride until he was a hundred per cent recovered, so a little bit of soft scrambling was just the tonic. Anyway, there was also a side of him that was anxious to get away and out in the open by himself for a while; since this whole engagement thing, Rachel had been coming on hot and heavy with the wedding talk and it was making him uncomfortable.

Gary couldn't understand the big deal about how many different layers of cake they should have, or what colour the bridesmaid's dress should be. While all this engagement stuff had sounded fine at the outset, already he was getting the distinct impression that he was way in over his head.

Just then Sean pulled up alongside him. 'Bloody fantastic, but I'm feeling thirsty,' his mate said. 'Fancy a pint?'

By rights Gary didn't like drinking when riding the bike,

but one would be OK as it was under the limit. And although he didn't like to admit any weakness to Sean, he could do with a bit of a breather. He followed his mate across the bog trail and through the fields out onto the main road, which led to a small village not far from picturesque Glendalough. It was a bit of a touristy spot but the pints were good, and there was always a roaring fire going in the lounge.

'So how's yer missus these days?' Sean asked Gary as they both hunkered down at the bar. 'Wrecking your head with all the wedding talk, still?'

Gary grimaced. 'Ah, you know yourself.' He felt a little bit guilty for moaning to Sean about that, really; he figured he should start showing a bit more loyalty to Rachel, seeing as they were supposed to be together for good now. 'I suppose she's just excited.'

'Ah, they all get like that,' Sean replied knowledgeably, and Gary wasn't sure how his friend would know when he'd never gone out with any woman longer than a couple of weeks. 'She give you any grief about coming out on the bike today?'

'Not too much.' Actually, Rachel had been OK about that, considering. Gary had expected her to nag him about his injuries, but instead she'd just urged him to try to take things easy.

'For your own sake,' she'd said. 'You don't want to miss out on the big ride when it does happen, do you?' Which was a good point, in fairness.

'So have you thought any more about suing that tool who knocked you down in New York?' Sean asked, referring to the taxi driver.

Gary had done a lot more than that. First thing after the New Year's break he'd phoned his solicitor to ask him about it and, like Sean, Frank Donnelly was confident he had a

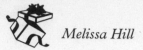

very good case. 'Yep, it's all in hand. My solicitor's setting the wheels in motion.'

'Proper order. I'd say you could be looking forward to a nice little payout from that.'

'Hopefully there's nothing little about it,' Gary joked. 'Would be nice to get some new wheels out of it, at least.'

'Assuming the missus doesn't get her hands on it first, of course! You know how demented they can get with all this wedding business.' Sean laughed. 'Good party last week, though. Rachel sure knows how to put on a proper spread.'

Gary nodded and supped his Guinness. 'Yeah, all things considered, she's not a bad catch, is she?'

Sean looked at him curiously. 'Sounds like you're still weighing it up. Bit late to be doing that now, isn't it?'

'Nah. Was just saying, that's all.'

Although the decision had been more or less forced on him, Gary found he was increasingly OK with the idea of settling down with Rachel. For one thing, he was relieved that her meeting his mam was over and done with. It had worked out well getting his mother to come to the party like that. It meant that any conversations she and Rachel had would have been short and sweet, which was the way Gary liked it.

What was bothering him now, though, was the call she'd got recently from that English guy, Greene, the one who'd helped him in New York. The notion that the guy was enquiring after his health didn't sit right with him for some reason, and the fact that he'd supposedly phoned a couple of times since seemed a bit too full-on for Gary's liking.

He looked at Sean, wondering if he should just throw the idea out there and get his take on it.

'Remember I told you about that do-gooder in New York?'

Sean looked at him. 'The fella that called the ambulance for you?'

'Yeah.'

'What about him?'

'Well, it's a bit weird but he followed me to the hospital afterwards and has been sort of sniffing around ever since.'

'What do you mean "sniffing around"?'

'I don't know . . . that's what I'm wondering. He met Rachel at the hospital while I was out of it, and I don't know if maybe he took a fancy to her then or something.'

'Why would you think that?'

'Just a notion. He rang her a couple of times since we came back and the other day he said something about calling into the bistro next time he's in Dublin.'

Sean raised an eyebrow. 'I get you. You're wondering why he's been ringing your missus, not you.'

'Well, he doesn't have my number to start with, and I've never met him. Rachel's been going on at me to ring him and say thanks and all that bullshit, but I just couldn't be bothered.' Gary took another sip. 'The way I see it, any eejit could call a bloody ambulance.'

'Too right. But I get what you're saying; it does seem a bit suspect.' Sean looked thoughtful. 'And there's no denying that Rachel is one hell of a looker, so who could blame him?'

Gary nodded, a strange combination of pride and possessiveness running through him. So he wasn't imagining things. Clearly Sean thought there was something to the idea too.

'Maybe you should give this fella a buzz all the same, suss out exactly what he's up to,' Sean went on.

Gary looked into the fire. 'Maybe I will.'

Chapter 19

Ethan's flight arrived in Dublin exactly on schedule, and now he stood in the taxi queue at the airport, waiting for a free car. For what seemed like the hundredth time, he looked at the paper in his hand and read the directions to the bistro. Getting into the cab, he explained to the driver where he was going, and the man grunted in agreement and pulled away from the kerb.

Despite himself, he was full of anxiety. Why he was feeling so nervous he didn't know; after all, he was in the right here, and the ring was his property. He just hoped that he'd be able to get all this dealt with, with the minimum of unpleasantness.

Thinking of Gary Knowles, he felt another jolt of anger. What kind of man would do such a thing? Take a piece of jewellery, a very expensive piece of jewellery, and blithely pass it off as his own? Even worse, what kind of man would give a stolen ring to the woman he supposedly loved?

A thief would, that's who, Ethan thought. What a nasty piece of work this Gary Knowles must be. He thought again about Rachel and their meeting in New York. She seemed like an incredibly sincere and kind woman; how could she be remotely attracted to such an obviously flawed character?

Then he sighed. Perhaps he shouldn't make assumptions about her. For all he knew she could be in on the whole thing, and all those offers of cookies for Daisy were merely a smoke-screen to throw him off the scent.

No, he decided then, Rachel *was* nice; she was an absolutely genuine person, he knew it. Why else would she have been so open about her engagement, and so willing for him to visit them at the restaurant?

He was sure that by now she would have mentioned to her fiancé that he would be in the city, and he wondered what Knowles would have made of that.

Maybe the man couldn't care less; goodness knows he'd been brazen about everything else so far. Notwithstanding the ring, he hadn't had the decency to even bother picking up the phone to thank Ethan for helping him out at the accident, so why should Ethan expect him to feel ashamed about nicking his ring?

Because Gary Knowles *must* have realised that this was what had happened.

Rachel seemed adamant that he hadn't suffered a brain injury, or anything that might cause him to believe that he had somehow, unbeknown to himself, spent a five-figure sum on a ring.

Ethan couldn't help but wonder about that too. If Gary had intended to propose to Rachel then surely he (and ergo Vanessa) would have ended up with a diamond ring, albeit a different one, instead of the silver charm bracelet. So what on earth was the guy's game?

He looked out of the window as the cab approached central Dublin.

It had been almost a year since he'd visited the city, and he'd forgotten how much he liked it. Maybe it would make a good location for his 'novel' after all. Ethan felt a weight in the bottom of his stomach as he thought again about his

lies to Vanessa, and he sorely regretted having to bring Daisy in on the ruse too.

But of course it would all be worth it in the end; and with regard to the novel, Ethan could always pretend afterwards that he'd had second thoughts, and that Dublin didn't suit the storyline after all.

Or that 'the New York agent' had had second thoughts about representing him as an author. That kind of thing happened all the time, didn't it?

At the end of the day, Ethan was here to get the ring back, nothing else. This wasn't research, nor a pleasure trip – far from it. If anything it was to conclude a business transaction. He needed to obtain the ring, and then return to London, where he would propose to Vanessa and get on with the rest of his life.

Minutes later the cab pulled up to the kerb near Dublin's Ha'penny Bridge and Ethan thanked and quickly paid the driver.

He took his case out of the car, and looked around for the purple building Rachel had mentioned, finding it easily a little way down by the river. Arriving at the premises, he focused on the establishment in front of him.

To the right of the entrance, behind a large plate-glass window was a wicker-basket display of every type of freshly baked bread imaginable, alongside a large selection of pastries as well as the cookies Rachel had mentioned. Just by the door, the lunch menu announced a tantalising selection of Mediterranean dishes, and the wood-panelled interior, colourful leather-banquette seating and soft lighting looked cosy and inviting, unlike the harsh monochrome look favoured by the majority of modern restaurants.

Strange, but Stromboli was almost exactly how Ethan had pictured it. Warm and welcoming.

A bit like Rachel, the thought came, unbidden.

Stop it, he told himself, mentally smacking his forehead. He needed to stop thinking of this woman as a friend, and instead start treating her and her boyfriend as the foes they were, at least when it came to the matter at hand.

Taking a deep breath, Ethan steeled himself to go inside, willing her to be there. Despite what he'd said about phoning beforehand, he didn't want to give Rachel or her fiancé too much advance warning of his visit, just in case they decided to make themselves scarce.

The bell above the front door of the restaurant jingled as Ethan walked inside, and he immediately saw that even though it was well past lunchtime, the dining room was still abuzz with customers. He was impressed. Rachel obviously did a booming business here. The feel of the place, in addition to the smell of fresh baking from the artisan bakery section, was enticing; it was rather old-fashioned and charming. To Ethan the atmosphere was almost like a mixture of cosy nights by the fireplace and breakfast in bed all wrapped into one, and he felt like he could stand all day there in the entrance, just breathing in the delicious aromas.

'Hello there, can I help you?' a pretty red-haired woman asked, and immediately he broke from his daydream and focused on her. She was dressed in jeans with a chef's jacket over her top, and really was incredibly striking. It was the eyes, he realised. She had the biggest, widest green eyes he had ever seen.

'Hello, yes. I'm here to see Rachel. Is she in?' He sounded nervous, he realised, and once again he mentally smacked himself for being so hesitant.

'She's not due back until this evening, actually. Is there anything I can help you with?' she asked warmly. 'I'm co-owner of the bistro.'

He saw that the name tag on her shirt read 'Terri'.

'Oh.' Damn. Ethan had gambled on Rachel being here, what with it being a busy Saturday afternoon and all that. 'Well, I suppose I should really have called first. You say she'll be here later?'

'Yes. She's away catering an event.'The woman was watching him with interest. 'Can I take a message, maybe get her to give you a call when she arrives back?'

'No need, thanks. Perhaps I'll just pop back later.' Again, Ethan was banking on the benefit of surprise.

'Well, it shouldn't be more than an hour or so till she gets in.' The woman's gaze dropped to the carry-on case Ethan held by his side, and she looked at him speculatively. 'In the meantime, you look like you've been on the road. Fancy a bite to eat while you wait?' she suggested.

Ethan thought about it. He'd missed lunch and hadn't eaten since breakfast, and the food here really did smell awfully appetising . . .

'If you have a free table, yes, I'd love that. Thank you.'

'Not a problem. Just this way.'Terri led him through to an empty table near the back of the dining room. 'You'll have to forgive me but this is all we've got left; we're so busy at the moment. Usually the rush tapers off after lunch, but today is particularly busy,' she said, motioning to the crowded room.

'Well, if the food tastes anything like it smells, I can understand why,' he replied, and Terri smiled as she handed him the menu.

'Thank you. Now are you sure I can't do anything for you myself? My name is Terri. As I said, I'm Rachel's business partner.' She held her hand out, and Ethan somehow got the impression that he was being railroaded into an introduction. Well, if he was going to wait around, he supposed it wouldn't matter.

'Nice to meet you, Terri. I'm Ethan Greene.'

A flutter of recognition immediately dawned on her face. 'Oh,' she said. 'Yes, Rachel was expecting you.'

He was slightly taken aback. 'Really? Because I wasn't entirely sure I'd be able to call—'

'I've heard all about you.' She smiled broadly. 'I think what you did for Gary was wonderful.'

'Excuse me?' Ethan looked up, momentarily wrong-footed.

'Well, for helping him out in New York, of course.'

'Oh, yes, of course.'

'And very nice of you to come by to check up on him too.'

'Yes. Would he be here by any chance?'

Terri chuckled. 'No, no, Gary doesn't work here. Actually, he doesn't spend a whole lot of time here at all, unless it's to be fed or watered,' she added, her tone wry as she fussed over the table setting. 'But I'm sure he'd love to see you, so he could thank you again and you two could catch up. After all, if it weren't for you, he might not be with us at all.'

Ethan noticed something in Terri's voice, something that sounded like sarcasm, but he wasn't sure if it was directed towards him or Gary.

He shifted uncomfortably in his seat. 'Well, I haven't met Mr Knowles at all as it happens.'

'Not at all?' she repeated, coming to an abrupt stop.

'Well, no, not officially. He was unconscious when I reached him, and I didn't manage to speak with him at the hospital either.'

'You've never even spoken to him?' Terri narrowed those expressive green eyes slightly, and for some reason Ethan almost felt like he was under a microscope.

'Well, no. As I said, he was unconscious.'

He wasn't sure where this was going and was reluctant to say too much just in case this woman was in on Gary Knowles's scam. 'I tried, of course . . . because my daughter was anxious to see if he was OK in the end. She's only eight, you see, and was a little shaken by it all.'

'I see.' Terri smiled then and there was definitely something behind it, Ethan was sure of it. He felt awkward. The conversation was rather strange and it certainly seemed like Terri was fishing for something. Was it possible that she knew about the mix-up and was in on the deception? He wanted to ask her point-blank if she knew about the ring, but realised he couldn't realistically divulge such information, not yet anyway, and especially not to anyone other than Gary or Rachel.

'So, seeing as I'm here on a spot of business this weekend, I thought I'd call by on the off chance—'

'Oh I almost forgot, let me get you our wine menu,' Terri said, interrupting him.

All of a sudden, she rushed off and Ethan watched her go. Near the entrance to the kitchen, he saw her tap an older man, who looked to be some sort of chef, on the shoulder. She whispered something in his ear, and then both of them turned back to look at Ethan.

Immediately, he felt himself blush and turn away. He had no idea what was going on here, but hoped that Rachel would appear soon, so he could do his business and leave.

Seconds later Terri was back with another menu, and for some reason also with the man she had been speaking to. 'This is Justin, he's our chef. Justin, this is Ethan Greene, the man responsible for saving Gary's life on Christmas Eve.' This time there was no mistaking that undercurrent to her tone, he was certain of it.

Justin nodded and smiled at Ethan. 'Ah, our famous New York hero. It's so nice to meet you.'

By now, Ethan wasn't sure who the butt of the joke was, but he sorely hoped it wasn't him. He nodded briefly at the chef. 'Yes, nice to meet you too.'

'So Ethan was just telling me that he and his daughter took care of Gary after the accident. Wasn't that good of him?'

'Very good of him,' Justin agreed sagely.

Ethan looked up. Something was going on here; these two knew something, didn't they? But what to say or do? Should he admit to these strangers the real reason he was here, or just wait until Rachel arrived and speak to her? The problem was that Ethan had no idea which, if either, party would be on his side.

'I'm sorry, but is there any chance I could order some food?' he asked pointedly. 'I'm actually quite hungry.'

'Of course, of course,' Terri soothed. With that, the chef duly headed back towards the kitchen and Ethan breathed a momentary sigh of relief.

'So what can I get you, Mr Greene?' she asked, her tone now all sweetness and light. So much so that Ethan wondered if he'd been imagining that she and her colleague had been interrogating him.

Feeling rather light-headed and more than a little stupid, he looked down the menu.

Clearly this entire thing was messing with his mind and driving him crazy.

Chapter 20

Daisy was worried, although she tried to tell herself there was little reason to be. According to her best friend, Tanya, her dad had a greater chance of being stampeded by a herd of donkeys than he did of being killed in an airline crash, but still she didn't like the idea of him being so many miles up above the ground like that, and especially not without her.

Once her dad had left for the airport, Vanessa had suggested that after returning from Daisy's piano class after lunch they should load up on popcorn and junk food and watch movies on the couch for the rest of the afternoon. Daisy thought this was a great idea; normally, she always tried her best to eat healthy food as a good example to her dad. It would be nice to just gorge out on ice cream and crisps without having to worry about being a bad influence. As far as she knew, eight-year-old girls didn't have to worry about cholesterol or heart problems, not yet anyway.

About halfway through the second *Pirates of the Caribbean* movie, Vanessa put her hands in the air and yawned. 'I wonder how your dad will get on in Dublin?' she said casually.

Daisy shrugged and spooned out some ice cream. 'Fine, as long as he gets the ring from Rach—' Too late, she paused, immediately realising she'd forgotten herself and spoken out of turn.

Vanessa sat up ramrod straight and turned to stare at her. 'What did you say?'

Daisy reddened furiously, and looked hard at the Ben & Jerry's carton she was eating from. 'I mean, as long as he gets to do his *research* for Rachel.'

'That's not what you said, Daisy.' Vanessa's voice took on an edge that Daisy didn't like. 'What's going on here? I thought Rachel was supposed to be an agent in New York. Why would he be seeing her in Dublin?' She paused slightly. 'And what's all this about a ring?'

Daisy wouldn't meet her gaze. 'Nothing. That's not what I meant. I meant that Dad just has to do loads of research for his book . . . so he can get it *ready* for Rachel,' she mumbled, but inside she was panicking like mad.

Oh no, her dad would *kill* her!

Although not if his girlfriend did first, and from the way Vanessa was looking at her, Daisy was worried that this was a real possibility.

Vanessa was silent for a moment, then she spoke again. 'Daisy, there's something going on here that I don't know about, isn't there?'

Daisy's eyes were glued to the TV, where Johnny Depp was doing something silly. 'No.'

'Come on, you can tell me, I promise. I'm thinking your dad hasn't gone to Ireland to do research like he said. We both know that, don't we?'

'He has, honestly.' Daisy's lip trembled. 'Look, I don't know why I said that . . . about Rachel, I mean. I just got confused because we were talking about Dad's book, and she was talking about it when we met her in New York . . .' She really wished Vanessa would stop going on about it. Why did she have to be so suspicious about what her dad was doing? It wasn't as if they were married or anything.

Yet.

'So this Rachel, she's the agent from New York?'

'Yes.'

'The one in your drawing? The pretty woman?' Vanessa asked and Daisy looked at her. Why did she have to go and put Rachel in her drawing? Now it seemed like Vanessa was suspicious about that too.

She nodded vigorously, trying to make it all look innocent and normal, and hoped that it would be enough to make Vanessa stop talking and just watch the movie. There was this big fight scene between Johnny and Orlando Bloom going on, and she tried her best to concentrate on it.

'So she's definitely an agent from New York – not from Ireland?'

'I think so.' Daisy was deliberately non-committal while she thought like crazy, trying to remember what her dad had told Vanessa about Rachel being an agent.

Oh this was all her dad's fault for not telling Rachel everything that day at the hospital. She was so nice and she would have understood. Daisy was certain of it. And maybe then Vanessa wouldn't be pestering her with all these questions now.

'Honey, what were you and your dad *really* doing in New York?' Vanessa asked.

'What?' Daisy mumbled, feeling decidedly cornered now.

'All of those times you two kept disappearing, where were you really going?'

'Erm . . .' She was now staring intently into the bottom of the ice-cream carton again, willing herself not to say another word.

'Daisy, you can tell me. Honestly, it's OK.'

'No. My dad said—'

Vanessa went very still all of a sudden. 'Your dad said what?'

Her heart pounded in her chest. 'My dad said not to tell,' she replied in a very small voice. Oh God, Dad was seriously going to *kill* her!

'Not to tell me what?' Vanessa's voice was stern, sort of the way Daisy's piano teacher sounded when she got the notes wrong. 'Daisy, look at me. I asked you a question.'

Tears filled her eyes. 'I can't!' she cried. 'I really can't! It was supposed to be a surprise.'

Then Vanessa's face changed, as did her voice. 'A surprise?' she repeated, sounding much more like the old Vanessa. 'What kind of a surprise, darling? For you, for your dad . . . or for me, even? And who is Rachel really . . . how does she come into it? Daisy, you have to tell me. Please.'

But by then Daisy had had more than enough of the questions. She tossed the carton of ice cream aside and stood up, tears stinging her eyes. 'I don't want to watch movies any more.' She headed towards her bedroom but Vanessa stopped her.

'I'm sorry, darling. I didn't mean to upset you . . . I just—'

'Leave me alone,' she said, shrugging her off. 'I don't feel like talking any more either.'

'Of course, of course, whatever you want.' Vanessa ran a hand through her long hair, as Daisy stomped past.

In the safety of her bedroom, Daisy fretted about what had happened and a knot of worry settled into the pit of her stomach. She'd ruined everything, hadn't she? She'd said something very stupid, and even though she'd tried to cover up the part about the ring, she knew Vanessa would be even more suspicious now and would probably be able to guess.

She stood by the window and looked out across the park in front of their house. Why, oh why did that stupid man have to get knocked down in New York? And why did her

dad have to help him? If they hadn't done that then he would have given Vanessa the ring on Christmas morning, and everything would have happened the way it was supposed to.

Instead, he had to go and try to get it back off that woman they'd met at the hospital, who seemed really nice.

Of course, if she'd taken better care of the Tiffany's bag . . .

Then Daisy thought of something. She pictured her mother showing her the various necklaces and bracelets she'd collected over the years, and remembered what her mum used to say about Tiffany's being a special, magical place.

Daisy had always been fascinated by her mum's jewellery collection as well as all her lovely clothes and shoes, which she vaguely remembered playing with when she was small and her mum was still here. She knew her dad had kept some things in storage for her when she was old enough to wear them, and she couldn't wait. Her mum had the nicest things.

But she thought again about her mum's exact words.

'A little bit of Tiffany's magic sprinkles happiness on everything, Daisy,' she'd said, and the man Daisy and her dad had spoken to in the store had agreed.

Which meant that maybe the things that came from Tiffany's were magical too – enchanted . . . kind of like the enchanted forest in *Sleeping Beauty*.

So maybe everything that happened in New York happened for a reason, like in a fairy tale. Maybe the bags getting mixed up hadn't been her fault at all? Maybe it was magic that had made it happen so that really it was Rachel and not Vanessa who was *supposed* to get the ring?

After all, if the ring fitted Rachel's finger, then maybe she was the one her dad was supposed to marry, like in *Cinderella*, when the glass slipper would only fit the right girl for the prince?

Daisy's heart raced with excitement. She would get her dad to find out if the ring fitted Rachel's finger, and if it did then . . .

Suddenly realising she was being silly, she shook her head, trying to make the stupid thoughts go away. Chances were the ring didn't fit Rachel at all. Daisy might only be eight, but she really should be old enough to realise that life wasn't quite like it was in the storybooks.

Instead, her dad would straighten things out with Rachel in Dublin, and come back with the ring. Then he would ask Vanessa to marry him, she would accept and they would all be a family, like her dad always wanted. That's the way it would work out, Daisy told herself.

That was real life.

'Ethan – hello!' exclaimed a voice behind him, and Ethan turned his head to see Rachel standing in the doorway of the kitchen, smiling at him. 'Terri and Justin told me you were here. Delighted you had time to call in and see us.'

'I hope you didn't mind my arriving unannounced. My meeting ended earlier than expected, you see, and . . .' He trailed off, not wanting to get into too many details.

'Not at all; it's lovely to see you again. And I hope Terri and Justin have been taking good care of you?'

Ethan looked down at his near-empty plate. The paella he'd chosen was one of the most delicious he'd ever eaten, and the accompanying sourdough was almost literally out of this world. 'Yes, they've been great. This is magnificent.' He wasn't about to add that her colleagues had also played twenty questions upon his arrival.

He stood up and offered his hand. 'It's so nice to see you again.'

Rachel smiled easily and took the seat opposite. 'Oh please,

sit down and finish your meal. So how have you been? Happy new year, by the way.'

'Same to you. Is Gary here?'

She blushed furiously. 'I'm afraid not. He needed to do something important this afternoon, and of course we weren't entirely sure when or even if you'd be visiting . . .'

Ethan felt deflated. Hell! On second thoughts, perhaps he should have been more specific instead of trying to catch them out. 'Of course, I understand.'

'He'll be kicking himself now, as I know he really wanted to see you, and thank you.'

'Oh well, not to worry.' Forget Gary; Ethan had hoped to keep Rachel out of this, but now it seemed he'd just have to get her involved, regardless. He took a deep breath. 'I was wondering –' he glanced around the bistro, which had become a lot quieter since his arrival '– I know you're working now, but would you have time for a quick coffee, perhaps? There's something I wanted to talk to you about.'

Rachel looked so apologetic, he felt like a heel. 'Oh I'd love to, Ethan, but I need to cover Terri's break now, and then we've got to prep for the evening sitting . . .'

Right at that moment, as if on cue, the aforementioned Terri appeared at the table.

'Was the food OK?' she asked him. 'Can I get you a coffee or some dessert, perhaps?'

'It was delicious. I really couldn't eat any more,' he joked, handing Terri a plate that couldn't be any cleaner if he'd licked it. And Ethan had almost been tempted to.

She laughed. 'Yes, I can see that.'

'But a coffee would be lovely, thank you.' He hoped that, given the circumstances, perhaps Terri might urge Rachel into joining him.

'Such a pity Gary isn't around, isn't it, Rachel?' Terri

said. 'Oh, and have you told Mr Greene about your engagement?' she added, indicating her friend's left hand. She smiled at Ethan. 'After all, you played such a large part in the whole thing, rescuing Gary like that. If you hadn't come along when you did, who knows what might have happened?'

But Ethan barely heard her. Instead, he just stared at Rachel's hand.

There it was. His ring, exquisite and sparkling just as he remembered it, but on another woman's finger. Immediately he was reminded of what Daisy had said earlier, and saw that it did indeed fit Rachel to perfection.

Then he quickly shook himself out of his stupor, realising that Terri had unknowingly given him the perfect opportunity to raise the subject. All he needed to do was explain the situation, and he could be on his way.

But for some reason, mostly down to Rachel's beaming, radiant expression, he just couldn't get the words out. 'It's beautiful. Congratulations,' he mumbled.

Noticing Terri giving him a speculative look, he squirmed uncomfortably, worried that he might be betraying himself.

'Thank you. We're so thrilled.' Rachel looked at Terri and stood up. 'OK, OK, I'm coming now,' she said, laughing. 'Ethan, again I'm so sorry. I really wish we had more time to chat but . . .' Then she stopped short, looking thoughtful. 'Actually, what are you doing this evening? I'll be finished here by seven, and Gary should be back by then, so if you're free it might be nice for the three of us to meet up for dinner somewhere, that's if you're not rushing back to London later?'

Ethan's heart lifted. Bingo. 'No, I'm not flying out until tomorrow afternoon, and I don't have any plans for tonight, as it happens.'

'Fantastic! Where are you staying? I'll give Gary a call

and arrange to book somewhere nice close by. That way the two of you can have a good chat, and he'll finally get the chance to thank you properly. Does that sound OK?'

'Sounds wonderful.' Having quickly filled her in on where he was staying, and told her what kind of cuisine he might like to try, Ethan sat back and relaxed a little.

He felt a whole lot calmer now that he knew he'd be seeing Gary, and definitely much better about not having to unburden himself to Rachel.

Because tonight, when the truth about the mix-up was finally revealed, wasn't it only right that Gary Knowles – and not he – should be the one worrying about the fall-out?

Chapter 21

Back in the kitchen, while Rachel was making dinner arrangements with Ethan, Terri nudged Justin hard on the shoulder. 'Did you *see* that?'

He drew back. 'Hey, stop the abuse; you know I bruise easily.'

She put her hands on the counter and started drumming incessantly. 'Well, did you?'

'I sure did. He's cute, isn't he?'

'That's not what I'm talking about,' she replied, exasperated, although yes, there was no doubt that Ethan Greene was *extremely* cute, in that open, earnest sort of way. With his soft blue eyes and sculpted masculine jawline, he certainly looked like no professor Terri had ever encountered. 'I knew it,' she said.

'They say you always know when you've found the One,' Justin teased in a sing-song voice.

Terri chuckled. 'Could you be serious for just one second? Forget what he looks like, you and I both know that there's something out of kilter about this guy's visit. Any fool can tell that he isn't here just to enquire after Gary's health. Hell, he'd hardly sat down at the table before he started asking about him.'

It was also pretty obvious from Greene's jumpiness when he asked about Gary that there was something else at play

here. The problem was that Terri couldn't quite put her finger on it. Yet.

Justin considered her statement. 'OK. Well, yes, I agree with you that there's certainly something fishy about the way he's just turned up out of the blue.'

'*And* you should have seen how Gary reacted the other day when I told him that his "rescuer" had phoned here looking for him. He didn't look at all happy about it, even though the same guy is supposed to have done him such a favour.'

'So what do you think, Sherlock? Is it that there's more to this accident story than we've been told?' the chef wondered.

'Or Rachel's been told . . .'

Justin narrowed his eyes. 'Well, that wouldn't surprise me in the least, knowing our Gary's ability to . . . ah, make friends and influence people,' he muttered sarcastically. 'But what could have happened? Does this Greene guy have some kind of bone to pick with Gary, do we think?'

Terri shrugged. 'It wouldn't be the first time, would it?' Goodness knows, Gary had a habit of rubbing people up the wrong way.

'But didn't he say that he'd never actually met Gary?'

'You're right.' She thought hard. 'But something is going on nonetheless. Ethan Greene is here for some reason other than to enquire after Gary's health. That much is obvious. We just need to try to figure out—'

At that moment, Rachel rushed into the kitchen. 'Terri, I'm so sorry,' she began, flustered. 'Go ahead and take your break; I'll get cracking here.' She grimaced apologetically. 'I didn't think he'd just arrive unannounced like that, and seeing as Gary isn't around to deal with him . . .'

'It's not a problem,' Terri assured her. She grinned.

'Anyway, I wouldn't blame you for wanting to chat longer; he's gorgeous.'

Rachel nodded. 'Isn't he? And such a lovely guy too. I'm so glad all three of us will get a chance to chat properly tonight, especially after what happened in New York.' She looked at Justin. 'Will I start on the pastry for the aubergine tarts?'

'Good idea.'

'What did happen?' Terri asked, fishing. 'I know you said Greene gave Gary first aid and all, but for someone who's supposed to be a complete stranger, he seems very interested in Gary's well-being, doesn't he? I mean, to come all the way over here from London just to see him . . .'

Rachel opened a fresh bag of flour. 'Well, it wasn't just to see Gary; he was going to be here anyway and . . . Oh hell!' She grasped at the diamond on her finger. 'I keep forgetting to take this off when I'm here.'

'I know. Knuckledusters can be *such* a drag!' Justin gasped dramatically and the others laughed.

On her way out, Terri looked across to where Ethan Greene had been sitting, but his table was now vacant. Pity. She would have liked the opportunity to pick his brains a little further. This thing was intriguing her more and more, and she wasn't going to rest until she got to the bottom of it.

'So how is everything going?' Vanessa asked when, later that evening, Ethan called to say hello from the comfort of his hotel room.

If he was being honest, he had to admit that he was still somewhat rattled from seeing Rachel with his ring on her finger, and was hoping that a well-timed phone call home would ground him and bring him back to reality.

He smiled into the phone, wanting to sound enthusiastic. He truly hoped that Vanessa wouldn't detect the strain

in his voice. 'It's going well. I'd forgotten how charming Dublin is, actually. We really should visit your parents more often.'

'I'm sure we will,' she said, sounding uncommonly enthusiastic, given that she was usually rather lukewarm about the idea. 'So how's the . . . er, research going? I know you're not long on the ground, but has the Muse struck yet?'

There was something about the way she said this that put Ethan on alert. The way she'd accented the word 'research', as if she knew that the so-called reason for this trip was all nonsense.

Then Ethan realised he was probably just being paranoid; heaven knew it was the day for it. 'Well, like you say, I've only just got here, but I'm getting lots of ideas, all the same,' he muttered quickly. 'How's Daisy?'

'She's great. She's reading in her room at the moment.' She sighed. 'Did her best to pretend earlier that she wasn't worried about you flying, but I know she couldn't really relax until you sent that text.'

Ethan had suspected as much, which was why he'd sent them a text message as soon as the plane had landed, a reassuring text for his little worrywart daughter.

'Like I said before, I'm not entirely sure you should entertain this type of behaviour from her,' she continued, and Ethan knew that Vanessa felt that by trying to counter Daisy's fears he might actually be validating them.

The truth was that he didn't know the best way to approach this kind of long-term neurosis, but how could he not do his best to set his daughter's mind at ease?

Nevertheless it was a relief to be able to discuss and make decisions about Daisy's emotional well-being with someone else. As she grew older things would undoubtedly get trickier, and it could only be good for his daughter to have a strong female influence in her life. And Vanessa was certainly that. With her determined no-nonsense approach, and especially given her sharp rise in London publishing, she was a force to be reckoned with, and he'd seen glimpses of that same single-mindedness at various times in their relationship too.

'I know, but I don't like to have her worrying.'

'No need to be concerned. She really was fine. This afternoon we had a good girly time watching movies and eating rubbish.'

Ethan had to smile. Daisy – eating rubbish? 'That's great, Vanessa. Thanks again for staying with her. I really appreciate that.'

'Don't be silly; it's a pleasure. You know I see her as practically my own daughter. She's the closest thing I'll get to it anyway!' she joked, in a thinly veiled reference to her inability to have any children of her own. Once again Ethan had to admire the way she'd come to terms with this fact, when he knew it was such a difficult thing for many others to bear. Apparently it was down to some gynaecological problem she'd had in her teens, and it was strange, but this knowledge made him even more eager for her to be part of their family. Silly too, especially when Vanessa was so easygoing about it, but it felt to Ethan almost as if they could somehow complete each other's missing parts.

'Well, I'm glad you both had a nice day.'

'So, speaking of the book,' Vanessa said, returning to the subject, much to his discomfort. 'Have you heard anything else from Rachel?'

Ethan's heart hammered. 'Rachel . . . ?'

'Yes, the agent you met with in New York. I figured she might have been the one who suggested the Irish angle? For the *manuscript*, I mean.' While her tone sounded completely

casual, Ethan could practically hear the italics. Were they actually still talking about a manuscript? Or was there some double meaning, a meaning of which they were both fully aware but neither could confess?

Ethan bit his lip, not sure what to think now. Something had happened since they last talked, he was sure of it. Could Daisy have spilled the beans?

No, he thought, shaking his head. She would never have revealed to Vanessa what was going on, not in a million years. Unless she happened to let something slip by accident . . .

It was unlikely and chances were that Vanessa was only asking about the manuscript again because she was in the publishing business, not to mention genuinely supportive of his writing ambitions.

'Not at all, but as I said I still have quite a bit of work to do to convince her. That's what this weekend is all about really,' he continued.

'Great. Well, good luck with it all. I can't wait to hear how it goes,' Vanessa said breezily. 'What are you up to tonight, then?'

'Nothing much. Just planning a little more location-scouting. There are some beautiful country estates in the vicinity and I thought I might hire a car and check those out.'

This notion had come straight from a tourist brochure that was sitting in front of Ethan in the hotel room, but he thought he should try to at least make his research sound authentic.

There was a tiny pause. 'That sounds like a lovely idea. I went to one a couple of years back for a wedding, although this was more of a castle than a country estate. Perfect for weddings really, those places.'

Now she sounded so much more like herself that Ethan

felt stupid for thinking she'd suspected something before. Clearly she was all for this research idea.

'Yes, I'm sure they are.'

'So you're thinking an old country estate might be a good setting for the story? I think you're right; it would be absolutely stunning.'

'Well, I have a few things in mind, but it's certainly worth checking out in any case,' Ethan said, not wanting to commit himself too much to this idea. Otherwise he really would have to visit some random Irish country estate, and bring back brochures and whatnot so as to prove to Vanessa that he really was doing research.

He sighed heavily, realising that all this subterfuge was becoming too much for him. He couldn't wait to get the plane back to London with the ring in his pocket. The ordeal had gone on long enough.

'You sound tired, darling. Don't do too much all at once, OK? As it is you really shouldn't have taken all of this on yourself. You know I'd love to help, if you'd let me. That kind of thing would be right up my street.'

'I'm sure. Well, anyway, I just wanted to call and see how you and Daisy were getting on. I'm heading out again soon but it might be a bit late when I get back so—'

'No problem. I'm sure you have lots to do and plan. Ethan, I must admit I just can't wait to read this book,' she said happily. 'I realise a lot of planning has to go into it beforehand but, believe me, when everything is done, I know you and I are going to have such a wonderful time . . . reading it together.'

Ethan wrinkled his brow. This conversation was definitely borderline odd.

'Well, it's all a long way off yet, of course, and I don't want to take anything for granted,' he said, chuckling nervously.

'This weekend is just to hammer out the idea, get the ball rolling and so on – you know how it is.'

'Of course. But just keep in mind that I'll be very happy with whatever ideas you come up with. Anyway, I'd better dash. It'll be Daisy's bedtime soon. Have a lovely time and see you tomorrow night.'

'Give her a kiss goodnight from me, won't you?'

'Of course.'

They said their goodbyes and Ethan hung up, thoroughly confused about the conversation they'd just had. Well, if nothing else, at least it had succeeded in putting tonight's confrontation with Gary Knowles out of his head, albeit briefly.

In truth, he was absolutely dreading going out to dinner with him and Rachel tonight. He despised conflict and there was no doubt that this conversation was going to be messy. He just hoped that the guy would be man enough to confess to the mix-up and reassure his fiancée that their engagement wasn't just a spur of the moment affair. It certainly sounded like that to Ethan and, from what little he knew of Rachel, she didn't deserve that. Hell, what woman did?

Taking a shirt and a pair of chinos out of his bag and laying them on the bed, Ethan turned on the shower and commenced preparations for tonight's battle.

Chapter 22

'Gary, no . . . I can't believe you would do this to me.'

Rachel wanted to scream. Having finally got Gary on his mobile (the reception could be dodgy in the Dublin mountains) to tell him about the dinner with Ethan, she'd discovered that he and Sean had spent much of the afternoon knocking back pints with some 'old mate' they'd met in the pub!

'Sorry, babe, but there's nothing I can do,' he said contritely. 'There's no way I can take the bike back to Dublin tonight with more than one in me. It wouldn't be responsible.' Although she was annoyed, she had to admit he had a point. 'So you mean to tell me that you and Sean are going to stay the night with this . . . mate of yours?'

'Yeah. Liam says we can leave the bikes overnight in the car park here and get a cab back to his place later. Then he or the missus will drop us back to collect them in the morning.'

'And where does this Liam live?'

'Not far. It's only a few miles from here, so it makes sense.'

It all sounded so rational and sensible that Rachel really couldn't argue.

Granted, he couldn't have known that she'd arranged to meet with Ethan Greene, but he could have at least called and told her he was planning on pulling an all-nighter. But that was Gary, wasn't it? Impulsive to the last. Then she

figured she should remember that his unpredictability was one of the things that had made her fall in love with him in the first place; actually, it was probably this very character trait that had led to their now being engaged.

'Please don't be mad at me, babe. It wasn't as if I planned this, and it's been years since we've seen Liam. Me and Sean were just having a bite to eat for lunch and couldn't believe it when he walked into the pub. Then, one pint led to another, and you know yourself . . .'

'I can imagine.' Rachel knew exactly how it went. The more pints that went down, the more reminiscing there would be, and the craic would be mighty too, no doubt. It always was where Gary and his boys were concerned.

Still, she supposed she couldn't be too annoyed; what with the accident and the injuries, he'd had a tough time of it recently, so a Saturday night out with the boys was probably exactly what he needed. She just wished it didn't leave her in such a pickle.

'Anyway, we didn't have anything on for tonight, did we?' he asked, and Rachel figured that it mightn't be the best idea to confess that she'd actually planned something without consulting him. It would make her look just as thoughtless as him, if not worse.

Better to just say nothing about the dinner with Ethan Greene, and Rachel would call and cancel it, tell him that something had come up. Although by now she was sick to the teeth of making excuses to the poor man.

'Not exactly, it's just . . . oh it doesn't matter. You're right: I wouldn't want you to drink and drive. Just take it easy on the beer too, OK? You're still on painkillers, remember.'

'Yes, Mammy,' Gary chuckled and despite herself Rachel felt a slight bubble of irritation. She hated the way he sometimes poked fun at her like that in front of his friends. She knew it was typical Irish male bravado, of course, usually harmless and merely a facet of a personality that was for the most part loving but also sometimes hopelessly immature. 'Hey, I promise I'll make it up to you. OK, babe? We'll do something nice when I get back tomorrow.' But the comment was almost drowned out by more background laughter, and Rachel figured there wasn't much point in continuing the conversation.

'OK then, have a good night and I'll see you tomorrow. Tell Sean I said hi.'

Hanging up the phone, Rachel returned to the kitchen, where Terri was getting ready for the Saturday-night-dinner rush.

'What's up with you?' her friend asked, obviously noticing her vexed expression.

Rachel harrumphed. 'Just Gary. Again.'

'Oh? Sounds ominous.'

'Ah, it's nothing really.' Rachel went on to explain about his afternoon drinking exploits. She shook her head. 'It's my own fault for arranging that dinner without asking him. The problem is that I couldn't get him on the phone before now. You know how bad the reception can be up there in the bog lands.'

Terri looked thoughtful. 'So it's just going to be you and Mr Blue Eyes tonight, then.'

'Hardly. I'm going to phone him now and cancel. There's little point in him meeting me again when it's Gary he really wants to see. I'd wager that he's had enough of talking to me and listening to me apologising on Gary's behalf.' She shook her head. 'God, anyone would think that somebody somewhere is trying to keep those two apart.'

Terri was silent for a moment. 'He seems like a really nice guy, though, and it sounded to me like he was at a

loose end tonight. Maybe you should just go along and meet him for dinner anyway?'

Rachel frowned. 'Would it not seem a little . . . weird, though? Without Gary, I mean?'

'Not necessarily. You're the one he knows, at least you're the one he's met and spoken to before. He mentioned that he hadn't actually spoken to Gary. Not unless he managed to before the accident?'

'Not as far as I know. Gary was unconscious for a couple of days afterwards and by the time he woke up Ethan had gone back to London.'

'Well, for what it's worth, I think you should go,' Terri insisted. 'You said yourself you felt grateful to him, so why not? Anyway, it's not as though he's hard on the eye either.'

Rachel was shocked. 'Terri!'

'What?'

'Why would you say something like that? I'm an engaged woman now.'

'Oh stop it; you're still human, aren't you? Ethan Greene is a hunk and a half and if I had the opportunity to go out to dinner with a guy like that . . .'

'Why don't *you* go, then?'

'Because none of this has anything to do with me. Plus I kind of get the impression that he's spoken for.'

'Really? Why do you say that?'

'I'm not sure; it's just a hunch. Anyway, it's after six now and it would be very last minute to cancel at this stage, not to mention rude – to Ethan and the restaurant you're going to. Where did you book?'

'Venu. It's near his hotel and he said he quite likes seafood, so . . .'

'Oh just go. It's Saturday night and, unlike me, you've

got a free pass from this place for a while. He seems like a nice guy and you'll have done your duty by bringing him to dinner on Gary's behalf. What harm can it do?'

Rachel thought about it. Maybe Terri was right. Ethan was a nice guy and she really did feel beholden to him. Yes, what harm could it do?

Ethan took a deep breath as he opened the door to the restaurant. He couldn't understand why he was so nervous. These people had something that belonged to him, something important and personal, not to mention expensive.

And, to add insult to injury, he wouldn't even be in this position if he hadn't gone out of his way to help a complete stranger. Talk about rotten luck!

He supposed he was just nervous about coming face to face with Gary, as he was the wild card in the entire scenario, whereas Rachel seemed like a rational, normal person and, Ethan figured, would be horrified when she found out the truth.

So really all he had to do was go in there and politely explain the situation, and refuse to leave until everything was resolved to his satisfaction.

He drew in a deep breath and steeled his nerves. He could get through this. Still, there was a side of him that wished he had brought Brian along for company. From what he remembered of Gary at the scene of the accident, he was rather well built, and Ethan could do with some brawn on his side if things got messy.

Oh well, too late now . . .

As he walked into the dimly lit room he looked around. Rachel had mentioned something about meeting them at the cocktail bar beforehand, but he didn't see either of them there. Maybe they were already at the table?

As he waited to enquire at front of house about the reservation, he heard a voice behind him.

'Ethan, there you are!' Looking in the direction of the sound, he swallowed hard. There was Rachel, leaving her coat at the cloakroom and wearing a red dress that could stop traffic.

Her smiling face took on a slightly confused expression and Ethan realised he was standing and staring at her with his mouth open. He quickly tried to compose himself and cleared his throat. 'Sorry, I was a little early.' His thoughts were moving slowly, taking in every aspect of her appearance. Then the bright flash of the diamond on her hand as she smoothed her hair down all at once reminded him of the purpose of this dinner. He was here for the ring. His ring . . . Vanessa's ring.

Then he noticed something. 'Has your fiancé been delayed?' he asked.

Rachel coloured, and her eyes wouldn't meet his. 'I'm so sorry, but Gary couldn't make it in the end. Long story.' She made a face and Ethan's jaw tightened. What was going on here? The guy was avoiding him on purpose, wasn't he? Why else would he refuse to return his phone calls and then cry off on this so-called 'gratitude' dinner?

But what Ethan really wanted to find out was whether or not Rachel knew what was going on. Was she also part of some plan to try to stop him retrieving the ring?

Well, forget that. Lovely as she might be, there was no way he was allowing himself to be played any longer.

Still, judging by the look on her face, he could tell that Rachel was deeply uncomfortable about the situation, and the fact that once again she had to make excuses.

'Oh. I see.'

'I'm so sorry. It was really my own fault for making plans

without consulting him.' She went on to explain about Gary being marooned in some pub miles away from civilisation, and although it sounded an unlikely story, for some reason Ethan believed her. She was so apologetic and seemed so genuinely embarrassed that he could hardly question it. 'It was late by the time I found out and I knew it would be rude to call and cancel so, if you don't mind, I guess you're stuck with just me for company.' She laughed lightly and, despite himself, Ethan found he was not altogether resistant to the notion.

'Of course not, but you really shouldn't have worried about being rude. If it's not convenient of course we can cancel.'

'Oh no. Truly, it's fine. We're here now, and to be honest I'm always glad of any opportunity to check out the competition,' she added wickedly, and Ethan smiled.

'Well, based on what I ate today, this place has a hell of a lot to live up to.'

'That's kind of you, thanks. You didn't have any problems finding it, did you?' Rachel asked as they were led to their table. 'I figured it was best to go for something close to your hotel. That way you don't have to worry about taxis and all that.'

'No, not at all.' There was silence for a moment as they took their seats and Ethan looked around the restaurant.

It was a nice place, not as cosy or intimate as Stromboli but the menu looked good. Then, reminding himself that his real purpose here tonight was not pleasure but pure business, he tried to focus on the situation.

When the waiter had taken their drinks order, he decided he should dive straight in and get to the point. The problem was that he had no idea how to start.

'So do you and your fiancé come here a lot?' he asked.

She shook her head. 'Not really. Gary isn't a big fan of restaurants, apart from ours, of course.' She smiled sheepishly. 'He's actually much more of a pub-grub kind of guy.'

'I see. And have you two been together long?' He figured he might as well lead into the subject by getting as much background on these two as possible. That way, if it became clear that Rachel genuinely didn't know about the mix-up, it might make dropping the bombshell that much easier.

'No, it's all been a bit of a whirlwind romance really,' she replied, explaining that they had been seeing each other for less than a year. 'New York was actually our first trip away together.'

'Had you two spoken about marriage before he proposed?' Ethan pressed, trying his utmost to keep any sarcasm out of his voice.

Rachel smiled. 'Absolutely not. It was a complete surprise, actually; possibly the last thing I expected.'

'Really? Why's that?' Then, thinking that he might sound too pushy, he added, 'It's just that I'm in a similar position myself and hoping to propose to my girlfriend soon.'

'Oh how lovely. Congratulations.'

'Well, I haven't actually done it yet, but I hope to very soon.'

Rachel smiled. 'Well, for what it's worth, it's such an exciting time, and I'm sure she'll be thrilled. How long have you two been together?'

'A little over a year.' She was so approachable and easy to talk to that, somehow, Ethan found himself telling her all about Jane's death and how much it had affected him. And before he knew it, they had eaten their starters and were on to the main course by the time he'd finished.

Rachel had tears in her eyes. 'She sounds wonderful. I'm

so sorry for your loss. And poor Daisy, losing her mum so young like that . . .'

'Yes, well, we were very lucky to find Vanessa.' Realising he had spent all this time taking about Jane but had barely mentioned Vanessa by name, he felt guilty. 'She'll be a great mum.'

Rachel cocked her head to the side. 'I'm sorry, and please don't take this the wrong way, but you keep saying what a great mum she'll be. Isn't that a little unfair?'

Ethan put his fork down. 'What do you mean?'

'Well, and again forgive me for speaking out of turn, but it sounds like your main rationale for marrying Vanessa is so you and Daisy can be a family again. I can completely appreciate you wanting that for Daisy's sake, but surely you must love her as much as you loved Jane?'

Ethan looked at her, realising that this woman, who was practically a complete stranger, had pretty much hit the nail on the head. But no, he realised then, it wasn't all just about being a family again. Of course he loved Vanessa just for herself; yes, maybe not quite as much Jane, but he honestly didn't think that was possible.

'I'm so sorry,' she added then, looking horrified. 'You barely know me and here am I, sticking my oar in. Forget I said anything.'

'No, it's fine,' he replied easily. 'It's my own fault for making it sound that way. I do love Vanessa, very much, and I can't wait to marry her.' He figured this was as good an opportunity as any to get the conversation back on track. 'The only problem is—'

'Of course, and again don't mind me, I guess I'm just projecting really.'

Ethan looked at her, curious. 'How so?'

'Well, I sort of have the same hopes for me and Gary,

about a being a family, I mean. I lost both of my parents a while back, and since then I've always felt a bit lonely . . . slightly cast adrift, I suppose.' She went on to tell him how Terri and the staff at the restaurant were the closest thing to a family she had. 'So now that Gary's proposed, it means I'm finally going to get the chance to be part of a proper family, or help build one of my own – if we're lucky enough to have kids, that is.'

'I understand.' There was so much longing in her voice that Ethan's heart went out to her.

'And this,' she said, lovingly caressing the ring. 'This signifies the start of all that, the start of everything I've always wanted. It's just so precious and so incredibly beautiful that I can hardly believe it's mine.'

'Actually—'

'It's something I can see myself passing down to my children, and perhaps on to their children too, sort of like creating a tradition. Sicilians are big on tradition, and having never been able to take part in all that, it feels important, almost essential, that I start my own, you know?' Then she laughed self-consciously and shook her head. 'Sorry, I don't know why I'm telling you all this; you must think I'm a complete loolah.'

And just like that, Ethan knew that there was no way he could shatter this lovely woman's dreams by telling her the truth. He just couldn't do it, and it wasn't his place to, in any case. Gary was the one who should be here listening to Rachel pouring her heart out about how much all of this meant to her. Despite his failings, at least Ethan knew his intentions towards Vanessa were honourable, whereas the cad that Rachel was marrying . . .

'It doesn't sound crazy at all to me, and I'm sure Gary is looking forward to those things just as much as you are.'

'Well, honestly, I don't think he really understands any of that "mushy stuff", as he calls it.' She laughed good-naturedly. 'You wouldn't exactly describe Gary as the type of guy in touch with his feelings. Your typical Irish macho male, I suppose.'

Again, Ethan felt maddened on Rachel's behalf that she'd ended up with a guy who sounded like some kind of knuckle-dragging idiot.

'You should tell him in any case. Let him know how much all this means to you, at least.'

'Well, first I have to try to get him to set a date for the wedding!' she said jokingly, and pushed her plate away. 'Goodness, Ethan, I can't remember the last time I opened up to someone like this. And you're supposed to be an English lecturer? Are you sure you're not really a psychologist in disguise?'

He smiled bashfully. 'No, definitely just a boring old professor. But really, despite what you think, you really should share some of this with Gary. He is the man you're going to marry, after all.'

Maybe then the guy would have a crisis of conscience and admit that their engagement was all a sham. Ethan would certainly be urging him to do so anyway.

He sighed. He supposed the best option now was to stop all the pussyfooting around, and just get Gary's telephone number from Rachel. Then he could talk to him straight and accuse him outright of taking the ring and trying to pass it off as his own. He'd like to give him a good ear-bashing too about resorting to such a mean course of action with this lovely woman, but he knew it wasn't his place to do that.

Rachel blushed. 'I know, and he really is a special person, although I realise a lot of people don't see what I do.' Ethan

didn't know how to respond to this so he remained silent. 'It would be nice if you could meet him.'

'I'd very much like to meet him too,' he replied wryly. 'So, you two haven't actually made many plans for the wedding, then?' he asked, feeling somewhat relieved that they hadn't set a date, not when everything might well end up having to be cancelled.

'Not yet. I've started looking into the arrangements, and Terri and I are going shopping for dresses soon, but Gary thinks it's all a bit girly.'

Of course he does, Ethan grumbled to himself.

It was all beginning to sound as though there would have been no prospect of an engagement at all if it hadn't been for this ring. He decided he'd try to tease out the specifics of the proposal. That way he'd know for sure if the engagement had been on the cards or if it had been precipitated entirely by the mix-up with the bags.

'So how did you react when he proposed in New York?' he asked. 'You mentioned before that it was something of a surprise.'

She beamed widely. 'Honestly, Ethan, I couldn't believe it. When I saw the Tiffany's box I nearly fell down.'

'I can imagine.' Ethan's fists clenched involuntarily. 'So he asked you to marry him, and then gave you the box?'

'No, no. Actually . . .' Her eyes dropped to the table and she hesitated slightly, as if she was about to say something but then decided against it. 'No, after he was released from the hospital we were exchanging Christmas gifts and he just produced that stunning little blue box and . . . well, when I saw what was inside I nearly lost it.'

'I know exactly what you mean,' Ethan said through gritted teeth. 'I mean, I can imagine,' he clarified quickly, but it seemed she hadn't picked up on anything untoward.

Rachel was still smiling at the memory. 'So while it took a bit of prompting – it was so funny because I've never seen Gary so nervous – he finally popped the question and the rest is history.'

Based on this account of events, Ethan now knew for certain that a proposal had never been in the offing, and from what he could tell this guy was making a complete fool out of this poor woman. She deserved so much better and Ethan sorely wished he had the courage to tell her that. But he really couldn't.

'Ethan? Are you all right?' he heard her ask and he immediately snapped back from his reverie.

'Yes, of course. Sorry, I was miles away. Just thinking, really.'

'About what?' Rachel took another sip of her wine and as she did so the ring on her finger glistened in the candlelight.

He swallowed hard.

'It is a beautiful ring,' he said, wishing he could somehow snatch it back without her noticing.

'Yes, it is,' she said, holding up her hand. 'It's so incredibly elegant, and nothing like I'd expected from Gary, actually.' She smiled. 'He can be a bit . . . what's the word?'

'Gaudy?' Ethan prompted, his mouth tightening.

She laughed. 'Well, no, I was going to say careful – with money, I mean. And I'm pretty certain this ring must have cost a fortune.'

Ethan knew all too well how much it had cost, right down to the very last cent.

'It's such a classic setting and a beautiful design, and from Tiffany's of all places . . .' She stared dreamily at her finger. 'I really had no idea a guy like Gary would even know about these things – you know, how a Tiffany diamond ring really is the last word in romance.'

'So I've heard,' Ethan muttered.

'But anyway –' she shook her head '– besides listening to strange women bleating on and on about their personal lives, how has your visit been? I hope the meeting went well. Was it something to do with your work?'

'Yes.' The question caught Ethan off guard. 'It was fine but . . . well, I'm actually here researching a book.' Now that he'd decided he was going to wait until he could broach the subject with Gary, he thought he might as well use this tried and tested cover story, instead of coming up with another to explain his visit here.

Her eyes widened. 'You're writing a book? Sounds fabulous! What's it about?'

Just at that moment, a waiter passed the table carrying a basket of bread and he caught Ethan's eye. 'It's about . . . bread,' he replied impulsively, his mind racing. Why the hell didn't he just stick with the same explanation he'd given Vanessa? 'Erm . . . a kind of exploration of bread in different cultures throughout the world. I'm researching Ireland now.'

'Wonderful.' Rachel smiled politely, and he figured that such an uninspiring subject matter had in fact been a brainwave. How boring did a book about bread sound?

Good, the last thing he wanted was for her to start asking too many questions; it was hard enough trying to keep up with the porkies he'd been telling to Vanessa about his 'research'.

'Well, considering the business I'm in, I know a thing or two about that, so don't hesitate to ask,' she added pleasantly, and out of nowhere Jane's dying words hit Ethan with the force of a thousand blows.

Go and find a woman who'll bake you bread.

He stole another look at the kind, sweet-natured woman

sitting across from him, whose gentle heart he was finding it impossible to break. Then Rachel moved her hand again, and the Tiffany diamond flashed so brightly it almost blinded him.

A woman who'll bake you bread.

The same woman who was currently wearing his engagement ring . . . ?

Chapter 23

Having finished the last of the Saturday-night rush, Terri said goodbye to Justin and the waitresses, and was just about to lock up and go upstairs when none other than Gary appeared at the doorway of the bistro.

She frowned, wondering what he wanted. And what was he doing here anyway?

Hadn't Rachel said something about him not being able to drive the bike back home tonight because he'd been drinking? Terri pursed her lips suspiciously.

Approaching the door, she could see that he did indeed look a little worse for wear. 'This is a surprise,' she said, letting him inside. 'I thought Rachel said you were staying in Wicklow somewhere?'

He grinned sheepishly. 'I was going to, but then I felt bad about letting my baby down. Is she still here?'

'No, she's off tonight. I thought you knew that.'

'Oh.' He looked puzzled. 'I thought she'd stay on if she knew I wouldn't be around.'

Not for the first time Terri wondered how a supposedly smart woman like Rachel had ended up with such a self-obsessed moron. She couldn't be certain but was pretty sure that her friend didn't have any low self-esteem or insecurity issues. After all, she had no reason to. Rachel was beautiful, had a successful business, was a lovely person and everyone adored her. So what did she see in this guy that nobody else seemed to? Her friend had alluded now and again to the fact that they had a scorching sex life but surely this wasn't enough to keep a relationship going? Although that wasn't something she'd know much about, Terri thought forlornly.

'Nope, definitely not here.' For some reason Terri felt like making things hard for him, and decided not to immediately reveal that Rachel was currently out to dinner with Ethan Greene.

Slightly crestfallen, Gary looked at his watch. 'Shite. It's a Saturday night. I don't really fancy just sitting in by myself and watching telly.'

'Well, I suppose you should have organised your day better, then, shouldn't you?' Terri said pointedly.

'Ah, don't you start. I got enough of an earful from Rachel earlier. And I came back in the end, didn't I?'

'Yes, how did you get back? I sincerely hope you didn't drive.'

Gary shook his head. 'Nah. Turns out Liam's missus wasn't as cool about us staying over as he'd thought, what with the new baby and everything. So myself and Sean had to get a taxi back. Cost us a bloody fortune, *and* we have to go back up there in the morning to collect the bikes.'

'Really.' Terri wasn't particularly interested in the ins and outs of Gary's exploits. 'So where's Tonto, then, seeing as you're on your own?'

'Ah, he was feeling a bit under the weather so he went on home. Bad pint, I reckon.'

'Right.' Terri deliberately jingled the keys. 'Well, Gary, much as I'd love to chat all night, I've got a few things to do here and—'

'Hey, any chance of a late one?' he interjected and Terri

felt like throttling him. As if she had nothing better to do than wait hand and foot on him because he fancied a free drink!

Then again . . .

Terri thought about it. She'd been wondering all week about this bizarre situation between Rachel, Gary and Ethan Greene. She just knew something was up and was desperate to figure out what it was. Now, and particularly when Gary's guard was down, perhaps this was the perfect opportunity to do a little digging?

'Oh go on, then,' she said, standing back to let him inside. 'I've still got a bit of cleaning up to do, so as long as you stay out of my way . . .'

He grinned. 'You're a star, Terri; did I ever tell you that?'

'Yeah, loads of times.' Going behind the bar, she took a bottle of beer from the cooler, grabbed a bottle opener and popped the top. Showtime.

'Glass?'

'Nah, I'm good.'

Terri slid the bottle across the granite-topped counter and Gary lifted it to his lips, gulping it down as if it were the elixir of life.

'Good woman.' Still standing, he practically drank the entire bottle in one go, then exhaled loudly. 'After the day I've had, I needed that.'

'I can imagine.' Terri had to bite her tongue. Instead, she proceeded to sweep the floor of the dining room. 'So how's life with you these days? I suppose you're all excited about the wedding?'

He rested the beer bottle on the bar. 'Ah, you know yourself. Hey, any chance of another one of these? I can get it myself.'

Of course you can, Terri thought. 'Sure, go ahead.'

'Thanks. It's been a really long day. Besides, nothing better than beer when it's on the house.'

Terri shook her head. Again, she just couldn't fathom how someone like Gary would spend thousands on a ring when he was so cheap that he couldn't resist the opportunity to get drunk at someone else's expense. Namely her and Rachel's, Terri thought bitterly to herself. Still, needs must . . .

'Well, I have to admit that you really threw us all for a loop,' she went on, determined to keep him on the subject of the engagement. 'Who knew you were so good at keeping secrets?'

'You have no idea,' Gary groaned, and Terri gave an interested glance, wondering what on earth he could mean by *that*. 'Oh about the engagement, you mean,' he added quickly, sitting up straight. 'Well, I suppose I am good at keeping secrets, and I wanted to make sure she was surprised.'

'Consider it mission accomplished.'

'Well, as far as all the wedding stuff goes, that's really Rachel's thing. Besides, she'll have to stump up and play her part in paying for all of that now. I've done my bit.'

Terri worked hard to keep the smile on her face.

Such a Romeo.

'I know you have. I mean, that rock must have set you back a fair bit, and from Tiffany's too.'

'Yep, I really went all out. She must be feeling pretty lucky having a ring worth at least . . . um, a grand or so on her finger.'

Leave it to Gary to talk about the price, Terri thought, prickling at his bad taste; but at the same time the figure he'd thrown out stopped her short. A grand, my ass. Not for a diamond that size and certainly not from the likes of Tiffany's! That ring must have cost twenty at least . . .

Then she paused, thinking that if Gary knew this for a fact wouldn't he be bragging about it, rather than trying to be modest?

Right away Terri knew something was up. Gary was hiding something – and she couldn't be sure if it was to do with the engagement or something else, something even bigger. But whatever it was, she was determined to find out.

'Right.' She stopped sweeping and leaned against the brush. 'You know, it's been a long day for me too, so I think I might join you. Fancy a shot of something stronger?'

Gary's eyebrows shot up. 'Of course.'

Putting the brush aside, Terri took a bottle of whiskey off the shelf and grabbed two shot glasses, pouring them each a nice-sized shot. 'Bottoms up,' she smiled, throwing it back and trying not to grimace at the taste. She hated whiskey but there was a method to this madness.

Gary threw his back too, and immediately she poured another, noticing him stumble slightly against the bar.

'Sit down at a table and relax,' she fussed. 'Unless you're in a hurry or anything?'

'Of course not.' Gary beamed. 'Anyway, I wouldn't dream of leaving a lady drinking all by herself on a Saturday night.'

Crikey, was he flirting with her? Terri's stomach churned and this time, it wasn't down to the whiskey.

'Yes, I have to applaud you for committing to Rachel. I hadn't figured you as a one-woman man,' she cooed, deciding to play along. 'You and Rachel are just so good together that I have to admit I'm a little jealous. I'd love a man like you in my life.'

He looked at her, trying unsuccessfully to focus on her face, and Terri tried her utmost to keep her smile steady and her distaste at bay. Now he was wondering if *she* was flirting with *him*. When she thought she might burst out laughing, she poured him another shot, which he again drank quickly.

'Nice one.' Gary now wore a satisfied expression, the combination of flattery and whiskey going straight to his head, it seemed.

She poured him yet another shot and got him a fresh beer for good measure.

Gary sat forward unsteadily. 'You know, I like this side of you, Terri, I really do. You're usually so . . . I don't know, serious all the time.'

'Well, I suppose every now and then everyone needs to get a little crazy.'

He hiccupped, and his words slurred slightly. 'Good woman.'

She poured him another shot and he looked at her speculatively, as if about to say something.

'What's wrong?' she asked.

'I was wondering . . .' Gary drank down the whiskey but then seemed to lose his train of thought.

'Yes?' she prompted.

'Ah, it's nothing really.'

'No, go on, you can tell me.'

'Well, it's just this bloke, Ethan, that keeps ringing her . . . He's starting to annoy me.'

Terri paused. Finally, she was getting somewhere. 'Really? Why? Are you jealous or something?'

'Nah!' He guffawed loudly. 'Why would I be jealous? Rachel's crazy about me.'

'Of course she is. But, actually, I was wondering about that too. Why *does* he keep ringing her?'

'Dunno. I reckon he took a fancy to her at the hospital while I was under.'

'I see.' Terri was disappointed. She was hoping for some

grand revelation from Gary about Greene, some explanation as to why he was so adamant about keeping in touch.

Could it be that Ethan Greene had a thing for Rachel that had somehow begun in New York? It certainly didn't look that way today, although, thinking about it, he did seem quite nervous around her, as well as being overly concerned about Gary's whereabouts. Was this because he wanted to see Gary, or was actually afraid of him?

No, there was something else going on at the back of it all, Terri was sure of it.

Again, she decided to bide her time and wait until the moment was right to reveal to Gary that at this very second Rachel was out having dinner with Ethan Greene.

'So you're worried that Greene might steal Rachel away from you, is that it?'

Gary guffawed. 'You must be joking! Nah, I just don't like the way he's sniffing around her, that's all.'

'I can imagine. Still, I suppose it's funny how these things work sometimes. If Greene hadn't come along when he did, then who knows what might have happened? With the accident, I mean.'

'Yeah, who knows?' Gary snorted and slurred. 'Well, all that seemed to work out well for Rachel, that's for sure.'

Terri narrowed her eyes. She was about to learn what was going on, she knew it. 'What do you mean? Of course it worked out well, but for both of you, surely?' She pretended to be shocked, egging him on.

He laughed. 'Well, to be honest, I can't really remember much of it myself, but the one thing I do know is that if that accident hadn't happened, we probably wouldn't be engaged.'

'What do you mean?' Terri sucked in her breath, but he didn't seem to notice.

He smiled and motioned her closer. 'Can I tell you a secret?'

'Of course. My lips are sealed.'

He scratched his head, reminding Terri of a gorilla she'd seen on a recent visit to Dublin Zoo with one of her nephews. 'I don't know where the hell that ring came from.'

'What? What do you mean?'

His eyes were glazed. 'As I said, I don't know where it came from. It just appeared in my stuff after the accident.'

Terri blinked, confused. 'You mean you can't remember buying it at Tiffany's?'

'Nah. I bought something there all right, but it wasn't that rock.'

Now her mind was galloping like a racehorse. 'Back up there for a second. You're telling me you bought something from Tiffany's, but when you got back from the hospital the same thing wasn't in the bag?'

'Bang on. I think there must have been some mix-up in the shop.' He raised his glass. 'Worked out well for me, though.'

'Hold on. You mean that you somehow ended up with the ring that Rachel's now wearing instead?'

'Yup.'

'But, Gary, surely you took the ring back to the store and told them about the mistake?' Terri was flabbergasted. 'Or explained it to Rachel, at least?'

'How the hell could I, when she was doing a jig over it?' He gave a self-satisfied grin. 'Anyway, the way I see it, it's finder's keepers.'

'But . . .' Terri was finding it hard to get a handle on this. It wasn't what she'd expected at all and yet it made sense. 'And what did you actually buy?'

He shrugged. 'Just some charm bracelet that I thought

Rachel might like. Didn't cost me much, and look what I ended up with!' He grinned again. 'I dunno . . . it was late, and I was rushing to get back to the hotel . . . Then next thing I know, I'm lying in some hospital bed.'

Terri was silent for a minute, while she tried to think this through.

'So it was right after you left Tiffany's that you got hit?' She hadn't known the specifics before, but now that she did this was starting to make a hell of a lot more sense. It was all falling into place. The ring – it wasn't meant for Rachel, and never had been. Which must mean . . .

Suddenly Terri recalled Ethan Greene's wide-eyed expression earlier today when Rachel was showing off her magnificent diamond.

Oh hell . . .

She tried to picture the scene in her head. Two men shopping on Christmas Eve, both laden down with packages. One gets hit by a cab and the other tries to help out, and somehow the shopping bags get mixed up.

Terri couldn't believe it. Poor Ethan Greene. He must have almost died when he realised that his massively expensive diamond ring had gone astray, and, even worse, that he'd ended up with a simple charm bracelet.

And poor Rachel too. Talk about adding insult to injury: Gary thought so little of her that he was willing to pass off the ring as his own and commit to marriage on a random whim!

'I don't understand. The ring isn't yours, so how could you use it to propose to Rachel?'

'What was I supposed to do, Terri? Believe me, I was as shocked as anyone when I saw what was in there, but I could hardly tell Rachel when she was mooning all over it, could I? Besides, it all worked out OK, didn't it? Rachel's happy, and yeah, OK, so it might not have been on the cards right now, but what can you do?'

Terri was so disgusted she thought she might gag. To think that he could blithely go along with something so awful . . .

'Gary,' she began, deciding to throw the idea out there, as clearly he wasn't clever enough to put two and two together. 'Did you ever consider that *maybe* the reason this Ethan Greene guy has been hounding you as you say, is not because he fancies Rachel but because the ring is actually his?'

He looked completely bewildered and she knew the idea had never even once crossed his mind. 'Huh? But how could it be? It was my bag.' But she could see his eyes grow wary, now the subject had been raised.

'Yes, but perhaps he'd been carrying a Tiffany's bag too, and the two of them got mixed up in all the drama?'

Gary shrugged. 'Nah, I don't think so. Anyway, it's not my fault if this guy can't keep track of his own stuff.' He was seriously slurring his words now, and Terri figured it was pointless trying to get him to see sense at this stage. She wondered if he would even remember this conversation tomorrow.

Well, however dishonourable his intentions regarding Ethan Greene, Terri now needed to know his true intentions towards her best friend.

'So this whole engagement only came about because the ring turned up out of the blue? You hadn't planned it all along?'

'Nah. I mean, I don't mind going along with it, though. Rachel's great, easy on the eye, good craic, dynamo in bed,' he added and Terri seriously had to restrain herself from throttling him. Clearly he'd forgotten whom he was talking

to at this point, and this must be how he talked about Rachel to his 'boys'.

Terri was so annoyed she couldn't think straight. She wasn't sure what to say next. Gary was an even bigger numbskull than she'd realised.

At that moment he laid his head on the table and closed his eyes, muttering something that sounded like 'I could get used to all this free stuff – beer, diamonds . . .' and then he let out a huge snore.

Terri waited for a moment, making sure he was out cold before she could even contemplate her next move. Her first instinct was to whack him over the head with something, she was so shocked by what she had just learned.

While she'd suspected all along that something wasn't right, she certainly hadn't anticipated this. Should she tell Rachel? Break the news to her friend that her so-called fairy-tale engagement was a complete sham, and had only come about because Gary had come out the better end of a mistake? She had to, didn't she? Although, thinking about it, no doubt Ethan Greene was doing exactly that himself right now.

Trying to imagine that conversation, Terri's heart went out to the poor guy. Why should he have to suffer the consequences of all this, when dumbass Gary was the one completely at fault?

Terri looked again at the love of Rachel's life, drunkenly snoring his head off. She hoped he had the mother of all hangovers tomorrow morning and would be wracked with shame and guilt over what he'd just told her. Or would he even remember?

Terri shook her head. Poor Rachel, and her big dreams about tradition; with an oaf like Gary for a husband what kind of traditions would she have to look forward to now?

Chapter 24

Gary could hear someone calling his name. He was in a murky place; something cold and hard was pushed against his face and for the life of him he couldn't figure out what it was.

'Ah, Ma, give it a rest . . .'

'Gary, wake up.'

There, he heard it again. Why couldn't he open his eyes? They seemed glued shut. He was slowly becoming conscious and the first thing he noticed was the shooting pain in his skull; it was as if his head was locked in a vice. Why did his head hurt so much? And again, where the hell was he?

'Gary, come on – wake up!' There was an insistent tapping on his shoulder and, blearily, he realised he knew that voice.

Finally, he was able to open one eye, then the other one. There in front of him stood Rachel. His fiancée, he remembered. She didn't look happy, though. He wondered why.

'Gary.' She shook his shoulder. 'What are you doing here?' It was more of a demand than a question.

He had still not uttered a word but was trying to focus on his surroundings. There was a whiskey bottle in front of him, along with two shot glasses. He appeared to have his head resting on the dark wood of a table and was sitting on a chair. He noticed that not only did his head hurt, but so did every other part of his body. He could only imagine it

had to do with the fact that he had slept practically upright all night.

'Hey, babe,' Gary mumbled as he started to slowly pick his head up from the table.

Rachel's nostrils flared and her eyes narrowed. He tried to think of a time when he had last seen her mad, and realised he couldn't recall a single moment. Sure, there had been times when she had been stressed out about this and that with the bistro, but her anger had never been directed at him.

'What the *hell* are you doing here?' she asked again.

Good question, he thought to himself, what *was* he doing? He tried to think back to the previous evening. He remembered getting a taxi back from Wicklow with Sean, and then arriving at the bistro looking for Rachel, but she wasn't there. Terri had been, though, and she'd given him more drink. More importantly, Terri had been *nice* to him; she'd invited him in for a beer and, of course, what man would turn down free beer?

It was strange because Terri never really talked to him, and he'd always thought she didn't particularly like him, but last night . . . had she *flirted* with him? Gary tried desperately to think back. Yes, there could be something to that. She'd certainly been over-friendly anyway. He tried his best to remember the rest. But he was missing something; there was something important he couldn't recall. They had started doing shots of whiskey; he remembered being surprised when she'd pulled the bottle out. They'd done a couple – no, it had been a lot more than a couple. Terri had kept refilling his glass.

And she had kept asking questions.

He hadn't thought anything of it at the time. After all, it just sounded as if she was jealous of Rachel getting married, and he hadn't realised this before, but maybe she'd fancied him too.

Then Gary's skin broke out in a cold sweat as the most important part suddenly came rushing back to him. He'd told Terri about buying the bracelet and ending up with the ring. He had told her the *whole* bloody story. And was he imagining it or did Terri have some kind of theory on exactly how that had happened, something to do with that guy Greene.

Christ . . .

He wondered if Terri had already told Rachel about the mistake. If she had, it would certainly explain why she seemed so mad at him now. And he hoped to God he hadn't shot his mouth off about anything else.

'Well? Do you plan on answering me?'

Gary snapped back to the present, realising he still hadn't said anything to Rachel. She was tapping her foot on the ground. He looked up, wondering if he had the presence of mind to bluff his way out of all this.

'Ah, well . . .' He wasn't sure what he was supposed to be explaining: why he was here, or why he'd proposed to her with a freebie engagement ring.

'Why are you sleeping on one of my tables?' Rachel entreated, and he breathed a sigh of relief.

'What time is it?' he asked groggily. It was starting to get bright outside. Had he been here all night?

'It's seven a.m. And you still haven't answered my question.'

'I came here last night, looking for you.'

Something crossed Rachel's face very briefly. Gary caught it and it piqued his interest. Was it guilt? If so, he wondered if he could maybe turn this around.

'But you weren't here so I decided to stay for a while,

229

and I had a drink with Terri.' He thought if he played up this aspect maybe it would distract her, make her a bit jealous even? 'We had a couple of drinks and—'

'Looks like it was a hell of a lot more than a couple of drinks,' she said, incredulous.

Gary blinked. Now he wasn't sure if she was angry about him drinking with Terri or sleeping at the bistro. He decided to wing it.

'Come on, babe, you don't need to be jealous or anything.'

'Oh please. I'm not jealous of Terri, I'm just wondering how you ended up sleeping all night in my restaurant.'

OK, she wasn't jealous. Gary shifted gears. 'Well, it's not my fault. Terri got me drunk and then left me high and dry here, so blame her.' If he shifted most of the blame onto Terri then Rachel could take her anger out on her.

Instead, Rachel rolled her eyes and sighed. 'Gary, come on. Last time I checked you were an adult. It's hardly Terri's fault that you got drunk. Didn't you tell me yourself you were drinking all day yesterday? Besides, how could she have possibly moved you? And I can't imagine she'd want to put you up upstairs either.' She put her hands on her hips. 'The problem is that I need to open up soon and I can't have you in here looking and smelling like you do. It wouldn't be good for business. So scoot.'

Was she really kicking him out? Couldn't she at least offer him some coffee to help him wake up first? Or maybe a bite to eat, while she was at it? What had got into her?

He started to open his mouth to ask these questions, but Rachel held up her hand. 'Gary, please, just get a move on. I don't have time for any of this right now. It's after seven and I have too much to do. Go out the back way.'

So now she was making him exit through the back, like she was ashamed of him or something? What the hell?

Shaking her head in irritation, Rachel started to clean up around him, taking away the shot glasses and placing the whiskey bottle back on the shelf. Gary sat there, confused and unsure of what to say. She had never acted this way around him before; usually she was all over him.

He started to panic, wondering if Terri had in the meantime told her the truth about the engagement; but she wasn't saying anything, expecting him to just guess why she was cheesed off, like women often did. He glanced at her left hand for the diamond but thankfully it was still there. He breathed an inward sigh of relief. OK, that wasn't the problem. Nice one. At least he didn't have to face all that now too.

Rachel came back over and starting making shooing motions. 'Come on, come on. What are you waiting for?'

She herded him through the doors that led to the kitchen and then to the back service door. When he reached it, he turned around and tried to summon his most charming grin. 'Don't I get a goodbye kiss?'

Rachel made a face. 'Gary, you stink. Just go and maybe I'll talk to you later.' She pushed him out of the door and closed it behind him.

Alone in the back alley, Gary sniffed inside his shirt. She was right: he did smell bad. He felt a growing sense of unease in the pit of his stomach. He seriously wished he could remember more about last night, what he'd said to Terri or more importantly what he didn't say. He didn't think he'd been drunk enough to blab everything, or shoot himself in the foot, not at this stage. Yet who could tell? One thing was for sure, he didn't like this – having Rachel mad at him, that was. Usually, she was delighted to see him and so happy to be around him. Should he try to make it up to her? Buy her flowers or something?

Walking around the front of the building, he peered in

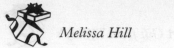

the windows to the inside of the bistro, where Rachel bustled among the tables, getting ready for business. He waited for her to look in his direction, but she didn't. It was as if she was purposely ignoring him.

He stepped out into the road, looking to hail a taxi home. He just hoped he could make it all the way there without puking.

As a cab pulled up, he got in and tried to rid himself of the worry that was starting to creep up on him big time. It wasn't so much that Rachel was mad at him; he'd had many women mad at him over the years.

But if she was this annoyed at finding him passed out on the table, what would she be like if Terri told her about the ring?

Chapter 25

Rachel could practically feel Gary's eyes on her from the other side of the window.

She knew he was looking in, but she'd already decided that there was no way she was acknowledging him. She felt as if she were holding her breath, waiting for him to leave. She had never treated him that way before; she had never cajoled or been angry with him. It was a completely new feeling.

She felt a little out of kilter today and she tried to convince herself it was only because she'd walked in to find her fiancé passed out after a drunken night.

But regardless of how much she tried to convince herself of that, a little voice in the back of her mind was telling her something else. She felt differently towards Gary today, and the scary thing was that she figured it might be related to last night's dinner with Ethan.

He was so different to Gary, so warm and easy to talk to. Last night, they'd stayed on for a very long time after dinner and had talked for ages over coffee. She still couldn't believe she'd opened up to him like that about her desire to have a real family and to create real traditions. She was sure he'd thought she was some kind of loon, but no, he actually seemed to understand perfectly what she meant. After all, he was hoping for the very same thing with his soon-to-be fiancée.

Despite herself, Rachel couldn't help wondering what the woman was like. She would no doubt be intelligent, stylish and definitely very beautiful, considering that Ethan was himself an incredibly handsome man. He was also gentle and courteous with impeccable manners, insisting after their meal that he saw Rachel safely off in the taxi.

Taking a wet rag she wiped down the area of the table where Gary had been drooling all night. Talk about a stark contrast . . .

She went through to the kitchen to start on making bread and pastries for their breakfast offerings, which of course immediately reminded her of the subject matter of Ethan's book. Damn it, no matter what she did this morning, her thoughts kept drifting back to him. What was wrong with her?

For some reason she felt uneasy. Not because of the dinner with Ethan – far from it. Actually that was the first time in a long time that a man had sat down and showed a real interest in her and her life. Ethan had asked questions and listened patiently to the answers. He wanted to know everything about her life and business – even her dreams – and for once she had no problem sharing.

It wasn't as if she didn't share things with Gary; it was just different. Their relationship was one of extremes and excitement. He made her laugh, even when he was being ridiculous, and normally she loved the fact that she never really knew what he was going to say or do. But she thought again about what Ethan had said last night about sharing her hopes and dreams with Gary, and she realised that she had never actually done that. Of course, this was mostly because her fiancé was a man's man and had no real interest in all that kind of malarkey. And for the most part Rachel liked that.

Still, as she thought now about some of the sacrifices she'd made, her mind suddenly seemed to focus clearly on the little oddities that she'd brushed off: Gary's reluctance to eat in some of her favourite restaurants because they were 'too fancy, and they never give you a decent feed'; the fact that he rarely complimented her on her appearance; the way that he often didn't notice the things she did for him; how it had taken so long for him to introduce her to his mother . . .

Rachel felt almost surprised by the realisation. Was Gary inconsiderate?

Her head said no, but deep down her heart seemed to argue the opposite. Yet, if he was, it certainly wasn't intentional; his behaviour could really be described more as clueless than anything else.

She sighed, deciding to turn some of this sudden reflection back on herself. Maybe the problem wasn't Gary at all, but her. Was she really so shallow that the first time another man paid her some attention, she immediately began picking faults in her partner?

No, that wasn't the case at all, she told herself. Anyway, and notwithstanding the fact that he was already attached, Ethan wasn't even her type.

In fact he went completely against the norm in terms of her history with men. She usually went for the strong, masculine and largely unpredictable kind, not the staid, straightforward, open type that Ethan seemed to be. The type that Terri kept insisting no longer existed.

Thinking about last night, she felt slightly guilty that after saying goodbye to Ethan and getting a cab home, she hadn't thought once about Gary until she'd actually crawled into bed. It was only then that she realised she hadn't heard from him all evening.

Rachel scowled. Little did she know then that her beloved was here, dead drunk and fast asleep in her restaurant. What had he been doing here and why didn't he call? Of course,

she remembered ashamedly, she hadn't called him either, and in fact had neglected to tell him that she was out for dinner with another man. Hell, she was hardly one to talk about inconsiderate behaviour, was she?

At that moment, she heard movement and the jangling of keys from outside, signalling Terri's arrival downstairs from her flat.

'Well, good morning!' Rachel greeted her with a smile. 'How are *you* feeling today?' What with the state Gary had been in, she expected Terri to be just as hung-over; however, her friend looked wide awake and bright as a button.

Actually, she realised, Terri looked slightly wired.

She smiled. 'I feel fine. Why do you ask?'

Rachel raised an eyebrow. 'Well, considering you and my darling fiancé had a late night of it, I figured you'd be the worse for wear.'

Terri shook her head. 'Nope. I know how to control myself. I take it his lordship was still here this morning when you arrived?'

Rachel nodded and rolled her eyes. 'And *I* take it you were forced into a spot of babysitting last night. I'm sorry about that.'

'It's not a problem.' Terri took off her fleecy top and put on her chef's whites. Then she seemed to look carefully at Rachel. 'How about you? Did you have a nice night?'

'Yes, it was great, actually. Ethan is such a nice guy and we had a lovely time.'

'I see.' Terri kept looking at her strangely, and for a moment Rachel worried that her earlier thoughts were written all over her face.

'I mean, it was a shame that Gary couldn't be there too but . . . What was he doing here anyway? I sincerely hope he didn't ride the bike back from Wicklow after all?'

'Yeah . . . I mean no, he and Sean took a taxi.'

She seemed strangely distracted, Rachel thought. 'I get the impression that he outstayed his welcome last night, sorry about that.'

Terri shrugged. 'Well, he was kind of worse for wear when he arrived, and then after a few more here he fell asleep so I couldn't really move him.'

Once again, Rachel felt an odd surge of distaste at her fiancé's rather boorish behaviour. 'Again, I'm so sorry. I'm sure Gary rolling up like that after a mad night was the last thing you needed.'

'It was fine. Actually, we had a chance to talk a little.'

'About what?' Rachel asked, completely perplexed by this. Gary and Terri rarely 'talked'.

Again, some kind of look passed over her friend's face, but Rachel wasn't sure what to make of it. 'Nothing really, just this and that. But anyway, tell me more about your night. What did you and Ethan Greene talk about?'

'The usual. He told me about this book he's researching, about bread. Can you believe it?' She smiled. 'And all about Daisy, his daughter, and of course his fiancée.'

Terri stopped halfway to the fridge. 'His fiancée? You mean he's engaged too?'

'Not yet, but he's planning to propose soon, apparently. Seems you were right about him being attached.'

'Right.' Terri seemed to be thinking very hard about something. 'And was she with him in New York?'

'The girlfriend? I'm not sure. I think so. His little daughter certainly was. Actually, now that I think of it, remind me to hold back about a dozen cookies or so from today, will you? Preferably the chocolate-chip ones. I promised Daisy I'd make her some to thank her for looking after Gary's bags, and Ethan's calling in for them before he leaves this afternoon.'

Terri stopped what she was doing. 'The daughter had his bags?'

'That's what Ethan said. Anyway, look at the time; it's almost eight. We'd better stop nattering and get cracking on with breakfast.'

'Yeah,' her friend agreed. 'Time flies when you're having fun. I don't know about you but, thanks to that fiancé of yours, last night was a late one for me.'

'You and me both.'

'What? You were out late too?'

'Yes, it was almost one by the time we finished.'

Terri's eyes widened. 'Wow, the conversation must have been good.'

'It was. He's a lovely guy, so easy to talk to and we just didn't realise the time.'

'Because you were so busy talking.'

Despite herself Rachel coloured a little, and Terri noticed. 'Oh my God, you're blushing!'

'I am not.'

'You are! What the hell happened last night? What did Ethan Greene say to you?'

'What are you talking about?' Rachel shook her head, mortified. 'Nothing happened. It was just a nice night. Jesus, Terri, I barely know the guy. Besides, in case you've forgotten, I'm engaged to Gary.'

'Hmm. And Gary didn't seem to know you were meeting another guy for dinner.'

'Honestly, it wasn't like that,' Rachel insisted, but she couldn't escape Terri's probing gaze.

'Look, Rachel, it's OK. I'm not trying to get at you, so don't be so hard on yourself. Ethan seems lovely and I'm glad you had a good time. And for what it's worth, I didn't say anything to Gary about it either,' she added meaning-fully and Rachel glanced at her.

Why was she sounding almost like a co-conspirator in some kind of cover-up? Because there was no cover-up. Ethan was a great guy but he was attached, as was she. The simple fact was that they'd been thrown together by circumstance, and she'd owed him a debt of gratitude for saving Gary's life in New York.

Last night, they'd had a laugh, exchanged stories and enjoyed one another's company but that was all there was to it.

End of story.

Chapter 26

Terri felt like a cat on a hot tin roof. She couldn't believe that this morning, far from crying into her coffee about Gary's deceit, Rachel had actually had a great night with Ethan Greene.

She had to smile at the irony and while, of course, she hated the idea of her friend being embarrassed or humiliated, she took some pleasure in the fact that after a nice evening with Ethan, Rachel had found her errant fiancé passed out the next morning, drunk and drooling all over the place.

After Gary's revelation last night, there was no question that Rachel was being deceived, but even Terri couldn't have conceived that the guy might well get his comeuppance in a very different and unexpected manner. She thought again about what Gary had told her, how he had knowingly proposed to Rachel with a ring meant for someone else. Terri thought about the amount of money Ethan must have spent on that ring, which raised another set of issues.

What was Ethan playing at? He obviously hadn't told Rachel about the mix-up last night, because she was still wearing the ring this morning and had no idea about anything untoward.

Terri wondered what he was waiting for; after all he must have realised the mistake fairly soon after it occurred. She thought again about the frantic phone calls he'd been making and then his sudden appearance at the bistro yesterday.

Clearly he was here to get the ring back, so why hadn't he said anything? Especially when the mistake had cost him a lot in more ways than one. According to Rachel, he was thinking about proposing to his girlfriend, but that plan would have gone awry once he discovered he'd ended up with the charm bracelet. Talk about bad luck! To think that the poor guy had gone out of his way to help the likes of Gary Knowles and then got shafted in such a horrible way.

She still couldn't believe that Gary hadn't copped the true cause of the mistake and had instead been going around thinking it was through some stroke of random luck that he'd ended up with a diamond that cost a small fortune. So much so that he'd even gone along with an engagement he had no notion of beforehand.

But again, why hadn't Ethan confessed all to Rachel? Terri could only imagine how anxious he must be to get the ring back, so why the delay?

She thought about the quietly contented expression on Rachel's face this morning. Could it be possible that the two of them had clicked last night at dinner, and as a result Ethan was afraid to hurt Rachel?

Granted, it was a long shot, but anyone who spent enough time in Rachel's company would realise that she was a romantic soul who didn't deserve to be crushed in any way.

That had to be it. Ethan obviously couldn't bring himself to tell her the truth and, Terri had to admit, she knew how that felt. With her new-found knowledge she too was reluctant to broach the subject, especially when it was all Gary's stupid fault and he should never have allowed the situation to get this far in the first place.

She wondered if she should try to contact Ethan some-

how, tip him off that she knew about what had happened, and say she would help him get to the bottom of it.

That was tricky territory, though, especially when she barely knew the guy, and had no idea about his reasoning for not saying anything.

Terri went on with her morning routine, but her mind was elsewhere. It was as if overnight she had turned into Cupid, desperately trying to orchestrate a very odd and intricate love triangle . . . or maybe it should be a love square, she thought, recalling that Ethan's girlfriend was stuck somewhere in there too.

Well, whatever it was, it involved one very big, very expensive diamond worthy of Ms Audrey Hepburn herself.

'Have you heard from Dad today? What time is he coming home?' Daisy asked.

Vanessa's eyebrows automatically shot together, but then she quickly smoothed her expression. After yesterday's discussion, she didn't want to come across as impatient towards Daisy, but she had to admit that she was actually way past impatient and now full-on agitated.

It was almost midday and Ethan hadn't called since the day before.

She'd expected him to phone, if not late last night, then at least first thing this morning, to update her on how his 'research' was going. But he never did.

She had tried calling him herself but it had gone straight to voicemail. She knew his phone was working fine in Ireland, so why wasn't he answering or returning her calls?

'I'm not sure, darling. He hasn't phoned yet.'

Daisy smiled weakly, and Vanessa knew she was still feeling upset that she had let the cat out of the bag. She'd been quiet for most of the day afterwards and had confined herself to her bedroom, barely speaking to Vanessa, other than briefly over dinner and at breakfast this morning.

'Are you going to tell him I told you about the surprise?'

'Of course not, darling,' Vanessa was quick to reassure her. 'After all, you didn't actually tell me anything, did you?'

That was the most frustrating part really. When Daisy had inadvertently revealed something about a ring, Vanessa had been so curious she'd wanted to shake the information out of her!

Her imagination had been running away with her, and she sorely wished she knew what Ethan was up to. Based on what little Daisy had said, though, Vanessa was almost certain his so-called research was merely a cover story for something else: namely some kind of intricate plan to propose. If there was a ring involved, she thought excitedly, that had to be it, didn't it?

She wasn't quite sure where this Rachel person came into it, if at all (perhaps she was some kind of wedding planner?), but knowing Ethan as she did, chances were he'd gone to Dublin to visit her parents and officially ask them for her hand.

He was such a traditionalist that was *exactly* the kind of thing he'd do, and it had taken every ounce of restraint in her not to phone her mother in the meantime and find out if he'd been in touch. But she really couldn't risk Ethan knowing that she was onto him, or indeed risk falling flat on her face if her suspicions weren't correct.

But then, on the phone yesterday, when Ethan started talking about visiting Irish country estates, she was pretty sure he was researching wedding venues, although she really would have preferred him to include her in that.

Still, if all the subterfuge meant that a proposal was immi-

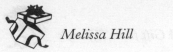

nent then Vanessa could certainly forgo that much. She wanted to marry Ethan. She'd known from the start that he was perfect marriage material: mature, well respected and talented. And possibly best of all, with Daisy they would be a ready-made family.

Then, as if on cue, the phone rang and she jumped.

'There, that must be him now,' she said to Daisy. With any luck she would find out all she needed to know very soon.

Vanessa flipped open her mobile phone and held it to her ear. 'Hi, darling. How are you?'

'Hey,' Ethan said into the phone and was it her imagination or he did he sound a little . . . distant?

'Are you having a nice time? And how's everything going with the research?'

'Yes, well . . . I'm doing as much as I can in such a short space of time.'

'I can imagine. I really can't wait to hear all about it. It sounds like such an interesting project.'

'Well, of course, everything is still in the very early stages,' he replied.

Vanessa stayed silent, feeling somewhat disappointed. Damn, what did *that* mean? She didn't think she could wait much longer; the suspense was killing her.

'Actually,' Ethan continued, 'it now looks like I may have to rethink the idea behind it altogether.'

'Why would you need to do that?' she asked. 'Especially after going to so much trouble . . . you know, going all the way to Dublin.'

'Let's just say the first idea I had didn't go quite according to plan, so now I think I may need to look at a different one.'

The first idea? If he hadn't arranged the visit to her parents in advance, and then had maybe missed them at the house when he called . . .

'Really? Why didn't your first idea work?' she enquired.

'Well, I'm a bit worried that some people might be upset about the outcome.'

She frowned. What the hell did that mean? 'What outcome?'

'Of the story, of course. I suppose I don't want to upset the reader.'

Vanessa shook her head. This conversation was truly bizarre. 'You don't want to upset the *reader*?'

'Yes.'

If by some chance her father had said or done something stupid, she would *murder* him!

'Well, there will always be critics, Ethan. You can't please everyone.'

'I know.'

'So perhaps you should worry less about readers liking the outcome, and concentrate on making sure that you and I are happy with the outcome?'

'As I said, it's early days and I'm not sure I'm ready for you to read it.'

Damn. Now Vanessa's thoughts were all over the place. What the hell was he trying to say here?

'I see, so where does that leave us in the meantime?' she asked, momentarily forgetting that they were supposed to be speaking in code. Although Ethan couldn't know that, of course.

'What do you mean?' he asked, and she could hear panic seeping into his voice.

She deliberately lightened her tone. 'Well, I should hope you're going to let me read it sometime.'

'Of course I will. It's still just a bit messy at the moment, that's all.'

'I see.' Vanessa's heart sank. It seemed there might be nothing forthcoming in the near future when it came to a ring or a marriage proposal or whatever the hell this was supposed to be. Could Daisy have misread the situation? Or had she completely misread it herself?

She turned to look at Ethan's daughter, who was sitting quietly at the breakfast bar.

'Well, we're looking forward to seeing you soon. When are you due back?'

'My flight's booked for this evening at seven. Are you and Daisy having a nice time?'

'We're having a lovely time,' she said, catching the little girl's eye and giving her a knowing wink. 'Do you want to talk to her?' Vanessa was rather hoping Ethan might confess to Daisy what was going on over there, and then she in turn might be able to enlighten her.

'Yes, if she's there.'

'Hold on.' She held out the receiver to Daisy, who clutched it eagerly.

'Hi, Dad. Yes, we're having a great time. No . . . not really.' At this, Vanessa could see the guilty shadow that crossed her face, and she realised that Ethan must be asking something about the secret they were keeping. She clenched her hands into fists. What was going on? And how could she get it out of Daisy? 'Yeah I miss you too. See you soon, Dad.'

With that, she handed the phone back to Vanessa.

'When exactly is your flight due in, Ethan? We can come to Heathrow and collect you, if you'd like.'

'No, it's fine. No need to go to any trouble. I can get a cab.'

'Well, as long as you're sure.'

'I am. Listen, I'd better go. I have quite a lot to get

through today. Some more options to explore, as I'm sure you can imagine.'

But she couldn't, Vanessa thought with frustration; that was partly the problem.

'Of course. Well, enjoy the rest of the trip and if there's anything I can help you with – any research I can do from this side or anything – let me know.'

'Ah, thank you, but after today I should have it all under control,' he said, sounding highly uncomfortable.

'That's good to know. See you soon, darling.'

But as Vanessa disconnected the call, she wondered how much longer she would be able to stand the suspense.

Chapter 27

Ethan knew that he should have bitten the bullet and got the ring back from Rachel last night, but he couldn't do it.

He was just too soft – or too bloody stupid, more like. By rights, he should be on a plane back to London now; instead he was heading back to Stromboli in one last-ditch attempt at getting the job done. But if it meant he could go home with Vanessa's ring in hand, it would be worth it.

'Ethan, hello again!' Before he could ponder his predicament any further, he was greeted with Rachel's beaming smile. She couldn't have got to bed until after two last night, and yet she looked beautiful. All thoughts of getting the ring back suddenly left his mind as he stood there stupidly staring at her. He felt a spasm of something go through his stomach; he couldn't put his finger on what it was exactly, but knew it was no longer just about the ring.

The truth was that he was still hugely bothered by last night's recollection of Jane's words and their significance in what was happening now. Jane would have laughed if she'd known what was going through his mind. She was the one who'd always believed in fate and the alignment of the universe and all that mumbo-jumbo. But wasn't it odd that fate had indeed led him here to this strange woman's door? A woman who had inadvertently ended up with an engagement ring that belonged to him and who also happened to be a baker by trade.

A woman who'd bake him bread . . .

And even stranger that such a random excuse for a book topic had led him to recall his beloved girlfriend's words in the first place.

A rush of panic and confusion flooded through him as the feeling settled. This was ridiculous, he thought. What was wrong with him?

'Sleep well last night?' Rachel asked and Ethan willed himself to snap out of it. 'Yes, very well, thanks.'

'So what are you up to today?' she asked. 'More research for your book, presumably.'

He nodded uncomfortably at the mention of his pathetic cover story. 'Yes, well, as much I can, really.'

Earlier that morning at the hotel Ethan had passed some time Googling any practical knowledge that he should have if he were writing a book about the history of bread in other cultures. He now felt that not only could he list hundreds of different types of bread across the world, but he also had a working knowledge of symbolism, rituals and ingredients. Just in case anyone starting asking questions.

'Well, as I said last night, if you need my help with anything in that regard, don't hesitate to ask.'

He smiled. 'Thanks, that's very kind of you and I'll certainly keep it in mind.'

There was a slightly awkward moment as the two of them stood there in the middle of the bistro staring at one another.

'Oh!' Rachel exclaimed, as if remembering. 'Are you here to eat? You must be hungry. Here, let me get you a table.'

'Thanks, but no, I had a huge breakfast at the hotel earlier.' He looked hesitant. 'Erm, I just wanted to pop in

to thank you for a lovely evening. It was really good of you to spend your Saturday night off babysitting me.'

'Not at all. I had a lovely time.'

'Me too. But I just wondered . . . could I possibly have a contact number for your fiancé? I'd really like to talk to Gary today if I could.'

Was it his imagination, or did a shadow cross her face at the mention of him?

'Ethan, again, I really have to apologise on his behalf. I don't know what's got into him lately, and it's just not good enough that you should have to chase him. When are you going back to London? I'll make sure he calls you today. If not, it'll definitely be this evening.' She pursed her lips. 'Let's just say Gary is a little . . . under the weather at the moment.'

'I see. But I'd quite like to be able to get in touch with him myself, just in case it slips his mind again.'

Damn it, couldn't she just give him the blasted number? Having her as the go-between was becoming tedious; irrespective of how much he enjoyed talking to her, it wasn't getting him anywhere.

'Believe me, I'll make sure that doesn't happen, but here –' Rachel walked over to the bar area and grabbed a notebook '– this is his mobile number.' She wrote down a sequence of digits, and Ethan wanted to punch the air.

Finally, he'd be able to talk to Knowles on his own, man to man.

'Thank you.' He put it carefully into his wallet, as if it were made of gold. 'And again, best of luck to you both – with the wedding plans.'

Rachel met his gaze. 'You too. Don't wait too long to do the deed either. You don't want your girlfriend to get tired of waiting,' she added, laughing.

'Believe me, I won't.' He went to shake her hand, but

once again she stepped forward and engulfed him in a warm hug. Ethan felt almost dizzy as he breathed in the smell of her hair, and the scent of her skin.

'Well, it was so lovely to see you again, Ethan. And please do keep in touch. You have my number too, and, as I said, if you ever need to know anything about bread . . .'

He smiled. 'I know exactly who to ask.' He looked at his watch, suddenly reluctant to leave. 'I suppose I'd better get a move on. Lots to do today.'

'I know what you mean. Weekends can get a bit mad around here.' She smiled and ran a hand through her hair, and once more Ethan saw the diamond sparkle in the light.

'Goodbye, Rachel,' he said, but as he turned to leave the thought struck him that, having seen how well it suited Rachel, he was finding it increasingly difficult to picture it on Vanessa.

As she moved between tables, serving customers, Terri studied the encounter between Rachel and Ethan with interest. It wasn't as though she was eavesdropping; no, it was more like 'accidentally overhearing'.

And whatever the words, judging from Ethan's enraptured expression and Rachel's coquettish laughs, there was little doubt that last night's dinner had had quite an effect on both of them.

Which of course went a long way towards explaining why Ethan hadn't told Rachel about the mix-up.

If Ethan behaved like that every time Rachel smiled at him, how would he ever be able to confess the truth about the ring? And how was Rachel ever going to see the light about Gary?

Terri bit her lip. She didn't want to interfere in her friend's business, but at the same time this was a tricky one. Knowing

Rachel, she would continue to go about planning this farce of a wedding, while at the back of it all her knucklehead fiancé was just playing along for the sake of it.

They were supposed to be going out shopping for dresses soon but there was no way Terri could allow her friend to spend another cent on a wedding that by rights should not happen. '

And on top of that, Ethan really needed to wake up and tell Rachel once and for all about the entire fiasco. He knew what had happened yet was still dragging his heels. And what was all that nonsense he'd been spouting to Rachel about being here in Dublin to research some book? Did he really expect people to believe it was all about *bread*?

Terri shook her head. She was a baker and had no interest in reading such a thing, so where was the market for that? What a sorry story.

She took off her chef's cap and shook out her hair. Obviously this was going to need some interference, she decided, heading for the front door. And it looked like she was the only person qualified to help the process along. After all, if she left it up to Ethan the situation would hardly be resolved before the next century.

Ethan was almost halfway down the street when she caught up with him.

'Hey there,' she called out cheerfully and he turned to look at her, surprised. It was only then that she noticed he had a mobile phone to his ear and a piece of paper in his hand.

'Yes?' he replied, quickly shoving the paper into his pocket.

'Hi! Remember me from yesterday?'

'Well, yes, of course. Terri, isn't it? I must admit I almost didn't recognise you with that hair hidden under your chef's hat. It's extraordinary,' he said, almost under his breath.

'Sorry to interrupt, I didn't realise you were on the phone.'

'No need to apologise. I was just about to call someone . . . in London,' he added mumbling.

Probably the girlfriend, Terri thought, and wondered if she too knew about the problem with the ring. Not likely; otherwise the woman would have come here in person to get it back, and no doubt taken not only the ring, but the hand off Rachel too! Terri certainly would anyway. She still couldn't believe that this guy was so soft that he hadn't managed to sort this out. But English people could be like that, couldn't they? All manners and not wanting to upset people. Admirable traits but maybe not with a diamond that size at stake.

Anyway, Terri was convinced that there was now a lot more to it than just good manners where Ethan was concerned. He had clicked with Rachel and clearly didn't want to hurt her. It was plain to see that he had hugely conflicting feelings about what he should do and what he wanted to do. Terri was impressed; in her experience it was rare to come across a man – never mind a complete stranger – who actually cared about someone else's feelings, rather than just stomping all over them in order to get what he wanted. And of course it was Ethan's consideration for his fellow man that had got him into all this trouble in the first place, wasn't it?

So what would his next move be?

'I see,' Terri said. Well, unlike Ethan, she believed in straight talking, so she decided to come right out and say something; unless she did, nothing would ever be resolved. 'Do you mind if I talk to you for a moment?' she said, and his gaze shifted nervously from side to side.

'To me?' He looked perplexed, clearly wondering what she could want with him.

'Yes. I know why you're here.'

Ethan's face grew wary. 'What do you mean?'

'I know that your visit here this weekend has nothing whatsoever to do with research for a book.'

His stared at her, wide-eyed. 'I really have no idea what you're talking about.'

Terri smiled and shook her head. 'Sweet, but that whole big blue eyes thing isn't going to work on me. I know everything. I know about the accident in New York, and I know about the mix-up with the engagement ring. I know you bought an expensive diamond from Tiffany's, but that your girlfriend ended up with a silver charm bracelet.'

His face went white. 'How could you possibly—'

'And I also know that you've been trying to tell Rachel the truth but for some reason have come up with this random story about researching a book.'

For a moment he looked as though he was about to argue, but it was as if he couldn't find the words.

She rolled her eyes. 'A book about the history of bread? Sounds tantalising!' She was gratified to see a slight smile break through his facade. 'Anyway, I know all of this because I got Gary drunk last night and, as they say in the movies, he sang like a canary.'

Ethan's head shot up. 'He admitted to stealing the ring?'

'Not exactly. Look, take it from me: Gary Knowles isn't the sharpest tool in the box. In fact he's so stupid that the thought the ring might have been someone else's never even crossed his mind.'

Ethan's eyes widened. 'He didn't know? Honestly? Well, I must admit that's a bit of a relief. I'd thought he was avoiding me on purpose.'

'No, I'll give him that much; he honestly didn't have a clue.'

'Then why did he give it to Rachel?' Ethan demanded, those blue eyes now flashing with irritation. 'And why ask her to marry him when it's pretty clear, to me at least, that he had no intention of doing so?'

'As I said, he's an idiot. And Gary was never one to look a gift horse in the mouth.'

'Still, it's a horrible thing to do.'

'Which, I take it, is why you haven't said anything to Rachel about it?' she enquired gently. 'That's the real reason for your visit, isn't it? Or was, at least.'

He nodded, and exhaled a deep sigh. 'Believe me, I've tried to tell her a number of times. But for some reason I just can't bring myself to do it. It would be a terrible thing to find out that your engagement is all a big mistake, and from what I can tell it *was* a mistake, wasn't it? He never intended to propose at all.'

'Unfortunately for Rachel, no.' Terri was again touched by the guy's obvious concern for someone who was a stranger to him. You just didn't get that these days. And for this reason, perhaps more than any other, she found herself wanting to help Ethan Greene even more.

'Anyway, I didn't think it was fair to put this on Rachel, not when it's Gary Knowles who caused the problem.' Ethan held up his mobile. 'I was about to phone him just now but, to be frank, I wasn't sure what to expect. I really can't believe he had no idea how it happened.' He looked at Terri. 'Where on earth did he think it came from?'

She rolled her eyes again. 'Who knows? From the great ring fairy in the sky?' She grinned. 'But the fact is that now he does know, as do I, so what are we going to do about it?'

Ethan looked surprised. 'We?'

'Yes. The truth needs to come out. Gary's a liar and ultimately a thief, if we're really being honest. He also seems

to think that he can manipulate Rachel to the hilt and I can't stand by and watch him do it.'

'Well, that's really none of my business.'

'Ethan, please. I'm also guessing that you haven't said anything to Rachel for another, slightly more personal, reason?' she suggested gently and Ethan's cheeks flared pink.

He lowered his gaze. 'I have no idea—'

'Don't be embarrassed; it doesn't surprise me in the slightest. Rachel's amazing and I think it's wonderful that you two got on so well.' But, oddly, Terri felt slightly deflated that this lovely man seemed to have fallen hook, line and sinker for her friend. Not that anyone who knew her could do otherwise . . .

Then he cleared his throat. 'This is all so surreal. The only reason I came here was to get back what's rightfully mine, but . . .'

Terri smiled kindly. 'But you've got a little more than you expected?'

Ethan was silent again, clearly lost in thought and Terri could only imagine the internal struggle he was having. He might have been all set to propose to his girlfriend but he was undeniably taken with Rachel.

'Look, I just didn't expect to be in this position,' he admitted, sounding baffled.

'I'm sure you didn't and it's not your fault. You were being a nice guy, helping Gary out, and he should have been honest with Rachel about the ring, but he's a prat.'

'Did he really admit everything to you?'

'In so many words. But he was very drunk and I'm not even sure he'll remember telling me.' She smiled wickedly. 'I left him passed out in the bistro. Rachel wasn't too happy to find him there this morning, I can tell you.'

Ethan shook his head in disbelief. 'I still can't believe she would agree to marry this guy.'

'You and me both. I was never his number-one fan, but I must admit the engagement threw me a little. I don't know what Gary has done to pull the wool over her eyes, but believe me, the rest of us see right through him. She's usually a great judge of character. Maybe, though, she's beginning to see the error of her decision,' she added meaningfully.

Ethan shrugged. 'Well, I must admit I really don't know what to do. I'm in a tough spot. I've never been in this position before. I mean, there's Vanessa at home, who I love and want to marry, but –' again he dropped his gaze '– you're right: there is something about Rachel and I can't quite put my finger on it. I just feel that if I tell her about the ring I'll crush her, particularly when she's been so wonderful.' He shook his head. 'Then there's this whole fiasco about the book . . .'

'Ah, yes, the book that is sure to be a *Sunday Times* bestseller.' Terri laughed. 'I take it all back. Maybe Rachel really is that gullible if she truly believes anyone is interested in the history of bread.'

He smiled bashfully and Terri realised that if Rachel *was* having second thoughts about Gary after last night's dinner, she could completely understand why. There was something incredibly appealing about Ethan Greene; he had the perfect combination of sensitivity and masculinity. 'I was on the spot and it was all I could think of.'

'Well, then I think we need to work on your storytelling abilities.'

'Believe me, Terri, I don't normally have to lie about anything.'

'That's not a bad thing,' she said softly.

'Thanks.'

'So, Ethan, I think this is where you might need my help because, unlike you, I'm actually quite good at coming up with plausible stories.'

'I don't know what you mean. Obviously, now that Knowles is aware of the problem, it's up to him to tell Rachel the truth and—'

'But you don't know Gary. If anything, he's even more likely to put his head in the sand about all of this.'

'But that's stealing, surely?'

'Yes it is. Again, perhaps something that isn't entirely beyond our Gary?' With what she knew about Gary at this stage, Terri wouldn't put it past him.

'Well, I'm not sure how it involves me – beyond the ring, that is.'

Terri eyed him. 'Are you absolutely sure about that?' Once more, he couldn't meet her gaze. 'You're happy just to stand by and watch Rachel get hurt?'

'Terri, it's absolutely none of my business.' He looked at his watch. 'Look, thank you for telling me this; it's good to know I'm not alone in thinking badly of Gary Knowles but, really, that's as far as it goes. And now that he knows the extent of the problem I'm sure I'll have the ring back in no time. What happens after that is nothing to do with me.'

'But—'

'As I said, I'm very sorry that Rachel had to get stuck in the middle of this, but I'm sure it will all work out.'

But even as he said the words, Terri guessed that Ethan Greene didn't mean any of them. She knew he cared about Rachel's feelings almost as much as she did.

Chapter 28

On his way back from collecting his bike in Wicklow, Gary felt his mobile phone vibrate in his riding jacket. He smiled to himself, pleased that he was such a connoisseur of bikes that he could distinguish between the vibrations coming off the riding machine and those of the mobile phone in his pocket. Actually, he was pleased that his brain could distinguish anything at all this afternoon, given that he was nursing such an almighty hangover.

This was probably Sean ringing him about where to meet up for a cure. Gary reckoned a pint was the only way he'd be able to relieve the ache in his bones and the persistent twinges in his ribs. Sleeping slumped over the table in the bistro last night hadn't helped, and while he'd tried his best to sleep off the worst of the after-effects at home earlier, he reckoned the only thing for it now was a good spin on the bike, followed by an afternoon in the pub.

Rachel was annoyed with him anyway so he might as well be hanged for a sheep as for a lamb. And after he'd gone out of his way to come back from Wicklow last night to see her! Sometimes you just couldn't win, especially with women.

Although Terri had been sound enough to him last night, what with the free gargle and good company. She blew hot and cold sometimes, Terri, but was all right at the back of it all. Gary smiled, figuring she must have always had a bit

of a thing for him, but because he was with Rachel he'd never really noticed.

He brought his bike to a halt, spraying gravel as he stopped. Still sitting on the saddle, he reached into his pocket and brought out the phone. Then he paused, suddenly worried it might be her again . . . but no, this looked like an international number. The calls had been coming thick and fast since the new year and while he'd managed to avoid most of them, he knew he wouldn't be able to do that forever. He didn't recognise this number but his curiosity got the better of him and he decided to answer it anyway. He could always claim it was a wrong number if needs be.

'Hello.'

'Is that Gary Knowles?' The voice was male, with an English accent and sounded posh. Shite, Gary thought, realising immediately that it had to be that Ethan Greene guy.

'Speaking,' he replied.

'Well, it's nice to talk to you finally. It's Ethan Greene here.'

'Right. Er, hello.' Gary tried to sound nonchalant but the truth was his nerves were in bits. Was there a chance that, as Terri tried to point out last night, the piece of luck that had landed in his lap (or at least in that Tiffany's bag) wasn't that at all? He didn't want to think too much about it.

If something had gone amiss then it was an innocent mistake and had nothing to do with Gary; him being unconscious and all.

'I'm not sure if you remember, but our paths crossed in New York,' Greene went on, not sounding particularly friendly. 'I've tried to get in touch with you a number of times since but it seems you're a very hard man to pin down.'

'Right, yes. I think Rachel might have mentioned something.'

'Mr Knowles, let's not beat around the bush. I'd like my property back.' Gary's eyes narrowed defensively. He didn't like this guy's tone. Who did he think he was, ringing up out of the blue like this and making demands? 'I don't know what you're talking about.'

'Oh I think you know very well what I'm talking about. The diamond ring that is currently in the possession of your girlfriend, Rachel? You and I both know that you didn't buy that yourself.'

'As I said, I don't know what you're—'

'Mr Knowles, we can do this the easy way or the hard way. The ring is mine and I want it back. I'm also more than happy to return your own Tiffany's purchase – a silver charm bracelet, I believe?'

'I really don't know what you're on about.' Gary knew better than to admit anything upfront. 'Thanks for looking after me following the accident and everything, but as far as this stuff goes it's all news to me. I bought that ring myself.'

'Really? So why did you admit to your friend Terri that you had no idea where it came from?'

Shite! Gary couldn't believe he'd been so stupid as to let his guard down like that. There was no way he could ask Rachel for the ring back now, not when she thought the sun shone out of his backside for giving it to her. No, what was done was done, and how was he supposed to know that the stupid ring belonged to someone else? Surely it was your man's fault for not looking after his own stuff? Gary was annoyed. It was bad enough that he'd been put in the awkward position of having to propose – unprepared! – because of this bloody ring, so for this guy to just turn around and expect him to hand it back after all that was a bit rich!

For all Gary knew any stranger could ring up and claim the ring was his, but where was the proof?

'Look, I don't have time for this,' he said in an attempt to get the guy off his back. 'I don't know what you're spouting off about, to be honest.'

'Fine, then you leave me little choice but to go to the police.'

'Grand. Do what you like.' Gary didn't know what else to say. Anyway, what could the cops do? He'd committed no crime, and in all honesty, he'd also been the victim here, considering that the appearance of this ring had led to him being engaged without having the chance to think properly about it. So the last thing he wanted to do was have to fork out a fortune for another diamond just because some stranger had taken the notion to blame him for losing one. Never mind the fact that he hadn't a hope of being able to afford even a small one, let alone something to match the size of that rock.

It was important that Rachel continued to think well of him. Gary didn't know how she'd react if she knew that his property business was in serious trouble and the debts were piling up. Especially when her own business was going so well. Women like Rachel wouldn't look twice at men who didn't pull their weight; Gary knew that much.

'You're seriously refusing to give it back?' Greene said, and Gary knew that he'd been calling his bluff about the cops. Clearly he had no proof and so hadn't a leg to stand on.

'Look, mate, I'm sorry for your troubles, but I really haven't a clue what you want from me. I don't know you from Adam, and here you are ringing me up and accusing me of all sorts and—'

'You stole my engagement ring, for crying out loud!'

'Now hold on a moment,' Gary said, his hackles rising.

He'd had just about enough of this. 'I didn't steal anything. If you've lost something then I'm sorry but, as I said, it's nothing to do with me.'

'I saw the ring on your girlfriend's finger just now. There's no question that it's mine!'

Gary frowned. What the hell? How could Greene have seen it on Rachel's finger?

'And quite frankly I cannot understand what such a lovely woman is doing with someone like yourself. We had dinner last night and she told me all about your so-called proposal and how you had it all planned. Planned, my foot.'

Gary was incredulous. Right. That was enough. First, the guy accuses of him of stealing some ring, and then he has the audacity to sneak around with his fiancée? Rachel hadn't said a word about going out to dinner with anyone last night, especially not this guy.

Was this his true game at the back of it all? Was all this talk about a ring a mere front for him to get into Rachel's knickers? Gary wouldn't put it past him.

'OK, Greene,' he said, his tone steely. 'I'll tell you one thing. I don't take kindly to strange men sniffing around my girlfriend. So if you know what's good for you, you stay away from her.'

'For goodness' sake, all I want is to have my ring,' Ethan said, backing down immediately, much to Gary's satisfaction.

'Well, good luck with that,' he said, hanging up on him.

Stupid prat obviously didn't know who the hell he was dealing with, and if he thought he could just roll up in Dublin and use some cock and bull story to try to swipe Gary's woman from him, he had another think coming.

Gary put the phone back in his inside pocket and revved up the bike again.

He needed to talk to Sean about this, get his take on it. This all seemed a bit too convenient for his liking. Granted, the ring had appeared out of the blue, but that didn't mean anything. He was only sorry that he'd admitted as much to Terri, and hoped she wouldn't go blabbing to Rachel. After all, the ring did belong to him; well, once it landed in his bags anyway. And although the proposal hadn't been as planned as everyone thought, he had asked Rachel to marry him – and in front of half the country on New Year's Eve! And he'd got used to the idea now, and was happy enough about settling down with her.

So surely she couldn't get too upset about a technicality?

With any luck Terri wouldn't say a word, and he was worrying for nothing. She'd been pretty drunk herself last night so maybe she wouldn't even remember. But in the meantime, just in case she did blab, he supposed he'd better start thinking about his own version of events.

Gary zoomed down the road in the direction of Sean's place.

And he shouldn't waste time worrying about that idiot Ethan Greene either. Rachel would believe him over some crackpot toff from London; he knew she would.

Chapter 29

'What the hell am I supposed to do now?' Terri said to Justin. She'd quickly filled him in on all that had happened in the last twenty-four hours, how she had got Gary drunk to get the truth out of him, and about the mix-up with the ring. Then she proceeded to bring him up to speed on her discussion with Ethan. Justin's eyes grew as big as saucers, and when she'd finished he let out a long, low whistle.

'Well, I have to say that it all completely beggars belief, even for Gary. But of course we knew all along that there was something fishy about this whole engagement.'

'Yes, but besides the fishiness, you really should have seen the look on Ethan's face. He thinks Rachel is the best thing since . . . erm, sliced bread,' she added.

Justin looked sceptical. 'But he already has a girlfriend, doesn't he? Who would be his fiancée by now if our Gary hadn't messed it all up.'

'I know.' Terri bit her lip. 'Lucky her, whoever she is. He's a dote and Rachel would be so much better off with someone like him than with the likes of Gary.'

'Come on, Terri, Rachel barely even knows him. And neither do you, for that matter.'

But Terri thought that sometimes you didn't need to know a person all that well to have a good feeling about them. She put her hands on her hips. 'Stranger things have happened, Justin. You didn't see Rachel this morning.

Something happened with those two last night; I'm sure of it.' When Justin's eyes widened again, she quickly clarified: 'Oh not that kind of something. I mean a spark, a connection, whatever you want to call it.'

His gaze narrowed suspiciously. 'When did you turn into such an old romantic?'

'Since I realised that my best friend has become engaged to the biggest shit in the world.' She kneaded her forehead. 'I'm her bridesmaid and we're going out shopping for wedding dresses soon. How am I supposed to tell her that Gary had no intention whatsoever of proposing, and that she's wearing – for all intents and purposes – a stolen ring? This is all such a mess.'

'So *are* you going to tell her? About how Gary came by the ring, I mean.'

Terri grimaced. 'Can you imagine that conversation? I don't want to upset her, but of course I don't want to see her get hurt either. You know what Rachel's like; she'd be devastated. Anyway it's not up to me to tell her, is it?'

'Well, surely Gary will say something now that he knows the game is up.'

Terri wrinkled her nose. 'I wouldn't bet on it.'

Justin continued making up some fresh salad. 'One thing I will give you: it is pretty telling that Ethan Greene didn't break the news to Rachel. Especially considering the size of that rock. If it were me, by now I'd have been ready to hold her down and prise it off her finger.'

'Exactly. Which has to mean that he feels something for her, or at least enough to worry about her feelings. He admitted as much to me on the street earlier.'

'So what are you going to do?'

'What can I do, Justin? Rachel's convinced that Gary's the man of her dreams, when in reality he's the stuff of most women's nightmares. Whereas Ethan, on the other hand . . .' She smiled, picturing the earnest face, the deep blue eyes. 'This could be fate.'

Justin raised an eyebrow. 'Well, for what it's worth, I think you should take a step back for a while, see how this plays out. I wouldn't go running to Rachel about it just yet; you've already done your bit in getting Gary to admit the truth, and maybe that'll be enough to shame him into telling her. If he does, then you'll be around to help pick up the pieces.'

Terri looked at him. 'When did you get so *sensible*?'

'I've always been sensible. You're the one getting carried away with all this "fate" business, which really isn't like you.' He picked up a chopping knife. 'But if you truly believe in that, then you also have to let fate do its own thing. The problem is that, in my experience, sometimes fate can have a strange sense of humour.'

Terri sighed, but she knew deep down that Justin was right.

Throughout her conversation with Ethan Greene, she'd already tried her best to give fate a helping hand.

What the guy did next was entirely up him.

Terri was surprised to see Gary at the bistro later that evening and even more surprised when, after speaking briefly to Rachel, he came into the kitchen and asked if he could have a private word with her.

'What's up?' she asked, drying her floury hands on a nearby tea towel. He looked preoccupied and uncomfortable, a notable change from his usual cocky demeanour.

'I, ah, just wanted to talk to you about last night,' he began, his tone cautious.

'Last night? What about it?'

'Well, I had a few in me and I might have said some things . . .'

'I'm not sure what you mean,' she said, feigning innocence. Was he worried she might tell Rachel about their
so-called flirting? Or did the concern stem from elsewhere,
namely the sorry truth about the ring?

'Well, as I said, last night is a bit fuzzy but you know the
way we were talking about the engagement and I was telling
you that it all happened a bit fast?'

Aha! So he *was* worried about that, she realised with some
satisfaction. He'd obviously had a good think about it all
after last night and had finally copped on to the reality of
where the ring had come from. Maybe she'd misjudged him
and he was about to come good after all.

'Yes, you might have mentioned something about it all
being a bit of a surprise for both of you.'

'Yeah. It's just that . . .' Then he looked at her, as if trying
to figure out something. 'Actually, did Rachel mention to
you where she was last night?'

'After work, you mean? As far as I know she went out
to dinner.'

'Any idea who with?'

Terri was all innocence. 'Well, now that you ask, I think
it was with that guy who saved you, Ethan Greene.'

There was a strange look on his face. 'Don't believe
everything you hear, Terri. That guy didn't save me.'

'Of course he did. You know that.'

Gary grimaced. 'I don't know. I think he's a bit of a
player, this fella, making up stories about losing some ring
to try to get into Rachel's pants.'

She shook her head, bewildered at his reckoning. 'Gary,
I really don't think so. And you yourself admitted that you
don't know where the ring came from.'

'Still, there's nothing to prove it came from him, is there?'

Terri couldn't believe what she was hearing. Was Gary

seriously trying to justify keeping the ring even though he knew it belonged to Ethan Greene? And was he now trying to accuse Ethan of moving in on Rachel? Admittedly, there might be something to the latter, but that was only through circumstance and certainly not by design.

'Gary, I'm not sure what you're asking.'

'If this Greene guy was so anxious to speak to me, then why did he go behind my back and ask her out to dinner?'

'Because you weren't here and Rachel thought you were staying overnight in Wicklow. Anyway, he didn't ask her; she asked him, to thank him for helping you out.'

He rubbed a hand across his stubbly jaw. 'I don't know, Terri; this guy seems a little too cute for my liking. And if he thinks I'm going to fall for that sorry story he fed me earlier . . .'

'So you have spoken to him, then?' Terri was relieved that the two men had at least been in contact. It meant that Gary would now have no choice but to be upfront about what had happened. Granted, Rachel would be hurt and feel very deceived but the truth needed to come out sooner rather than later. 'I'm glad. The sooner Rachel knows about this the—'

Gary looked at her. 'Rachel doesn't need to know anything, as there's nothing to know.'

'But . . . but we both know that the ring isn't yours!' she replied, wide-eyed. 'You must give it back to Ethan.'

'Forget it, Terri. There's nothing to prove it's his. It's Rachel's now, and none of us wants her to get hurt, do we?' He looked at her closely, and Terri realised that behind his Neanderthal bluster was a calculating mind. This worried her even more.

Even worse, he was calling her bluff, daring her to admit what she knew to Rachel, when he was sure she wouldn't

be able to back it up. He was right in a way: there was probably no firm proof that the ring belonged to Ethan. And,
by the looks of things, Gary was planning to suggest that
Ethan was using it all as a cover story to get closer to Rachel.
Perhaps he was even convinced of it himself.

Either way, it looked like Ethan wasn't going to get the
ring back any time soon.

Just then Rachel arrived back in the kitchen. 'Hi, what
are you doing hiding away in here?' she said, sidling up to
Gary.

'Just thanking Terri for keeping me company last night,'
he said, putting an arm around her, and Terri was amazed
at the ease with which he could lie. 'Anyway, I'd better go
and let you ladies do some work.'

'Are you sure you don't want to throw on an apron and
give us a hand? I've got some fresh pastry that needs making,'
Rachel teased him, going to the storeroom.

'Nah, best to leave all that stuff to the experts,' he joked.
Giving Rachel a kiss on the cheek, he eyed Terri briefly as
if to challenge her.

With a sinking heart, Terri knew that, realistically, even
if she wanted to tell Rachel the truth, she didn't have a leg
to stand on. The story would seem so unlikely and far-
fetched that there was a chance Terri might simply come
across as jealous or spiteful.

What made it harder was that Gary was willing and (it
appeared) well able to cover his tracks, and after talking it
all over with Justin, Terri knew that by saying something to
Rachel she ran the risk of ruining not only their friendship,
but also their business relationship.

So what was she going to do?

Rachel came back out of the storeroom. 'Making more
sourdough already?' she said, noticing that Terri was knead-

ing out fresh dough. 'Damn, it must be doing a bomb today.'

She and Terri had an unofficial competition going on over how well each of their speciality breads was doing in the artisan bakery. Today Rachel's olive bread was lagging behind.

'Doesn't it always?' Terri replied jokingly, hoping her despondency didn't show in her tone.

'We're still fine on cookies though, and – oh blast!' Rachel added, her face falling. She wiped her hands and fished around in the pockets of her apron for her mobile.

'What's wrong?'

'I don't know how many times I promised Ethan I'd make some for his little daughter. I should have given them to him when he was in earlier, but I completely forgot. Maybe he can pop back and collect some later.'

Terri watched as Rachel waited for the call to be answered.

Rachel rolled her eyes. 'No answer. I'll just leave a message and hope he gets it before he goes back to London.'

Terri idly wondered why Ethan hadn't taken the call. Although, given Gary's response to his plight, he was perhaps down at a Garda station trying to make a complaint, or worse, she thought with a woeful grin, down by the River Liffey trying to decide whether or not to hurl himself in.

'When is he due to go back?' Terri asked. 'Doesn't seem that he's had that much time for research.'

'Not sure. I think it's this evening. And I know,' Rachel chuckled, 'I just didn't have the heart to tell him that a book about bread sounded about as interesting as paint drying. But I did tell him that we'd help out, if he'd like – given our own superior knowledge of the subject!'

'Good idea.' Maybe Ethan would take Rachel up on this and use it as a pretext for staying in touch. If so, the guy would be rightly stuck with his lame cover story. 'But we

both know I'm the real baker around here,' she teased. 'Seeing as my good old sourdough's left your olive bread for dust, again.'

'Well, get cracking on making more of it then, instead of rubbing my nose in it!' Rachel retorted. 'Anyway, I told Ethan in the message to collect the cookies whenever he can, so if he calls back later when I'm finished here will you make sure he gets them?'

'Of course.' Terri now wondered if Ethan would be back with a policeman, given his recent stonewalling by Gary. Yet she knew he wouldn't make a scene, for Rachel's sake if nothing else. Either way, she wasn't entirely resistant to another encounter with Ethan Greene. It meant she could find out exactly what had been said when he'd spoken to Gary.

Rachel was using her fingers to break up pieces of fat for puff pastry. 'Damn, I keep forgetting to take this off,' she said, catching the ring as it was just about to slide off. She laughed lightly. 'If I'm not more careful, one of these days it'll end up in somebody's dinner!'

Terri looked up and watched Rachel place the ring on a nearby shelf before resuming what she was doing.

'Yes, we wouldn't want that, would we?' she replied distractedly, turning back to the dough she was kneading.

Chapter 30

Ethan was so angry he thought he might burst. The gall of the man to deny outright that the ring was Ethan's, when Knowles had to know full well he had come by it in unlikely circumstances!

Enough was enough. There was nothing else for it now but to take this whole thing straight to the police. But there was a problem: which police? The incident had happened in New York so why would the Irish, or indeed the British police, be interested?

He wondered if he might be able to claim the loss back on his credit-card insurance. There would be visual proof (as well as witnesses) to his buying the ring in the store, and he could ring Tiffany's and ask them to send him copies of the security footage of Gary Knowles buying the silver bracelet. Yes, he supposed he could try that. Ethan was annoyed he hadn't thought of this before now, but, stupidly, he'd thought he was dealing with reasonable and rational people, not a thug with no morals, who thought nothing of pocketing such a valuable item.

He was delighted to have been offered another excuse to visit the bistro, and by Rachel herself, when he picked up her message about collecting cookies for Daisy.

So this afternoon he'd go and see Rachel one last time

and then tell her straight out exactly the kind of man her
fiancé really was.

And this time nothing was going to stop him.

'She's not here,' Terri told Ethan when he arrived at the bistro
again. His flight was due to leave at seven, and he figured he'd
have ample time to pop back and explain all to Rachel before
heading to the airport. 'She's out catering another event tonight.'

He ran a hand through his hair. 'I don't believe this.'

Terri looked at him. 'I hear that things didn't go so well
with Prince Charming earlier?'

'You could say that.' He glowered. 'He completely denies
that the ring is mine!'

'I'm so sorry, Ethan. I tried my best to make him see
sense. But Gary can be stubborn, not to mention stupid.'

'We'll see how stubborn he is when Scotland Yard are
breathing down his neck,' Ethan said brusquely, although it
was a threat that held little water and they both knew it. He
looked at Terri. 'I appreciate your help, though. You're the
only one who seems to believe me.'

'Of course I believe you. I just wish things could have
been different. Anyway,' she said, taking a white cardboard
box from beneath the counter. 'Rachel asked me to give you
these. They're cookies for your daughter, she said.'

'Thanks.' Ethan absently tucked them under his arm.

'And this is for you,' she added, offering him a parcel
wrapped up in purple paper, Stromboli's logo emblazoned
upon it in orange writing. 'It's some more of that sourdough
you liked so much at lunch yesterday. I think you might
enjoy this even more.'

'Thanks, but that's really not necessary,' he said reluctantly. In truth, Ethan didn't want anything to remind him
of this godforsaken place.

'I know Rachel would really like you to have it,' Terri continued, pressing it into his hands. There was something in her voice that caused him to look at her more closely, but then he wondered if he might be imagining it. God knows his head was all over the place this weekend. Her green eyes bored into his. 'Please, I insist. And try to eat it as soon as you can, won't you? It won't stay fresh for long. Maybe have some on the flight back?'

'Thanks, that's very kind of you.' Ethan took the parcel, more for her sake than anything else. He actually quite liked Terri; he knew exactly where he stood with her, and she was ultimately the only person besides Daisy with whom he could share his frustration.

But now he just wanted to get out of this blasted place and back to London, where first thing tomorrow he would talk to the credit-card company, and indeed his lawyers, to see what other options he could explore.

'Again, I'm so sorry about what's happened. I know Rachel would be horrified if she knew and—'

'I know.' At this point, Ethan was almost past caring about what Rachel did or didn't think, but he appreciated Terri's kindness. 'Thank you for the bread, and for trying to help me too. That means a lot. I don't know what I'm going to do next, but . . .'

She smiled and patted his hand. 'Try not to worry, Ethan. Things have a way of working themselves out in the end.'

'Welcome back!' Later that evening, Vanessa hugged Ethan warmly upon his return to London. He was so exhausted by the weekend's events that he felt almost relieved to be back, despite not achieving what he'd set out to do.

Daisy stood in the background, smiling and obviously waiting for a moment alone to find out how everything had

gone. Ethan lifted her into his arms and hugged her tightly until she squealed. 'I missed you, buttercup,' he said, before whispering into her ear that he'd tell all later. 'And you too, darling,' he said, kissing Vanessa briefly. Was he imagining it or did she seem a bit . . . giddy?

'I wasn't sure whether you'd eat on the plane so I made a light supper,' she said.

Actually, Ethan was starving. He hadn't fancied any of the options they had on the plane and had (stupidly in retrospect) packed the cookies and bread in his checked luggage. Then, seeing as the cookies were for Daisy he opened his bag and withdrew the box.

'These are especially for you,' he said, winking at her. Then, remembering he couldn't make any mention of Rachel, he mumbled something about picking them up at the airport.

'Yay, thanks, Dad.'

But immediately realising that now it looked like he hadn't sought out a similar treat for Vanessa, he meekly picked up the sourdough. 'And this is for you. Well, for us really. There was a lovely bistro with an in-house artisan bakery near the hotel and I thought you might like it.'

'Bread?' Vanessa looked suitably underwhelmed.

'Yes, sourdough. It smelled so delicious I couldn't resist . . .' He shrugged, thinking that making up pathetic excuses and sounding like an idiot seemed par for the course these days.

'Lovely. Well, I suppose it'll do nicely with supper, then. Shall we eat?'

Ethan nodded and followed her into the kitchen. He tried to avoid Daisy's still-probing gaze, too weary to try to get the message across that his visit to Dublin had been a complete and utter waste of time.

Vanessa had laid on a very nice spread of olives, cheese

and Parma ham and Ethan set to it with gusto, pleading hunger as a good excuse not to talk about his trip. Making up more stories was the last thing he wanted to do, given that the entire thing had been such a disaster.

Taking the bread out of its Stromboli paper packaging, Vanessa sniffed it approvingly. 'You're right: this does smell delicious.' She tore a large piece from one side. 'Daisy, would you like some?'

'No, thanks.' Daisy seemed put out that her father was keeping her in the dark, but Ethan just didn't have the energy for explanations. He didn't have the energy for anything at all. In truth, what he needed now was a good night's sleep and the chance to recharge his batteries.

'Ow!' Vanessa cried out and he saw her put a hand to her mouth. 'What the hell? I almost broke a tooth . . .'

Then Ethan watched wordlessly as she extracted something solid from her mouth. 'Goodness, I could have choked on something this size,' she said disapprovingly.

'What is it?' Daisy asked, and on closer inspection Ethan saw that Vanessa was holding up something small wrapped in greaseproof paper.

'Oh my God, Ethan . . .'

Then his heart skipped a beat as, having unwrapped the paper, and with her eyes widening, Vanessa held up a diamond ring. *The* diamond ring.

Ethan's jaw dropped, and he suddenly remembered Terri's insistence that he take the bread and her cryptic assertion that everything would turn out OK.

'How did you . . . ? Is this what . . . ?' Vanessa's eyes were out on stalks and she was grinning from ear to ear, while Daisy looked on in amazement. 'I can't believe this!'

Although he was knocked for six, Ethan automatically felt a huge weight lift from his shoulders. How had Terri

done it? And why? She must have somehow pilfered the ring from Rachel, possibly because she knew he was getting nowhere with Gary . . .

Vanessa was still staring at the ring, a look of complete and utter delight on her face. 'Ethan, is this what I think it is?' she said, beaming at him. 'Forgive me, but it's not a . . . joke or anything, is it?'

He forced himself out of his reverie. 'No, darling. It's exactly what you think it is,' he reassured her, unsure why his tone sounded so leaden when this was what he'd wanted all along. Perhaps because it was just all so unexpected.

'Oh my . . . I don't know what to say. What an absolutely amazing surprise!'

He could see Daisy watching him carefully, as if she sensed that he was just as surprised as Vanessa. The whole scenario felt almost like a replay of that Christmas morning in New York.

'So,' he said, clearing his throat. 'I haven't actually asked the most important question. Will you marry me, Vanessa?'

She stared at the ring, and her eyes glistened with tears. 'Of course I will!' she cried, jumping up to embrace him. 'Oh Ethan, this is just the best surprise!'

And as he held her in his arms, Ethan wondered why the moment felt so surreal, and so . . . anticlimactic, almost.

Then, taking the ring, he slipped it onto the third finger of her left hand, where it should have been from the start.

'Oh,' Vanessa said, giggling, when the ring failed to glide smoothly into place, like it was supposed to. 'It seems a little tight.' She tried to force it more firmly onto her finger but still it stayed wedged above the knuckle. 'It doesn't matter; I can always get it resized,' she assured him blithely, but Ethan was baffled.

His mind went back to the sight of the ring on Rachel's

finger, where it had fitted perfectly, a rather strange coincidence given that Tiffany's had sized it especially for Vanessa.

Once again his gaze met Daisy's; the squinty-eyed look out in force as she watched the scene with interest. He suspected she was thinking the same thing.

Wasn't it strange that the ring didn't fit Vanessa, but was somehow perfect on Rachel?

Chapter 31

Rachel was frantic. How could she have lost her beautiful ring? And where? She distinctly remembered taking it off yesterday morning before she went to work . . . or had she removed it *at* work?

Maybe she'd taken it off when she returned home after that dinner with Ethan Greene on Saturday night. She might have been a little tipsy, but surely not so much so that she wouldn't remember taking it off. And if she had, then where else would she have put it other than on the nightstand?

She couldn't be certain, she admitted, panicking as she checked down the side of the bed and on the floor beneath to try to locate it. After that, she went out into the living room and began turning over all the cushions on her sofa, but to no avail.

She'd noticed it wasn't on her finger at the anniversary dinner Stromboli had catered for last night. The happy couple had been married for forty years, and during the speeches Rachel, instinctively imagining her and Gary's forthcoming anniversaries, remembered looking down at her engagement finger, only to find that her gorgeous ring wasn't there. She hadn't been able to relax until she returned home to find out if she'd left it there.

But since there was no sign of it, she decided now that she must have removed it at the bistro and it was probably in the kitchen there. Perhaps Justin or Terri had spotted it lying around, hidden under a tea towel or a bag of flour or something, and put it somewhere else for safekeeping.

Rachel took a deep breath and tried to calm herself. That had to be it, she thought, feeling better already. Goodness knows what she'd do if she had to tell Gary she'd misplaced it. He'd go ballistic.

She'd check with the others at the restaurant today, but first she needed to make an appointment with the bridal store to coincide with her day off next week.

She couldn't wait, and still couldn't quite believe that all this – the New York proposal, huge Tiffany diamond – was truly happening. It was fairy-tale stuff really. This time last year she didn't even know Gary and look at her now, running a successful business and planning the wedding of the year. It was everything she'd ever wanted – or at least it would be again, Rachel thought, worriedly caressing her engagement finger, once she'd located her ring.

Looking around her beloved little mews house, she wondered what she and Gary would do about their living situation.

They'd be moving in together, obviously, but where? They hadn't yet discussed these practicalities. No doubt they'd start looking for a house in the future, but what to do in the meantime? Gary's place was too far out of town for her – she'd not even stayed over at his for months, she thought guiltily – and her own little one-bed house would never be big enough for the two of them.

Not to mention Gary's beloved bike.

He was even talking about buying another one once the money from the accident came through and she groaned inwardly, already having visions of their future home being strewn with engine parts.

Rachel was in two minds about the lawsuit; once Gary was OK she didn't think there was anything to be gained from suing the taxi company, but of course she wasn't the one who'd ended up with aching ribs and concussion. Thank goodness he'd had health insurance, though; who knew what would have happened if he'd had to pay out a fortune for the hospital bills? Her precious ring may well have been making its way straight back to Tiffany's before she'd even got a chance to see it, she thought, smiling.

But once the idea of legal action had entered his mind, Gary couldn't be dissuaded, and apparently his solicitor had readily agreed to take on the case on his behalf.

Rachel couldn't help but feel sorry for the poor New York taxi driver and she hoped the lawsuit wouldn't get him into trouble with his employers or, worse, cause him to lose his job. Ethan had mentioned that the man seemed incredibly remorseful at the time, and Rachel really couldn't see the point in punishing him even further; but it wasn't up to her and there was no reasoning with Gary.

'Are you mad?' he'd argued when she'd suggested it might be best to just move on and forget about it. 'The fool almost killed me! Anyway these guys have insurance for this kind of thing.'

She also wished Gary would spend less time on pursuing a case against the person who'd hurt him, and instead show some gratitude to the one who'd helped. These musings made her think again of Ethan.

As she and Gary hadn't spoken today she wasn't sure if the two men had been in touch over the weekend. It was so embarrassing having to make excuses for Gary, particularly when Ethan had gone out of his way to follow up on everything afterwards. Terri was right: he was such a gentleman and a kind-hearted old soul. Rachel was amazed by his thoughtfulness, which was all the more impressive considering everything he'd been through.

She couldn't imagine what it would be like to experience the sorrow of losing the person you knew was 'the One'. And despite not knowing Ethan's current girlfriend, and soon-to-be fiancée, she couldn't help but feel a little sorry for her. It must be difficult having to live in the shadow of a past love, a love that obviously still weighed heavily on Ethan's mind. Even Rachel, who didn't know him from Adam, could see that, and she hoped the girlfriend was strong enough to deal with it.

She shook her head. There she was, worrying about complete strangers and trying to imagine what they were or weren't feeling. How stupid was she? Especially when it was highly unlikely she'd ever come across Ethan Greene – never mind his girlfriend – again.

'It was you, wasn't it?' the voice on the other end of the line said without preamble when Terri answered the phone at Stromboli on Monday morning.

'Ethan, hi.'

'Why? I'm hugely grateful, of course, but why did you help me?'

Terri sighed. She still wasn't sure of the answer to this question herself.

Already she'd been having second thoughts about intervening, and was feeling worse now that Rachel had realised the ring was missing and was frantic about it.

What had she been thinking, swiping it like that? It had been crazy and irrational and above all totally foolish, especially given that it was really none of her business.

Still, Terri couldn't just sit by and let her friend be made a fool of. And seeing as there was no question that the ring

was Ethan's, and he was too bloody nice to spill the beans, something had to be done.

So on Sunday afternoon at the bistro, when Rachel's ring had almost slipped off and she'd subsequently removed it and placed it on a nearby shelf, Terri had seized the opportunity. Rachel had gone out front to the bakery to replace some stock and before Terri knew it she'd slipped the ring in with the dough she was making, and then later passed this on to Ethan.

Terri realised now that she hadn't really been thinking at all; if she had she would have considered Rachel's feelings and how upset she'd be once she realised the ring had gone.

'Because you would have never got it back from Gary,' she told Ethan now. 'And you certainly wouldn't have taken it back from Rachel.'

'Still, it was exceptionally decent of you, especially when you don't even know me.'

She knew enough to know he was a good person, though. His reluctance to hurt Rachel demonstrated that. When Terri told him as much, he gave a soft laugh. 'Too much of a wimpy old sod, you mean.'

'Doesn't matter. Your intentions were good and ever since I got the truth out of Gary I knew I couldn't let him get away with it.'

'But what will happen now? With Gary and Rachel, I mean. I take it Gary's confessed everything?'

'As far as I'm aware Gary doesn't know it's missing yet.' But he soon would, Terri realised, biting her lip.

'Poor Rachel. She'll be up the wall.'

'I know.' But it was for the best; Terri was sure of that. 'It's not something you have to worry about any more.'

'Thank you again, truly. Although I must admit I do wish you'd told me you'd put it in the bread,' he said, a slight twinge in his voice that Terri thought sounded like regret.

She frowned. 'Well, I couldn't say it out straight, but I thought I did in so many words. Remember I told you to eat it on your flight back?' She chuckled. 'I just hoped you wouldn't break a tooth or anything.'

'In fact it wasn't quite like that.' Ethan went on to tell her about how Vanessa had actually been the one to find it. 'It rather caught us both by surprise.'

'Oh dear. That ring really does seem to have a mind of its own. So all's well that ends well for you, then? I guess congratulations are in order.'

'Yes, yes, absolutely,' he agreed.

For some reason, this sounded forced to Terri. Crikey, had he gone and fallen *that* hard for Rachel while he was here?

She had to admit that Ethan and Rachel would be quite a good match, though. Both dreamers, romantics, afraid to offend and always willing to see the best in people.

In other words, completely out of touch with reality.

She breathed a deep sigh. 'Look, I know that intervening in the way I did might not have been the best strategy, but the truth is that I wasn't thinking straight. It just made my blood boil to think that Gary's been stringing Rachel and the rest of us along about that ring, and then when you show up he doesn't even have the decency to admit to what happened.'

The problem was that Terri hadn't thought clearly enough about how *Rachel* would feel once she realised the ring was missing. Still, once Gary realised, he'd sort things out. He'd have to.

'I know. I must admit that as I went back to the airport I was at a complete loss as to what to do. I was so sure that Gary would acknowledge that it was all a big mistake and . . . well, I suppose I wasn't prepared for how terrible I felt for Rachel.'

Hmm. *Definitely* something going on there, Terri thought. And she wondered now if she should somehow try to act on this knowledge. No, no: she'd interfered enough as it was. If Ethan was interested in Rachel then he could sort it out himself. Anyway, hadn't the guy just got engaged? Christ, were all men – even the nicer ones – so bloody fickle?

'The truth about this engagement will need to come out sooner or later,' she said. 'Rachel's going to be upset no matter what. But at least you've got your ring back – at last.' She smiled. 'I'm sure your girlfriend got a lovely surprise. It's not every day a girl finds something from Tiffany's in a loaf of bread.'

'Yes, she was very surprised. I rather was too.'

'Well, the best of luck to you both. When's the wedding?'

'Oh. Not until next year, I would imagine. Plenty of time yet.'

Again Ethan sounded a million miles away from a loved-up groom-to-be.

'Still you must have been glad to see the ring finally on the right woman's finger.'

'Well, funnily enough it doesn't fit Vanessa, which is odd, given that I'd had it sized especially for her.'

'I see.' Just then, Terri was distracted by Rachel's appearance in the kitchen, and she knew she'd better end the call. 'Well, it was nice talking to you again, but I'd better go. Lots to do here.'

'Of course. Thank you again. And give my best to Rachel, will you? Although no, maybe she won't want that. I'm sure the poor thing will never want to hear my name again once the truth comes out.'

Whenever that might be, Terri thought, grimacing guiltily.

Chapter 32

For Ethan, the following week went by in a daze. He still couldn't believe that after all the worry, all the hassle of going to Dublin and trying to get the ring back, he'd had it returned to him just like that.

And although he was hugely grateful to Terri for intervening, in truth he'd rather she'd told him upfront what she was doing; that way, he could have fished out the ring himself and decided what to do with it afterwards.

Yet what was there to decide? The ring was meant for Vanessa; it was bought with her in mind and with the intention of a proposal. But now, given all that had happened in the meantime, for some reason the whole idea just wasn't sitting well with him.

What must Rachel be thinking? She must be going out of her mind, wondering where it was and how she could have lost it. Especially when she already had such an attachment to it. While Ethan knew that what Rachel was and wasn't feeling was none of his business, still he couldn't help but feel partly responsible.

Would this mean that Gary would finally own up to the truth? Based on the conversation they'd had in Dublin, Ethan couldn't see it. He was sure that guy was the type who'd try to slither his way out of anything.

He thought again about Vanessa's delighted reaction to his 'surprise proposal'.

'Well, I knew you had a great imagination, but even I'm taken aback at this level of creativity!' she'd teased, after the rather awkward moment when the ring didn't fit her finger. 'So this whole going to Dublin for "research" was just an elaborate ruse to throw me off?'

'Yes, absolutely,' Ethan agreed, still trying to get over the shock of it all himself.

She laughed lightly. 'So what did Mum and Dad say?'

'I'm sorry?'

'Mum and Dad. What did they say when you told them what you were planning? That's the real reason you went to Dublin, yes? To officially ask Dad for my hand?' When his expression revealed his surprise, she raised an eyebrow. 'Oh I honestly thought . . . Why did you go to Ireland, then?'

'For the ring, of course!' Daisy piped up, and Ethan looked at her worriedly. 'We tried to get it at Tiffany's in New York, but they didn't have the special one he wanted for you, did they, Dad?'

Ethan agreed, at this point resigned to just going with the flow. There had been so much drama and palaver surrounding all this that he felt he could no longer keep up.

'I see. So that's why you two kept disappearing all the time!' Vanessa seemed delighted to have her suspicions confirmed. 'Well, I'm even more impressed now. I had no idea you had such specific taste, Ethan. But you couldn't get it at Tiffany's on Old Bond Street?'

'No, not that particular setting. But I'm sorry, because of course I should have asked your parents first.'

'Don't be silly! It's fine. It was the only reason I could pinpoint for that sudden jaunt to Dublin, and it's not as though you didn't put a huge amount of thought into all this in any case!' She indicated the sourdough, and then reached across the counter for the wrapper. 'Stromboli,' she read out loud from the sticker on the front. 'Do they do this kind of thing on request?' she added, picking up the ring again. 'Specialised proposals, I mean. How did you hear about them?'

'Just read something on the internet a while back,' he mumbled, not wanting to get into any specifics.

'It was a brilliant idea, Dad,' Daisy chimed in. She met Ethan's eye and a smile of understanding passed between them. 'See, I told you he had a great imagination,' she said to Vanessa.

That night, Ethan slept better than he had in weeks. The ring was back in his possession; he and Vanessa were back on track and all was once again right with the world.

Until his new fiancée dropped another bombshell the following morning.

'Don't get me wrong, the way the proposal happened was so romantic and really original,' Vanessa said over breakfast. 'But forgive me if I admit that I'm also rather partial to tradition. What about the little blue box? It would be nice to have it so I can keep the ring safe when I'm not wearing it and it's silly perhaps, but I'd quite like the whole Tiffany's package too.'

'I'm sure it's in my luggage somewhere . . .' Ethan fudged, knocking back his early morning coffee.

Bugger Tiffany's and their little blue box! Of course Terri wouldn't have been able to return both the ring and its packaging. As it was, he was lucky enough to have got anything back at all. But Ethan's stomach lurched as he realised another visit to the store beckoned. At this stage, it felt like he should be buying shares in the place.

He'd head down to Old Bond Street after his last lecture that day and try to pick up something small and inexpensive, perhaps a silver dress ring for Daisy? Then he could

give the packaging to Vanessa so that she could have her precious paraphernalia. Sometimes he didn't understand women at all.

'Don't worry about it for now. I just thought I'd mention it, in case you decided to throw it away or something.'

Now Ethan wanted to kick himself, wishing that he'd thought of saying he'd done exactly that. It would be just the kind of thing any man worth his salt would do. Well, at least those who were supposed to have no appreciation of the little things that seemed to mean so much to women.

At this rate, Ethan would be happy if he never saw a little blue box again in his life.

Gary was in the middle of his latest building job when he got a call on his mobile from his solicitor.

'Frank, what's the craic?' he said, positioning the handset under his chin.

He hoped it was news on the New York taxi lawsuit. Frank Donnelly was a viper by reputation and Gary suspected he would go all out to ensure his client got a big payout.

It was no more than he deserved. He'd missed nearly two weeks' work over it *and* he'd had to shell out for those extra nights in the New York hotel, as well as the flights home.

OK, so Rachel had actually taken care of all that, but seeing as they were engaged now, it was practically the same thing. She was the one who'd started talking about opening a joint account to keep track of the wedding expenses, something that put the fear of God into Gary in case she'd put two and two together and figure out what was going on.

He couldn't for the life of him understand why she didn't approve of him going after the cab company, calling it 'bad karma' and all that crap. Wasn't it bad karma that he'd been hit in the first place?

'Just a bit of an update on the cab thing,' Frank replied and Gary straightened up in anticipation.

'Oh?'

'Well, there's good news and bad news. From our point of view, the CCTV footage looks good.' Gary recalled that his solicitor had asked the relevant New York authorities to send the CCTV tapes of the area along Fifth Avenue, hoping these would show the incident in its entirety. 'Looks straightforward enough and it's easy to make you out on the side of the road trying to hail a cab. Then, out of nowhere – bang, you're on the ground.'

Yep, that was exactly the way it had happened. From what little recollection Gary had of it, anyway.

'So what's the bad news?' he asked.

'Well, seems the taxi company have a witness to the accident. A passenger in the cab. Seems this guy reckons that *you* were at fault.'

'What the hell?' Gary fumed. 'How could I have been at fault? I was only walking down the street, minding my own bloody business!'

'Their witness is saying you were distracted when you stepped out into the road. The way he saw it, the driver couldn't have avoided you.'

Gary remembered how that day he had been distracted, as well as a little flustered by that call that had come through on his mobile. 'Frank, it all happened so fast it's hard to remember exactly how things went,' he told his solicitor quickly.

'Of course. Especially with the concussion and everything. That's what I told the New York suits. Sure, how are you supposed to know what happened? All you remember is waking up in hospital.'

'Exactly.' Gary was pleased Frank seemed to understand.

'All right. I've requested a copy of the so-called witness report and when I get that, pop into the office here and we can have a chat. Then we can take it from there.'

'Sounds good. Cheers, Frank.'

'And even if it does look like you were caught unawares, we should be able to nail the guy for speeding, or reckless driving, or something like that.'

'Perfect.' Witness or not, Gary was confident that Frank would interpret the situation in some way that would turn this to his advantage. Although if the issue of fault wasn't as clear-cut as he'd thought then maybe the payout wouldn't be as lucrative.

Well, whatever it was, it would be better than a kick in the arse, and he was sure he'd get the price of a new bike out of it at least.

Gary grinned. The one good thing about Rachel being so against all this was that she wouldn't be looking to get her hands on the money to spend on this wedding. Already he had it up to his neck in quotes for hotels and flowers, and soon she'd be shopping for dresses that would no doubt cost half the national debt of a small country.

That was the problem with bloody expensive engagement rings, Gary thought, getting back to work; they set the bar sky high for the rest of the circus.

Chapter 33

Sitting in the bridal studio and watching the delight on Rachel's face as she tried on wedding dresses, Terri sorely wished she'd minded her own business.

This was supposed to be one of the happiest times in her best friend's life, and if she thought about it properly Terri knew she'd been just as deceitful as Gary in hiding the truth from Rachel.

The poor thing had been distraught at the bistro on Monday morning, when she'd confessed to Terri and Justin that her beloved ring had gone astray.

'I can't remember if I took it off here or at home. You know the way it's always getting in the way while I'm baking . . . ?'

Terri still felt sick to her stomach when she thought of how she'd lied barefaced to her best friend as she'd said: 'Can't remember the last time I saw it on you. Are you sure you didn't leave it at home?'

Rachel had shaken her head, and with obvious distress had confessed she couldn't remember the last time she'd had it on. 'Gary will kill me,' she gasped. 'How am I supposed to tell him I can't find it?'

'I'm sure he'll understand,' Terri soothed, privately hoping that when Gary realised Rachel's anguish about losing the ring he would finally come clean. He would surely confess everything once he knew how distraught she was, wouldn't he?

But it had been almost a week now and still nothing had changed.

As it was Terri hated having to go along with this whole wedding charade, not least because of her own deceit. How could she realistically tell her friend that her dream engagement was all a lie? And that the wedding she was so excited about was a complete sham? So much for being a loyal bridesmaid . . .

Her friend was currently standing in a slinky mermaid-style gown that looked like it was literally made for her curves. She was holding her hair up and examining herself in the mirror. 'What do you think of this one?' she asked.

While under normal circumstances Terri would have suggested that Rachel bought it straight away, instead she grimaced and shook her head. 'I'm not sure. Do you think it might be hard to walk around in all day?'

Rachel walked a couple of steps and then turned around. 'No, it's fine actually.'

Terri wrinkled her nose. 'I dunno. I'm still not sure if it's really you.'

'You've said that about every single one I've tried today!' her friend said testily and again Terri felt like a heel. 'Maybe, but you know I won't let you settle for second best,' she said, even though Rachel would have no clue that there was a deeper meaning to those words. But the comment also seemed to annoy the sales assistant and the atmosphere in the bridal studio grew tense.

Rachel turned around to let the woman unzip her, and she and Terri waited in silence as she put the dress back on its hanger, and got out the next one.

It was a strapless, princess gown made of ivory silk. It had very little detail, just yards and yards of the luscious material. Rachel stepped into the dress and the bridal assistant pulled it up and over her breasts. Once it was all zipped up, she stood on a small riser to examine herself in a three-way mirror.

'Oh my goodness, this one is beautiful!' she gasped, staring at her reflection.

Terri's mouth dropped open. She had to admit that it was. There was no way anyone could find fault with that dress.

'Ah, I almost forgot the finishing touch.' The saleswoman rushed forward with a simple ivory veil, which had the smallest amount of lace running around the edges. The result was spectacular.

'This is the one . . . I know it,' Rachel whispered.

Terri swallowed hard. 'It is pretty,' she said evasively. Rachel continued to stare at her reflection. 'I know it's cheesy, but this is the type of dress I've always pictured myself in. It's not too fussy or fashionable – more sort of . . . timeless, isn't it? The kind of dress that could be passed down through generations.'

Bloody hell. Terri knew how much this sentimental stuff mattered to Rachel and she also knew that if she was looking for tradition, Gary Knowles was the last person she should be marrying. The guy's notion of tradition was drinking the same pint in the same pub every Saturday night. She pursed her lips together, not sure how to respond.

Looking radiant, Rachel turned around and smiled. 'Isn't it wonderful?' she urged. 'Do you think Gary will like it?'

Terri waited for a moment and then decided to ask the question. 'Rachel, are you absolutely sure about this?' She looked meaningfully at the sales assistant, who caught the look and reacted appropriately.

'I'll give you both a minute,' she said and moved away.

Rachel stared at her. 'Sure about what?'

'About marrying Gary.'

Her friend coloured. 'Why wouldn't I be?'

'Well, it just all seems to have happened very quickly, doesn't it? I mean, you two haven't been seeing one another all that long, and then in New York he just proposed out of the blue?'

Rachel paused ever so slightly and there was a strange look on her face that Terri couldn't identify. Was it hurt, or could it be doubt? Rachel turned back to the mirror and squared her shoulders. 'Look, I know you don't particularly like Gary; you've made that perfectly clear. And that's fine, you don't have to, but the truth is that I'm committed to the idea.'

Terri sat up straight. 'Committed to the idea? What the hell does that mean?'

'It means . . . it means that yes, of course I love him. OK, so he might seem a little . . . brash at times, but at the back of it all I know he's a good man. And I know that he loves me. He wouldn't have asked me to marry him or bought me that amazing ring if he didn't want me to be his wife.'

Terri took a deep breath, desperate to blurt out the whole sorry truth so that her friend would finally be able to see the light. But, looking at Rachel's face, again she knew she couldn't do it.

'Rachel, I'm sorry. Maybe you should take that dress,' she said finally.

'Do you really think so?'

'Yes, it's lovely; it was made for you. Wait there and I'll go and get the sales assistant.'

When Terri found the woman, she offered an apology. 'Sorry about that,' she said, smiling. 'My friend and I just needed a minute to chat about it, but I think we're ready now.'

'Marvellous.' The saleswoman started to walk back to the

fitting room to take Rachel's measurements. 'Has your friend decided what she wants?'

Terri's mouth tightened. 'Well, she seems to think so and I suppose that's all that matters.'

Chapter 34

Rachel was truly going out of her mind. It was almost two weeks since she'd lost her engagement ring and she'd long since run out of places to search.

When she'd first noticed it missing, she'd turned every room in the house upside down, checked the pockets in all of her clothes, and gone over every nook and cranny in the restaurant. The only explanations she could realistically come up with at this point was that it had fallen down the plughole when she was washing her hands, or been swept into the bin at work with a pile of rubbish. At this stage, though, what had happened to it didn't seem to matter nearly as much as what she was going to do about it.

Gary didn't appear to have noticed anything amiss just yet, although he had commented on its absence on her finger during a recent visit to the bistro. She'd quickly reminded him that she didn't wear the ring at work in case she damaged it, which was the truth, of sorts.

But seeing as it had been missing for some time now, and she was running out of places to search, Rachel knew she'd have to broach the subject soon.

'I just don't know how I'm going to tell him,' she confessed to Terri now. They were in the kitchen getting ready for Stromboli's lunchtime trade.

Her friend shrugged. 'It's not as though you lost it on purpose. These things happen. I'm sure Gary will understand.'

Rachel looked at her. While Terri had been sympathetic initially, Rachel got the feeling she wasn't taking the ring's disappearance seriously enough. Didn't she know how much it meant to her, or, more importantly, how much Gary had spent on it?

'I really don't think he will understand,' she replied, somewhat more testily than she'd intended. 'When I think of how much he must have paid for it, it makes me sick to my stomach.'

'Well, I'm not being smart, but maybe it didn't cost as much as you think?' Terri ventured. 'Anyway the ring, or indeed the price, isn't the important thing; it's the sentiment behind it, isn't it? I'm sure Gary understands that.'

But the comment got Rachel thinking. Maybe Terri was right and she could be worrying for nothing. It was an expensive-looking ring and a big diamond, certainly, but maybe not so expensive that she couldn't replace it herself without Gary realising?

That's what she'd do, Rachel decided. Instead of confessing to Gary that she'd lost the ring, she'd first see if she could try to replace it. That way he'd be none the wiser. OK, so it would be an unexpected expense on top of all the others they were facing this year, but wasn't it her own fault for not taking good enough care of it?

There was a small Tiffany & Co. store in Brown Thomas, and she could pop down there during her break after the lunchtime rush and see if she could find a replacement or at least some kind of alternative. And not that it mattered, but she was also slightly curious as to exactly how much Gary *had* spent on the ring.

No doubt that would correlate exactly with how bad Rachel would feel about having lost it.

'Can I help you with anything?' the smiling assistant asked as Rachel perused the display at Tiffany's later that afternoon. Her eyes eagerly took in the display case and the stunning jewellery laid out there. Rings, bracelets and earrings that coloured the dreams of women around the world, jewels so beautiful that they were really only a fantasy to most, unlikely to ever be a reality. So how lucky was she to have been given one and how idiotic was she to have lost it?

Her heart sank afresh.

'I'm looking for an engagement ring,' she told the assistant. 'It's a style from your Fifth Avenue store but I don't think I see it here.'

'Well, because of our size, we can carry only a select range in this store, but all jewellery is available to order. Maybe you'll recognise it from our catalogue?' The woman reached under the counter and brought out a copy of Tiffany's famed *Blue Book*. Rachel felt an automatic shiver of delight at the instantly recognisable robin's-egg blue on the elegant catalogue cover. 'Was it three-stone or solitaire? Or perhaps a diamond band?'

'Solitaire,' Rachel told her, and her breath caught a little at the beautiful photographic array of diamond rings of every shape, setting and design in the catalogue. The photographs were so vivid and the diamonds looked so real she almost expected them to sparkle on the page in the same way they did in real life.

The woman turned to the solitaire section and Rachel almost immediately recognised her own platinum marquise design. 'That's the one,' she said, pointing to the picture.

'Classic marquise,' the assistant clarified with a nod. 'Yes, that's a very popular one. It's gorgeous.'

Looking at the photograph Rachel felt sick to her stomach yet again, to think she had lost such a stunningly beautiful item. But perhaps with luck (and a thus far unknown amount of cash) she just might be able to recover the situation.

'And you definitely don't have this one in stock at the moment?' she asked.

The assistant looked rueful. 'I'm afraid not. We'd be happy to order it for you, and can have it instore and ready for collection by the end of the week. Although we do require a deposit for special orders. Two thousand for this one.'

'Two thousand?' All of a sudden, Rachel's heart lifted and her face broke into a huge smile.

It wasn't as though she had that amount of money lying around in loose change anywhere, but the ring was nowhere *near* as expensive as she'd imagined. Yes, replacing it would mean sacrificing the majority of her share of the income from Stromboli for the next few months, but it would be worth it. She shook her head. Trust Gary to surprise her *again* by managing to choose an amazingly beautiful diamond ring that looked like it cost an absolute fortune, but in reality was actually rather reasonable.

'For the deposit, yes,' the assistant continued, taking out an order book. 'I can take it today, if you'd like. Or maybe you'd prefer to wait for your fiancé and let him be the one to injure the credit card,' she joked easily.

Now, Rachel felt nauseous. 'Two thousand? For the deposit?' she repeated in a whisper, all thoughts of replacing the ring suddenly going right out of the window. Her face went pale.

'Yes, ten per cent of the overall price is standard for booking deposits.'

Rachel's head grew light and she began to see stars in front of her eyes. It didn't take a genius to work out that if two thousand was ten per cent of the overall price, then Gary had spent twenty thousand – *twenty thousand* – on the ring.

And she had lost it.

Oh Christ . . . oh Christ . . . oh Christ. Her head spinning, Rachel held on to the edge of the glass display case. She was so dizzy she was sure her legs would give way beneath her.

'Are you OK?' the woman asked, seemingly unaware that she'd as good as felled her latest customer.

'I'm fine,' Rachel managed. She tried to compose herself as best she could. 'And . . . actually, I think you're right; it's probably best to wait for my fiancé to do the honours.'

The woman chuckled. 'Wise decision. Pop in any time you like, both of you. We'd be delighted to look after you, and of course we provide a glass of bubby to all our happy couples to really get the celebrations going. Would be a shame to miss out on that!' she added with a wink.

'Yes. A shame.' Desperate to get out of there before she did something stupid, like collapse in a heap on the ground, Rachel bade the Tiffany's sales assistant a quick goodbye. She stumbled her way through the store and back out onto Grafton Street as fast as her woozy legs would carry her.

Twenty thousand! The ring had cost twenty thousand euro, and she'd gone and lost it. What was she going to do? And why had Gary spent so much? She felt inexplicably angry at him.

As it was she'd have *died* if she'd known she was walking around with something that valuable on her. And to think that she'd been wearing that ring while blithely kneading dough and getting it covered in flour and eggs and all sorts.

It was *far* too much to spend on her. It was far too much to spend on anyone or indeed anything that didn't at the very least have four wheels or a roof on it!

There was no *way* she could tell him she'd lost it now, Rachel knew that for certain. Especially when she knew that times were tough in the building trade and she'd suspected for a while that Gary was just about keeping the business afloat. He was much too proud to admit it, of course; but Rachel wasn't stupid, and reading between the lines she'd figured things were bad when he was so anxious to return from New York quickly in order to get back to work. She sighed, everything suddenly becoming a hell of a lot clearer. No wonder he'd been so reluctant to participate in her enthusiasm for the wedding preparations; no doubt all he could think about was how much more he'd need to shell out for that too!

But what had possessed him to spend so much on the ring? He knew she wasn't one of those high-maintenance types who expected the best of everything. And really this was a very long way from the chocolate red rose he'd given her on Valentine's Day.

And to think that he'd never said a word, never even let on that he'd spent so much. That was unusual, actually. Much as she loved him, she knew Gary did have a tendency to brag about things like that.

She looked blankly around her at all the people rushing past on the street, trying to figure out what to do. Maybe she could try to replace the ring with some kind of cheaper version so that Gary wouldn't notice the difference? But it was Tiffany's, so of course he'd notice.

Rachel's head spun, not knowing what she should do now. Was there a chance she'd got it wrong back there and picked out a ring she only *thought* looked like hers? But in

all honesty there was no mistaking it; Rachel knew deep down that the solitaire she'd just learned had a twenty-thousand price tag was exactly the one she'd been wearing on her finger up to a fortnight ago. It was just so hard to believe or even imagine Gary spending so much money on a single item.

'I had no idea you could even spend that much on a single transaction with a credit card,' she said afterwards to Terri and Justin, who both seemed just as shocked as she was upon hearing how much her engagement ring had cost. At least, that's how she assumed Gary had paid for it; he couldn't realistically have taken that much in cash with him on their trip.

'Are you sure?' Terri asked, looking decidedly shell-shocked, and Rachel was somewhat gratified to think that at least *now* Terri'd understand why she was so frantic about losing it. 'Christ, that's a hell of a lot to spend on a rock.'

'I know. What should I do? There's no way I can afford to replace it myself now and Gary will hit the roof when I tell him I've lost it. He might even call off the wedding.' She bit her lip in an effort to quell impending tears.

Terri put a comforting hand on her arm. 'Ah, no. I'm sure he wouldn't do that.'

'What about insurance?' Justin suggested, looking thoughtful.

'No good. I didn't have a chance to get it insured before I lost it,' Rachel replied mournfully.

'Well, what about Gary's credit-card insurance? I know my Visa card has some kind of purchase protection included; maybe his does too.'

'Yes, that sounds . . . interesting,' Terri said quietly.

'It is,' Rachel said, heartened. 'How would I find out about that, Justin?'

'You'll need to get your hands on Gary's statement,' he told her. 'There's a monthly fee charged on the card, so if that's listed on the statement and he bought the ring with the same card, there's a good chance it's covered.' He draped an arm around her shoulder. 'So maybe you're worrying for nothing, sweetheart.'

Rachel wanted to hug him. Justin was right; if the ring was automatically covered by Gary's credit-card insurance then chances were he wouldn't get too upset about her losing it, since it could be replaced.

'Yes, I'm sure you're worrying for nothing,' Terri repeated, and Rachel immediately began to feel better.

'Of course now you'll have to find some way of getting the statement without alerting Gary,' Justin pointed out. 'And I don't know about you but Bernard would leave me for sure if he knew how much I rack up on mine! Or on second thoughts,' he grinned, 'maybe he'd be proud, who knows?'

'Well, we'll need to share stuff like that soon enough,' Rachel replied, wondering how she might go about purloining Gary's credit-card statement without him knowing what she was up to.

And notwithstanding the insurance, there was a second advantage to checking it too. On the off chance that she'd been mistaken about the ring in question today at the store, she could check the Tiffany's transaction on the statement; that way she'd know for certain if her future husband had indeed spent the best part of a year's salary on it.

Yes, a peek at Gary's credit-card bill should draw a line under all of this, one way or another.

Now all Rachel had to do was figure out the best way to get hold of it.

Chapter 35

Vanessa was still walking on air. There was so much to do, so much to plan and she was already itching to get started on those plans.

Not to mention so much to celebrate, which she, Ethan and Daisy would be doing in spades soon. Her mum and dad were over the moon about the engagement and she was really looking forward to going home at the first opportunity and showing off her gorgeous Tiffany diamond.

She glanced down at her newly resized ring, still finding it hard to believe that Ethan had actually proposed. She was delighted she'd got to the bottom of Ethan and Daisy's little secret and also relieved that there was a reasonable explanation as to why he'd been acting so strangely in New York.

After the New York trip, she'd truly believed that something wasn't right, that perhaps Ethan had gone off into one of his dreary fugs about Jane. In truth, and despite her best attempts to hide it, Vanessa couldn't help but always feel threatened by Jane's memory, and for this reason she had never been entirely sure of Ethan's feelings for her, or if there was a serious future for them. Vanessa knew that she'd never replace the love of his life, but now that she was sure he was committed to her, she would try her utmost to be a good stepmother to Daisy and a good wife to him.

At least the future didn't include the prospect of other children, and Vanessa felt comforted that this had been headed off at the pass from the outset, as the truth was that she had no real desire to procreate, and no interest in all the hassles and inconveniences that went hand in hand with babies. A ready-made family would do just fine.

Yes, Vanessa was confident that Ethan was absolutely the right man for her, the perfect person with whom to share the rest of her life, and she was pleased he'd finally come to realise that too.

And to think that he'd gone to such great lengths, first in New York and then in Dublin, just for a specific ring!

It was a beautiful ring, of that there was no doubt, but at the same time she couldn't quite understand why it had to be that and no other. But of course Ethan was like that: very exacting and, despite his mildness, hugely determined when he set his mind to something.

There was also another reason Vanessa was looking forward to their visit to Dublin. Ethan's comment about researching old Irish estates hadn't been lost on her, and if she was getting married at home, she was going to do it in style. Especially given that all her publishing friends and colleagues would be attending, and maybe some from New York too.

So now that Ethan had popped the question, she was determined to get the wedding plans moving. There was little point in waiting around and she hated those silly types who got engaged for the sake of it, and didn't take the trouble to actually set a wedding date. Because getting married was ultimately what being engaged was all about, wasn't it?

She'd have to check with Ethan, but she was already thinking of August. It was traditionally a rather quiet time in publishing, and of course he'd be on holidays from the university and Daisy from school.

The visit to Dublin later in the month would be the

perfect opportunity to scout out locations for the reception as well as suitable florists, caterers and all that. But nothing wrong with getting started in the meantime.

Picking up the telephone, Vanessa smoothed out a piece of paper she'd brought to the office that morning, and dialled the number.

A friendly male voice replied. 'Stromboli Bistro. Justin speaking. How can I help you?'

'Oh hello. I understand you have a catering service?'

'That's correct, yes.'

'As well as a sideline in quirky wedding proposals, apparently,' she added, laughing lightly.

'I'm sorry?'

Vanessa went on to explain about the ring hidden in the bread that had come from Stromboli's bakery. 'It was such a lovely idea, although a little risky too, I must admit. I did almost break a tooth.'

'I see.' The man seemed confused as if he wasn't sure what she was talking about, but that hardly mattered.

'My fiancé was raving about your food and, surprise apart, I have to say I thought your sourdough was absolutely delicious,' she went on. 'And seeing as your company has already played such an integral part in all of this, I'd like to get a sample menu and catering quote from you for our wedding. We don't have a specific date just yet but it should be sometime later this year, possibly August?'

There was a brief pause on the other end of the line. 'Of course. I'm sure we'd be happy to provide you with a quote, and a sample menu would be no problem at all. Terri, our catering manager isn't here just at the moment, but if you'd like to leave your details I'll get her to phone you back.'

'Thank you. That would be wonderful.' Already Vanessa was impressed with this level of professionalism. Having lived in London for so long, she was expecting it to be difficult to organise a wedding in Dublin from afar. Good recommendations were everything, and what better recommendation for a catering company than the establishment that'd been directly involved in the proposal? 'I'll be visiting Dublin shortly, so perhaps my fiancé and I could pop in for a chat.'

'We'd be delighted to see you. Can I take your name?'

'Oh yes, of course. It's Vanessa Ryan. And my fiancé's name is Ethan Greene,' she added, before giving him her telephone number. She couldn't help it; she just adored using the word 'fiancé' at every available opportunity.

She said goodbye to the man from the bistro and was just about to put down the handset when her internal line buzzed.

'Brian Freeman for you,' her assistant told her. 'Line three.'

Vanessa hesitated for a bit, her finger hovering over the button for line three, before eventually making a decision. 'Tell him I'm in a meeting.'

'Someone's been naughty,' Justin said to Terri. 'Or should I say very, very stupid?'

It was late afternoon and she'd just arrived for the evening shift. 'What are you talking about?' she asked, frowning as she tied an apron around her waist.

'I got an interesting call today from a lady who seemed very appreciative of our part in her fiancé's wedding proposal.'

'Did the guy pop the question over dinner here or something?' she replied easily. 'Can't say I recall anything like that happening recently but Rachel might.'

Justin put his hands on his hips. 'It was the strangest thing. Apparently *somebody* baked a Tiffany diamond ring into a loaf of our sourdough.'

Terri's mouth dropped open; she was unable to believe what she was hearing. 'The *fiancée* called here?' Then, realising she'd unintentionally landed herself in it, she blushed furiously. Finally she met Justin's gaze. 'Something had to be done.'

'Oh my God, Terri, what did you think you were doing?' he exclaimed disbelievingly. 'You had no right to take – or should I say *steal* – Rachel's ring!'

'It's not her ring,' she replied half-heartedly, but the words sounded weak and she knew it.

'Still, it's not your place to interfere. Just because you've gone gooey-eyed for this Ethan guy, it doesn't mean he was telling the truth!'

'What are you talking about?' Terri tried her best to ignore the first part of that comment. 'And of course he was telling the truth, something we both know Gary isn't capable of.' She folded her hands across her chest. 'I don't know about you, but I wasn't going to stand by and watch her mooning over that diamond for a minute longer.'

'So you just decided to steal it and give it away to some stranger with a sob story?'

'It wasn't stealing and Ethan isn't a stranger.' Terri felt she had to defend herself. 'Look, Justin, the guy was too nice to take it back from Rachel, and since Gary had no intention of handing it over either . . . I had to do something.'

'But you've seen Rachel moping around this last while. She thinks it's her fault the ring is missing and is terrified of telling Gary.'

'I know. So maybe this will bring everything out in the wash.'

'Well, something is going to come out in the wash soon, that's for sure,' Justin said, sighing grimly.

'What do you mean?'

'That woman I spoke to, your man Ethan's girlfriend, was asking about catering for their wedding. I told her you'd phone her back.'

'What? Oh Christ.' There were so many unpleasant scenarios that Terri couldn't get a handle on them. 'Why on earth would she want *us* to cater for a wedding in London?'

'Because apparently the soon-to-be-Mrs Greene is one of our own, so the wedding will be taking place in the 'oul sod.'

'Here in Dublin? You've got to be kidding me.'

'Nope.'

'Oh God.' Terri put her hand to her face and her skin broke out in a cold sweat. She didn't know what to think – or do – now. But surely Ethan wouldn't want them to cater his wedding? The last time she'd seen him he looked like he never wanted to set foot anywhere near the place again, and who could blame him?

She looked at Justin. 'Look, you're right. I know I was wrong to take matters with the ring into my own hands,' she admitted, shamefaced. 'But it's done now. Gary was never going to own up and I just couldn't stand by and watch Rachel get sucked in by his lies. He's a shyster, Justin; we both know that.'

'Hmm, shyster or not, it looks like you've landed us all in the middle of it now,' Justin said solemnly. 'Because when that girl comes in here wearing Rachel's precious ring, there's going to be one hell of a shit storm.'

Chapter 36

Rachel was looking through Gary's credit-card statement for December. Having puzzled for a while about the best way to get her hands on it, she quickly realised that a perfectly good reason was staring her right in the face.

She and Gary were in the process of setting up a joint account for the wedding expenses, and the bank had requested identification documentation and proof of address for them both.

'Bank statements, utility bills, passport copy, you know yourself,' she'd reminded him.

'Well, I can get you a bank statement, but I'm not sure about the utility bill,' he'd replied reluctantly. 'I, ah . . . think I threw out my last electricity bill.'

A light bulb went on in Rachel's head as she figured this was the opportunity she'd been waiting for.

'What about a credit-card bill, then? I'm sure that would also do as proof of address,' she said, trying to make her voice sound casual, but luckily Gary didn't notice anything untoward.

He'd duly dropped the necessary documents into the bistro earlier that afternoon and now, in the privacy of her living room, Rachel took the opportunity to look through the Visa bill for the insurance charge Justin had mentioned.

If it was there, then she would tell Gary straight out that

she had somehow lost the ring. If it wasn't there, well . . . then Rachel didn't know what she'd do.

She ran her gaze through a list of the most recent transactions, trying to pinpoint the New York purchases. There were loads of Fifth Avenue stores on there; one from Sachs, a couple from Bergdorf Goodman, and . . . ah, there it was: Tiffany & Co.

Rachel looked across the page to check the corresponding charge and blinked.

One hundred and fifty dollars? How could that be? She frowned. Gary couldn't possibly have bought a diamond ring for that. She looked again at the figure, perplexed. Rachel didn't think it was actually possible to spend so little in the store, unless it was for a souvenir or something.

Then, thinking of her own recent conversation with the Tiffany's assistant about the deposit, it hit her. Of course! Gary had probably ordered the ring in advance and had paid for it long before, so the visit to the store that day was just to collect it. Perhaps the transaction she was looking at was the remaining balance, or for a gift-wrap service perhaps?

Chances were that was exactly what she was looking at, but unfortunately this didn't help her in any way. If Gary had paid for the ring in increments, without the receipt there was simply no way of knowing how much it had cost in total.

She wasn't sure why it mattered, really; she already knew how much he'd spent on it.

But assuming that he'd paid for it bit by bit with the credit card, did that mean the insurance would still cover it?

She flicked through the pages until she came to the final

one. To her dismay there was no sign of the purchase-protection insurance Justin had mentioned.

Rachel gulped and looked again at her naked ring finger. It was coming up to three weeks since she'd last seen it, and having searched everywhere she could think of (not to mention avoided all Gary's questions), it seemed unlikely it was going to turn up at this stage.

She sighed. There was nothing else for it; she had to bite the bullet and tell Gary the ring had disappeared.

Rachel bit her lip.

Whether the admission would cause her fiancé to disappear too remained to be seen.

Daisy had a dilemma. There was something very important she needed to talk to her dad about, but she didn't think she could do it now.

Although she was pleased that he'd got the ring back, the truth was she'd been very concerned since that day Vanessa had tried it on and it didn't fit.

Why didn't it fit her, particularly when it was supposed to have been made especially for her?

'I'm sure they just made a mistake with the sizing at the store,' her dad said when he and Daisy spoke about it afterwards, and he'd explained how another nice woman in Dublin had helped him get it back. 'Anyway what does it matter? All that matters is we've got it back and we've done what we set out to do.'

But it mattered to Daisy, because it didn't feel right.

According to her dad, the ring had fitted Rachel. He'd told Daisy so when she asked him about it again on his return. And as far as she was concerned this was important.

Still, because her dad had gone to so much trouble to

get the ring back, and seemed relieved that everything was now back to normal, Daisy thought she'd better wait a while before mentioning her thoughts on the subject to him.

She knew her mum was a big believer in fate, and that the universe was supposed to always make things right.

So had the universe made sure that she and her dad were in the right place the day that man got knocked down in New York, so that the bags would be swapped and the ring would end up with the right person?

Maybe her mum had made sure that the ring had gone astray so that it would find its way to the person on whose finger it rightly belonged?

Up until this morning, Daisy had believed that, but now she wondered what the universe was trying to say when it had led her to find the box hidden deep in the rubbish bin.

Vanessa was all moved into their house now, but she still didn't understand how some things were done around the place, like how there was one bin for normal rubbish and a different one for recycling.

Recycling to help save the earth was important to Daisy, in the same way it had been important to her mum.

But while it had been bad enough trying to convince her dad to stick to the rules, it was even harder trying to teach them to a new household member, and Daisy was frustrated at yet again having to separate the recyclables.

This morning, while Vanessa was in the shower and her dad was out for a morning jog, Daisy had found more stuff in the regular bin that didn't belong. She'd taken the trouble to fish out the plastic bag and the pink and white box that it contained.

And it was when she realised what the box was that her dilemma began.

First Signs Pregnancy Test.

Daisy's heart skipped a beat. Did this mean she might be getting a baby brother or sister? It was something she'd have liked; but she had known it was impossible, given the circumstances. Until now.

Now that her dad and Vanessa were engaged they'd obviously decided to get started on being a family right away. She knew how much her dad wanted that too.

And in all honesty Daisy was pleased. Being an only child was lonely sometimes, and she had to admit that she'd felt even more alone since her dad had started going out with Vanessa. He didn't read to her as much, and they didn't get to spend a whole lot of time together, just the two of them.

So maybe a new baby would be a good thing.

But one thing was for sure: the discovery had solved her dilemma. Now Daisy knew about this, she couldn't possibly confess to her dad her worries about the ring, and that it might not be on the right person's finger.

Especially not if she, Dad and Vanessa were about to become a proper family in every way.

Chapter 37

Gary cranked up his bike and set off towards Rachel's. She'd asked him to call over to her place tonight, and he'd reluctantly agreed, anticipating yet another bombardment of wedding stuff.

He just wasn't in the mood for wedding talk, not after the day he'd had. Earlier this afternoon, he'd been to his solicitor's office to check out the CCTV tapes and read the witness report from the accident, and things weren't looking good.

It seemed there had been a couple in the cab at the time, and the guy who'd given the report was adamant that the driver couldn't have avoided Gary, and had described in great detail how the whole thing had played out.

Nosy bastard. Gary couldn't understand how some stranger could have such a perfect memory of an incident that didn't concern him, when he himself could barely remember what he'd had for breakfast. In fact, immediately after he was hit, the passengers had just hopped out and left him to fend for himself.

The footage had also shown that guy Greene and his kid breaking their way through the crowds to help him. Gary had noted with some dismay that it looked like they had just exited Tiffany's, and were carrying lots of shopping bags, which, he had to admit, meant there might actually be something to Greene's suggestion that their bags had got mixed up after all.

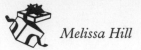

If that was the case, Gary felt a bit stupid now for thinking that the ring had been the result of some random stroke of luck. He supposed he should have thought a bit more about where it came from at the time, but what else was he supposed to do when at that stage Rachel was doing cartwheels over it? He felt sort of bad now for telling Ethan Greene to go and stuff it too, but he could hardly go and take it back off Rachel now because of some stranger's unlikely story, could he?

Anyway Greene had backed down in the end and, as far as Gary knew, hadn't been heard from since he called the guy's bluff about chasing Rachel.

But now that the situation had been made a little clearer, Gary figured the best thing to do was keep his mouth shut until he was forced to do otherwise.

He just wished that that so-called witness had done the same. The guy's account of events running up to the accident had been clear, concise and, according to his solicitor unfortunately, very damaging for their case.

Gary was livid. So much for his brand-new bike! Still, at least he'd got something out of it, he thought now, when Rachel opened her front door. Although he wasn't terribly enamoured of the fuss surrounding the wedding, he knew that his reluctance to admit to the truth that the engagement wasn't planned stemmed from the fact that he didn't want Rachel to realise the truth about him.

She'd be disappointed in him, that's for sure.

Another one to add to the list, he thought forlornly.

In fairness, though, it seemed that at least Terri had understood how important it was not to rock the boat, as it had been a good three weeks since he'd blabbed and yet nothing had come of it. Obviously Terri had also figured that what Rachel didn't know wouldn't hurt her.

But when his fiancée answered the door with a peculiar look on her face, Gary immediately had second thoughts. Rachel looked as if she had the weight of the world on her shoulders.

Shit, had Terri finally spilled the beans? Or had Rachel somehow found out about the CCTV footage of the accident, seen Greene and his bags and put two and two together? Or even worse, had she spoken to his mam?

His worries were allayed somewhat when Rachel put her arms around him and hugged him tightly. 'Thanks for coming over.'

'Hey, it's no problem. What's up?'

She was nervous, Gary noted, and this was so unlike her that it was making *him* feel nervous.

Her voice was soft. 'There's no easy way to say this . . .' She shook her head and tears filled her eyes. Gary's heart dropped into his stomach. Shit. Was she breaking up with him, calling off the wedding? He was taken aback by how resistant he was to this now, especially given the way the idea had been landed on him.

Yes, she could be a bit over the top with the soppy stuff sometimes, but weren't all women? She was one of the few people who made him feel good about himself; he liked having her in his life, and he realised that it was unlikely he'd ever find a woman like her again.

Rachel had faith in him, she looked up to him, thought he was genuinely wonderful, when all around him things were crumbling. Although she didn't know it, she was the one thing that kept him positive in the face of all the problems surrounding him. And right then, when it seemed as though he might lose her, Gary didn't want to imagine life without her.

'No easy way to say . . . what?' he repeated, stammering a little.

She looked down at her left hand, and with a start Gary copped that she wasn't wearing her engagement ring. Yikes.

'I lost it.'

'Rachel, I can explain—'Gary began, but the two of them had spoken at exactly the same time, and Gary honestly thought he'd misheard what she said. 'What?'

She looked up at him through lowered eyelashes. 'I've lost the ring somehow. I'm so sorry. I didn't want to tell you it was missing until I was sure, but I've searched high and low for the last three weeks and—'

'Hold on,' Gary interjected, flabbergasted, but also slightly relieved that it was she who was apologising. Still, alarm bells were going off in his head. 'It's been missing for three weeks?'

This was around the same time that Ethan Greene was in Dublin trying to get it back. Something was up here, he realised, in a rare moment of clarity.

Rachel nodded. 'I'm so sorry. I know I should have said something but I honestly thought it would turn up, that maybe I'd taken it off and left it somewhere at the bistro, but there's been no sign. Believe me, I've left no stone unturned. All I can say is that it just seems to have vanished into thin air.'

'No sign. Vanished.' Gary's mind was racing so fast he couldn't do anything other than repeat random words.

Rachel reached for him, misinterpreting his reaction for annoyance or anger. And the truth was that he *was* annoyed, but not for the reason she suspected. No, he was downright fit to be tied, because he was full sure that there was something else at play here. And he was equally sure that Ethan Greene, and most likely Terri too, were at the centre of it. No wonder he hadn't heard anything since!

Rachel was crying openly now. 'I'm so sorry. I've been going out of my mind these last few weeks and I haven't been able to sleep or eat just thinking about it and how much it cost.'

Gary could only imagine how bad she felt, and he really wanted to try to make her feel better. But this posed a bit of a dilemma. He couldn't very well throw his arms around her and tell her it was OK, not if he was supposed to have spent a couple of grand on a diamond, could he?

Yet at the same time he didn't have the heart to pretend to be angry, not when she was so upset and had obviously been stressing about this for a while.

Instead he stared at the floor in the manner of someone who was trying to get a handle on such news. 'I have to say this was the last thing I expected,' he said truthfully and Rachel nodded.

'I know, and I hate myself for not taking better care of it. I should have guarded it with my life, especially knowing how much you paid for it, and how hard you must have worked to pay it off bit by bit and everything.'

Christ, now Gary felt like a right heel, what with her going on and on about the cost.

'Look, don't worry about that; it's only money,' he said, in the hope of making her feel better.

'Only money?' she laughed through her tears. 'Oh you really are the most wonderful man. Thank you for trying to make me feel better when we both know that ring cost enough to bankrupt most people.'

'Erm . . . yeah.'

She bit her lip. 'I know this might be a long shot but was it insured, by any chance? Justin thought that maybe your credit-card insurance would cover it but I wasn't sure.'

'Hold on. Justin knows about this?' Gary asked. Which meant Terri did too, he was certain of it.

Rachel seemed to realise her slip of the tongue. 'I had to tell them because I had to ask if they'd come across it at

work. I would have told you first, only I couldn't bring myself to admit that I'd gone and done something so stupid.' She burst into tears again and Gary wasn't sure what to do.

'Ah, look, it's OK. I'm sure it'll turn up,' he said, encircling her in his arms and patting her gently on the back.

'Little chance of that at this stage,' she sniffed. 'Gary, I'm just so sorry,' she said again. 'I know I should have been more careful. Really, I shouldn't have been wearing it to work at all, especially when I had to take it off because it kept getting caught in my baking and—'

'When was the last time you saw it?'

'I'm really not sure. When I noticed I didn't have it, I could have sworn I took it off at work earlier that same day. But like I said, neither Terri nor Justin has seen it.'

'It does sound like you lost it at work,' Gary agreed, as things began to click into place. This was way too coincidental for his liking.

'I don't know. I just can't say for sure. Gary, I promise I'll make it up to you. I can only imagine the sacrifices you made to buy me that ring, and the last thing I wanted was for this to happen. I'll make it up to you, honestly. I went about trying to get a replacement but –' her face fell '– I just couldn't afford it.'

'Don't worry about it. It isn't your fault,' he replied, feeling like a right fraud now. He wished she wouldn't keep going on and on about how much the thing had cost; that only made him feel worse. 'I know it wasn't your fault.'

For once Gary was telling the truth. Given the timing and the circumstances, he was pretty sure that, however that ring had 'suddenly' gone astray, it certainly wasn't Rachel's fault.

Chapter 38

Ethan could have counted on one hand the number of times he'd been to Dublin in his lifetime, yet here he was in the place for the second time in the space of two months.

He was still reeling a little from all that had happened in the past four weeks. Much to his surprise, Vanessa was powering ahead with the wedding plans and had even gone so far as choosing a date.

This year.

He wasn't sure why, but for some reason this made him feel uncomfortable. 'What's the rush?' he'd asked, although he didn't know why he'd expected anything less of his driven and supremely organised fiancée. In life as in work, Vanessa wasn't the type of woman who waited around.

'I've never believed in long engagements, Ethan. What's the point? Either we're getting married or we aren't. Don't worry,' she added with a playful laugh, 'I'll take care of everything. You just need to turn up on the day.'

And it seemed that the day in question would be this coming summer. August, apparently. It all felt like a bit of a whirlwind to Ethan, but of course, what with all the fuss surrounding the ring, he'd barely had time to pause for breath since Christmas.

He, Daisy and Vanessa were on their way to Vanessa's parents' house, and now, as he sat in the passenger seat of the rental car Vanessa had arranged for them, he wondered

how everything had panned out for Rachel, and if her errant boyfriend had since told her the truth. He'd been tempted a number of times to phone the bistro and find out, but then he figured he'd better let well enough alone. It was none of his business after all.

He turned to look at Daisy in the back. 'How are you doing back there, buttercup? What do you think of your first visit to Dublin?'

She'd been quiet on the flight over, and in fact had been largely quiet about everything over the last few weeks.

The ring was back safe and sound, and she'd already given him and Vanessa her blessing in New York. So why did he feel once again that Daisy was somehow reluctant about it all?

'It looks really pretty, although not as pretty as New York,' Daisy replied, then blushed slightly as she remembered this was actually Vanessa's hometown.

'You're right about that!' Vanessa laughed. 'And I should warn you, Daisy, that my parents' place is small; don't expect any big mansions or anything like that.' She smiled at Ethan. 'I know your dad was amazed at how tiny it was last time we visited.'

'Don't be silly! Of course I wasn't,' Ethan argued, but he recalled how uncomfortable and slightly apologetic his girl-friend had been the first and only time he'd visited Vanessa's childhood home during a brief trip while Daisy had stayed with his own parents.

He realised that Vanessa was a little embarrassed by her working-class roots and couldn't figure out why; based on the one occasion he'd met Pat and Greta Ryan, he knew that they were warm, lovely and completely down to earth.

But Vanessa could be funny like that sometimes, and perhaps the circles she moved in at work and some of the very wealthy upper-class people she met inspired some deep-seated insecurities about her own upbringing. He didn't quite understand it himself, but as his own background was decidedly middle-class it was impossible to see such things from her point of view.

They arrived at the Ryan house shortly after eight on Friday evening, and Greta was waiting for them at the doorway of a small mid-terraced house on a quiet suburban street.

A short woman, who shared Vanessa's fair hair colour (although her shade was decidedly brassy compared to her daughter's platinum), she greeted them all with a round smiling face and arms wide open.

'Come in, come in, all of you!' After making a huge fuss of Daisy, whom she hadn't met before, she then pounced on her daughter.

'Show me that rock,' she exclaimed, and her eyes widened when Vanessa proudly extended her left hand. 'Jesus, Mary and Joseph, you must have paid through the nose for that!' she laughed, looking at Ethan.

If only you knew, he thought wryly.

'Well, if it isn't the happy couple,' Vanessa's dad Pat boomed, throwing his newspaper aside as they entered the living room. 'Congratulations, and fair play to you, boss,' he added, addressing Ethan. 'I must admit I never thought we'd get someone to take her off our hands.'

'Thanks, Dad,' Vanessa said petulantly and Ethan looked at her, having never heard her use that tone of voice before. It was pretty obvious, to him at least, that the man meant no harm and she was overreacting.

'Ah, sure, you know what I mean. I just never thought we'd find a man to tame you,' he said, winking at Ethan, but it seemed the damage was done and Vanessa's bubble of excitement was well and truly burst.

Despite Greta and Pat's best efforts over dinner to chat about wedding plans and potential venues, Vanessa seemed somewhat distracted.

'So ye're staying for the full weekend, then?' her mother asked hopefully.

'Yes, and we're going to try to organise as much as we can for the wedding while we're here.'

Really? Ethan realised this was the first he'd heard of it. He'd thought this visit was to celebrate the engagement and an excuse to spend some quality time with her parents. But, true to form, Vanessa was never one to waste an opportunity.

'We're going to check out some possibilities for the reception tomorrow,' his fiancée went on. 'I know Ethan has his heart set on an Irish country estate, don't you, darling?' She smiled, while Ethan tried to remember when he had uttered such a thing. 'I was thinking maybe Powerscourt might be ideal?'

'Oh that would be just gorgeous,' her mother agreed eagerly and Ethan could tell she was desperate to be involved in all the plans.

'And then after that I've booked us lunch at a place in town. It's a restaurant but they have a catering arm too, and I wanted to taste the food.' She winked at Ethan. 'I think you might be familiar with it.'

While he tried to figure out what she meant by this, she laughed and went on to repeat to her mother the story of his unusual proposal. 'So I thought it might be fitting for them to be involved on the day too. Of course I'll have to make sure the food's up to scratch first, but if that sourdough is anything to go by—'

'Hold on,' Ethan said, his stomach filling with dread. 'What restaurant are you talking about?'

'Stromboli. I thought they'd be perfect, all things considered, don't you?' his fiancée said, smiling. 'And I, for one, can't wait to see what all the fuss is about.'

Chapter 39

'I'm really glad Gary was OK about it,' Terri said into the mouthpiece. 'See, I told you he'd understand . . . Yes, he really is one in a million.' She rolled her eyes at Justin across the kitchen. 'But no need to come in today anyway. I insist. Now that it's all out in the open you should at least relax and take a breather.'

Having convinced Rachel that a busy Saturday at the bistro was the last thing she needed after the stress she'd been under in preparation for telling Gary about the missing ring, Terri hung up the phone. 'Apparently he was fine about it,' she told Justin sardonically. 'There's a surprise.'

He shook his head. 'Wasn't she even the tiniest bit suspicious about that? She loses a ring that supposedly cost tens of thousands, and tightwad Gary doesn't even raise an eyebrow?'

'I guess not. Anyway, cool or not, she agreed that the last thing she needed after such a stressful time was a busy Saturday lunch here. So she's still taking the day off. I told her to use it as a good opportunity to spend some time making it up to him.' The words had tasted bitter in her mouth but Terri knew she had to try to keep Rachel away from the bistro, today of all days.

Because today the newly engaged Ethan Greene and his fiancée were due to make an appearance for lunch.

When Justin had initially told her about the fiancée's catering enquiry, she'd thought about getting in touch with Ethan to ask him what the hell he was playing at, coming back here and flaunting the ring she'd taken such risks to help return.

But then she realised that it was unlikely that Ethan would have been party to such a thing, and in any case she didn't have a contact number for him. Rachel would have one, of course, but what reasonable excuse would Terri have for asking for it without arousing suspicion?

As far as Rachel was concerned, Terri had only met Ethan briefly, and while she considered concocting some random story about how he'd left something behind, she knew it wouldn't ring true.

So when she returned Vanessa Ryan's call and subsequently arranged a booking for her and Ethan to try a sample menu over lunch, her next priority was to make sure that Rachel was nowhere in the vicinity.

Notwithstanding the fact that it would be hugely coincidental for Ethan to choose Stromboli as his wedding caterers, his fiancée wearing an identical ring to the one Rachel had lost around the time of his last visit would be a coincidence too far.

And given that it was her actions that had inadvertently engineered the scenario, Terri figured the best she could do now was to let it all play out in her friend's absence. She really wasn't looking forward to it, though, and could only imagine how Ethan must feel about returning; she knew how worried he'd been about Rachel's reaction to the ring's disappearance.

And not for the first time, she wondered if the ring, currently in the possession of Ethan's fiancée, really did have a mind of its own.

Ethan was just about ready to climb the walls of the country estate he, Daisy and Vanessa were considering as a venue for their wedding.

Not because Vanessa had somehow got it into her head that he wanted to get married in such a place, but because he couldn't believe that out of all the companies in Dublin involved in catering, she had turned her attentions to Stromboli.

He supposed it was partly his own fault, given that he'd been the one to make her aware of it in the first place.

Damn that stupid bread, and damn Terri too for putting the ring in it and turning the whole palaver into a three-ring circus. Although that was unfair; he knew that Terri had only had the best intentions in doing so, and he was genuinely grateful to her for trying to help him out.

Still, gratitude was the last thing Ethan was feeling just then, and he wondered what on earth he was supposed to say when he, Vanessa and Daisy waltzed into the bistro today, Vanessa proudly wearing Rachel's lost engagement ring.

He could only assume that either Rachel or Terri was aware of the reservation, and saw no problem with it; so perhaps he was worrying for nothing.

Possibly the truth about the ring's origins had all come out in the meantime, and Rachel, far from being upset, might actually be anxious to apologise? Which left him with another problem he hadn't previously thought of. Obviously Vanessa knew nothing about the mix-up or the resultant hullabaloo, and Ethan didn't relish the thought of telling her that his 'surprise' proposal was as much of a surprise to him as it was to her.

Then again there was always the horrifying chance that neither Terri nor Rachel had any idea that the wedding in question was actually his. The enquiry had been made by Vanessa, presumably in her name, and as Stromboli catered events on a regular basis, why would anyone there bat an eyelid at today's lunch reservation?

After Vanessa had dropped the bombshell at her parents' house the night before, Ethan had tried his best to talk her out of it, dismissing Stromboli as a small enterprise, unlikely to meet her exacting standards. 'It seemed more like an individual or two-man outfit to me, fine for smaller events like parties, I'm sure, but hardly experienced enough for a full-blown wedding.'

'I disagree actually. The woman I spoke to on the phone sounded polished and confident, and from what I've seen on their website they look very professional,' Vanessa retorted, while Ethan tried to work out whether she'd been talking to Rachel or Terri. 'Not to mention that it would be fitting for them to take part on the day, given their important contribution to our engagement, wouldn't it?'

So Ethan had little option but to go along with today's lunch, and just pray that it didn't all explode in his face.

'What's wrong, Dad?' Daisy asked, taking his hand as they walked through the landscaped grounds, and he quickly rearranged his expression into what he hoped was a less anxious one. Sometimes his daughter was just too perceptive for her own good.

'Nothing, darling. Just lots to think about for the wedding. What do you think of this place?' he asked, indicating the estate's perfectly manicured gardens.

She shrugged. 'It's OK, I suppose.'

'Just OK?'

Daisy seemed to hesitate. 'It's sort of . . . posh, isn't it?' she whispered, and Ethan couldn't help but smile. Once again Daisy had hit the nail on the head.

'Are you looking forward to the big day in August?' he asked then. He still hadn't been able to tease out her feelings about the wedding taking place in such a relatively short time. 'I know it might seem fast but . . .'

'That's OK, Dad. I think I know why,' she replied ominously, but Ethan didn't have the opportunity to query this any further because Vanessa, who'd been chatting to the estate's events manager, came rushing over.

'Isn't it perfect?' she gushed. 'I just adore these grounds, and if the weather is kind we can arrange for a garden party on the terrace upon arrival, sort of like a grander version of afternoon tea. I'm thinking perhaps macaroons and champagne? Remind me to suggest this to the caterers this afternoon, won't you?' She smiled at Daisy. 'Does that sound good to you?'

The little girl looked dubious. 'I think most people would still be hungry. Maybe dinner might be best,' she suggested, her tone perfectly serious, and Ethan had to smile. Out of the mouths of babes . . .

'Well, of course we're going to have that too, silly!' Vanessa joked, and Ethan noticed that Daisy seemed hurt by what she'd obviously construed as a dismissal. He smiled at his daughter and reached for her hand.

Vanessa looked at her watch. 'In fact, that's what we need to investigate next, and seeing as it's almost midday we really should be heading back to Dublin soon. I hope everyone's hungry, as I've asked the caterers to let us try a little bit of everything. Although, we'd probably better not eat too much or we'll all explode!'

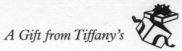

And as they followed Vanessa back to the main house Ethan mentally prepared himself for what lay ahead. He wondered if Stromboli's explosive name would today turn out to be prophetic.

Chapter 40

When he, Vanessa and Daisy arrived at the bistro, Ethan looked around nervously for Rachel, but he didn't have much of an opportunity to see anything at all before Terri sashayed over, a big smile on her face.

'Hello there! You must be Ms Ryan. Welcome,' she greeted warmly. Ethan noticed that she seemed to be going out of her way not to make any eye contact with him and he relaxed a little, realising that, given her reaction, Terri had indeed been expecting their visit. 'And you must be Daisy? Hi!' She reached down to the little girl's level and smiled, before finally looking at Ethan. 'Mr Greene, nice to see you again. I'm so pleased our little surprise worked out well.' With that she gave a surreptitious wink, and Ethan breathed a huge inward sigh of relief.

It was OK. He'd worried for nothing; Terri had it all under control.

'It's nice to be back. And yes, thank you, it worked well.'

'Good. I have a lovely table set up for you all back here,' she said, leading them towards the rear of the restaurant.

As Terri continued to chat good-humouredly with Vanessa and Daisy about the menu and the samples, Ethan kept a cautious eye out for Rachel.

'I must apologise because we're pretty short-staffed today,' he heard Terri say then, as if she were reading his mind.

'My colleague and co-owner, Rachel, is off today, so forgive me in advance if things are a little busy.'

'I see.' Vanessa looked slightly miffed by this, but Ethan immediately deduced that the information was for his benefit, to put his mind at ease about any potential drama over the ring. He made a mental note to try to get Terri alone at some stage so he could thank her yet again for saving his bacon.

'But in any case,' Terri smiled winningly as she continued her charm offensive towards Vanessa, 'I'm sure you'd all much rather eat in peace, and perhaps when you've finished sampling the menu we can discuss everything in more detail?'

'That would be wonderful, thank you,' he replied, when Vanessa failed to answer.

'Great. First, let me get you some drinks and then I'll have Justin, our chef, bring out the first platter.'

'Do you need any help?' he asked, and Vanessa shot him a look.

Terri squarely met his gaze and just then he felt profoundly grateful for all that she – a complete stranger – had done for him. If it weren't for her he might never have got the ring back, and without her intervention today could very well be like stepping onto a minefield. He realised suddenly how awkward and difficult this must be for her too, and indeed how much she'd risked in her efforts to help him. Rachel was her best friend and her business partner, yet she'd gambled all that to come to his assistance. Why?

'Thank you for offering, Ethan, but really I have it all under control,' she said.

'That's great to know. I – I mean, we,' he corrected, almost forgetting himself, 'appreciate that, don't we, Vanessa?'

His fiancée looked at him as if he were stark raving mad. 'Well, I'd certainly appreciate a drink, if it isn't too much trouble,' she said, smiling tightly.

'Of course!' Terri leapt into action. 'I'll be right back.'

'Is it just me or does she seem a bit odd?' Vanessa said, wrinkling her nose.

'I think she's nice,' Daisy piped up. 'I really like her eyes.'

Ethan nodded in agreement. Oddly, Terri's eyes were one of the first things he'd noticed about her too.

'Hmm. She seems a bit too overfamiliar for my liking,' Vanessa said, turning to look at Ethan. 'Did you notice she called you by your first name just now? A bit much for someone who's only met you once before.'

'Actually, Terri was the one who came up with the idea of baking your engagement ring into the bread,' Ethan said, feeling somehow bound to defend Terri. 'So I suppose she feels somewhat part of it all. Anyway,' he added pointedly, 'wasn't this personal touch the very reason you're considering the company's services for the wedding?'

'Yes, but there's a difference between that and over-familiarity.' Vanessa picked up the sample menu Terri had laid out for them. 'Still, I must admit that the food here really does sound delicious.' She sat forward in her chair and glanced around. 'Shame about the surroundings. Even for Dublin it's a little bit . . . twee, isn't it?'

Again, Ethan felt annoyed on behalf of Terri and Rachel. He suspected they had put a huge amount of thought and effort into the decor.

'I rather like it, as it happens,' he said. 'It's warm and cosy and, more importantly, it doesn't feel like you're eating in a science lab.' It was a thinly disguised barb at Vanessa's own preference for minimalist London eateries, which looked

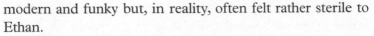

modern and funky but, in reality, often felt rather sterile to Ethan.

'It smells great too,' Daisy agreed. 'I'm so hungry.'

'Well, we're just in time then!' Terri chuckled, reappearing at the table with drinks; she was followed by Justin, who was carrying a huge platter of various savoury goodies. 'Now this is a broad selection of options we offer as starters, so I'll leave you three to dig in. Then, when you're ready, we'll bring out some mains. Sound OK?'

Already Ethan's mouth was watering, and he worried that if Terri kept serving them this great food, then Vanessa really would want to choose Stromboli for the wedding. Which meant that he wouldn't be able to avoid meeting Rachel again.

As they ate, Vanessa was determined to comment and rate almost every morsel she put into her mouth, and Ethan tuned out and wondered again how Rachel had reacted when she realised her precious ring had disappeared. He knew that he wouldn't be able to relax properly until he found out.

After a while he spotted Terri across the room, chatting to customers at another table near the bar. He vaguely recalled that the restaurant's toilets were situated in that area and figured that this was the opportunity he needed to get her alone.

'Back in a moment.' Excusing himself, he stood up and tried desperately to catch Terri's eye as he approached. Luckily, she seemed to sense his gaze and very quickly finished talking at the table and proceeded to a small alcove by the entrance to the toilets. Ethan followed, conscious that while the spot afforded them some privacy, it would still be all too easy for Vanessa or Daisy to spot him from their table.

'Terri, I'm so sorry,' he began. 'I had no idea Vanessa was going to do this. But thank goodness she spoke to you on the phone, otherwise I can only imagine how awkward it would be if Rachel—'

'How much trouble it would cause, you mean,' she interjected shortly. 'Seriously, Ethan, what the hell were you thinking bringing your fiancée and that ring back here? You've really made things very difficult. I didn't know if I should scupper the food on purpose, just to be sure we don't end up at the wedding!'

'I couldn't help it. It was all arranged without my knowledge. Believe me, I had no intention of going within a million miles of this place. Sorry,' he added quickly, noticing her slightly wounded expression, 'you must know what I mean. Don't get me wrong: I'm incredibly grateful that you're handling it all so well. And what about Rachel?'

Terri fixed those intense green eyes on him. 'What about her?'

'Well, she isn't here – on a busy Saturday. I take it that's also your doing?'

'Of course. We couldn't risk her seeing you again, to begin with, and then recognising what she believes is her ring on another woman's finger. Rachel can be a bit innocent at times, but any fool would be able to put two and two together.'

Ethan frowned. 'Knowles still hasn't told her the truth, I take it.'

'You take it right.' She shook her head. 'I know I did you a favour, but really, Ethan, if I'd known how upset she'd be I'd never in a million years have intervened like that.'

'For goodness' sake, how is Knowles getting away with putting her through this?' Ethan clenched his fists and Terri looked at him thoughtfully.

'I thought you said that none of it was any of your business,' she said, her tone implying in no uncertain terms that his reaction seemed over the top for someone who proclaimed he didn't care.

'It isn't, but I just can't bear to think that the man is still stringing her along like that. She's much too good for him.'

'I know, but I think that at this stage we just have to step back and let them get on with it—'

'Terri!'

Ethan started quickly at the sound of the voice, and he and Terri turned to see a tall, broad-chested man he vaguely recognised heading towards them, a thunderous look on his face. He realised that the very subject of their discussion had just stepped through the door of the restaurant.

'Oh shit! Just what we need,' Terri whispered

And to Ethan's dismay he realised that all attempts at controlling this situation had now gone right out of the window. There was no question that Vanessa would have heard; in fact, the majority of diners in the room were already glancing in his direction.

He took a deep breath. Here goes . . .

'What do you want, Gary?' Terri asked. 'Ethan, we'll talk again later,' she said, dismissing him.

'Ah, what a coincidence! So *this* is the famous Mr Greene,' Gary said, glowering at Ethan.

As the man stood in front of him, Ethan tried to remind himself yet again that he had nothing to be afraid of – Gary Knowles was and had always been in the wrong – but when the guy had a good twenty pounds on him, this was difficult.

'I knew it. I knew you two had to be behind this,' Gary boomed, and Terri grabbed each of them by the arm and (quite forcefully, Ethan noticed, considering her small frame)

pulled them into a quiet alcove nearby out of sight of her customers.

'Gary, what the hell are you doing?' she hissed. 'This is a restaurant, not your crappy Saturday-night local!'

'You should have thought of that before you helped Mr Do-Gooder here to steal Rachel's ring,' he growled.

Ethan was flabbergasted. Was this guy really so stupid as to have convinced himself that the ring actually belonged to him? 'Rachel's ring?' he retorted hotly. 'For goodness' sake, you know damn well that ring was never Rachel's, or indeed yours!'

Gary took a threatening step towards him. 'Where is it? What did you do with it? I'm warning you, Greene. You make sure she gets it back right now or I'll—'

'Ethan? What's going on here?' Vanessa interjected, white-faced, Daisy standing by her side. 'Who is this man?'

Suddenly Ethan saw his carefully ordered life come crashing down before his very eyes.

Gary crossed his arms, a slight smirk on his face as he realised that this was an awkward moment for Ethan in more ways than one.

'Don't worry, darling. It's a long story,' he replied, putting a soothing hand on Vanessa's arm. 'You and Daisy head back to the table and I'll explain it all later,' he added with a tight smile. The last thing he wanted was for Daisy to be upset by all this, so he prayed Vanessa would take the hint.

'No, I want to know what's going on right now,' she insisted forcibly. 'Clearly there's something that you're not telling me and—'

'Hey, Daisy, would you like to come into the kitchen and say hi to Justin? I know he'd love to meet you,' Terri interjected, swiftly taking the little girl's hand and turning her away from the spectacle, and once again coming to Ethan's rescue.

'Good idea, buttercup,' he reassured Daisy while she reluctantly followed Terri through to the kitchen.

'Well?' Vanessa looked from Ethan to Gary. Then she frowned. 'Excuse me, why are you staring at me like that?'

Ethan looked at Gary to find that he was indeed staring at Vanessa with a perplexed look on his face.

'Hey, I know you,' Knowles said then, his eyes narrowing.

'What? What are you talking about? I've never seen you before in my life. Ethan, are you going to tell me what the hell is going on here?' she repeated impatiently.

'Darling, I really don't think this is the time or the place,' he mumbled.

'Hold on! I *do* know you.' Knowles continued to stare at Vanessa with confused recognition.

'Don't be silly. I've never met you—' She glanced disparagingly at Gary as if he were a particularly annoying fly she wanted to swat away, and refocused her attention on Ethan.

'Vanessa—'

'Bloody hell!' Gary said finally. 'It's you.'

'Excuse me?'

'It *is* you. The bird in the taxi – the one from New York.'

'I'm sure I don't know what you mean,' Vanessa replied shortly, but Ethan noticed a faint blush creep across her face.

'No, no, I'm right! I know I am. I'd swear to it,' Gary insisted. 'I recognise you from the CCTV footage. You and that guy were in the taxi that ran me over.'

Ethan was now seriously perplexed. 'Knowles, what on earth are you talking about? How could Vanessa possibly have been . . . ?' But the rest of the question trailed off when he noticed that Vanessa was looking momentarily unnerved.

What the hell?

'Nonsense. You've clearly mistaken me for someone else. But never mind that, is anyone ever going to tell me what *this* is about? Why were you arguing?' she asked, her voice low so as not to disturb the other diners. 'And how do you know this man, Ethan?'

'You were with the guy . . . the witness – what was his name?' Gary was adamant that Vanessa had been in the cab. 'Freeman, that's it,' he recalled eventually. 'Brian Freeman.'

Suddenly the mood shifted.

Brian . . . ?

Confused by this, Ethan turned to look at Vanessa, who by now was looking exceedingly uncomfortable. Clearly there was something to Gary's story. Ethan's mind raced as he struggled to figure it out.

'Brian? He was in New York while we were there?' he said, ignoring Gary and addressing Vanessa. 'What were you and Brian doing in a taxi? You never said anything about it.' All too quickly, Ethan realised that his best friend had also failed to mention anything about seeing Vanessa in New York, or being in the city at the same time as them, let alone being at the scene of the accident that had preceded all Ethan's problems with the ring in the first place.

Suddenly he felt caught completely unawares. How had this happened? How had the tables been turned? Instead of demanding an explanation, Vanessa was now the one under scrutiny.

Was it really possible that she and Brian had been in the cab that knocked Gary over? And if they had been, why on earth hide it?

'Yeah, well, I'm sure you two lovebirds can sort the rest of it out in your own time,' Gary interjected, and if Ethan had had any inclination to punch the man before, he seriously wanted to do so now. 'I take it your missus won't be needing that now?' He indicated Vanessa's ring and she looked down, puzzled.

'Excuse me, I still don't know who the hell you are, but I do know that this is absolutely none of your business,' Vanessa said through clenched teeth. 'Haven't you caused enough trouble?'

'I want an explanation,' Ethan said to Vanessa, ignoring Gary. 'If you and Brian were in the cab that day, why didn't you mention it? You knew I was involved in the aftermath of the accident – I told you all about it – so why hide it?'

'Yeah, and why didn't you stay and try to help out instead of taking off like a rocket?' Knowles queried. 'I could have died, you know. The police call it "fleeing the scene", which I suppose is why your boyfriend finally came to his senses about making a statement.' He grunted. 'Fat lot of good it did me, though.'

Ethan tried to pretend the other man wasn't there. 'Vanessa, I asked you a question.'

She sniffed and looked away, refusing to meet his gaze.

'It's not how it seems, Ethan,' she began, her voice pleading, and Ethan's stomach dropped into his shoes.

'Nice try, babe, but this guy Freeman's already hung you out to dry,' Gary said, clearly enjoying the discomfort he was causing. 'It's on record that the cab picked you two up from some place uptown.'

Vanessa didn't even look at him. 'We were having a business meeting,' she explained weakly, but Ethan was by now an expert in lame excuses, given the ones he'd had to concoct himself recently.

'Really? A business meeting – on Christmas Eve? I wasn't aware Brian had become one of your authors, or indeed that he was in New York.'

'Brian was heading downtown and I had some shopping

343

to do so we shared a taxi back from . . . our meeting,' she continued, her hazel eyes shining with tears as she spoke. 'When we reached Fifth Avenue I spotted you and Daisy on the street outside Tiffany's. I started to panic, stupidly worried that you might see us, although of course this was impossible but . . .' She shook her head. 'Brian tried to calm me down and we started arguing, and then—'

'I knew it!' Gary proclaimed. 'I knew that gobshite driver wasn't paying attention! Walked out in front of him, my foot! Tell lover-boy thanks very much. His lies fucked up my lawsuit.'

Ethan couldn't believe what he was hearing. 'So you were actually there when the accident happened? But what about afterwards, when you saw Daisy and me trying to help? Did you just . . . sneak away, hoping we wouldn't notice?'

Obviously he wouldn't have noticed, though, Ethan thought; at the time, his only concern was for the injured Knowles. He remembered the cab driver mentioning something about his fare abandoning him, but the last thing Ethan would have expected was for someone he knew to be in the cab, let alone to have caused the very accident that had . . .

Then an uneasy feeling came over him and, just like that, he understood. One look at Vanessa's shamefaced expression told him everything. 'Oh my God . . .' he whispered. 'You – and Brian?'

Vanessa and Brian . . . having an affair?

Christ, did Vanessa's determination stop at anything? He knew well that she had her heart set on securing the great Brian Freeman for her publishing house, but would she honestly sink that low?

And of course good old Brian, who was used to women throwing themselves at him, would hardly refuse. Suddenly,

Ethan recalled Brian's rather odd reaction that time when he'd told him about his planned proposal going awry. *Make sure it's what you both want, and for the right reasons* . . .

Now, in retrospect, it made sense.

He couldn't believe he'd been betrayed in such a way, and by two people he cared for and trusted. Clearly care and trust didn't work both ways.

'Perhaps whatever went on at that meeting was your unique way of trying to poach him?' Ethan asked scornfully.

'That's not fair. Ethan, we didn't . . . Brian doesn't . . . Look, things are different now. You and I are engaged, whereas before I – I was never sure how you . . . if you really—' Her gaze dropped to the floor. 'Of course it had nothing to do with poaching him. Brian and I, well, we'd known each other for a while and it was sort of ongoing before you and I met. We bumped into each other a lot socially and it gradually became a . . . I don't know, a kind of habit, of sorts.' She shook her head, unable to explain it away, and Ethan couldn't believe that he'd been made such a fool of. 'Seriously, Ethan, it meant nothing, and it's over now. As soon as you proposed, I told him it was over.'

Ethan wanted to be sick. To think that he'd trusted Brian, confided in him all his doubts and worries about Vanessa, their relationship, marriage and of course the ring, and all along his so-called mate had been sleeping with her behind his back! God, he was an idiot!

And right then he wondered whether, on Christmas Eve, up there somewhere, darling Jane was having a word in the ear of her beloved universe.

'So,' Gary said, breaking the silence, 'about this ring . . .'

Chapter 41

At that moment Terri reappeared with a still perplexed-looking Daisy in tow. 'Look, you lot might be perfectly happy to stand around and chat all day, but might I remind you that this is a restaurant, and I have customers to serve?' Her voice was hard. 'If the three of you want to continue this, then please do so at a table instead of blocking up the place!'

Daisy stared at Vanessa's stricken face. 'What's wrong, Vanessa?' she asked and Ethan could see from her expression how her anxiety levels were rising.

'It's nothing, darling,' he soothed, reaching down to put an arm around her. 'Why don't we do as Terri says, and go back to our table and finish our food? Did you have fun meeting the chef?' Ethan was trying desperately to keep his voice light, while inside he wanted to put a fist through the wall.

'Ethan, I—' Vanessa began, but he held up his hand.

'Leave it. Now is not the time.'

There must have been enough in his voice to warn her not to push it, because instead of continuing to argue she quietly relented. 'I'm sorry,' she sobbed, turning on her heel and heading straight for the ladies' room.

Terri gave Ethan a quizzical look and he shook his head slowly as if to say 'Don't ask.'

He and Daisy made their way back towards their table

on the other side of the room, his legs weak and jelly-like. He was vaguely aware of Gary following them.

'Dad? What's going on? Why is Vanessa crying?' Daisy was clearly perturbed, and she looked at Ethan for reassurance.

'It's OK, honey,' Terri said, taking the little girl's hand again, somehow understanding that Ethan was struggling to cope. 'She's just upset about something.'

'Is it the baby?' Daisy asked, and right at that moment Ethan was glad that he was just about to sit down, because he really didn't think his legs would be able to hold him up.

He looked at his daughter. 'What?'

Terri raised an eyebrow. 'I think I'd better leave you to it. Gary, now that you're here, you might as well make yourself useful,' she urged, nudging him on the arm. 'I've got some tables that need clearing.'

'To hell with that, I'm in the middle of something.' But Terri's tone must have given Gary pause, as he hesitated for a brief moment before reluctantly moving away, leaving Ethan and Daisy alone.

Ethan looked at his daughter. 'Honey, what are you talking about? What's all this about a baby?'

Daisy looked around hesitantly, as if trying to locate Vanessa.

'We had a little argument,' he said by way of explanation. 'I think she might be gone for a while.'

Daisy sighed and looked down at the table, where the platter of wedding nibbles had long since gone cold. 'Please don't be cross, Daddy,' she said guiltily, looking up at him through her eyelashes.

'What? Why would I be cross with you?' At this point, Ethan had no idea what was coming. And what was all this about a baby?

'OK,' Daisy sighed again. 'Well, I think I'd better tell you everything.'

After prising Gary away from Ethan and whatever drama he and Vanessa were experiencing, Terri had strong-armed him into helping her clear tables by promising that she'd tell him what she knew about the ring's disappearance.

Despite what she and Justin might think, she realised Gary wasn't completely stupid and once Rachel had revealed that the ring was missing he must have put two and two together.

It was such bad luck that Ethan had to be here when he reached the obvious conclusion. Or was it? Clearly Gary's appearance had sparked some controversy between Ethan and his fiancée, and from the snippets she'd overheard while going to and from the kitchen, it wasn't just about the ring.

Poor Ethan, it seemed that his trip to New York had caused more than one problem for him. Her heart went out to Daisy too. She seemed a nervous little soul and had been hugely unsettled by the scene. That Vanessa woman shouldn't have made the child privy to Gary and Ethan's argument, irrespective of how curious about it she might have been herself. As it was, Justin had tried to cheer Daisy up and stop her worrying about Ethan by asking her to 'help out' with the cookie dough.

Now that the lunchtime rush was over and only a few occupied tables remained in the dining room, Terri turned to Gary in the kitchen. 'Why are you here?' she asked him again. 'It's Rachel's day off. Aren't you supposed to be spending time with her today?'

'I told her I had something else on,' he replied. 'Something important – like finding out how the ring she's so upset

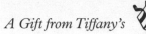

about could suddenly have disappeared into thin air.' He stared at her, his eyes narrowing suspiciously.

Terri looked away and continued piling used plates on top of one another. 'I have no idea what you're talking about.'

'Come on, Terri, you can't fool me. I saw the ring on Greene's missus. Isn't it a bit coincidental that it just "disappears" the last time he was here? The very same time the two of you came crying to me with some sorry story about it? And what is he doing here again anyway? Trying to rub Rachel's nose in it or something?'

Terri put her hands on her hips. 'Gary, how many times do I have to say it before it gets into your thick skull? The ring isn't yours; it never was. You admitted as much to me yourself that night you got drunk.'

Just then, Justin came rushing into the kitchen. 'You two, change of subject might be good right about now.'

They both ignored him.

'Look, as far as I'm concerned it *is* Rachel's; and however we might have ended up with it, she adored that ring,' Gary retorted. 'But I wonder what she'll think when I tell her that her so-called best friend conspired to steal her engagement ring from her. It *was* you who took it, wasn't it? You and that Ethan Greene were in it together. I wonder how Rachel will feel when she realises she can't trust her own friend. What do you think about that? How is Rachel going to feel?'

At that moment, the door from the dining room swung open.

'How is Rachel going to feel about what?' a voice asked.

Terri, Justin and Gary turned towards the doorway, where Rachel stood, a confused look on her face.

Chapter 42

'What's up?' Rachel asked, laughing lightly. 'Everyone's gone very quiet all of a sudden.'

She'd noticed that all three had become deathly silent upon her entry and she examined the scene in front of her more closely.

What was Gary doing here? Wasn't he supposed to be at Sean's, fixing up some problem with the bike? He looked worked up about something too; she recognised that vexed expression. And it seemed as though he and Terri had been having some kind of animated discussion. In addition, Justin seemed to have dropped whatever he was doing in the dining room upon her arrival and had rushed into the kitchen ahead of her.

'Well? How am I going to feel about what?' she repeated. She looked at Gary, then at Terri and a shiver of unease ran down her spine. Neither would meet her gaze.

She searched each of their faces. 'What's going on? And was I seeing things, or is that Ethan Greene out there? I thought I spotted him on my way in.'

Terri smiled, but Rachel could tell it was forced. 'Yes, Ethan's here with his fiancée. They were thinking of hiring us to cater for their wedding and are trying out some samples.'

'Oh so he did pop the question, then?' Rachel smiled. 'That's nice. I must go out and say hello.'

But her words were automatic because deep down she knew that there was something not quite right about Ethan's presence here, and the catering thing seemed very odd indeed. He was supposed to be from London, so why on earth would he want them to cater for his wedding?

Gary spoke then. 'Funny you should mention him,' he said scathingly and Terri shot him a look.

'Well, you've certainly no excuse for not catching up with him this time, Gary.' Rachel tried to keep her voice light, but every bone in her body was telling her there was something very odd here.

'Oh I've caught up with him all right,' her fiancé replied, and she didn't like the ominous way he said it.

'So, what were you lot talking about?' she asked again. 'I thought I heard my name being mentioned.'

'It was nothing, really,' Terri told her. 'We were all just chatting about the wedding.'

'Oh.' Of course, Rachel thought, relaxing a little. Terri was her bridesmaid, after all, so perhaps she was planning a surprise that needed Gary's approval? And then she'd walked in, right in the middle of it. Whatever it was Rachel was sure she'd find out in time. In truth, she was still so relieved that Gary hadn't hit the roof about her losing the ring that she was happy to let him and Terri plan anything they wanted.

'What are you doing here anyway, Gary?' she asked. 'I thought you said you'd made plans with Sean.'

'I did, and I just popped in for a sandwich on the way.' That wasn't unusual, but Rachel knew it annoyed Terri that Gary took advantage and often assumed the food would be

free just because of their relationship. So that could have been what they were arguing about.

'How come you're here, boss?' Justin asked. 'I thought you were taking the day off.'

'I thought I would, but I was bored.' She laughed. 'Can't keep away from the place! Anyway, I might as well give a hand with the clean-up while I'm here,' she said, looking at the pile of dirty plates on a nearby counter. 'But first, I might pop out and say hello to Ethan.'

'Ah, you'd better leave it for the moment.' Terri grimaced. 'Last thing I heard, he and the girlfriend were having a bit of a discussion,' she said, leaving Rachel in no uncertain terms that said discussion wasn't a pleasant one.

'Oh?'

'Yeah. Seems the missus had a bit on the side that Mr Schoolteacher didn't know about,' Gary added snidely, and Rachel wondered how he could possibly know this.

'Right. So you and Ethan have had a chance to chat, then,' she said.

'Yep, and we still have plenty more to say to one another, by my reckoning.'

Rachel couldn't quite get a handle on her boyfriend's tone but again knew it wasn't right.

'OK. Well, I'll go and get changed, and maybe I'll get the chance to say hi before they leave.'

'And I'll go back out and check on the tables—' Terri began, but stopped in her tracks when there was a soft knock on the restaurant's connecting door.

They all turned to see a little girl's head peek wide-eyed around it.

'Daisy, hi!' Rachel smiled, recognising Ethan's daughter immediately.

She smiled back. 'Hi, Rachel.'

'It's OK, *I'll* check on the tables,' Justin said, giving Daisy a light pat on the head as he passed.

'Everything OK, sweetheart?' Terri asked, going straight to her. She bent down in front of Daisy and took her hand.

The little girl shook her head and her bottom lip trembled. 'Vanessa came back from the toilet and now she and Dad are fighting. I think I really messed everything up.'

'Oh honey, I'm sure it's probably just a silly disagreement. Adults do that sometimes. Please don't think it's your fault.'

Rachel smiled as Terri gently tucked a lock of Daisy's blonde hair behind her ear. She was really so good with kids.

Gary just stood there, looking uncomfortable.

'No, it is all my fault. I told Dad.' Daisy began fiddling with the hem of her dress. 'I told him what I thought about the ring.'

At the mention of a ring, the hair on the back of Rachel's neck involuntarily stood up. And was it her imagination, or did Terri shoot her a nervous glance when Daisy said this?

'What ring, Daisy?' Rachel asked, coming closer.

Then again, she realised she was probably just hypersensitive about rings, considering what had happened to her own.

The little girl's eyes were filled with tears. 'Vanessa's ring.' She hiccupped loudly. 'The Tiffany's ring was supposed to fit Vanessa, but it didn't. Mum always said that she and Dad were the right fit, and that when you found someone you really loved, everything fitted. But the ring doesn't.'

Terri pulled her into a big hug. 'I understand why you might think that, honey, but I suspect your mum might have meant something other than jewellery.'

Rachel raised an eyebrow. Vanessa had a Tiffany's ring too?

'My mum also said that Tiffany's was a magical place, so maybe the ring my dad bought there didn't fit Vanessa because she's not the right person.' She looked at Terri, her eyes red-rimmed. 'I know she's been keeping secrets from my dad. That's why they're fighting now.'

Rachel struggled to keep up. 'Like Terri said, adults often fight, even when they love each other,' she soothed, wondering what on earth was going on with Ethan and his girlfriend. And what was all this about a Tiffany's ring that was supposed to fit, but didn't?

'It fitted you, though,' Daisy said, breaking away from Terri and looking directly at Rachel.

She frowned. 'What?'

'The ring. Dad's ring. The one you got by mistake. Dad said that it fitted you.'

Rachel wasn't sure what was going on but Daisy certainly seemed like one very confused little girl. 'Daisy, what makes you think that? How would I possibly—'

Gary stepped forward. 'Ah, Rachel . . .'

'What do you mean?' she whispered, approaching Daisy.

Terri stood up and put her arm around Daisy's shoulders. 'Rachel, I think you and Gary need to have a chat. Gary?' she urged and Rachel's fiancé moved closer.

'Terri's right. We need to talk,' he said gruffly. 'Something happened in New York, something really weird. I was going to tell you but—'

A knot of unease started to grow in Rachel's stomach. There was something very off about what Daisy had said, about this entire situation, actually. And she realised yet again that she was the only one in this room who didn't know what it was all about.

'A chat about what, Gary? What is it you were going to

tell me?' she asked, her mind racing. Just as she started to try to put the pieces together, Ethan Greene came rushing through the door.

'Daisy!' he cried, going to his daughter and engulfing her in his arms. 'What were you thinking, slipping away like that without telling me? I was afraid you'd— Oh Rachel, hi.' He stopped short when he caught sight of her standing close by, and again she knew instinctively that his multiple appearances at the bistro lately had nothing to do with concern for Gary after his accident. Nothing at all.

'Where's Vanessa?' Daisy asked.

'She went back to her mum's house, buttercup.' He looked embarrassed. 'I'll tell you all about it later.'

'I told Rachel about the ring,' his daughter said, and she saw Ethan cast a wary glance towards Gary, who stood impassive, now saying nothing.

As the tension in the room between Gary, Rachel and Ethan increased and seemed to make the air vibrate around them, Terri noticed that Daisy looked near to tears again.

'Daisy, I'm going on a break now. Do you fancy sharing a nice big hot chocolate with me – with marshmallows?' Terri suggested brightly and Daisy looked at her father for his permission.

'It's OK, honey, go with Terri. I'm just going to have a little chat with Rachel.'

Daisy beamed. 'That's great, Dad! Don't forget what I told you, OK?' she said, casting a conspiratorial glance at Rachel.

The problem was that Rachel seemed to be the only one who wasn't in on the conspiracy. Terri, Ethan and Gary were clearly all privy to what she herself was missing and whatever it was, it was becoming more and more baffling by the second.

Terri took Daisy back out front, leaving Rachel with the two men. There was a momentary silence as she looked back and forth between them, unsure what to think.

'OK,' she said finally. 'What's going on here that I don't know about?'

Chapter 43

'Quite a lot, babe,' Gary offered. He looked disdainfully at Ethan. 'I'm sorry to tell you, Rachel, that this man here and your so-called best friend have been lying to you,' he said solemnly.

Rachel looked at Ethan. 'What is he talking about?' she asked, and for the first time she noticed that Ethan seemed tired and defeated. Those typically lively blue eyes were flat and dulled.

'You're a good one to talk about lies,' Ethan said to Gary.

'Oh yeah? Tell us again about your book, Greene,' Gary replied with a sneer. 'The book you told Rachel all about at your cosy dinner.'

Rachel looked at Gary blankly, unable to figure out how on earth this was relevant. Gary knew all about her discussions during the dinner with Ethan that time, but she couldn't understand why he was bringing it up now. Jealousy? He hadn't come across as such before. 'What does Ethan's book have to do with anything?' she asked.

'There is no book, Rachel. There is no bloody book. It was just a big story, a big excuse to try to get into your knickers.'

'Oh for Pete's sake!' Ethan glared angrily at the other man. 'Why don't you tell her why I was forced to come up with such a story in the first place?'

Gary shrugged. 'Hell if I know. Because you were trying to manipulate her? And, anyway, if you were so sure, then

why couldn't you just say what you came here to say from the start?'

'Because I didn't want to hurt her, that's why! Although you seem to have no problem with that and you're supposed to be her fiancé.'

Rachel's head was spinning with confusion. 'There's no book?' she said to Ethan, who nodded grimly. 'So what was all that about you coming here for research? And if you didn't come here for that, then why did you? Clearly it's something to do with Gary's accident. Although Terri's right: in retrospect, your concern for his well-being does seem over the top.' Obviously there *was* more to Ethan Greene than met the eye, and for once Rachel realised that her friend's initial suspicions seemed to have been founded on something after all.

'I had a completely legitimate reason for coming here. But when it came down to it, I just couldn't tell you. It's stupid . . . I can't explain it.'

'Couldn't tell me what, for crying out loud?'

'About the ring.' Terri had quietly re-entered the room. 'Justin is looking after Daisy outside, and she's fine,' she told Ethan. Their eyes met and Rachel saw some kind of shared understanding pass between them. What was that all about? 'I figured Gary might try to slither his way out of the truth,' Terri went on. 'Looks like I was right.'

By now Rachel was utterly bewildered. 'My ring? The one I lost?' She looked at Gary. 'Slither out of . . . ? Can somebody *please* tell me what is going on as I'm completely lost,' she demanded, suddenly irritated.

'Gary didn't buy that ring,' Terri continued, before Gary could reply. 'Ethan did.'

'There's no proof of that—' Gary began, but Rachel cut him off.

'But why would Ethan buy me a ring?' Rachel said baffled. 'He didn't know me.'

'I bought it for Vanessa,' Ethan said gently, as if she were a small child who wasn't quite getting it.

He wasn't wrong: Rachel *wasn't* getting it.

'But how would a ring that you bought for your girl-friend end up with—'

Then Rachel suddenly remembered the conversation she'd had with Ethan back at the hospital, when he mentioned losing something at the scene of the accident . . . then Gary's half-hearted and, if she thought about it now, rather reluctant proposal when they exchanged gifts . . .

And just like that, coupled with Daisy's comment about Vanessa's ring being from Tiffany's, all the pieces finally fell into place.

'Oh my God,' she gasped, turning to Gary, feeling sick. 'It wasn't yours. The bag, the Tiffany's bag – it didn't belong to you at all, did it?'

'There's nothing to say it belonged to him either—' Gary began but Rachel put a hand up to stop him.

'I'm sorry, Rachel, but the ring *is* mine,' Ethan insisted quickly. 'There was obviously a mix-up when Daisy and I helped him after the accident, but I didn't discover it until the next day, when Vanessa went to open her gift and she got yours instead.'

Rachel tasted bile in her mouth. 'I can't believe that you gave me a ring that you didn't buy,' she said to Gary, tears filling her eyes. 'You stole a ring that was meant for some-one else? What kind of person would do something—'

'Hold on! I didn't steal anything.'

'What do you call laying claim to something that is not rightfully yours?' Ethan interjected hotly, and the two men glared at each other.

'What was my gift?' Rachel asked then, her tone robotic. There was silence and Gary stared at his feet.

'You said that you discovered the mistake when your girl-friend opened her gift,' she said to Ethan before turning to Gary again. 'What was I supposed to get?' she repeated forcefully, knowing deep down that although it was something from Tiffany's, it clearly wasn't a diamond ring.

There was a long, tension-filled silence until eventually Terri spoke. 'He bought you a charm bracelet,' said her friend, clearly wanting to put her out of her misery.

A charm bracelet.

Rachel's heart plunged to the depths of her stomach.

She wanted to die.

So Gary had been just as surprised as she was by the appearance of the engagement ring. Which could only mean one thing: he had never intended to propose to her in the first place.

And not only that, she realised now, mortified, but they all knew. Ethan, Gary, Terri, possibly even Justin, knew what had happened, had maybe even known all along. They had seen her dancing around like a happy loon about her so-called fairy-tale engagement, and yet none of them had bothered to enlighten her. And this, possibly more than anything else, hurt the hardest.

'A charm bracelet,' she said stonily, and in a quick flash of insight she recalled the Tiffany's transaction on Gary's credit-card statement, which in retrospect made perfect sense.

Ethan and Terri were telling the truth; this was no bad dream, no embarrassing nightmare from which she'd wake up and feel silly.

She looked at her fiancé with disdain. 'You proposed to me with a ring that belonged to someone else?' she said, her voice barely a whisper. 'How could you? How could anyone stoop so low?'

Gary was reluctant to meet her gaze. 'What was I supposed to do, Rachel? Tell you it was all a big mistake? You were over the moon about that ring and the proposal, and I knew that if I said something you would—'

'Of course you should have said something! Instead you chose to make a complete fool of me by going along with this huge . . . charade!' She wanted to die of embarrassment when she thought about her recent behaviour, all the plans she'd been making, not only for the wedding, but for the rest of their lives. She'd been such a fool.

'I didn't know what to do. It caught me by surprise too,' he said quietly, seemingly unable to offer any other explanation.

Then Rachel looked at Terri, unable to believe that her best friend could have kept such a thing from her. Especially when Terri knew very well what it was like to be betrayed, given how her last relationship had ended. 'So you knew about this too?' she said, her voice hoarse.

Terri looked distraught. 'Not until that first time Ethan came here. I had an inkling that something wasn't right and then –' she looked sideways at Gary '– he let it slip the night he came back from Wicklow, when you were out with Ethan. He'd had a few drinks and . . . Look, none of us wanted to hurt you, Rachel,' she finished sadly. 'We were just trying to figure out the best way to—'

'And you, you were going to propose to your girlfriend with this ring?' Rachel turned her attentions to Ethan. 'You knew the whole time, and you lied barefaced right from the beginning. All this nonsense about being concerned for Gary, and being in Dublin to research some book. Christ, you must all think I'm some kind of idiot.'

'Rachel, no, of course not,' Ethan replied earnestly. 'It's just that I didn't want to upset you. None of us did. And, to be frank, it wasn't up to me. Gary should have been the one to tell you.' Again he stared accusingly at Gary.

'Rachel, Ethan's telling the truth,' Terri said. 'He was trying to consider your feelings.'

'Why would any of you think that leading me on this . . . this *farce* is considering my feelings?' she exploded. 'What kind of imbecile do you think I am?' Much to her annoyance she began to sob and saw Terri move to comfort her. 'No,' she cried, stepping back. Tears stained her cheeks. 'Don't touch me. Don't any one of you come near me.'

Then she thought of something else. 'Where is the ring now?' she asked, realising that its sudden disappearance no longer seemed so inexplicable. 'Oh,' she said then, answering her own question, 'of course. I presume it's back where it belongs?' She remembered little Daisy's comment earlier about the ring not being the right fit for Ethan's girlfriend.

Well, how the hell could it be?

'So what happened? Did you have a crisis of conscience or something?' she asked Gary. But then why did he act so surprised when she admitted yesterday that it was lost? Christ, had he been upfront with her about *anything*?

'As far as I was concerned it was your ring, and there's no way I was handing it over just because some—'

'It was me,' Terri interjected guiltily. She looked at Ethan. 'I helped Ethan get it back that time he was here. I knew that Gary wasn't prepared to own up and I couldn't let you—'

Gary took a step forward. 'Look, there's no proof that it was ever Greene's.'

'Save it, Gary,' Rachel whispered. This was all becoming more mortifying and hurtful by the second. To think that

all along the people she cared most about had been plot-
ting and planning behind her back, and in the most
patronising ways . . . 'Don't say another word to me, any
of you. Stop trying to make excuses for your actions; you
are all liars. Every last one of you.'

Terri reacted as if she had been slapped. 'Please, Rachel
. . .' she began.

'No, not another word,' she said dully.

Gary went to move towards her and she held up her hand
to stop him.

'Ethan, I'm glad you got your ring back, and it's on the
right woman's finger now,' she told him.

Then she cast a withering glance at the two people she
loved the most, and whom up until today she would have
trusted with her life. 'As for you two, as far as I'm concerned
you've done nothing but lie, and I want nothing more to
do with you.'

With that, Rachel walked out of the kitchen door, straight
through the dining room of her beloved restaurant, and
didn't look back.

Chapter 44

When she was gone, Gary glared at Terri. 'Are you happy now?' he said. 'Do you see what you've done?'

Terri was gobsmacked. 'What *I've* done?'

'Yeah. You're the one who nicked the ring, to give it back to your boyfriend here.' He looked disdainfully at Ethan. 'The two of you seem to be in right cahoots these days.'

'How dare you?' Ethan replied, stepping forward, his jaw tight. 'How dare you accuse us when *all* of this is your fault! The only reason I didn't say anything right from the beginning was out of concern for Rachel.'

'Bullshit. You were trying to get into her knickers. And when that didn't work you thought you might try getting into Terri's instead.'

Terri stood rooted to the spot, unable to believe what she was hearing.

Ethan, though, seemed to have no such problems. He took another step forward and, quick as you like, caught the other man by surprise – landing a well-placed punch directly under his right eye.

Gary stumbled, fell back onto a nearby worktable and crashed heavily to the floor.

'Oh my God!' Terri put a hand to her mouth. She looked at Ethan. 'I can't believe you did that.'

Ethan winced and gingerly held his right hand, already looking like he was regretting it big-time.

'Well, after everything that's happened I think he had it coming, don't you?' he said. 'But disrespecting you like that, that was the last straw.' He met Terri's gaze, and was it her imagination or was there was a heavy charge to the air that hadn't been there before?

It was the last thing she'd expected from a guy who seemed so mild-mannered he would hardly swat a fly. And the fact that he'd done it to defend her honour . . .

'Especially when you've done so much to help me,' Ethan continued, and just like that the air went out of Terri's balloon.

Oh.

'What the fuck . . . ?' Gary was trying to stand up but still seemed dazed by the blow. And never mind being taken by surprise, Terri figured his male pride would have been seriously hurt from being decked by, for all intents and purposes, a schoolteacher. She smiled.

'You deserved it and you know it,' Ethan said, astounding Terri even further by going over and hauling Gary up from the floor.

She waited nervously for the other man's return blow, but no, the two just stood there staring at one another for a long moment.

Then, much to her surprise, Gary held out his hand.

'You're right, Greene. Maybe I did deserve that.'

After a moment's hesitation Ethan took Gary's hand, and gave it a light shake.

'But whatever you might think, I didn't steal that rock from you. It never even crossed my mind that it belonged to someone else. I honestly thought it was just a stroke of luck. And then when Terri came up with the notion that there might be more to it, I suppose I just buried my head in the sand.'

'Fair enough. While I don't agree with how you handled things, or how you treated Rachel, I suppose that's neither here nor there, nor indeed any of my business.'

Terri was wondering if she was seeing things. Were Ethan and Gary seriously in the process of making things up? Christ, she should have got these two together a long time ago! Despite her best efforts at making Gary see sense, clearly this was the only kind of language he understood.

'Yeah. I fucked up there all right.' Gary put both hands in his pockets and stared down at his shoes. 'And listen, I'm sorry about all that with your missus earlier. I wouldn't have said anything if . . . well, you know.'

Ethan nodded stiffly. 'Perhaps we both made a mess of things.'

'So, no hard feelings?' Gary was saying to Ethan, and Terri wanted to shake him – shake the two of them actually. No hard feelings? After everything that had just happened?

'I'm not sure Rachel will see it like that,' she said, reminding Gary of the fact that his fiancée had just run from the place in tears.

To his credit, he looked shamed. 'Honest to God, Terri, I just didn't know what to do. If I'd told her the truth, she'd have left me. I know she would.'

'You must know Rachel well enough to realise that she isn't with you for the sake of a diamond ring,' she said, flabbergasted.

'She'll get some shock if she is,' he said regretfully, and at that point Terri saw a side to Gary Knowles that she had never noticed before. It was as if the tough-man mask had finally slipped, and behind it was the face of an immature schoolboy who'd been caught out in a lie. 'Things have been very slack for me work-wise this last while,' he continued sheepishly. 'Rachel didn't know. And I didn't want to say anything, particularly when this place was doing such a bomb. No woman wants a man who brings in less dosh than she does.'

Terri rolled her eyes, doubly frustrated that it now seemed that much of this was about male pride. 'Come on, Gary. Rachel doesn't give a damn about things like that. All she cares about is you, not what you earn! That's why she's so hurt by what happened. As far as she's concerned, your engagement – maybe even your whole relationship – was a lie, especially if you couldn't tell her the truth.'

'It's not too late, though,' Ethan ventured. 'OK, so she's upset now but maybe if you tell her what you just told us . . .'

Gary looked from one to the other, unsure.

'Go after her, for God's sake,' Terri urged, unable to believe what she was suggesting. But, looking at it now from Gary's point of view, she could see that he honestly hadn't intended any malice; through no real fault of his own he had simply got caught up in a situation from which he couldn't escape.

Gary nodded and rubbed his cheek. 'Hey, any damage to the old noggin?' he asked, quickly returning to form, and Terri had to smile.

'No need to worry; you're still gorgeous,' she replied wryly as Ethan looked on in amusement. 'Now go and sort things out.'

When Gary had gone, Terri and Ethan were left alone, facing one another.

'I thought you might be the one to go after her, actually,' she probed gently, trying to tease out his feelings where Rachel was concerned.

He gave a short laugh. 'Me? Hardly. Don't get me wrong;

I mean, last time I was here you were right when you suggested I might be a little . . . confused about Rachel. Distracted, more like.' He sighed. 'It's silly, but . . .' Ethan's words trailed off as he tried to explain. 'Well, I must admit I was a little wrong-footed when it sank in properly that she was a baker. I hadn't really thought about it before, but Daisy's mum, Jane, and I had this sort of in-joke.' He went on to tell her about Jane's instruction about finding someone to bake him bread. 'I suppose I could be accused of taking it rather literally for a while,' he said, shaking his head. 'Nonsense really.'

'I think it's actually quite sweet,' Terri said truthfully, realising that he must have loved Daisy's mother very much indeed. 'I'm so sorry for all this,' she said then, feeling strangely uncomfortable in his presence now. 'I'd imagine after everything that's happened you'll be glad to see the back of this place.'

Ethan sighed, his expression unreadable. 'I'm not entirely sure how to feel at the moment. It's all been such a mess, certainly, and . . . Oh my goodness – Daisy!' he gasped as if suddenly remembering that she was here too. 'Heaven knows what she's making of all this.'

'It's OK. I know Justin will be keeping her well entertained outside. And I made sure she was out of earshot for most of what went on before, and definitely for the worst of it.'

'I noticed that. Thank you.' He looked directly at her and again Terri wondered why the conversation felt so awkward all of a sudden. 'She can be a real worrier.'

Terri had suspected as much, which was why she'd endeavoured to keep the little girl away from the squabbling.

'Don't worry; I'm sure she'll grow out of it. And poor

thing, I suppose she has good reason to be fretful, what with losing her mother, I mean.'

He nodded, obviously deeply troubled by this. 'It's just that I've never been entirely sure of the right way to deal with it. Vanessa says I shouldn't indulge her, that it'll only make things worse, but . . .'

'Sounds to me like Vanessa wouldn't be the best role model when it comes to parenting,' Terri retorted quickly, and then, remembering herself, she put a hand to her mouth. 'Oh Ethan, I'm sorry. I shouldn't have said that; it was completely out of turn.'

'No, you're right. I think that could have been part of the problem, actually. I fell so hard for Vanessa and at the same time I was so intent on trying to give Daisy what I thought she needed – a strong role model and some kind of replacement for her mum – that I didn't look closely enough to see if Vanessa truly was the right one for the job,' he admitted. 'It wasn't fair on Daisy or Vanessa,' he added and Terri realised that despite his little 'blip' about Rachel, he really did love Vanessa.

'Well, to be fair, it is a big responsibility.'

'And looking increasingly like one I'll continue to bear on my own.' He smiled sadly. 'Not that it's such a terrible thing. That little girl is my world.'

'She's very lucky to have such a great dad.'

Ethan squirmed. 'Well, I'm not so sure about that. Not when she believes in such nonsense as a diamond ring that supposedly has magical powers.'

'That stuff she was saying about Tiffany's being magical? She told me she got that from her mum.'

He nodded sadly. 'Jane filled her head with a fair bit of fanciful nonsense, and she's at the age where she believes in all of it, unfortunately. I thought she'd grow out of it,

come to understand that much of what her mother used to say was entirely metaphorical, but . . .'

'Well, if you think about it, it seemed for a while like that ring *was* magical and *did* have a mind of its own.' Terri laughed, trying to make him feel better. 'Anyway, she's still very young. If it were me, I'd try to let her hold on to that innocence for as long as I could. Real life is hard enough sometimes.'

'Perhaps you're right.' Ethan smiled back and Terri felt her nerve endings tingle in response. What the hell was wrong with her? 'But I've never been a big believer in fairy tales,' he continued, his voice tinged with regret, and Terri couldn't be sure if he was thinking about Jane or Vanessa.

'Me neither,' she replied truthfully.

Chapter 45

The following afternoon, Ethan landed at Heathrow, his heart heavy. He walked through the airport as if in a trance, Daisy at his side.

He thought again about Vanessa and Brian and wanted to take his so-called friend and tear him limb from limb. Talk about betrayal. But of course that wasn't the only secret Vanessa had been carrying; there was something else that, much to his humiliation, he'd discovered from Daisy.

During all that hullabaloo at the bistro yesterday, when his daughter had mentioned a baby and explained about the pregnancy-test kit she'd found, Ethan hadn't known what to think. As far as he was aware it wasn't possible for Vanessa to have children, so why the pregnancy test?

So when Vanessa had returned to the table at Stromboli, he knew it was the first thing he had to ask her, even before discussing Brian. Her eyes were still red-rimmed from crying and her face was pale, but when he broached the subject, her skin turned so white it was almost translucent.

'What do you mean?' she asked, looking rather like she had when Gary had accused her of being in the taxi in New York. Like a rabbit caught in headlights.

'It's a simple question.' His voice was hard. 'Why was there a pregnancy-test kit in our dustbin?'

'What?' She continued to look at him, her eyes unsure. 'How did you—'

'It was supposed to go in the recycling,' Daisy put in guiltily, by way of explanation, but Ethan patted her hand as if to quieten her.

'It's OK, buttercup, you don't need to explain.' Turning to Vanessa again he said, 'Is there something important I should know?'

She shook her head, her eyes downcast. 'No. I thought there might be. With the US time lag, I thought I might have made a mistake with contraception, but I hadn't.'

'Contraception? How odd. I was under the impression that you couldn't have children.'

But Ethan realised now that this too had been a barefaced lie, same as all the other lies she'd been telling him right from the beginning of their relationship.

In fact, when he thought about how Vanessa was so dogged about getting what she wanted professionally (or to avoid what she didn't), he wondered why it had never crossed his mind that she might do the same in her personal life.

'Well, yes, but there's always the chance . . .' But her words were weak and they both knew it. She had played him along all the time, played on his gullibility.

'Why, Vanessa? Why did you agree to marry me, know-ing that our relationship was built on lies?'

'I don't honestly know,' she replied, tears in her eyes. 'I did – do – want to marry you. But I never wanted to go through the whole childbirth thing and I suppose I thought that, with Daisy, we were a ready-made family. I wouldn't have to be a mum, and nobody would expect me to replace Jane. Not that I could have done, even if I wanted to,' she added, her tone bitter. 'No one could replace that paragon of virtue.'

'How dare you!' Ethan said, his tone hardening. He was so enraged by this that he hadn't noticed Daisy quietly slip-ping away towards the restaurant's kitchen.

Vanessa stood up to leave. 'I'll be staying at my parents' house, if you need me,' she said. 'Believe what you like, Ethan, but no one will ever fill the shoes of your precious Jane.' She put on her coat and there were fresh tears in her eyes. 'I'm sorry that this happened. For what it's worth, I do love you, and Daisy. But you were never truly going to let me in.'

Ethan thought about that now, and wondered if there was any truth in it.

She loved him with too clear a vision to fear his cloudiness . . .

But obviously not enough.

And whatever he'd thought before about his daughter's crazy notion of the ring being definitive proof of true love if it fitted, perhaps she'd been onto something all the same.

As expected, his daughter was still confused and upset about what had happened. She was so young, and had no idea about the complexities of an adult relationship. Despite Vanessa not being the right fit for the ring, the little girl had accepted her as part of their lives and Ethan knew she had been looking forward to being a family. Now it would never happen. They weren't a family and Vanessa would not be a replacement mother.

After the incident at the bistro yesterday they'd gone their separate ways, Vanessa back to her parents' house and he and Daisy to a nearby hotel. They'd spent today just enjoying the sights and each other's company, before getting the Sunday-evening flight back to Heathrow, as planned.

Ethan tried to clear his head as they got into the back of a taxi and told the cabbie their address. Maybe there had been signs for a while that things weren't right, and all this business with the ring had helped him realise it. As Jane

would no doubt have said if she were here, everything happened for a reason.

He spent the rest of the journey so deep in thought about what had happened that he didn't even realise that the taxi had come to a stop in front of their town house in Richmond. He was staring out of the window, but he did not register where he was or recognise any of his surroundings.

'Mate? Is this the address?' the taxi driver asked.

Daisy nudged him. 'Dad, we're here.'

Ethan snapped to attention, surprised. How could the place look so different after only a few days? How could so much change in such a short amount of time?

'Oh yes. Sorry. I'm a bit tired,' he explained quickly, so he wouldn't look like a lunatic.

He paid the driver and grabbed his and Daisy's bags. Then he trundled up the steps slowly and extracted his key from his pocket. After placing the key in the lock he turned the door handle. Walking into the hallway, he immediately realised that something was different.

Going straight into the bedroom, he realised what it was. After what had happened, Vanessa must have taken the next available flight out of Dublin rather than spending the last day with her parents. It hadn't taken her long to remove the few boxes she had brought with her when she moved in. In retrospect, her decision to keep her old apartment and all of her furniture should probably have been the first indication that this arrangement wouldn't be forever.

'She's gone,' Daisy said unnecessarily. 'Vanessa's gone.'

'I know, buttercup,' Ethan said, his heart sinking. 'Looks like it's just you and me again.'

'I'm sorry, Dad,' she said, through a large sob. 'It's all my fault for losing the ring, isn't it?' Suddenly she began to cry openly, and Ethan's heart went out to her. She took so much on herself, when really none of this had anything to do with her.

He pulled his daughter close to him and led her towards the sofa. 'No, no, of course not. None of this is your fault. These things just happen sometimes and it's nobody's fault.'

Daisy buried her head in his shoulder. 'I'm sorry for not taking better care of it,' she mumbled through her tears.

'Honey, it doesn't matter. The ring has nothing to do with this.' But of course that wasn't strictly true, was it? It was precisely because of that damned ring that all of this had happened.

'Are you cross with me?'

'No, darling. Of course, I'm not cross.'

'But you and Vanessa aren't going to get married, are you?'

'No, we're not. And that test you found? There was no baby. It was only a test to see if there might be one.'

She nodded thoughtfully. 'That's a pity. I think I might have liked a brother or sister.'

'I know, poppet.' Ethan sighed. 'I would have liked that for you too.'

'Vanessa's never coming back.' It was more of a statement than a question.

'No. But it's OK, Daisy. You and me, we're a team; you know that. We only need each other, don't we?'

Daisy sniffed. 'Did Vanessa give you the ring back?'

'Yes, she did.' She'd taken it off and placed it on the table right before she'd left the restaurant. Given all that had happened, Ethan was almost reluctant to pick it up, afraid that the cursed thing might scald him.

'Can I see it?'

Ethan pulled the ring from his pocket and placed it in Daisy's hand.

'Dad?'

'Yes, darling?'

'Do you like Rachel?'

'Rachel from the bistro? Yes, of course I do.'

A woman who'll bake you bread . . .

Ethan no longer knew how to feel about that and he was still haunted by her reaction to the truth. That wasn't because of any personal feelings for her; he knew that now, and guessed that any imagined feelings he'd had were merely a side-effect of his desperate quest to get the ring back. Really, if he thought about it, he was no better than Daisy for creating significance and meaning where there was none.

'Does she like you?'

Ethan knew where she was going with this; she was still fixated on the fact that the ring had fitted Rachel. He tried to fudge it. 'Well, unfortunately Rachel is very angry with me at the moment.'

'Why?'

Ethan explained how Rachel had thought the ring had been bought for her and was naturally upset when she realised it hadn't been.

Daisy digested the information. 'But that wasn't your fault.'

'No, that's true. It doesn't stop her from being angry anyway.'

'You should call her and keep telling her you're sorry. I'm sure she'll forgive you.'

Ethan smiled. 'I'm afraid it's not like that.'

'Yes, it is! Call her, Dad. Call her now and tell her you're sorry. Then she'll like you again and you guys can be happy ever after.'

'Please stop, darling. I need to leave Rachel alone now. Goodness knows I've caused her enough problems.'

Daisy's face crumpled and she turned to look at him. 'But she's the right one, Dad. I know she is.'

'Daisy, just because the ring happened to fit Rachel doesn't meant anything.'

'But—'

'Daisy,' Ethan repeated sternly, tired all of a sudden. Of the ring, of Rachel, of everything. 'Let it go. I know you mean well, but you have to remember that things don't always work out like they do in your storybooks.'

Chapter 46

'You know, staring at it won't make it ring,' Justin said, passing Terri on his way to the storeroom.

'Tell me about it,' she replied with a sigh.

He shook his head sadly. 'No word from her yet, I take it?'

'No.' Terri was climbing the walls. It was two days since the big bust-up at the bistro and they still hadn't heard anything from Rachel.

While Terri hadn't expected her to turn up for her shift yesterday, she'd been hoping for at least a phone call to let them know how she was. When that wasn't forthcoming she'd phoned Rachel at home, but her friend wouldn't pick up.

'I just wish she'd talk to me,' Terri sighed. 'She's right, you know. I'm as much to blame as Gary for this. I should never have kept the truth from her, and I definitely shouldn't have interfered like that.'

'You were just trying to help. At the end of the day you had her best interests at heart.'

Had she, though? Terri wondered now whether she had just been blinded by her distrust of Gary and sidetracked by Ethan Greene and his endearingly bumbling attempts to resolve the situation.

She wasn't sure. But one thing was certain; although she was sorry Ethan had been hurt, she was glad that that Vanessa looked to be out of his life. Terri had disliked the silly woman on sight, and what she'd subsequently learned about her reaffirmed this.

'Heck of a day, wasn't it?' Justin said, echoing her thoughts. 'Talk about drama! Such a pity the little kid got caught up in the middle of it, though.'

'Yes. She's a sweet girl.' Terri was still thinking about Daisy's childish insistence that the ring had found its way to the 'right' person.

Was there any truth in that? She had to admit that fate had got it right when it came to Vanessa, hadn't it? Clearly, given her lies and infidelity, she wasn't the right person for Ethan and definitely didn't deserve that ring. But did that automatically mean that Rachel did? Terri had suspected before that there was some spark between the two of them, but given Rachel's genuine devastation the other day, and Gary's insistence that he was ashamed to tell her the truth, it seemed that there was another element to *their* relationship that Terri had never been aware of.

Maybe Gary wasn't just some thoughtless buffoon who'd been deliberately underhand; maybe he was genuinely afraid of losing her?

In all honesty, Terri was afraid of losing Rachel too. They had been through so much together and were such an integral part of each other's lives, yet now, because of Terri's actions, their friendship (as well as their business) was seriously under threat.

She just wished Rachel would talk to her.

'Has Gary spoken to her, I wonder?' Justin asked.

'I don't know. I never thought I'd say this, but I actually felt sorry for him on Saturday. I don't think I've ever seen a man look so crushed.'

'He truly thought that coming clean about it meant he would lose her?' Justin shook his head.

Terri nodded. 'I can't understand why he couldn't have been straight with me about it from the start, instead of trying to keep up this hard-man image. I don't know – bloody Irishmen.'

'Hey, don't tar us all with the same brush, sweetheart. You know I'm totally in touch with my feminine side,' he said, winking, and Terri raised a smile.

'I don't know, Justin. It's all such a mess.'

And because Terri didn't know what else to do, she went to the cupboard and took out some flour, intent on finding comfort the way she always did in times of trouble – by baking bread.

Later that evening Terri knocked on Rachel's door, praying her friend would answer. She held her breath, listening for approaching footsteps, but heard nothing.

She knocked again, this time more forcefully. Eventually, she heard light footsteps coming closer to the other side of the door.

'Who is it?' Rachel called out.

'It's me. Please let me talk to you.'

There was silence and Terri was sure her heart was going to pound out of her chest. Please open the door, she willed.

'Leave me alone. I don't want to talk.'

'OK, fine. But maybe you'd like to eat?' She tried to keep her voice light but inside her nerves were in tatters. If Rachel didn't respond to this – their mutual in-joke – then their friendship was well and truly over. 'I've brought some of my famous irresistible sourdough.'

It seemed as if several minutes had passed when the door finally opened just a fraction. From what little Terri could see of her, Rachel's face looked drawn and she had her hair pulled back.

'Well, I am hungry . . .' she said, and Terri saw some of the old Rachel sparkle behind the miserable facade.

'I thought you might be.' Terri handed her the loaf and immediately began fidgeting with her newly empty hands. She looked at her friend. 'I really need to talk to you. Please?'

'Then talk,' Rachel replied, stonily.

'Can't I come in?'

'Nope.'

Terri took a deep breath and stared into her eyes. Although she'd always known that this whole thing was going to end badly, she hadn't anticipated how guilty she'd feel, and how much Rachel would suffer. But from Rachel's point of view the people she loved, and who were supposed to love her back, had betrayed her.

And Terri realised it was all because of Ethan Greene, a man who was practically a stranger. Justin was right, and she wondered what had come over her that she'd put her friendship and her business at risk by sticking her oar in.

She couldn't believe how everything had gone so terribly wrong so quickly.

'Rachel, I'm sorry. I know I should have told you the truth about that ring as soon as I found out about it. I know that. But the truth was that I didn't know what to do. You were so happy about the engagement—'

'Exactly. I was so happy. And you knew it was all a lie. Why didn't you tell me? Why let me go on thinking that I was in some kind of fairy tale and Gary was my Prince Charming? To think that he was basically railroaded into a proposal . . .' Her hurt and embarrassment were plain to see. 'Everyone knew the truth, except me. Imagine how I feel. Manipulated. Lied to. Now I see what all of this was, I realise I wasn't allowed to make up my own mind. Everything was manufactured by you, Gary – even by Ethan,

pretending at that dinner that he was interested in my hopes and dreams. None of it was real.'

Terri hung her head. 'I know. You're right and I'm sorry. Even now I'm not sure why I didn't tell you, but please believe me when I say that the last thing any of us wanted was to hurt you.'

'But why treat me like a child, Terri? I really hate the way everyone does that all that time. I'm thirty-two years old, not some toddler who needs protecting.'

'I suppose . . . I suppose I've always thought that you're too quick to see the best in people, whereas I'm—'

'A complete cynic who's suspicious of everyone's motives?'

Terri looked down at her shoes, ashamed. 'Again, you're right. Maybe I am too quick to think the worst. I'm sorry.'

'How's everything at work?' Rachel asked, her neutral tone still not giving much away.

'Fine. Justin is holding the fort at the moment.' Terri paused, realising they were treading on dangerous ground here. What if Rachel had decided she wanted out of Stromboli, that because of Terri's deception she was prepared to give up the business they'd so carefully built up? Or, even worse, that she wanted Terri out? 'We're looking forward to having you back, though,' she added delicately. 'The place isn't the same without you.'

'Hmm, just as long as our customers aren't choking on foreign objects in their food,' she replied archly, and Terri breathed an inward sigh of relief at the brief glimmer of humour in her tone. Everything was going to be OK.

'So are you going to share this with me, or what?' Rachel said, moving aside at the doorway, indicating that Terri should come in.

'I'd love to.' Terri stepped past her and the two proceeded into Rachel's tiny living room. She turned to face her friend.

'Look, again, I'm sorry. Taking the ring the way I did was especially stupid of me. But Gary was adamant he wasn't going to own up, and I felt so bad for Ethan.'

'Yes, it was kind of strange of you to go to such lengths for some guy you barely knew,' Rachel said, raising an eyebrow. 'Is there something you want to tell me?'

Terri reddened. 'What? No. Of course not. Actually, to be honest, Ethan was so concerned about not upsetting you that I wondered if you two might have had some kind of connection from that night you went out for dinner.'

'As if.' Rachel snorted. 'He's not my type, Terri. Way too straight for my liking. I prefer them complicated.'

'Yes, I suppose you do have a particular type, all right,' Terri said lightly.

Rachel gave a wan smile. 'I'm Sicilian, don't forget. We're genetically programmed to be attracted to challenging men.'

'So has Gary been in touch?'

'He's been trying morning, noon and night, but I don't want to hear it.'

Her friend's tone was hard but Terri could hear sadness behind it. Whatever flaws he might have, Rachel truly, genuinely, loved this guy.

'I just don't understand what he was playing at, Rachel. Surely he must have known it would all come out in the wash at some point.'

'He can be funny like that, and despite what you think,' she added meaningfully, 'he's always been massively insecure at the back of it all.'

'I kind of gathered that. Who would have thought it?'

'Well, it was always obvious to me. Where do you think all the bluster comes from? He carries on like some big-time property tycoon, but we both know he's just a man with a van,' she added, and Terri giggled, realising that

perhaps Rachel wasn't quite as gullible as they'd thought. 'I don't know, I suppose I've always found it quite endearing in a way. And thinking about it, I'm not surprised he didn't own up. He must have thought all his Christmases had come at once when I opened up that ring box. There aren't many men who have something like that landing in their lap, are there?'

'Are you going to forgive him?' she asked Rachel.

'I don't know. It's not something I can decide right away. I do love him, but I'm not sure I can put this down to simply macho bluster. It was very hurtful, finding out that he'd never intended to propose at all.'

'Well, for what it's worth, I do think that he genuinely didn't know where it had come from at the start and was worried that Ethan was chasing you.'

'No, Ethan was chasing his twenty-thousand-euro investment.' Rachel gave a sad smile. 'I feel sorry for little Daisy, though; she seemed to think that the whole thing was fated somehow. Sweet.'

Terri agreed. 'Yes.'

'I remember Ethan saying something about her mother being a bit airy-fairy. And then when things went awry, poor old Daisy must have taken what she'd said about Tiffany's to heart. But the ironic thing is that the ring didn't fit me either,' Rachel admitted and Terri looked at her in surprise. 'It was too big. I figured Gary hadn't thought about that side of things, and I had it resized before we left New York.'

Terri shook her head. 'No wonder it didn't fit Vanessa, then. Poor Daisy. All this had nothing whatsoever to do with Tiffany's magic.'

'I know. That poor fiancée really got a bum deal, didn't she?' Rachel gave a sardonic chuckle. 'And there's me, not only ending up with her engagement ring, but getting it resized so that her future stepdaughter thinks I'm some kind of Cinderella and she's the ugly sister.'

'I'm not sure Vanessa's completely blameless in the entire scenario,' Terri said, explaining what she'd overheard at the restaurant.

'Poor Ethan,' Rachel said. 'Maybe I was a bit hard on him the other day. He's come out on the wrong end of this too, hasn't he?'

Terri nodded sadly. 'Well, if nothing else, at least he still has his glass slipper.'

Chapter 47

Daisy lay on the floor of the living room, drawing a picture. It was a nice lazy Saturday afternoon. Her dad was in the shower after being out for a run, and she was enjoying the peace and quiet.

She had to admit, though, that things had been a bit weird lately. Her dad had tried acting like everything was back to normal, and had gone about his days as if that whole thing with the ring had never happened.

He and Daisy had continued doing activities together at the weekends, like a normal father and daughter. They hadn't spoken again about Rachel or Vanessa but, while Daisy tried to do as her dad said and forget about what had happened in Dublin, she was still convinced that he had made the wrong decision by not trying to make things up with Rachel, when it was obvious (to Daisy anyway) that they were supposed to be together.

She caught him sometimes, sitting in his room looking at the ring, and knew that he was sad, but she didn't know if he was thinking about Vanessa or Rachel, or maybe even both.

She didn't understand some of what had gone on and wished that her mum were still here to explain it to her. Then again, if Mum were here, none of this would ever have happened, would it? Daisy sighed. People were always telling her she was a clever little girl, but sometimes she thought that adults made their lives way too complicated, her dad especially.

At that moment, the phone rang, and Daisy got up to check the caller ID. She didn't recognise the number so she let the answering machine pick up, like her dad always told her to if he wasn't available to answer it. Still, she hovered nearby to listen to the message. It was a woman's voice and she sounded rushed.

'Hi, Ethan. It's Rachel,' the voice said and Daisy's ears pricked up. 'Are you there?' The voice paused for a moment, waiting. 'OK, you must be out,' Rachel continued. 'I just wanted to say that I'm so sorry about what happened.' There was a nervous laugh. 'As I'm sure you can imagine, it was all incredibly embarrassing for me, especially finding out like that. But I feel bad for taking it out on you, particularly when you were so lovely about trying to protect my feelings and . . . Anyway, I hope you're OK, and Daisy too. Terri told me about Vanessa and . . . Well, look, I just wanted to apologise.'

The sound of Rachel's voice had made Daisy feel all warm inside. She was definitely the right person for her father; she knew it! Without thinking, she picked up the handset and spoke into it. 'Rachel, hi.'

'Daisy? Hello, sweetheart! How are you?'

'Fine, thanks.'

'Is your dad there? I wasn't sure if . . .'

'He's in the shower,' Daisy told her. 'I'm glad you phoned. I know he'll be really happy to hear from you.'

'Oh. Well, that's nice. I think I might have been a bit rude to him that last time you guys were in Dublin.'

'I know. You were upset about the ring. I get upset about things too sometimes. Like the other day when my scary

piano teacher gave me a really hard piece to play and I couldn't do it.'

Rachel laughed. 'I see. Well, it was lovely to talk to you, Daisy, and do tell your dad I was asking for him, and that I'm sorry. I'm really glad he got the ring back. Oh and –' Rachel paused, and Daisy wondered what she was going to say '– remember that thing you said about your dad's ring finding its way to the right person?'

'Yes?' Daisy grinned, realising that everything was going to be OK. Rachel understood what it all meant and she was really calling so that she and her dad could get together.

'Well, I wanted to tell you that I wasn't the right person, Daisy. The ring didn't fit me either. I had to get it resized.'

Daisy's face fell. 'What? But how can that be right? Vanessa's the wrong person. My dad knows that now and—'

'Daisy, what on earth are you doing? Who are you talking to?' She realised that her dad had come into the room and overheard her. He held out his hand for the phone, an irritated expression on his face.

'It's Rachel,' she told him in a small voice, her thoughts all over the place.

'Rachel, hello. I'm sorry about that . . .'

Daisy moved away, barely hearing her dad talking into the phone in the background.

She slumped down on the sofa. If what Rachel had just said was true then what had happened? Why had the Tiffany's bags got mixed up in the first place if it wasn't to lead her father to Rachel? Daisy kicked away her drawing, a picture of a pretty blue box tied up with white ribbon. Why wasn't the Tiffany's magic working?

It had been a hell of a time, Ethan thought. But now, two weeks later, at least life had got back into that normal comfortable rhythm he was used to. No surprises, no drama.

For Daisy's sake he tried to appear OK. Every now and then he caught her staring at him with a peculiar look on her face. She seemed very aware of what he was doing and of his moods. He tried not to think about Vanessa and the fool she'd made of him.

Clearly she'd tipped Brian off that he'd found out about the affair, and Ethan had been avoiding calls from his so-called friend for the last fortnight. Ethan wasn't interested in excuses and explanations, and although he was hurt by their betrayal, he was also slightly taken aback by how little it actually bothered him.

And if he truly did love Vanessa, if he really felt deep down in his heart that she was the right person for him, then by rights he should be inconsolable. But he wasn't. Instead he felt almost numbed by the events of the last couple of months. The mix-up with the ring, the complications in trying to get it back – it was all such a big mess it was as though there was no rhyme or reason to it.

However, he knew he needed to be strong for Daisy now, and he couldn't be constantly mooning over what might have been.

It was now the end of a long week, and he was wrapping up his duties at the university. He left campus and took a cab to the house of one of Daisy's friends, Tanya. She went there after school each day until Ethan finished lectures.

He knocked on the door and it was answered by Janice, Tanya's mother. 'Oh hello, Ethan. Come inside. I'll get Daisy. The girls are playing upstairs.'

Ethan walked in. He knew the routine. After the girls came downstairs and Daisy collected her things, Janice would try to insist they stay for dinner. Although it was never said, he knew Janice was convinced that Ethan was a clueless

bachelor who couldn't possibly understand his daughter, let alone cook her a good meal.

As soon as the girls thundered into the room, Janice looked at Ethan and smiled. 'Tell me that you and Daisy will stay for dinner. We have plenty.'

He shook his head apologetically. 'Thank you again, but Daisy and I have things to do tonight.'

Ethan had planned a fun evening for the two of them. He was going to cook his daughter her favourite meal, and then allow her to eat junk food and stay up late to watch a movie, whatever she liked.

Janice nodded. 'Well, perhaps another night, then?' she suggested, a faint note of hope in her voice, and Ethan idly wondered if the woman had taken some kind of shine to him now that he was once again unattached. He hoped not. More woman trouble was the last thing he needed at this point.

'Ready to go?' he asked Daisy, who nodded and smiled in agreement.

They left Janice's house and started their walk home. 'So how was your day?' Daisy asked.

He reached out to hold her hand. 'It was pretty good. The best part, though, is that it's Friday and I get to spend tonight with my special girl.'

'And who's your special girl?' Daisy asked, looking sideways at him.

'Well, I don't know . . . Let me think for a minute,' he said in a playful tone, figuring she was teasing. Then he looked down and saw that her expression was solemn. 'Why, you are, silly!' he insisted, starting to tickle her. 'Who else?'

She sighed. 'I wish I knew.'

Ethan regarded his daughter silently. He wondered if this was yet another phase she was going through. Since the incident in Dublin, Daisy had seemed dissatisfied with it being just the two of them. It had never been that way before. He didn't think she was missing Vanessa or anything; it was more that she was disappointed in him about something.

'So, what movie do you fancy watching tonight?' he asked, deciding to change the subject.

Daisy looked up at him as if he hadn't spoken. 'Are you upset about Vanessa?' she asked out of the blue.

Ethan looked at her. 'Of course I was, at first,' he admitted, realising that his daughter wasn't in the mood for fun just then. 'But afterwards I realised we weren't right for each other.'

Daisy furrowed her brow; she was thinking hard about this statement. 'So who is right for you, Dad?'

He grinned. 'You are, buttercup. You know that. You're the only lady in my life and I'm happy to keep it that way.'

'What about what happened in New York, though?' Daisy insisted again. 'What about the Tiffany's magic that Mum talked about?'

'Sweetheart—'

'And if you say you're happy just being my dad, then why are you so sad all the time?'

Ethan was slightly taken aback by his daughter's observation. 'What makes you think I'm sad?'

Daisy rolled her eyes. 'Dad, I am not an idiot.'

He raised a small smile; there was nothing like being told off by an eight-year-old.

But she was right. Lately, Ethan had indeed been feeling sad and bereft about something, and he wasn't entirely sure what that was. The ache of Jane's absence seemed to have returned, this time stronger than ever, and as each day wore on he wondered how long it would be until those feelings

faded and were lost to time. How long would it be until he was truly happy again?

He didn't know the answer and he figured there was a good chance he would still be thinking about Jane when he was ninety years old, wrinkled and alone.

And if – as Daisy insisted – Jane had been intervening from above to set things right, he truly wished that he understood what she was trying to say.

A woman who'd bake him bread? Ethan didn't think so. Because, as far as that was concerned, he felt nothing for Rachel Conti other than sympathy.

Back at the town house, while Daisy was in the shower, he set about making dinner. He gathered together all the ingredients for her favourite – chilli con carne – but it was a light meal on its own and Ethan knew he'd need some kind of accompaniment to fill him up. Either that or he would end up gorging himself on chocolate and ice cream later and he knew that wouldn't go down well with Daisy.

He opened the freezer and rummaged around at the back of it for the frozen garlic bread he kept for situations just like this. Then he paused, spotting the purple wrapping with which by now he was almost too familiar. Half a loaf of bread from Stromboli. He hadn't put it there, so he deduced it must have been Vanessa who'd frozen the remainder. For posterity, perhaps?

Taking it out, Ethan couldn't help but think that the place seemed determined to haunt him. Just when he thought he'd left it behind, Stromboli (or at least its bread) reared up again. Still, however it had ended up here, there was no denying that the bread was amazing, and it would go nicely with tonight's meal.

Ethan put the frozen loaf into the microwave for defrosting. He'd freshen it up by warming it in the oven. He smiled, thinking that Terri would have a heart attack if she could see him now, microwaving her precious bread, particularly this one, which she'd baked especially for him so he could . . .

Suddenly Ethan stopped short. He stared at the loaf, wondering why he hadn't figured it out before.

Terri.

It was *Terri* who'd baked him bread, not Rachel.

The same Terri who'd been on his side and had helped him through this entire nightmare, first by returning the ring, then by covering for him in front of Vanessa at the bistro, and again by protecting Daisy from the arguments that ensued . . .

A woman who'd bake him bread.

Ethan raised his gaze skywards. For the first time since his beloved's death, the cloudiness had lifted and he could finally visualise his future.

'Thank you, Jane,' he whispered with a smile. 'Now I get it.'

Chapter 48

It was a crazy Sunday lunchtime at Stromboli and Terri sorely wished she hadn't so readily agreed to swap shifts with Rachel today.

But she'd had little choice, given that part of her penance for lying to her friend was that she became 'her undying slave' for the next few months.

Terri didn't care; she was just glad that Rachel had forgiven her, and that things were back to normal around the place.

Well, mostly normal. Rachel and Gary's wedding was very definitely off, and while they'd begun talking about what had happened, Rachel was unwilling to let him off the hook for what he'd done.

Especially as it seemed this wasn't the only secret Gary had been keeping from her. He'd now admitted to everything he'd been hiding over the last six months: the fact that his business had practically gone to the wall, he was being hounded and harassed by the bank because of the scale of the debts that had built up, and, perhaps most embarrassing of all for someone like Gary, that he was back living with his mother and had been for some months.

Which of course completely explained Mary Knowles's shocked and rather annoyed reaction when faced with Rachel's super-expensive engagement ring on the night of the party, Terri recalled with a smile. Not to mention Gary's reluctance to introduce Rachel to any member of his family. He was terrified of being made a laughing stock.

'So by all accounts that ring brought him about as much luck as it did me,' Rachel told her.

'Or Ethan,' Terri pointed out. 'So much for the famous Tiffany's magic.'

For some reason, Terri found herself thinking more and more about Ethan Greene, and that brief moment they'd shared the day everything had gone crazy and he'd decked Gary, partly in her honour.

She knew the idea was stupid and had absolutely no basis in reality, but Terri could no longer trust her own judgement these days. The truth was that she almost missed the drama; missed carrying the secret that only she and Ethan had shared. It was an intimacy of sorts and despite not being especially deep or meaningful (at least as far as Ethan was concerned), she was fully aware of its absence.

She'd also been completely unprepared for how much she'd disliked Vanessa on sight, and how vindicated she'd felt to learn of the woman's betrayal.

Then there was Daisy, a little girl who was so serious and literal that Terri could understand why Ethan was so eager to give her some stability. The poor thing was terrified of losing her father, which was understandable, given what had happened to Jane.

But now that all the drama was over and things had settled back to normal, she felt dissatisfied and somewhat . . . adrift. Was it because Ethan was out of their lives?

Terri didn't really understand the feeling and didn't even want to try to put her finger on what it meant. She was also

 *Melissa Hill*

annoyed with herself for yielding to it, but the fact remained that it was there whether she liked it or not.

Rachel mentioned that she'd spoken to Ethan recently to apologise for all that had happened, and Terri had to do everything in her power to stop herself from picking up the phone too. Of course, she and Ethan no longer had that mutual secret, or any real reason to stay in touch.

Just then Jen, one of the waitresses, rushed through to the kitchen from out front, a harassed expression on her face.

'Terri, I'm really sorry to do this to you as I know you're busy, but there's this customer at the bakery counter giving me terrible grief.'

She frowned. 'What's the problem?'

'Well, he's complaining about the bread on display, saying it's stale.' She shook her head wearily. 'I don't know what his problem is, to be honest.'

'Stale? But everything's made fresh in the kitchen each morning.'

'I know, and I told him that, but I think he's just an asshole really.' She grinned. 'Nice-looking, though, although that hardly makes up for it.'

Terri's eyes narrowed. Nice-looking or not, there was no excuse for being rude to her staff.

'Anyway he's insisting the stuff he wants isn't fresh but won't accept my assurances that everything we sell is freshly baked.' She put her hand up to her forehead. 'He won't entertain anything from me, to be honest, and is demand-ing to talk to a manager. Do you mind?'

'Oh brother!' Terri could feel the beginnings of a serious headache. She wiped her hands on her apron, repositioned any flyaway hair under her cap and, happy that she looked confident and in control of the situation, prepared to face the music. 'At the bakery counter, you said?'

Jen nodded apologetically. 'Sorry.'

Putting on her best managerial smile, Terri went outside and headed directly for the bakery counter near the front of the restaurant. Then, spotting who was standing behind it, she stopped short.

'Ethan?' she gasped, her eyes wide. 'What are you doing here? And Daisy too. Great to see you, but what . . . I think there's some mistake.' She looked back towards the kitchen, uncertainly. 'I mean, my waitress said a customer was complaining.'

He looked at her, his handsome face solemn and unreadable. 'Yes. As I explained, I'm not at all happy with this bread.' She was taken aback by his serious tone, but noticed that Daisy wouldn't look at her and seemed to be trying not to smile.

'OK. Well, I'm very sorry about that,' she replied automatically, trying to figure out why he was being so formal. 'What seems to be the problem?'

This felt very surreal. After everything that had happened, why were Ethan and Daisy back in Dublin at all, let alone complaining about bread from Stromboli's bakery?

'It's not fresh,' he said, pointing to the sourdough, *her* sourdough.

'Of course it's fresh,' she replied defensively. And Terri should know too, as she'd spent the best part of this morning baking it.

Daisy started to giggle and Terri felt as though she was the butt of some weird joke.

'Ask her, Dad!' she blurted, and then glanced quickly at her father as if she'd said something out of turn.

Terri looked at the little girl, wondering what was going on. Ask her what?

'Well,' Ethan began, and there was a smile in his voice, 'I was wondering if there was any chance you might make a fresh batch.'

'I don't understand.'

'Perhaps . . . just for me?' he added meaningfully, and Terri's heart skipped a beat as she immediately realised exactly what he was referring to.

A woman who'll bake him bread.

And more importantly, a woman who understood what he was trying to say.

She gulped.

'You want . . . me . . . to bake . . . for you?' she asked, her voice robotic as she tried to figure out if this was real or if she was imagining things.

'Yes, and for Daisy too. If you'd like to, that is.' Ethan's voice was gentle and Terri raised her gaze to look at him. His blue eyes were soft and hopeful as they met hers. 'I know my being in London might be a problem, but I'm sure we'll find ways to keep it fresh.'

Terri honestly felt like she was in some kind of weird dream. Nothing was making sense any more. She knew what he was saying, knew exactly what he was asking, yet it was the very last thing she'd expected. This kind of thing didn't happen to her; she hadn't shared her life with anyone for eight long years.

She stared back at Ethan, not sure where this had come from, or where it was heading; but whatever it was, she already knew she liked it.

Smiling at the man she knew she'd already fallen for, Terri gave him the only answer she could think of. 'I'll be happy to bake you two all the bread you want. But I must warn you,' she added lightly, 'there'll be no surprises this time. With me, what you see is what you get.'

'And it's exactly what we want,' Ethan replied gently, reaching for her hand.

Epilogue

Here he was, back in New York again on Christmas Eve. It felt weird – a bit surreal really – but at the same time it felt completely right too.

Hard to believe that it was only a year since he'd last been here. It felt almost like a lifetime, considering. Everything had changed; perhaps most importantly, *he* had changed. No more running around chasing his tail and trying to keep everything going. Life was much simpler now, much more easy-going.

And it was all down to her.

How had it taken him so long to see what was in front of him? That the key to being happy wasn't about all those things he'd thought were so important before, but about finding the person who was, as little Daisy joked, 'the right fit'.

He knew he was unbelievably lucky to have found her at all; but even luckier not to lose her, after all the craziness that had happened in between.

OK, so it had taken him a while to see the wood for the trees, but once he had seen it there was no stopping him.

He paused for a moment and stood back, letting the throngs of passers-by on the street go round him.

He heard a few muted sighs and some not-so-muted mutters of annoyance as people manoeuvred past him, trying to move quickly in the freezing cold. The air was sharp, the

temperature in the minuses, and there was a scattering of snowflakes in the sky.

A loud laugh from nearby startled him out of his reverie, and he noticed some tourists taking pictures. A woman piled her dark hair up into a high bun on top of her head and put on a big black pair of sunglasses. 'There! Do I look like Audrey?' she giggled to her friend.

The distraction helped shift his focus back onto what he was here to do, and taking a deep breath he moved towards the rotating doors.

'Good afternoon, sir, and welcome to Tiffany's,' a man in a top hat greeted him when he was inside.

'Thanks.' He smiled in return and quickly glanced around.

It was mad to be back here again after everything that had happened, especially given the luck that his last visit had brought him. But at the same time, how could he go anywhere else?

This time would be different, though. This time he knew exactly what he wanted.

He gulped when he thought again about the money side of it, but it would be a fair exchange.

He'd put much more thought into it this time, and was going to get her something that suited her, something she could wear while at work, or wear anywhere really. He just hoped that she *wanted* to wear it.

Half an hour later, he reappeared on Fifth Avenue, clutching the little Tiffany's shopping bag like his life depended on it. The snow was falling heavier now and he gave a little laugh as he watched the sea of yellow taxis snaking along the road.

This time, he was taking no chances.

He turned right and headed towards the park. It must be strange for her being here too; she had taken some convincing about the trip, and he supposed he could understand that too. But if all went well, maybe they could make a Christmas visit to New York a new tradition? He shook his head. There he was, getting ahead of himself again, he thought ruefully, instead of just seeing how things went.

Heading into Central Park, he walked slowly along the side of the lake towards the Wollman ice rink, where they'd agreed to meet. From his vantage point he could see that she was already there, standing off to the side a little.

As he approached, she looked up and smiled at him. 'How incredible is this? Snow on Christmas Eve . . .' Then her words trailed off as her gaze dropped to his side. 'What have you been up to?' she asked, her eyes widening.

He chuckled, giving her a light kiss on the cheek. 'Just a little bit of last-minute shopping. For you.'

'I don't believe it! For me?' She stared up at him. 'Well, as long as it's only something small.'

'Oh it's something small, all right.' He brought out the little blue box and, without warning, dropped to one knee. 'I know how big on tradition you are, so . . .'

'What? What are you doing?' she gasped, her expression one of complete bafflement. 'Don't tell me that's . . . You can't afford—'

'I sold the bike,' he said, and at his words something changed in her expression.

'What? No! Gary, you love that bike.'

'Yeah, but I love you even more, and I figured that all this – the trip back here, a return to the scene of the crime – was as good a way as any to convince you.'

'There really was no need. You know we've got past all that now and . . .' Her eyes sparkled and her words were giddy. 'You really sold the bike – just for me?'

'Yep.'

Sean and the boys thought he was mad, but Gary didn't care so much about what the boys thought any more. Rachel was the most important thing in his life, and he wanted to make sure she knew he didn't take her forgiveness for granted. It had taken her a long time to let him back into her life after what had happened, and now he wanted her to know exactly how much she meant to him. And, more than that, he wanted to give her the proposal she deserved.

'So what do you think, Rachel?' he asked. 'Will you marry me?'

'You know, Daisy would just love this,' she laughed. 'Just wait till I tell her and Terri, and Ethan too. They won't be able to *believe*—'

'Rach?' The ground was damp, his joints were starting to strain a bit from crouching and people were staring, but Gary didn't care. All he was interested in at that moment was her answer. 'You're killing me here. Yes or no?'

Rachel looked at the ring box in Gary's palm, before her gaze rested on his face.

She shook her head. 'Gary Knowles,' she said, smiling, 'by now, you of all people should know that a girl would *never* say no to something from Tiffany's.'